Ghost Diamonds

By

Keith Hoare

GHOST DIAMONDS

Copyright © 2024 Keith Hoare.

All characters in this publication are fictitious. Any resemblance to real persons, living or dead, is purely coincidental. Certain locations mentioned in this publication are fictitious and do not exist. Laws and regulations controlling industries and country law in this publication are fictitious and do not represent reality.

All rights reserved. This literary work may not be reproduced or transmitted in any form or by any means, including electronic or photographic reproduction in whole or in any part without express written permission of the author.

The right of Keith Hoare to be identified as the author of the work and has been asserted by him in accordance with the Copyright, Designs and Patent Act 1988.

Published by: Ragged Cover Publishing

I

ISBN 978-1-908090-72-0

Chapter 1

Lisa gripped the edge of the seat when, yet again, the small passenger aircraft hit an air pocket with a thud. Alongside her, Jenny, her penfriend since she was fourteen, over four years ago, sat unconcerned. She was used to the turbulence.

Jenny lived in South Africa, and only two days before this flight, she met Lisa, who had arrived on a direct flight from the UK. The two girls stayed in Pretoria at Jenny's parents' house before boarding the aircraft for the internal flight to stay at the family farm, close to the border of Mozambique, in the Kruger National Park.

Lisa felt sure the air in the cabin seemed to be fogging up, and there was a distinct acrid smell of burning. She turned to Jenny, who was also looking around the cabin. "Can you smell burning?"

"I can, and it's getting worse," Jenny replied, standing and looking towards the back.

Other passengers were also doing the same, and the flight attendant urged them to remain seated, saying there was nothing to be concerned about. Yet, no sooner had she expressed those words than there was a deep and muffled bang from under their feet. The plane shuddered, already beginning to lose altitude fast. Passengers screamed as the aircraft plunged. Jenny sat back down and tightened her seat belt, urging Lisa to do the same, besides having her lean forward with her head downwards.

Immediately, the loudspeaker came alive, and the pilot ordered everyone to brace themselves for an emergency landing while assuring them he had everything under control.

Lisa wanted to scream. Her life began flashing in front of her eyes, nothing tangible, just images of her childhood, her father before he passed away, her mum kissing her goodbye at the airport, her brother giving her a book to read for the journey, but the fear was too much, she couldn't get the scream out and just kept leaning forward, her eyes tightly shut.

Around the cabin, other passengers were realising, whatever the pilot had told them, the seriousness of their position. The initial screaming was slowly replaced by a strange, eerie silence as people lost themselves in their thoughts, perhaps of their families, many praying. Couples grabbed each other, and two children buried their heads in their mother's lap.

What must have only been seconds for Lisa seemed like hours. She dared open her eyes and turned to look towards Jenny and the gangway—then gasped in disbelief. Someone was standing there, a man in his sixties, his short black beard contrasting with his grey hair. His clothes were of the type she had seen in the old black-and-white movies of the mid-forties.

"Sit down," she called, but he didn't hear. He stared forward, apparently apathetic to the impending catastrophe.

"Who has to sit down?" Jenny asked, looking up.

"Him," pointing at the man. "He'll be killed if he doesn't return to his seat."

Jenny looked to where she was pointing, but no one was there. She covered Lisa's hand, which was gripping the armrest between them, to calm her, Deciding Lisa must be hallucinating, terrified like her of the inevitable.

"There's no one there, Lisa. It's just the fear in you that makes it seem there is," she said quietly.

Lisa wanted to object to her assessment, as the man still stood there, but decided to play it down. "I suppose you're right. It must be my mind playing tricks. We will be all right, won't we?" she asked, her voice trembling.

"Of course we will. The pilot knows what he's doing. Now, please, put your head down. We must brace for impact."

In the cockpit, the pilot had managed to pull the plane out from its steep dive; even so, to carry on would not be an option. They were still losing height, and he was frantically looking for level ground to land the aircraft. All he could see was dense forest, with small open patches strewn with large stones. Such a landscape spelled disaster. It was at that moment that he spotted a lake. Even though the forest surrounded it, there was a chance he could skim over the top of the trees to bellyflop onto the water, far safer than any current alternative. Not hesitating, he pulled the aircraft around, heading directly towards the lake.

While Jenny put her head down, Lisa had only closed her eyes. Mainly worried about the man standing there, she opened them and looked at him. He turned, and their eyes met. A slight smile flickered across his face, and he raised a finger to his lips.

"Please sit down," she whispered under her breath. "You'll be killed."

He never replied but leaned over Jenny, placing one of his hands on Lisa's forehead before gently moving it down and closing her eyes. She felt strangely calm. His hand was cold, in a way lifeless, but the fear had gone as if she was drifting, becoming detached from her body. Then, the impact came.

The eerie silence was replaced with screams as the plane bounced over the top of the water before the nose came down, throwing the aircraft into a somersault and snapping the fuselage in the center. Each half suspended for a second before sinking fast into the lake. The water rushing in spurred Lisa into action. She was a good swimmer, aware that the cold would soon slow and dull her reactions if she delayed too long. Pulling her seat belt free, she gestured to Jenny to follow. Behind them was the gaping hole of the shattered fuselage and safety. Except the cold of the water was overtaking Lisa's efforts. Her arms seemed heavy, no longer responding, her legs slowing and beginning to lock up.

Jenny also felt the cold, finding every movement more difficult, even to release her seatbelt. Her reactions slowed as the plane sank deeper and deeper. Jenny blacked out; soon, she'd take an impromptu breath, dragging the water into her lungs, then, certain death.

Only the emergency lights inside the fuselage guided Lisa toward the way out; everyone else was lifeless in their seats, but the cold was winning, even with her determination to escape. Lisa, too, had lost control; the distance was a little too far to escape the fuselage and rise to the surface. Then, just as exhaustion and failure were inevitable, someone grabbed her hand. Lisa couldn't see who was helping her in the murky waters, except whoever it was dragged her out of the shattered fuselage and up to the surface. Gulping the life-giving air, she trod the water, looking round to thank the person, but there was no one; then suddenly, Jenny broke the surface and gulped at the air, filling her lungs. Lisa swam over to her. Jenny, already recovering, looked around.

"Can you swim to the shore, or do you want help?" Lisa asked between gasps.

"No, I'm okay. I'll follow you," Jenny replied.

They swam to the lake's edge, and Lisa helped Jenny out as she came up behind. They pulled off their wet clothes and laid them on the ground before collapsing on the bank, lying in the sun's warmth.

"Thanks for the help, Lisa. I thought I was finished down there."

Lisa looked at her. "For what?"

"You dragged me to the surface."

"Excuse me, Jenny, I was going to thank you for dragging me to the surface, not me you."

"How could I do that? I was blacking out?"

Falling silent, both girls looked out across the unbroken surface of the lake for signs of other survivors, in particular for the one who had helped them both. But there was no sign of life.

Jenny was confused by Lisa's admission that she'd not helped her to the surface. "But if you didn't drag me out, and I didn't help you, then who did, and where are they?" Jenny persisted, obviously still confused.

"I don't know; it was dark, and the water was murky. Surely whoever helped us couldn't have drowned... could they?"

Jenny placed her hand to her mouth. "God, that's awful, risking their life for us and not surviving."

"I agree with you, but what's even more awful, Jenny, is there's only us left from twenty-five souls on that plane." She looked down, tears coming to her eyes. "Someone saved us at their own cost. I'd rather they'd have saved those two children."

However, Jenny was having none of it. "Those kids were dead the moment the plane hit the water and broke up. Only God knows how or why we were chosen to be pulled from that plane, but believe me, Lisa, we're not out of the woods by a long way. We are in a dangerous and unpredictable area. One moment, it's sunny; the next, we'll be in downpours bringing spontaneous rivers of fast water or mudslides—besides wild animals, insects, and snakes. A snake or insect bite can make you very ill, maybe kill you. Those children alone would possibly last a day if no help arrived. We might survive."

Lisa could understand her argument; it was a silly comment. "So what do we do? Sit here and wait for rescue, or make our way to civilisation and help?"

Jenny stood and gazed around the landscape before replying. She was trying to figure out where they were, but she could see no prominent landmarks. Then, assuming the plane had remained on course and a fault developed only hours into the flight, they should be reasonably close to help. She also noticed, over the distant hills, a gathering of storm clouds. That was never a good sign.

"We should make our way out of here," Jenny began. "With the plane completely hidden from view, the odds of a rescue directed to this point are very remote, but I don't believe we're far from help."

"Well, you know this country far better than me. Let's get going. We may even find a village. I'm starving."

Chapter 2

The two friends made their way to the far end of the lake, following the setting sun. Jenny decided that was the direction they should take. However, the terrain had become far more difficult. The light scrub surrounding the lake was fast giving way to trees bordering the edge of a forest, which initially seemed impenetrable.

Jenny was looking for the tell-tale footprints of animals using the lake, and she soon found a well-worn track that they probably used or maybe a route smugglers would use between South Africa and Mozambique.

"How far do you think we need to go?" Lisa asked.

"I don't know. Small tracks like this often join larger tracks, maybe a river. Either way, they are a route to help. Are you hungry? Some berries on the bushes are edible, although sometimes bitter."

Lisa glanced at the bushes and tiny berries, deciding that perhaps she wasn't hungry. "No, I'm okay, but a plate of fish and chips would go down well."

Jenny laughed. "Don't say that. Now I'm feeling hungry."

The rain, which Jenny had been concerned about earlier, came without warning. One moment, there were clear skies. The next, they were in a torrential downpour. Jenny didn't want to waste time sheltering, wanting to continue.

It was Lisa who heard the deep rumble first. She shouted to Jenny above the rain noise, asking if it was thunder, believing it sounded more like a herd of elephants. However, this was said jokingly rather than as a serious comment. Jenny had come to a halt and was stood listening. The ground began to shake, and at the last moment, she grabbed Lisa's hand and dragged her off the track. The two girls stumbled down a small embankment as three elephants thundered past them.

Lisa fell face down in the mud. She was livid at Jenny's impromptu action, not realising that maybe it had saved her life. Raising her head, rubbing the mud from her face, she stared down for a moment before screaming in terror. Inches from her face was a skull, its sockets alive with ants, the remains of matted hair hanging like a stage prop from its head.

Jenny moved closer to Lisa to see what the screaming was all about, seeing the skull. She shuddered involuntarily before grinning. "Why... it's a skull? How cool's that?"

Lisa spun around. "Cool... bloody cool! It scared the shit out of me."

Jenny shrugged. "This is Africa, Lisa. A country littered with skeletons. Life's cheap and unfortunately expendable."

Lisa shook her head. "No, Jenny, life is not cheap. We're all God's children."

Jenny wasn't listening. She'd seen something far more exciting and began pulling undergrowth away, revealing a vehicle similar to a Land Rover with two more skeletons still in the front seats.

"Hey, look at this. Judging by the state of it, I think it's been here ages," Jenny said, at the same time pushing her way through the undergrowth along the side of the vehicle and looking into the back, now open with the remains of a canvas roof in tatters on a twisted frame. She pulled off the forest growth and looked at three steel boxes. One was on its side. The contents of what looked like dirty stones had fallen out onto the floor of the vehicle. She picked up a stone and studied it carefully.

"I wish Dad were here; he'd know what this was for certain, but I think it's a diamond."

Lisa leaned over and picked one from the box, rubbing it on her jeans to remove the dirt. She was rewarded with a stone that glistened in the sunlight. Yet she wasn't convinced it was a diamond. It looked nothing like the diamonds she'd seen in jewellers' windows back home.

"Are you sure these are not glass, like beads for the natives?" she asked, throwing the stone back and picking up another.

Jenny turned and looked at her, her eyes shining. "Come on, bartering glass beads were when explorers like Livingstone were around, not when people were driving vehicles. I think these are from the mines, Lisa. They are diamonds; if these boxes are full, this lot's worth millions."

Lisa looked at a second one more carefully. "So why aren't they in separate bags rather than just thrown in a box as if they're worthless?"

"They're not cut diamonds; this is the raw stuff from a mine before they work on them to make rings and things. I reckon they have been pinched," she replied slowly. "Either way, Lisa, even the smallest one, cut, would be at least three carats in size, certainly bigger than what Mum has on her finger."

Leaning back on the truck side, Lisa looked up at the sky. The rain had stopped, and the sun was breaking through.

"Well, whatever they're worth, we can hardly take them with us, so let's move on, shall we?"

"I agree we can't take them now, but soon, this track will be full of rescuers going to the aircraft, and if we've found this vehicle, so can they. I vote we move the boxes to hide them well away from the crash site and come back later. After all, we only need our bearings and some transport. Dad would help, and we'd be rich, Lisa, stinking rich, believe me."

Lisa frowned. "But surely someone owns them? They'd hardly let us walk away with their property and sell them, would they?"

"Who owns them? Look around. The owners are dead!

Anyway, give me a hand to get the boxes out, then we'll move them to a place only we know."

It took the girls nearly twenty minutes to move the three boxes onto the track. They both stood for some time as they caught their breath, trying to decide where to put the boxes so they could find their place again.

"The problem as I see it," Jenny began, "if we use trees as landmarks, the tree could be gone tomorrow, knocked down by an animal. Then, if we hide them in the fast-growing undergrowth, the landmark wouldn't be there anymore. We need something that will not be affected by weather or growth."

"Then we should return to the lake. There's lots of rocks and things around there, so we could easily fix a landmark," Lisa suggested.

Jenny wasn't for walking back, so they left the boxes at the side of the track and walked on further, taking more notice of the terrain before Jenny stopped dead.

"There, that's where we'll put them," she said excitedly, pointing at a huge rock nearly hidden by trees all around.

Lisa looked at the rock for a moment. She couldn't quite see how they'd get the boxes there with the deep undergrowth blocking their way, but it was a landmark, and even if they didn't get to the rock, at least they could line the hiding place up from the track.

Bringing the three boxes from where they'd left them back down the track, they counted twenty big paces from the track towards the pointed rock before stopping. Lisa thought it more logical to count from the rock, but the undergrowth was far too dense. The ground was soft, partly a mixture of rain and years of rotted leaves, so they found it easy to dig out with their hands. Soon, they had a hole big enough for the three boxes. But before they buried them, Jenny opened the broken box and handed Lisa ten stones, and she took ten.

"We'll need them to raise some money and prove to Dad that the diamonds exist." Then she looked Lisa in the eyes. "Only you and I know about this place. I trust you, Lisa, as you'll have to trust me. We both return together."

Lisa placed her arms around her and hugged her tight. "I'm not greedy or dishonest, Jenny, so you can count on me. What worries me is, like you see in the films, when other people get involved, it can become some sort of free-for-all."

"Well, we can only do what we can, but Dad will be discrete, and he is a botanist, often going out in the forest. No one would think differently if he took me and you out on a purported field trip. He has many boxes for plants and things, so even a few boxes after a trip won't raise any suspicion. But you have a point by mentioning a free-for-all. I think we'll not put all our eggs in one basket, so to speak. We'll leave two of the boxes here and put the third open and part filled in another location."

Making their way back to the track with the part-filled box, they counted seventy paces further on before burying the box. Both happy they'd done all they could, they set off again. After another five miles, they were exhausted, deciding to take a rest on the side of the track. Jenny found some safe fruit from a tree to eat, and they sat there quietly.

"You know, I don't think anyone's been here for years," Jenny remarked. "I know rain washes surface marks away, but if it had been well-used by vehicles, there would be ruts, like every other track seems to have in this country, but there's nothing. I think the only thing that's holding back the forest is the animals going to the lake."

Lisa looked at her, concerned. "So you're saying it could go for miles, and we'd not meet a person or another wider, more used road?"

She shrugged. "I don't know. I'm not used to being away from the safety of the farm. Dad tells me things and shows me plants, so at least I know enough to ensure we don't poison ourselves, but that's more luck than anything. I wasn't interested, listening to him going on more to humour him, as you do."

"Well, I, for one, am glad you took some notice of him. At least we can eat."

Jenny stood and stretched. "Right, another hour, and that's it for the day. We then find somewhere to settle down for the night. It gets cold at night, and with both of us wearing only jeans and T-shirts, a night without shelter would be pretty bad."

Not arguing, Lisa followed Jenny as the track closed, forcing them to walk single-file. However, a further hour brought them to a river. They'd heard the roar of water for quite a distance, and Jenny was excited. She knew that once at the river, they just had to follow it and would soon come across a village.

It was even better than Jenny had hoped when they arrived at the river. Running alongside was a wide track suitable for vehicles.

"I half expected this," Jenny began. "After all, the crashed vehicle on the track had to get there somehow. Besides, Lisa, we're directly opposite the falls, so we have a landmark to find the track again."

"So, what do we do now?" Lisa asked as she shivered. "It's already getting cold."

"We must try to find some sort of shelter."

Following the river in the direction it flowed, the other bank rose steeply, trees clinging precariously to its steep banks and often small, flat, dry areas below, which obviously would flood in heavy rain. It was in one of those areas Lisa saw a figure of a man. He seemed to be standing watching them and closely resembling the man she had seen on the aircraft. She stopped dead, staring at him. Then called Jenny. "We're saved. There's a man on the other bank watching us. He must be from a village."

Jenny, a short distance ahead of her, came back. "Where's this man? I can't see him?"

Lisa pointed to the other side of the bank. "There... Oh, he's gone. That's strange. You'd think he'd see we weren't like locals and come to find out who we are?"

"Yes, I suppose you would," Jenny replied slowly, suspecting Lisa was perhaps hallucinating again. But Jenny, while looking in the direction Lisa had pointed, saw what she was looking for. On the far shore, where Lisa claimed she'd seen a man, a cave was just above the bank. A cave meant shelter for the night. She pointed it out. "That's what we want. Come on, the water's shallow here. Take your jeans off before we cross, then you won't be sitting around all night in wet clothes."

Lisa needed no urging. After all, it had taken close to two hours for her clothes to dry after climbing out of the lake, followed by the rain. She had no intention of getting them wet again. Soon, they were across the river, and Jenny was exploring the cave, ensuring no other residents might object to them being there. She looked out as Lisa finished fastening her shoes.

"All clear, no snakes or anything obnoxious. It's really dry and cosy."

The dark came fast. Inside the cave, it was pitch black. The girls had collected dry leaves and moss to have something to lie on. Jenny had even found more fruit, scooping out one to act as a cup so they could drink water. Now both were silent, deep in their thoughts, cuddling close together to keep warm. It was not that Jenny felt particularly warm toward Lisa, but she gave comfort at least.

Moments before Lisa fell asleep, she thought she saw the same man she had seen on the aircraft. Later, he was standing at the entrance, watching her. It was as if he was protecting them. Still, this time, she said nothing, convinced her mind was playing tricks, and she had no intention of making a fool of herself again in front of Jenny.

Chapter 3

When Lisa woke the following morning, Jenny was already up.

"Morning, sleepy; you were zonked out last night," Jenny said, handing her something that looked similar to an apple.

Lisa stretched and took the fruit from her. "You're right. I was knackered. I don't remember a thing after falling asleep."

"Well, it's a nice day at least, so we'll make good progress on this track, and I've got a feeling we'll be sleeping in a real bed tonight. Anyway, I'm going for a swim. The river opens out and deep enough. Are you coming?"

Lisa was all for it. Within ten minutes, both had thrown their clothes off and were swimming in the cool, still water of a small backwater of the river. Eventually, they flopped down at the side, drying out quickly in the warm sun. Lisa then sat up and slipped her T-shirt back on.

"You know it's fantastic weather in this country," she began, pulling on her jeans. I'd love to live here. Where I live now, it's cold and drab. Two months of decent weather, and that's your lot."

"Yeah, I know what you mean. At the farm, I swim nearly every day when I get up," Jenny replied as she dressed. "Anyway, when you're ready, we'll move on."

They walked side by side following the wider road, meeting nothing or even seeing any signs of life. After around an hour and a half, Jenny decided they should eat something, so she left the road and looked around for edible fruit or berries. Lisa was sitting on the grass, throwing small stones into the river, watching the ripples spread. Then she heard a scream. It was Jenny, coming from the undergrowth behind. She stood quickly, at the same time shouting Jenny's name and asking where she was, but there was no reply. Making her way gingerly into the undergrowth, she kept shouting her name, soon rewarded with a weak reply. Within minutes, she was at her side. Jenny was lying still on the ground. Her body was shaking, saliva dribbling from her mouth.

"Jenny, what happened?" Lisa asked in a panic.

"I've been bitten," came back a weak reply.

"How, what's bitten you, and what shall I do?"

Jenny gave a weak smile, ignoring her questions. "You're safe now, Lisa. It's all up to you. My part is finished, and people are waiting for me. I know you won't let us down."

"Excuse me, what's this 'it's up to me' thing, and who's these people waiting? Then you say I won't let you all down? Why will I be letting you down?"

But Jenny didn't seem to hear. Her eyes had closed, her breathing becoming irregular. Lisa, afraid whatever had bitten Jenny could still be around, slipped her arms under the girl and, with a great deal of effort, lifted her before struggling to get her back on the track. Lisa flopped down, exhausted. She was well aware that Jenny was slipping away, and she could do nothing about it. How long she was at her side, Lisa didn't know or care. This was her friend, a girl who'd been full of life less than a couple of hours before, a girl she'd travelled halfway across the world to meet. But more importantly, her skill and understanding of plants had kept them alive.

It was at that moment she heard a voice, or rather not exactly heard, more sensing a voice speaking inside her head.

"There's nothing you can do. Jenny has fulfilled her destiny. It is time to move on and fulfil yours."

Lisa looked up. She'd heard no one approach, but the man she'd seen on the plane and the same one she'd seen standing on the other bank was now only feet away.

"What do you mean, she's fulfilled her destiny? This is my friend. She can't die," Lisa replied, tears running down her face.

But it was as if he'd not heard her in how he replied. "You will come to a small village two miles further up this road. There is a hospital in the square. When the doctors come, tell them what has happened, and they will help. Don't delay; the rain is returning. Say goodbye to your friend. I will look after her."

Lisa looked down at Jenny and then up to ask a question, but no one was there. She stood in a daze. Whatever he said, she was sure if the village was that close, they would help Jenny. Beginning to walk away, Lisa stopped, then returned; slipping her hand into Jenny's pocket, she removed the stones. What made her do this, she didn't know, but she'd suddenly become frightened of someone finding Jenny before she returned, as well as the stones in her pocket. Then, it was almost certain the finder would come after her to find out where they'd come from.

***

The walk to find the village alone gave her time to think. Enabling her to put what had happened into perspective. The aircraft, why did it suddenly go so wrong that it crashed into a lake and virtually guaranteed little or no survivors apart from her and Jenny, saved from certain death by someone or something? Then the elephants… came out as if from nowhere, and since that incident, no other animals had been seen. Coupled with all this was the coincidence that they ran into the bush just where the truck had crashed and a box conveniently broken open to reveal the contents. But it was Jenny and only Jenny who'd led her to safety before she, too, was expendable.

Lisa felt she was in some sort of deadly game that killed people without remorse to keep her alive, but why should she be kept alive? What was the significance of the diamonds, and, more importantly, what was her destiny? In this deadly game, would she be the next one to die?

Lisa gave an involuntary shiver. She didn't want to die. Not alone in a strange country away from her family, for the sake of what, a few diamonds in her pocket. After all, once she was dead, the rest of them would be lost forever again.

The stranger, or vision as Lisa had decided it was, had been correct. She found a village within two miles. It shook her that they were so close to help, and if he'd told her earlier, Jenny would never have needed to look for food, and they'd still be together.

The children were the first to show their faces, running to meet her as she came to the outskirts of the village. Their shouts brought her out of her thoughts, but she didn't stop to talk. Carrying on as the man told her until she entered a square. People had emerged from their small houses with corrugated roofs, gazing at her as she passed and began following at a discrete distance. To the far end of the square was a brilliant white single-story building with a large red cross painted on either side of the doorway. Lisa headed for it. However, to her dismay, the single room was clean but bare, apart from a few stacked wooden framed beds in the far corner.

A man entered the room after her, and she turned. "Do you speak English?" she asked with some trepidation.

"Of course, my name is Joshua. What is it you want? There is no hospital due for two days. Where have you come from?"

"I'm Lisa. I was in a plane crash. My friend and I are the sole survivors, but something has bitten her, and she needs help. I was told the doctor would be here to get me home. If no one's coming for another two days, can you help my friend? I'll pay?"

"We will help, Lisa, but we don't want your money."

"Thank you. Can we go now? I'm really worried she'll die?"

Joshua nodded and left the room. Lisa followed, standing around while he talked to the other villagers.

He came back to her. "We should leave before it is dark. Can you lead the way?"

She smiled. "I'll do my best."

Lisa left the village with Joshua and eight others, soon arriving at the place where she'd left Jenny.

Lisa stood for a moment, frowning. "Bloody strange. I'm sure this was the place," she said aloud, at the same time looking around, attempting to get her bearings.

Joshua was now at her side. "This is where you left your friend, Lisa?"

"Yes," then she looked down. "Well, I think it was, but the grass is not flattened as expected."

Lisa began climbing the small embankment to where she'd first found Jenny. Again, nothing had been disturbed, not even broken blades of grass where she'd struggled to pick Jenny up and bring her down to the track.

Joshua had followed, seeing the confusion on her face. "Perhaps you are mistaken, and your friend is somewhere else?" he suggested.

"I'm not stupid, you know?" Lisa came back at him curtly, annoyed at the suggestion that she was some idiot. "Jenny was here. I carried her down to the track, away from whatever had bitten her." She pushed past him and returned to the track, looking at her distinct footprints on the dirt. "Look, the area is disturbed, with one track coming from the other way and one going off to your village."

He looked down at the ground. "I agree. You stopped here briefly, but as you say, only one set of footprints came and left. Where are your friends? After all, you must have come together, with you leaving alone?"

Lisa could see his logic; she felt a little stupid about

her last outburst. "I suppose not that I remember stopping once more after leaving Jenny. It has to be further down the track," she replied, setting off alone to backtrack.

Joshua and the other villagers followed a short distance behind, allowing her to search independently.

However, after just under two hours, she came to a halt, looking across to the cave where they had stayed the night. There was no way Jenny would be further down the track than this location.

When the men from the village caught her up, she pointed across the river. "That's where we stayed last night," she said confidently.

He frowned. "You swam across then?"

"No, paddled, it's only inches deep. Go and check yourself if you don't believe me."

"We don't disbelieve you if that's what you did, but paddle. I don't think so. The river is very dangerous, with fast undercurrents after heavy rain, and yesterday the rain was very heavy."

Lisa spun around, obviously very annoyed. "I'm getting fed up with being called a liar all the time. I slept in that bloody cave last night. Just because the river is swollen now does not alter that fact."

Joshua didn't answer her directly but began jabbering to the others in a language she couldn't understand. "If this is where you began, we will retrace our steps and search for you, Lisa. If she is here, we will find your friend."

They spread out, working up and down the banks. Eventually, they were back where Lisa claimed she had originally left Jenny. A villager, along with Joshua, approached her.

"I'm sorry. While we agree you did come to the first location and remained a short time and, as you said, left towards the village, we can assure you there was no one else here."

Lisa wasn't giving up. She knew they were wrong, but how could she prove to them Jenny existed? "What about animals? Could they have dragged her away?"

He shook his head. "No, Lisa, no animal has been around. You can see for yourself. There are no tracks."

Tears were coming to her eyes. She'd trusted the man's word that he'd look after her. Now Jenny had been taken by something or someone. "She can't just disappear. Besides, a man who directed me to your village told me he'd look after her."

Joshua looked confused. "There was someone else? I thought you said there were only you two?"

"There was, but he kept appearing and then going away. Is someone from your village playing tricks on me because it's no longer funny? Particularly when a girl's life is at stake." Then Lisa looked directly at him, suddenly realising the truth. She began grinning, giving a slow clap. "I see, you had me going then, and I fell for it. This is all a trick, Jenny's with you, isn't she?"

Joshua shook his head slowly. "We don't play tricks, Lisa. Our life is hard enough to waste time with childish pranks. Look at it from our side. You tell us there's been a plane crash with only two survivors, you and Jenny. But no one in authority has been to our village asking if we have seen a plane come down. You arrive at our village, claiming Jenny has been bitten. You left her to look for help. We can accept that was the right thing to do. Then we came to help, and there was no indication anyone else was here. Now you dream up another person. You should return to the village and wait for the doctor. It would seem you are suffering confusion, perhaps from a bang to the head. Then, where is the aircraft?"

"At the bottom of a lake, I told you."

"You did, but what lake? It all sounds very convenient."

"What does?"

"This plane disappeared completely, as did all the passengers; surely some broken bits would be floating around?"

"How do I know? It would be pointless looking for broken parts. I could hardly put it back together. Anyway, Jenny said we needed to find help." Then she gave an indifferent shrug. "Some help you are. I must have come from somewhere. I didn't just appear. Well, that's not quite true. I dropped out of the sky, but hardly on my own; I'm not a bloody bird."

Another man from the village had been listening and spoke to Joshua in a language Lisa couldn't understand.

"This man you saw, he spoke to you?" Joshua asked.

Lisa shrugged. "Sort of, why?"

"He either spoke, or he didn't?"

"When I say sort of, it's not that he talked as such, like you and I, but more like it was in my head. Then, his clothes were old, not scruffy, similar to those worn in the forties or fifties. Is this important?"

If you could see the fear in someone's face, Lisa could see it now with Joshua.

"Can you describe him? What was his race? Did he have a beard? His clothes, were they the clothes of a landowner rather than a farm worker? What did this man look like, and what did he say?" he asked, his voice virtually a whisper.

She thought for a moment. "I suppose, thinking about it, he'd be European, maybe Dutch. Well, he sounded like Dutch when speaking English. As for the clothes, he certainly wasn't working class." The more she described the man, the more nervous Joshua became.

"And his words?" he asked.

Lisa sighed. "I can't be sure; like I said, he spoke with a funny accent. Something about Jenny has fulfilled her destiny, and I need to go on and fulfil mine. Then he said the doctors at the Red Cross would look after me and that I must leave now as the rain was coming. But more importantly, he said he'd look after Jenny, but he lied. He didn't, but, thinking about it, Jenny also said some funny things."

"Why funny?"

"Well, it was not funny as a sentence; more that the words didn't sound logical. She told me her part was finished, and people were waiting for her. I put her words down to her being confused with the poison in her body."

Joshua turned and jabbered to the others. As they listened, they, like Joshua, seemed to get more agitated by the minute. Then he turned back to her. "We must leave this area."

"What about Jenny? She's got to be somewhere. Ask your friends to keep looking. I'll pay good money if they find her. Besides, how can I tell Jenny's parents I left to get help, and now I can't find her? They'd think I was some sort of idiot when I could lose someone just laid at the side of the road?"

"You should have told me about the man you saw back in the village. We cannot help you, Lisa. Your friend is no longer here. You must come with us."

They argued for some time, and then Lisa finally gave in. There was nothing she could do to convince them to keep looking. These villagers were terrified of something she'd said.

"Then go. You're useless at tracking when you can't even find an injured girl. I'm staying. I'll find Jenny, myself."

Joshua looked up at the sky. "The man you spoke to was correct. The rains will soon be upon us, and the river can rise quickly. It is very dangerous to be on this road when it comes; often, it is covered."

"I'll take my chances, thank you. You may have given up. I've not, I'm staying," she retorted.

"You are a very foolish girl to ignore the warning given to you. Our ancestors have walked these lands for hundreds of years. Often, they are seen and spoken to like you. You should take the man's advice."

"Yes, we get the same sort of claims, particularly from drunks or people on drugs back home," Lisa mocked. "As it is, I'm not drunk or hallucinating. Jenny is around here, and I'll find her without you. This is the age of the computer and the mobile telephone. Don't even suggest I've been talking to ghosts or whatever. I'll not believe it."

Joshua sighed. People from outside never understood. He handed her a small bag and a blanket. "Take this food. When you are certain she is not here, you can return to our village to wait for the Red Cross." With that, he walked away, the other villagers following.

Soon, Lisa stood alone, watching them until they finally disappeared around a distant bend. Sighing, she walked in the opposite direction, convinced that she'd show Joshua he was wrong. She must have been confused, and Jenny was further on, or maybe she had woken after the snake bite and was heading in the wrong direction away from the village. After all, as far as she could see, the villagers were even worse at tracking than she was when they could stand there and tell her a girl could just disappear without leaving tracks. It was a human being they were looking for, not a bird that could fly away.

Lisa eventually came to a halt. She'd seen nothing, not even an animal. It was as if she was the only person in the world. Even so, she wasn't scared. There was nothing to be scared about. She was confused, unable to believe or even contemplate Joshua's words about ghosts talking to her and possibly the man she met taking Jenny. It was ridiculous to even think that way. Even so, it was true she'd seen the man more than once, and then there was the crash. Was it he who grasped her arm and guided her through the fuselage and up to the surface?

Sitting down on the bank of the river, she opened the bag Joshua had given her. It contained dried fruit, some strange-looking dried meat, and a broken piece of bread. Lisa discarded the meat and chewed on the bread. The sky had become so much darker in the last half hour, and she suspected, as Joshua said, a thunderstorm was coming.

Knowing she wasn't far from the cave she and Jenny had sheltered, Lisa gave up her search and made her way there. It was lucky she went when she did. The last time she crossed the river, it was easy, now it is difficult. Not only was it faster flowing, but the water had risen and was well above her hips. Making the other bank, she was soon sitting at the cave entrance as the first rain spots came.

Neither the man nor Joshua had exaggerated about the storm. Never in her life had she seen such a downpour. Yesterday's rain was nothing to this. As she watched, the river began to rise, soon completely covering the road. But for Lisa, it also meant something else. Jenny would have been washed down the river if she had stayed on the road. The search for her was looking very bleak, besides pointless. If Jenny had come round, would she have enough about her to get to high ground? Lisa had no idea, only that she wasn't competent enough to find Jenny on her own and could only return to the village and wait for the Red Cross to arrive.

Chapter 4

In Pretoria, the loss of the aircraft was making headlines. For four days, the search went on. With very important people on board, speculation was rife, from a bomb to it being shot down. No one suggested the obvious that there may have been a failure with the aircraft. Although it was understandable, with no communication or a mayday, it indicated a failure could have been instant, such as an explosion or the plane being shot down.

Bapota, a senior officer in the South African police force, had been tasked with running the search operation. He was in the air traffic control office with a man named Chika. They knew each other well, living on the same street, and often sat on each other's porches with a beer.

"Is it strange not to receive any mayday communications?" Bapota asked.

"It happens. But it was a fine day, with no reports of excess turbulence or a storm brewing in the mountains when they set off. We have radar sighting reports from our early warning systems on the border, picking them up on the logged route in the flight plan, but suddenly, they were not there anymore. Air reconnaissance of the last known area they were in radar contact has yielded nothing. Our infrared onboard cameras would have picked up the latent heat from burning fuel or even a burning wreck, but there's been nothing. The aircraft has disappeared off the face of the earth."

Bapota shook his head slowly. "I don't believe they can just disappear. There's always an explanation."

"Maybe, if you need anything from us, just ask. The country wants to know the fate of this aircraft."

"Tell me about it. Powerful people in the government are constantly calling. I think they suspect a terrorist plot, most if not all, afraid of getting onboard an aircraft until there is an answer."

***

Bapota returned to his office later that day. When he entered the building, the duty officer approached him.

"We've had a call from the Red Cross. Their coordinating officer has reported that one of the field units, on their six monthly visits to the village of Umbra, was told of an English girl who came to the village, claiming she had been in an aircraft that had crashed. Wasn't there an English girl aboard the aircraft that went missing?"

"There was. Could this be the breakthrough we've been waiting for? If one has survived, there may be others. Where is this village?"

They went up to a large map pinned on the wall, and the officer pointed to the area. "It's a tiny village, not even marked, but just about here."

"That's miles away from where we've been searching. It's got to be another hoax by someone trying to claim the reward for information?"

"Possibly, but when I spoke to the doctor in the field, he said the man at the village only mentioned it because he felt the girl was confused and needed help."

"Why would he think that?"

"I asked the doctor the same. He said the villager told him that if there had been a crash, the police would have been around asking questions, or a farmer coming in to sell their goods would have known about it, but there has been nothing."

"He's correct. Someone would have known. It needs to be looked into. Besides being the only possible lead we have, if you discount the lunatic calls as well as the conspiracy theorists."

Bapota called Chika.

When Bapota was put through, Chika asked, "You're back quick. What can I do for you?"

"Would you believe I've just been told of a report from a doctor on his regular visits to remote villages of an English girl coming into the village claiming to be a survivor of an air crash?"

"You're joking. If there's a survivor, that means there could be more. Where is the village?"

"My thinking as well, apart from the location of the village. It's called Umbra and nearly sixty miles off the known route of our aircraft."

"Then it's a hoax. We have the aircraft's route precisely, ten miles maybe, but sixty, that's way off the plotted route. Someone's arse would be kicked if it were true. What do you want to do? Should I forget it or call the local police and have them follow up on the claim?"

"Before we involve others, I'll talk to the Red Cross on the ground and get more information, maybe even talk to the girl," said Bapota.

"I'll look forward to your call."

Bapota's next call was to the Red Cross office, where they linked him by radio with the team in the village.

"Who am I talking to?" Bapota asked.

"Danny Summers, I'm the doctor here, and you are?"

"The name is Bapota. I'm looking into the disappearance of an aircraft. We have been told you have an English girl there who was aboard an aircraft that crashed?"

"The girl isn't here. I was told by a villager, Joshua, who helps us out while we are here, that a girl had been to the village claiming she was in an air crash and wanted help with another injured passenger."

"I'm assuming the village responded with help?"

"They did, but a search found nothing, not even the injured passenger, so they returned to the village. The English girl refused to do that and decided to keep searching for her friend. Unfortunately, there has been a flash storm followed by local flooding since then, and she has not returned."

"That's outlandish. Are you telling me the villagers abandoned a girl from a city in the outback alone? How the hell is she going to survive?"

"I asked Joshua that as well. Joshua is very sensible, but no villager intended to remain with the girl once she'd said she wasn't returning with them to the village. The villagers around this area are very superstitious and easily spooked. Even to have someone just walk into the village unnerves them."

"It happens, I suppose. Did she give a name to this Joshua?"

"Yes, she said her name was Lisa."

Bapota went cold. Lisa was the name of the English girl on the fateful flight.

"Is this Joshua in the village at the moment?"

"He is currently helping unload our vehicle. Why do you ask?"

"Bring him to the radio. A girl called Lisa was on the missing aircraft, all the country's talking about. We need more information."

Soon, Joshua was by the radio.

"Joshua, the name's Bapota, I'm with the Pretoria police. You told Doctor Summers about a girl coming to the village. Can you describe her?"

As Joshua described Lisa, Bapota stared at a photo of Lisa sent from the UK. He couldn't believe what he was hearing. They had been searching the wrong area; the girl Joshua described was Lisa.

"That was a good description, Joshua, but why didn't you insist she return to the village? She is at great risk out there alone."

"It is what Lisa told us. Our elders would not have allowed her into the village to start with or even gone with her if we'd known."

"Excuse me, what are you talking about? The girl is just eighteen; she needed help, not aggression."

"Lisa did, Sir, but we could not give her the help she wanted. You should also leave her. She's among people who will look after her. I can say no more."

Doctor Summers came back on the radio. "Joshua's left the hospital, Bapota. I'll try to find out more for you, even send our transport to the area she's supposed to be."

"No doctor, do nothing. We're coming to join you. Keep in close touch with your office. If Lisa turns up, try to keep her in your hospital. She's almost certainly one of the twenty-five passengers. There could be more alive. We have to speak to her urgently."

"I'll do that. Remember, we're on a regular route and cannot overstay. We intend to leave this village tomorrow afternoon. Will you be here before then?"

"We most certainly will."

Bapota called Chika.

"Well, Bapota, is it a hoax?"

"No hoax, Chika. The description of the girl is certainly Lisa from the UK. Get search and rescue out there fast and sort me a helicopter. Four days is a long time without help. Now, time is of the essence."

Chapter 5

Lisa's intention to return to the village had a flaw. With crossing the river to shelter from the rain, crossing back was proving impossible. The river had risen so much; it was now fast-flowing and very deep, as well as the track on the other side of the river had been completely submerged. At first, Lisa considered waiting until the waters receded. However, in her estimation, judging by how swollen it was, it could be quite a time, maybe even days. She didn't have enough food to wait that long and had to find another crossing over the river in a safer location.

This would be difficult, as the terrain on this side of the river would make it far more difficult to keep close to the river bank. With no road like the other side of the river, it was particularly hilly, with steep inclines. Even so, there was no option. Lisa was also convinced by the way she had spoken to the villagers that it was unlikely they'd come back to find her, so she set off.

Using the same idea as Jenny, Lisa knew she had to find a track, but the terrain was steep, and her clothing and trainers needed to be more adequate. The going was tough, disorientating her, making it impossible to know where she would end up. Lisa wasn't even confident she was heading in the direction of the village. Eventually, she found what may be described as a track. It was long, narrow, and winding, and clear of vegetation. Lisa decided that it must lead somewhere, if only used by local animals, to find water.

After two hours of battling, Lisa was close to giving up and turning back. It may be a track, but she was still faced with constantly pushing overhanging shrubs and branches out of the way just to get through. At last, the path came out in a small area where she could sit down and rest. Taking the final piece of dried fruit from the bag

Joshua had given her, she chewed on it, contemplating her position. The man from the past who kept appearing had not returned, and she was already putting it down to stress. Then, after not finding Jenny, she convinced herself Jenny must have come around and found her way to safety. All that was needed now was to get back to the village herself, then she could leave Africa and return to normality. It was also very hot. She was soaking with the effort of fighting her way down the track, sitting down to rest.

After a short time, Lisa set off again. The track was not getting any better, then she came to a halt. The vegetation had disappeared, even the ground cover was non-existent, and the trees that once grew had left only dead and rotting gnarled branches and stumps. Directly in front was a lake. It was like a mirror; not even a ripple broke the surface. The air was still, and the sounds of the forest were not even intruding. Such warning signs on the landscape, added with a mildly acrid smell in the air, would ring alarm bells under normal circumstances, but not with Lisa. She could only see somewhere to wash the dirt and grime from herself. She threw her clothes off as she ran towards the lake, down to her bra and knickers, and soon she was in the water. It was freezing, but the banking sloped gently, and she soon started swimming, except the water disturbance increased the acrid smell, making her cough as it caught the back of her throat. In minutes, she was out of the water, constantly coughing and needing water to clear her throat. She was nervous about quenching her thirst from the water out of the lake. The heat of the day made her skin dry virtually immediately. Quickly, she pulled on her jeans and T-shirt before laying down to rest.

***

Lisa hadn't moved for two hours after coming out of the water. Her skin was burning, she could hardly see, and her entire body was shaking as if she had a fever. Also, her throat was very sore. Standing a short distance from her, the man Lisa had seen so many times was looking down at her. He had an understanding of what her problem was and looked up across the lake. He never took his eyes away from that direction until he saw a small line of natives appear from the edge of the forest heading this way. Satisfied with their progress, he slowly disappeared.

***

Lisa opened her eyes. Where was she? The mattress Lisa was lying on was old, hard, and flat on the ground. She was naked, her entire body covered in some sort of white grease. The room was a small hut. The walls looked like straw, plastered in mud, with a tin roof. Besides that, her body felt like it was burning up, and her throat was parched. As she tried to move, even a little, the pain was unbearable, making her scream involuntarily.

Her scream brought two women into the hut. Both were African and dressed in simple dresses. One carried a roughly handmade cup, putting it to Lisa's lips, allowing her to sip the water. The other woman looked over Lisa's skin, dipping her hand into a large pot left at the side of the mattress, spreading more of the grease onto Lisa's body.

Lisa tried to speak, but she couldn't. The woman gave her the drink, smiled, and spoke softly in a language Lisa couldn't understand.

They gently rolled Lisa over, spreading more grease over her back. After they finished, they rolled her back again. Lisa closed her eyes and soon fell asleep.

***

Three days had passed since Lisa woke in the hut. Today, after being given a dress, she ventured out. Parts of her body were still red, but the burning pain had all but gone, and with a little help from the women, she was able to sit outside the hut.

Lisa was in a small village with around twenty smaller

huts, similar to the one where she'd met Joshua. The food they had given her was cooked root vegetables with plenty of water. The water tasted of being boiled and allowed to cool. She decided this must be the only way they could make sure any parasites were not in it. Looking around, she couldn't believe the poverty, and yet they hadn't hesitated to help her. A man approached, aged around forty.

"I am called Kofi, you are?"

"Lisa."

"You are not South African?"

"No, I'm from England."

He frowned. "Why were you in this area as well as at the 'Lake of Death'?"

"I'm trying to get home. I was in a plane crash. Why is it called 'Lake of Death'?"

"The water is poisoned. Nothing can live in the lake or around it. If we had left you, your skin would have begun to fall off, and your inside would have burned up. We have learned the hard way, not understanding it was the water that was poisoned. When we brought you here, the women scrubbed you down, put plenty of fat on your body, and gave you water containing a healing herb."

"I'm very grateful to you all for saving my life. How I'm going to repay you for your kindness, I don't know, but I will. But how did you find me, and why would you go so close to such a place?"

"You are very welcome, but you owe us nothing. As for how we found you, I have no explanation, never do we go near the lake, because like I said it is very dangerous. Except this one time, something or someone guided us towards you during one of our hunting trips. You have healed very well; often, people falling into the lake can take weeks to recover or even die, yet in less than a day, you were healing. Soon, you will be able to go home. A doctor who comes to see us will soon arrive. We have heard he is in another village not far from us. We are due for a visit from him, and his people will take you home. Tonight, if you feel well enough, you are invited to join us in celebration, giving thanks for your astonishing recovery. We must follow such traditions in thanking our ancestors for their knowledge passed down through generations in how to help someone over an illness or injury."

"I'd love to join you. Thank you for inviting me."

***

When Kofi came to take Lisa to the celebration, it seemed like the entire village was there. Music was being played using converted oil drums, homemade flutes, and other sounds filling the air. She sat at the elder's side, accepting different foods handed to her and, at the same time, watching the dancing from the children through to the men dressed in colourful but scary clothing, their faces painted to frighten away the bad spirits during their celebrations.

Lisa was beginning to relax. She liked these people, their simple ways, and their generosity, with scarce and valuable food willingly given to a stranger. Deciding then, no matter what, as soon as she could, she would repay their hospitality. The music died down when dusk came, and Lisa walked slowly back to her hut, stopping for a moment at the entrance and watching the last of the villagers go into their own homes.

Then she gasped. Once again, the man she'd seen so many times was standing at the far end of the square. As the last door shut, he walked slowly towards her, coming to a halt feet away. Lisa was no longer frightened or nervous around this man, vision, or whatever, starting the conversation herself.

"You said you'd look after Jenny, but you didn't. Where is she?" Lisa demanded.

It was as if the man didn't hear what she was saying, as he spoke with no reference to her question. "You are now fully healed from the lake's clutches and beginning to learn our people's ways. Soon to be leaving these shores for a short time. When you return, what is written will be fulfilled. Only then can those lost in time who walk this land finally rest."

"Excuse me...," Lisa replied with some annoyance, "I assume you had a hand in bringing the hunting party to my rescue, so thank you for saving my life, but you could have saved Jenny, stopped her going into the bush for the food we didn't need, so I'm not coming back. This country frightens me."

When their eyes met, his were deep and black, giving nothing away about his thinking. Lisa shuddered inside.

"You will return," he replied. "Your future is already written, and as time progresses, you will need my help once more..."

"No... I don't want your sort of help. Neither will I return to help you or whoever else, no matter what's written or any other stupid notion."

He turned and began to walk away. "I will be waiting..." then he was gone.

Lisa stood there for some time. Deep inside, she was determined that, whatever the reason, she'd not return to Africa.

Chapter 6

The villagers of Umbra were in panic as vehicle after vehicle came through to the square in front of the hospital. The normal silence was further shattered by search and rescue helicopters descending, finding the few open spaces to land. In one helicopter was Bapota. Once down, he was directed to the hospital, which had now been taken over as the control room. Joshua was brought in to speak to Bapota.

Bapota, sitting behind a table with papers strewn across, looked up at Joshua. "I'm told you speak and understand English very well. Why is that?"

"I was helped by a charity that selected suitable children from the villages for training as a doctor, engineer, or any other useful career to help their villages. I obtained my degree in engineering and was engaged by another charity to locate suitable sites for drilling to provide fresh water. Unfortunately, the charity closed due to lack of funds. I'm looking for alternative employment to benefit the remote villages."

"Sounds pointless to me. You should get yourself employed by one of the major mining companies and send money back to your village like everyone else. Anyway, to business. I understand you met Lisa. It seems she walked into your village for help, but by the sound of it, you gave her very little and didn't even deem a reported plane crash important enough to send a runner to inform the local police. I assume you're intelligent and would have realised how important it was for the authorities to be informed, yet you chose to do nothing."

Joshua cowered back. "You don't understand, Sir. Many in the village believe she is not of this earth, walking with ghosts of the past. We could not help her."

"Don't talk rubbish, Lisa is an eighteen-year-old English

girl. How do you think our government is going to explain to the British authorities that she was abandoned because a group of illiterate villagers believed she wasn't human?"

He looked down. "I can understand your argument, except your world is not ours. I may be educated in your ways, but as the spokesman for the village, I must follow the old ways handed down through generations and portrayed in our celebrations and beliefs. In such beliefs, our ancestors don't go away; their spirits live on with us, even hunting by our side."

"Maybe so, but as an educated person, you are very aware that such education places responsibility on that person to ensure the village follows the law of the land. That includes informing the authorities of a murder or an accident where people are killed or injured."

"You are correct, and I take full responsibility for the failures of my villagers. But you must also understand my problem."

"Explain."

"We were surprised Lisa claimed that an aircraft had crashed in the area when no hunting party or water bearers reported this. Particularly when she said there were at least twenty passengers aboard, making it a large aircraft and not a small, privately owned single-engined plane. If such a large aircraft had come down, I don't think we would have needed to call the authorities. They would already be here. Like you are now."

"That is a fair point, except an aircraft in trouble can and does drift off their route, so you should have realised if no one was looking for a crashed plane, that may be because they are looking elsewhere. But let us not go down that route at this moment. What did you do when she asked for help?"

"At first, we did help, going immediately to the area where she told us an injured girl lay. Where she took us, there was no girl, footprints, or signs there had ever been another girl, only those of Lisa. We even widened the search, presuming she was confused about where she'd left the injured girl. Again, we found nothing. I suggested she may have been wrong, and only she survived. Lisa wouldn't accept that, then she began to talk about yet another person, a man not of this time. The villagers were scared of such talk, particularly in an area where, for hundreds of years, villagers claimed seeing people who were long dead. Many who saw such visions were never the same. Others went insane. I wanted to take her back to the village and wait for the doctor, but they were scared, convinced she was a bad spirit that had materialised, afraid she would wreak havoc in the village with her words and actions. I got an agreement that she could wait outside the village where she'd be fed and given shelter, except Lisa wouldn't come back with us, deciding to carry on looking for her friend. Many were relieved, convinced they were right, and she did walk with those of the past. All I could do was tell the doctor. At least he would send someone for her."

Bapota sighed inwardly, thinking about how he hated coming out to these areas and listening to such stupid beliefs. "Walking with the dead or not, get yourself ready. You will travel with me and show us where she took you."

"Yes, Sir, I will willingly go with you. But I never meant Lisa any harm. I found her a pleasant girl, not worried about herself more her friend."

"Maybe, but if she's died of exposure or drowned, caused by your village's stupidity in not informing the authorities, you can be sure important people will be clamouring for someone to pay. So, expect arrests to be made with long prison sentences. Now move yourself."

Joshua didn't comment. This was the reality of so-called civilisation, where a very real fear exists of the unknown among the uneducated, being overruled by the law that never considers such fear.

***

Bapota stood for some time in the spot Joshua claimed Lisa had taken them. The rains had washed any signs of tracks away. The searchers began spreading out, searching everywhere, in a way expecting to find her body. He looked at Joshua. "You mentioned while coming here that the aircraft crashed into a lake. Did she tell you what direction?"

"No, Sir, but she was insistent that was where the aeroplane came down."

"Were you not curious to find the crash site and check for yourselves what she was claiming. There is bound to be debris floating if what she claimed was true."

"We couldn't see the point. Lisa told us no one survived, only her and a girl she called Jenny. Life is difficult enough to waste time going on such searches for curiosity. If we had sent a runner to the police station, he wouldn't have arrived before the doctor arrived, who carried radio communication, which is why I decided to wait and tell him."

While Bapota could see the man's reasoning, he knew the authorities would take a different view. But he decided not to mention that possibility. "Did you at least find out where this lake was supposed to be? We've looked at the maps of the area, and there seem to be many possible locations. Most of the locations we suspect are long gone, often created from the mining that went on in the area, now to be taken back by the forest. Currently, I'm awaiting updated satellite photos."

"I believe it can only be one of two, less than two days of walking, both off the main road and difficult to access without stumbling on an animal track. One is known as the 'Lake of Death'; it contains acid from old mining, and nothing can survive after falling in it. Lisa couldn't swim out of that lake, as she had claimed. Then, getting here would be difficult, with steep areas to descend. She'd hardly come this way; far easier routes from the lake lead to villages as well as ours."

"And the second lake?"

He pointed the other way. "It would be a one to two-day walk, depending on the tracks being clear. Several tracks lead from the lake, used by animals when the rains have gone."

Bapota called for a map, and he, with another man, studied the area.

"That is where we find the aircraft, pointing to the lake. Take a helicopter and survey it for debris while the ground crews find a suitable route. Keep several searchers in this area and find Lisa. Not that I hold out much hope she's still alive."

Chapter 7

As Kofi told Lisa, the doctor had arrived to give the villagers their usual health checks for the children and adults with problems.

Lisa had not heard them arrive very early in the morning, and even when they set up the large tent for surgery, she was still asleep. However, the village was packed, with those who lived nearby swelling the numbers with long queues. The chattering and children's crying woke her. Not wanting to push in, she sat outside her hut for a while, eating fruit and drinking a very weak flat beer, which tasted good and was refreshing.

As soon as the doctors stopped for a break and went to sit outside the tent drinking coffee, Lisa approached them. The doctor and two nurses were quite shocked to see a white girl.

"You don't think this is the girl everyone's looking for, do you?" one nurse quietly commented to the doctor.

"Certainly a possibility."

"Hi, I don't suppose you can give me a lift when you leave? I'm Lisa. I was in a plane crash," she asked matter-of-factly.

The doctor answered for them all. "People have been looking for you for the last few days. Why didn't you go back to Umbra?"

Lisa shrugged. "I couldn't. I sheltered in a cave from the rain, but the river had risen, preventing me from getting back across. Then I had a slight accident—well, not quite an accident, more a foolish thing on my side. I swam in a poisoned lake. The villagers found me and sorted me out. Have you come from Umbra, then?"

"Not directly. We also don't return that way, but I will contact our control. They will make arrangements to have you collected. Then, if you've been anywhere near the poisoned lake, let alone swam in it, we should give you a quick checkover?"

"Yes, I'd appreciate something for a cough, which I still have, and I often feel sick first thing. Although the villagers here knew what to do, I'm much better now."

"You have to remember, Lisa, these people have looked after their ailments for thousands of years before we came. They know what they're doing, but sometimes modern medicine doesn't go amiss to finally eliminate any lingering infection. If you go with my nurse, I'll be in as soon as I've called our control to let them know you've been found."

Within the hour of the doctor contacting control, a helicopter settled outside the village to collect Lisa. After thanking everyone, they all waved farewell as she left.

***

Bapota stood watching the helicopter come down. He could not believe Lisa had been so close, and no one considered checking the local villages. When the helicopter landed, Lisa was taken to the hospital, which had become the operations room. Inside were several office desks brought by the searchers and a meeting table. By the time Lisa had sat down and brought coffee, all the other seats at the table had been taken. Everyone wanted to hear just what had happened and how she escaped.

"Perhaps Lisa, in your own words, tell us what happened to you right up to when you were collected by the helicopter?" Bapota asked.

She was just about to begin when a man interrupted. "I'm Doctor Harley, Lisa. Before you start? I have a medical team standing by. Can you tell me, are any other survivors still in the forest?" Everyone in the room had fallen silent, looking at her.

"I'm sorry, only Jenny and I survived the crash. Everyone else died," Lisa answered soberly. "Have you not found Jenny yet? She was on the track leading down to this village. She'd been bitten by something but had gone when I returned with help?"

"Jenny has not been found as yet, but we are still searching. Can you please tell us how you and Jenny managed to get out?" Bapota asked.

No one interrupted again after Lisa began her story, although she was careful to leave out that they had stumbled on the crashed vehicle and removed the diamonds from inside. She also didn't mention the man she kept seeing; after all, they'd think her mad if she admitted all that went on between them were one-way conversations.

After she finished, Lisa was taken to a tent set up as a dining area to eat while discussing her story. She would return later when they had put together questions for further clarification.

"It sounds unbelievable to me that out of all the passengers, with many more capable of escaping the aircraft, only two escaped, with one an inexperienced city girl," Bapota commented. "I say that because, in my view, others in the passenger cabin, like the two girls, might have still been alive."

"Why do you believe Lisa would be incapable of surviving? At home, we were given to understand that she was a good swimmer, which contributed to her escaping the wrecked aircraft. She's also gone on to prove to be level-headed in a crisis," another in the room said.

"I was saying that because of the UK police report after interviewing her mother. She claimed Lisa was more of a home girl. Her only holidays have been in the UK, and she has never been abroad. That is why I'm surprised a girl like her survived?" Bapota answered.

Carl Vissor, an army officer, cut in. "Maybe so, Bapota, but you are forgetting Jenny. She's a girl more than capable of looking after herself. I believe Jenny was able to help her out of the aircraft and survive in the forest. When Lisa is left to her own devices, the stupid girl swims in a poisoned lake, ignoring important pointers like no vegetation, dead trees, and lack of wildlife. All indicators would be ringing alarm bells to any South African girl."

"Very true, but where is Jenny? The search has been extensive. Even the helicopter using thermal imaging has not located her."

"I agree, except our initial scanning of the lake did not reveal the aircraft, nor have we located any debris in the lake or the bank. We must believe Lisa's claim the aircraft is at the bottom of the lake and send in diving teams. They will remove the victims and retrieve the all-important black box. What it does sound like is sabotage. If Lisa has told us correctly, the cabin was filled with smoke, and she heard a bang underneath."

"I leave that to you, Carl, while I concentrate on finding Jenny. She would be far more valuable in telling us what happened. Marcia, can you sit with Lisa and get a complete written statement from her?"

Marcia, a trauma specialist, had come with Bapota and worked at times for the South African police. "When will she be going back to Pretoria?"

Bapota shook his head. "Not immediately. We cannot allow her to leave the country or talk to the press until we have found the aircraft and can make a statement against the known facts. With the best will in the world, she would only complicate matters. We have reasonable facilities on site, so she'll be fine. Everyone, keep a discreet eye on her; we can't have her wandering off again."

Chapter 8

During the next few days, Lisa sat around reading books she had borrowed from people working to find Jenny and recover the aircraft. She wanted to go home and put everything behind her. However, Marcia had told her she needed to remain until they had completed the search for Jenny and the recovery of the aircraft's black box. Lisa had no option but to accept it. After all, she could hardly leave without their help.

With their austere lives, the village of Umbra Lisa had first come to was now what could only be called a tent city. Springing up for the teams coordinating the recovery of the aircraft. While she felt responsible for disturbing this village, realistically, no matter what, if the plane had been located without her help, this would have been an inevitable consequence because of the size of the operation.

There was one genuine advantage for the village. Drilling equipment had been brought to make a borehole, meaning the village would have a fresh supply of water when everyone eventually left. An engineer working on the well told Lisa that it was cheaper than bringing water in and safer for the workers due to the seepage of contaminants from old mine workings leaking into the streams and rivers. She was more than put out; they would only drill for water for their safety, yet the village had never been considered at risk.

Since returning to Umbra, Lisa tended to avoid the villagers, embarrassed by how she had spoken to them while searching for Jenny. However, the day before she was supposed to fly to Pretoria, Lisa decided to at least say goodbye and apologise. Lisa found Joshua sitting outside his family hut, carving. He looked up as she approached.

"That's a nice carving. Do you do a lot of them?" she asked in an attempt to strike up a conversation.

He shrugged. "We have an opportunity to sell our carvings to the people here from the city. Soon, they will leave, and the chance will be gone."

"May I sit with you?"

"Of course, you are always very welcome to join me."

She sat down. "I'm sorry for how I spoke to you last time we met. I know you were helping and had my safety in mind, but I had to carry on searching for Jenny. I owed her such a lot in getting me to the road. I live in a big city. This sort of environment is alien to me, so I didn't understand the dangers."

"It is forgotten, and I would have felt the same if my friend had gone missing. I've been told you swam in the poisoned lake. You are a fortunate girl to have survived. Many who don't know of its danger have not returned."

"So I understand. However, according to Kofi, the heavy rain could have weakened the acid on the surface, and the water was too cold to stay in any length of time. Either that or this run of luck I'm having has continued. It makes you very scared, wondering when it will suddenly end. I'll be glad to return to a world I understand."

He nodded in agreement. "I think if I came to your world, I would be scared."

They sat silent for a short time. Lisa watched as he turned a simple piece of wood into an African woman's figure. "May I buy a carving from you for a memento of my time here?" she asked.

"Just a minute," he answered, going into his hut and coming out with a carving. "This is for you," he said, handing it to Lisa. "It has been waiting for you to return to our village."

The carving, around six inches high, showed two female figures holding hands. One was African, the other European. She gasped. "It's beautiful. How much do I owe you?"

"It is a gift from our village. We will take nothing for it."

"I can't let you waste so much time for nothing when you could have been earning from your carvings to feed your family."

"To tell you the truth, most villagers are upset with how others from the village treated you, particularly those who should have known better. The problem in a civilisation that has remained unchanged for hundreds of years is that most of their beliefs are entwined in superstition and beliefs from stories of our ancestors passed down over the years. When you began mentioning seeing and hearing voices of people from the past, along with a girl who never seemed to have been there, they became frightened. Terrified that you could turn supernatural forces against them. I know it sounds naive, but you can see, living in a village away from the cities, lives are straightforward, along with their reliance on the land. Anything that risks this balance creates fear; believe me, any talk of supernatural happenings is at the top of the list."

"I'm sorry, I never intended to frighten anyone. I was desperate; my friend was missing, and no one believed she existed. Since then, I've had time to think and have concluded that when someone is overstressed, things often seem more real than they are. Since I've become less stressed, I've had no more visions." Lisa's last words were more tongue-in-cheek after the man's reappearance in the other village. Still, she decided it was best to downplay such events.

"That is good, but I hope your experiences have not put you off Africa. It is a great continent with many mysteries, beautiful landscapes, and wildlife."

"So I'm finding out, mind you, when you get forced off the track in a rain storm to avoid being trampled on by three huge elephants, I'm not into being that close. Back home, I leave the close-ups to the nature films on the telly."

He looked at her, confused. "Elephants in this area of the Kruger, are you sure."

Lisa grinned. "Jenny said they were, not that I looked, except they must have been large; even the ground shook as they thundered past. I think they'd been spooked in the storm."

"Interesting, it must mean they are finally returning after being decimated in the past during the mining operations. Will you visit us when you return to South Africa? You can be sure of a warm welcome."

She sighed, "I'd love to, but realistically, I'm no doctor or nurse, so a charity working in Africa would take little interest in me. I don't have any money. My education is abysmal, spending most of my life looking after my disabled mother. I'm returning to work as a hairdresser's assistant, washing hair all day for a pittance. What I earn will hardly feed me, let alone allow me to save enough for a holiday abroad. But you never know; one day, I may be able to save enough to come back." While she said those words to placate him, Lisa, as she told the man who kept appearing, had no intention of ever returning. This country frightened her.

Before Joshua could reply, Bapota walked over to them. "I've been looking for you, Lisa. Have you a few minutes?" he asked quietly.

Joshua watched her walk away, smiled to himself, then carried on with his carving. He felt this would not be the last time the village would welcome Lisa.

Bapota took Lisa to the hospital. Inside was Carl Vissor, the army officer, and Marcia.

"Please take a seat, Lisa," Bapota said before taking one himself.

"Is this about me going home tomorrow?" she asked.

"No, it's about more information coming to light. We

have an inconsistency in your statement that needs to be cleared up. You claimed Jenny escaped with you?"

"Not claim, she did. Have you found her?"

"We have found her body."

Lisa looked shocked. "She's dead?"

"That is why you are here, Lisa. Jenny's body was not in the forest or by the side of the road as you claimed; she was found in the aircraft," Carl cut in.

Lisa stared at him, obviously in shock. "That's not possible. You're mixing her up with someone else. We escaped, walked miles, swam, talked, and cuddled together at night to keep warm. If this is some sort of joke, it's not very nice."

"We don't make a joke over such serious issues," Bapota replied. "I accept we will require formal identification. But I can assure you the initial count of the victims still inside the aircraft tally with the list of names from the airline apart from you. Only your seat is empty, still belted up, and the victim beside where you are sitting, we believe to be Jenny. Even her seat belt is still closed."

Lisa brought her hands to her face, shaking her head slowly. "No, No... You're wrong. Jenny was pushing me out of the aircraft."

"I can only tell you what we found, Lisa. I can show you photos, but they would be too distressing. Victims underwater, even for a short time, are not pretty sights."

Lisa sat there quietly, visions of inside the stricken aircraft as it plunged into the lake flashing through her mind. Could she be wrong? Maybe she had been disorientated, and Jenny didn't escape? Then how could her belt still be fastened? Nothing made sense, yet everything had been so real, even her being dragged out of the aircraft and to the surface by unseen hands. Then, the final words from Jenny while she lay at the side of the road came back to her. "My part is finished, and people are waiting for me." What did they mean? Was Jenny dead, and her presence still so powerful she seemed real, allowing them to converse? Unlike the man who keeps appearing, who never seemed to hear anything she said.

"We are waiting for an explanation, Lisa," Bapota reminded her.

She looked directly at him. "How can I explain? Unless you're suggesting I should admit I've been hallucinating? If that's the case, how did I survive? I know nothing about survival or feeding myself from the different things growing. Finding my way to a village miles away would have been impossible."

"We don't know what was going through your mind or how you survived, Lisa, and that's a fact. Given the findings and your initial statement, you must remain in South Africa. If any reporter around here approaches you, give no comment referring them to me until we find the truth of what happened."

"This sounds like you're thinking I had something to do with bringing the plane down. Before coming to Africa, I'd never been inside an aircraft. I don't even know how they work or anything. It crashed. I managed to get out and wandered around this area until I found the village. That is not exactly difficult to understand."

"No, it isn't, except it could have been concocted, especially with you claiming you weren't alone all the time. Had you expected Jenny not to be found, or were you trying to create an alibi as to why only you got out?"

"That's rubbish. If I did not want the aircraft found, why would I tell you where it was? Then what did you think I did? Take a gas bottle onboard, along with a parachute. Then, when everyone was dead, somehow, I directed this aircraft to crash into the lake before jumping out. Or maybe I was the only one with the sense to bring diving gear, just in case the aircraft missed the runway and landed in a lake like it did?"

"We don't know, Lisa, although you are raising possible scenarios."

"Oh come on, I'm a bloody assistant hairdresser, that means I wash hair, make tea, and brush up, not a female James Bond. Where I come from, we call a spade a spade, and what you say is a long way from what is possible. Either that, or you're living in some fantasy world when you claim my seat belt was still fastened. I'm not Houdini, the celebrated escapologist, or that skinny I could afford to spend valuable minutes struggling out a seat belt when it clips open. I want to call the British Embassy, and then you can explain to them why you're holding a British citizen who has survived an air crash."

"You can do that when you return to Pretoria."

"And when is that?"

"We are delaying your departure while we investigate further. Until then, you remain close to the village and don't wander off alone. The last time you did, you nearly got yourself killed."

"Yes, well, that's my business, not yours. I also want to call home and tell my mother I'm okay."

"You can't. The world must not know there is only one survivor until we know the facts. Including how you managed to escape what all the divers are telling us would be virtually impossible at the depth the aircraft is resting."

"Then they're talking rubbish because I did. So am I under arrest for managing to escape a crashed plane without helping to get others out? Because I'll tell you this. Not one of you in here would have delayed in that watery grave to help others, knowing if you did, you risked death. If you claim you would, I'd not believe it."

Marcia decided to intervene to calm down the situation. "Conflict between you two is doing nothing to help us understand what happened to this aircraft. There are anomalies on both sides, which may never be answered. I say that because people have survived many times in the history of mankind, where situations when looking from a distance or even retrospectively, survival was deemed as impossible. It's as if they find a superhuman strength within, where the need for survival overcomes what can seem improbable. Please, Lisa, with the new information gained after finding the aircraft, allow Bapota a little time to talk to professionals and understand what happened to allow you to survive. We owe these answers to the relatives who lost their loved ones. There is no suggestion you had a hand in anything untoward. You, like those who didn't survive, are all victims, and I can assure you that will always be at the top of my agenda."

She sighed. "I'm sorry. Like you say, I'm not the only victim. Then, I'm interested in a possible explanation of why I survived and no one else did. I'll go now unless there is anything else."

"No, you're fine with leaving," Marcia told her.

Lisa stood and walked out of the tent.

"Thanks, Marcia, I never expected her to react the way she did," Bapota said after Lisa had left.

Marcia gave a slight nod. "It's obvious the girl is under a great deal of stress. And no matter what we suspect or claim, any defence in a court of law would claim the girl had just survived a horrendous crash. She'd be shocked, bewildered, and unable to accept she was the only survivor. The mind, under those conditions, would attempt to protect itself by tricking her into believing she wasn't alone and that people very close to her, such as Jenny, also survived. In her mind, that is."

"You are correct. That could be the answer. Even so, in Lisa's mannerisms, I don't think she is telling us everything, not that I can put a finger on what she's missing out. Except for the initial inspection of the aircraft, it does not look like sabotage. Still, that view could change, so the government wants everything kept under wraps for now. Without a satisfactory explanation as to why the smoke, the smell of burning, followed by the explosion are clarified, the press would be speculating about different terrorist groups, heightening tensions."

"How long do we hold her for?" Marcia asked.

"Let me answer that, Marcia," Carl said. "We have already removed the victims and slung straps around the two parts of the fuselage. We are ready for a lift tomorrow. By the end of the week, we expect to have loaded the sections onto transport trailers. Before we do, there will be an initial inspection of the fuselage. That will enable us to understand what probably happened. Lisa can go back to Pretoria by next Monday."

***

Lisa kept out of the way of Marcia and Bapota, spending all her time with the women and children of the village, even teaching them a little English. In return, they showed her their way of life. Children also took her on a long walk to show her where they would collect water, which was often contaminated, making them ill, and small patches of the forest they had cleared to grow food. Lisa thought her life was hard, but these people constantly lived on the edge all the time, never complained, and just got on with living.

She also spent time with Joshua, but neither of them mentioned the visions she'd had or the reality that she would never return.

The following Sunday, Lisa was again sitting in front of Bapota and Marcia inside a tent.

"I've talked to medical professionals, Lisa, about your belief you were with Jenny," Bapota began. "They think you did believe Jenny was with you. It is documented that people in shock and under severe stress or danger often create a companion they talk to and seek advice from. We believe you did that and survived on what you thought was edible fruit. Yet at times, you were eating berries or fruit that can give hallucinating effects, extending, or adding to your belief someone was with you."

Lisa wanted to go home, so if this was their explanation of how Jenny could exist, she didn't have the strength to argue, even though no one believed her. "Maybe you're right, particularly now it is certain Jenny died in the aircraft. I was in shock after the crash, and yes, I was terrified and didn't want to die. So, to create an imaginary person looking like Jenny and not feel alone sounds like a logical explanation. So you don't suspect I had anything to do with bringing the aircraft down?"

"No, the damage to the aircraft was caused by an external issue, which I don't want to go into detail about. The final question about the seat belt has been sorted out. A diver admitted that he snapped it closed, claiming he was trying the belt to ensure it wasn't faulty. He never told the other diver, who mistakenly claimed in his report that it was fastened. We are now happy for you to return to Pretoria and sort out travel documents with the British embassy to allow you to leave this country. A word of advice and perhaps even a warning. If I were you, I wouldn't mention Jenny was with you. The papers would have a field day. You will also upset her family, who are mourning the loss of their daughter, making it worse if you persist in claiming she didn't die in the aircraft. Put it down to shock and eating a few badly selected fruits to keep alive."

"Then what happens if reporters come here and talk to the villagers? I took them to find her."

He shook his head. "It has been arranged. If a reporter has heard rumours and, like you say, attempts to get information from the villagers, they will deny it ever happened."

She sat for a moment, then looked at him. "It seems

you have everything sorted out to make me look like a fool or insane if I claim to be seeing ghosts. On my part, I just want to get out of this country and never come back. So tell them what you want. I'm saying nothing."

"Not a fool or insane, Lisa. Only a logical explanation as to what happened, without attracting the conspiracy theorist or the supernatural contingency that would add their slant to the story," Marcia added.

Chapter 9

Following the funeral for Jenny, Lisa left on the next flight to Manchester, England. Jenny's parents had been pleasant with her, although she felt they didn't think she should have survived but rather their daughter. Of course, they hadn't said that, but Lisa could sense the resentment. So, she was glad when it came to boarding the aircraft. Inside her luggage were the diamonds packed in gift boxes. The boxes she'd hidden the diamonds in were from a tourist shop that initially contained a selection of different semi-precious stones from the region. However, that was before she'd replaced them with the diamonds.

Lisa's brother, Nick, and her mother were waiting at Manchester airport. Although crippled with arthritis, Lisa's mother was determined to make the journey and welcome her daughter back from what should have been the holiday of a lifetime.

Stepping off the aircraft and entering the airport, the authorities couldn't have been more pleasant. Customs waved her through, like when she'd left South Africa. However, in the arrivals area, her mum and brother Nick were not the only ones waiting; there were also many journalists. It was forty minutes before they finally climbed into Nick's small car.

"So, how are you feeling?" he asked.

"About what?"

"About everything that's happened."

"Bloody sick, if you must know. I held my friend as she died, and I couldn't do a thing about it. I saw children of less than five years die in their mother's arms. The passengers' screams as we hit the water still ring in my ears, so Nick, how would you feel?"

"I'm sorry, I didn't think. I just thought you'd like to talk about it."

"Well, I don't. I'd like to forget it. Anyway, what's been happening here then?"

"Not a lot. There's talk that the factory will close soon, which means I'm out of work."

"They won't let you go, Nick; you're too valuable," his mother said.

Nick sighed; his mum didn't understand this was closure, not redundancy or cutting the workforce. He glanced at Lisa in the mirror and winked. She shrugged.

"Yes, mum, you're right. I am too valuable, aren't I?"

"Has Carol from the shop rang?" Lisa wanted to know, changing the subject.

"No love, should she have?" her mother asked.

"I hoped she'd have called to say I could start next week, that's all. I put it on her answerphone to say I'm on my way home. This holiday has knocked a hole in my meagre savings, besides owing a load to the government, who put me in a hotel I couldn't afford. Apart from all that, I'd like to earn something for Christmas at least."

"So why didn't you stay with Jenny's parents?" Nick asked.

"They wouldn't have me. Made some sort of excuse that I needed to be near the police station to help with the investigation. In fact, besides seeing me off at the airport, they only came a couple of times, and that was to get me to go over what happened again and again. I'd got to the point of believing everyone thought it was me who crashed the plane, not the bloody pilot."

"I did tell you your penfriend was out of our class Lisa, what with their two houses and servants," her mother commented.

"What's the air crash got to do with Jenny's lifestyle? Anyway, they weren't servants but live-in domestics."

"Call them what you like. We couldn't afford a live-in daily even with my attendance allowance."

Nothing was said for a short time, and then Lisa's mother, after lighting a cigarette, spoke. "Don rang last week, wanting to know if you were dead. I told him no one knew and told him to call later in the week. He never did. It was headlined in the local paper you'd survived, so he may have decided it wasn't worth calling until you were back in the UK. You should ring him when we get home."

Lisa was fed up with Don. She'd known him for six weeks, and he took her out at first. But that soon faded to sitting in his or her house, giving the excuse that he wanted to save up for a car. She'd decided on the outward journey to break it off when she returned.

"I'll call him later, Mum."

"Did you have time to buy me a present then, Sis?"

"Yes, I've got you something, not much; I lost all my money and had to rely on the British consulate handouts. Again, like the hotel cost, they made it clear it was an advance and wanted it back. I've got you something as well, Mum."

"Have you, dear, that's nice, I hope you didn't spend too much?"

Lisa sighed, her mum was puddled; she'd just said that.

Then Nick asked a question that sent her cold. "So now you've been there. Do you fancy going back for a real holiday?"

"Why do you ask that?" she demanded.

"No reason. I was just wondering if you found the country okay or not," he said, taken aback by her aggression.

"You've got to be joking. I'm never going back. It's a bloody dangerous place. If the hordes of killer insects or snakes don't kill you, half the fruit-like stuff on the trees is poison. Besides, poverty outside the cities must be seen to be believed; it's as if people there live on two different planets. You'd cry, Mum, seeing what I've seen."

"I know love. It's on TV all the time. No sooner

have they sorted one starving group they are asking for donations than someone else has the same problem. It's all regrettable."

The rest of the journey was in silence. Just being home felt good for Lisa, and she stared out the window, her mind set on sorting Don out and then seeing Carol for a job.

After helping their mother into her wheelchair, Lisa went to her room and flopped on the bed. She soon fell asleep, exhausted from the long journey. But her sleep was not peaceful. Images of the crash, the journey through the forest, and even the skull inches from her face came flashing back. Everywhere she turned, the man stood silently watching her, his words 'she has fulfilled her destiny, it's time to move on and fulfil yours,' quiet at first and 'fulfil yours' repeating and repeating loudly in her ears, suddenly Lisa woke with a start. Her body was soaked in perspiration, along with a thumping headache. Glancing at the clock, it was only five in the afternoon; she decided to go into town after unpacking and showering. The fresh air may give her some relief from the headache.

Unpacking her bag, Lisa looked at a package wrapped in newspaper. She'd not packed such a package. She was sure of that. Opening it up, Lisa was taken aback. Inside was the carving of the two girls Joshua had given her, but she'd handed it back. So, how had it got in her luggage?

"This is getting out of hand. Either that or I'm losing my mind," Lisa said aloud, placing it on her dressing table.

Quickly showering and dressing in jeans and jumper, she left the house.

"Hey, Lisa!"

Lisa turned to see Patsy, her one-time best friend at school, waving furiously from the other side of the road. Patsy seemingly ignored the traffic and ran across to give Lisa a bear hug. Being a large girl, Lisa gasped.

"Hi...," she said weakly.

"You're a dark horse, going to South Africa and never telling us. We had to read in the paper about a local girl going missing following a plane crash, then find out it's you. Then I'm walking down the street, and you turn up as large as life on the other side of the road."

"Well, it's a long story, and I've not seen you for weeks since you left for Leeds Uni."

"Oh, that… I gave up. It was too much like hard work. University was supposed to be all about fun and partying every night. The lot in our class had other ideas; going back to the digs to work every night was dead boring, I can tell you. Anyway, I'm on my way to meet the girls. Are you coming?"

Lisa shrugged. "May as well, I've got nothing else to do."

They walked on together and soon arrived at McDonald's. Other girls she knew were there, and some were astonished to see her walk in.

"Aren't you supposed to be dead?" one girl asked with a hint of sarcasm.

"Do I look dead?" she retorted.

The girl just shrugged indifferently.

"So what was it like then?" another asked.

"What?"

"The crash thing, were you scared? Were there lots of bodies? Come on, Lisa, give us the gory details."

"You're bloody sick, you are. How do you think it was? There was only me that survived, women and children screaming as we hit the water before they drowned, besides my penfriend, whom I've been writing to since I was fourteen."

"So why did the papers say you were dead when you weren't?" the girl who thought she had been dead persisted.

"No one knew where we'd crashed, and we're not talking about England, you know, the country's so big this country would fit in the bottom of a park put by for animals. Besides, mobiles and fast food bars only exist in the cities; I had to live on weird types of fruit off the trees, not very clean water, and walking miles to find a village."

"Well, I'm not going if there's no fast food places. I live on the bloody stuff," Patsy said indignantly.

"You're not," Lisa replied. "I'll never go back even if my life depended on it."

"Don was around last night," a girl said, changing the subject completely, "he was chatting Cindy up, wasn't he Cindy?"

Cindy grinned. "Was he... I told him to get lost. After all, he was still with you. But he said you were dead, and he was a free agent again. That was sick when it was already in the local paper that you'd survived."

Lisa grinned. "He can stay a free agent, as far as I'm concerned. I'd decided to dump him when I came back anyway."

"You could have texted him..." Cindy said with disappointment in her voice. "There was me trying to get rid of him when I could have got a free meal out of him tonight. As it is, I'm stuck with Mum's offerings, and she's still on her healthy salad bit. Last night, I gave it all to my rabbit; I couldn't face more of it again."

All the other girls burst into laughter, Lisa decided she'd had enough and stood to go.

"I'm off. I'll see you all at the club on Friday. Being broke and the insurance whinging about paying me a few quid for my lost clothes, I need a job, so I'll catch Carol at Hot Cuts before she goes."

When she'd gone, Patsy sighed. "She's bloody weird. Who in their right mind rushes to South Africa to meet a female penfriend anyway. My penfriends were cool lads, especially the one from Sweden."

All the others nodded in agreement. After all, Lisa

wasn't that popular, and it wasn't cool to be seen backing her.

Chapter 10

Over the next four months, life for Lisa was as if she'd never been away. Carol had given her back her job, although, as Lisa suspected, it was still only washing hair, brushing up, and making tea for the clients. Lisa's father's death and her mother having to give up work and struggling with arthritis, among other problems, meant college was out of the question. She'd hoped to make something of herself as a hairdresser, except Carol wasn't that interested and didn't have the work anyway.

After sending Don on his way, she stayed in a great deal and was beginning to regret her hasty decision. She missed him. Friday night had come round, and once again, she was stuck in with nowhere to go.

Finishing cooking the dinner, she heard her brother come through the door.

"Hi, dinner's nearly ready," she said without turning from the cooker.

"Well, don't go mad, that could be our last," he replied abruptly.

She turned to look at Nick, confused. "What do you mean?"

"I've been sacked, or rather, the companies gone belly up; even the bloody wages aren't being paid. They told us the government would eventually cough up, but I'm to go to the job center in the meantime."

"I'm sorry, Nick, but you'll get another job easily; at least you've got a degree; I've nothing."

"I hope so. We've got no insurance, you know, so who's going to pay the mortgage this month?"

"I can give you a couple of hundred, the insurance sent me."

He smiled. "Thanks, Sis, but it's six hundred a month."

They said no more, eating their meal in silence. Lisa

wondered if she should show him the diamonds. After all, Jenny had told her they were worth lots of money, so at least they would help to pay the mortgage this month.

"I've got something that might help if we can sell them, that is."

"What?"

"Diamonds, I brought them from South Africa."

He grinned. "You're not talking about those boxes with the stones of the region inside, are you?"

"Yes."

"Lisa, they're worthless tourist stones you pick up off the ground."

"I know that. I'm not stupid, but what's inside is not the original content. I changed the mixed stones for diamonds to get them through customs."

"Yes... And pigs fly, where did you get the money to buy diamonds?"

"I didn't, I found them. It was Jenny who told me they were diamonds and worth loads. I'll show you."

She left the kitchen and was soon back, carrying a box and putting it on the table in front of him. He opened the lid and looked at the stones carefully. Lisa was right about one thing. These certainly were not what would have been in the box. The originals would have been various stones, but these were dull glass-looking stones, all the same.

"You say you picked them up, sounds a bit far-fetched. After all, they hardly leave diamonds around for tourists to pick up."

"They weren't on the ground; they were in a box. There were loads of them, but I couldn't carry them all."

"Where was the box?"

Lisa told him about the crashed vehicle and what she and Jenny found. While she told him he looked at the stones more closely, she also left out the fact that they'd moved the boxes and that there were three boxes.

"I don't know. They look like glass rocks to me. We need someone who knows about rocks to tell us just what they are."

"Should we take them to the jewellers on the high street?"

He shook his head. "No, they're only assistants, I'm thinking of going back to my old university and seeing Professor Walsh in the geology department, he's the only person I'd trust to tell us if they really are diamonds."

"So when can we go? I've got Wednesday off, but I might be able to change it."

"Don't change it yet, I'll call him Monday and see when he's available."

Nick called the professor as promised and arranged to meet him with Lisa the following Wednesday.

***

On Wednesday, they caught the train to Leicester and then a taxi. Walking through the University, Nick showed her places he'd hung out, ending up in the refectory for dinner before their appointment at two. A few minutes after that time, Nick knocked on the door of the professor's study.

Lisa smiled to herself when she saw him. He was typical: corduroy trousers, an old jumper, grey unkempt long hair, and a study with every surface covered in books or periodicals. He shook their hands and found Lisa a seat after moving several books onto the floor. Nick ended up standing behind her.

"So what can I do for you?" he asked Lisa.

"We have some stones, which have been in the family for years and Nick won't believe me that they're diamonds, so he said you knew all about geology and would settle our argument."

"I'll try. Have you got them with you?"

Lisa opened her handbag and handed him a small polyethylene bag with five diamonds inside. He took the bag from her, pulled the first one out, and studied it with eyeglass. Then he took out another to study.

Eventually, he looked up at her after he'd gone through them all. "They are diamonds. Just with a cursory inspection, they are first grade, and each would finally cut to well over three carats."

"Are they worth anything?" Nick asked.

"I would say you're looking at over a thousand pounds per stone, even in the raw state."

"So would we sell them at a jeweller's?" Lisa asked, picking one up and looking at it with renewed interest.

He laughed. "No… They would have to go to a specialist diamond dealer for cutting before a high-street jeweller would be interested. But why would you want to sell them if they've been in the family for years?"

Lisa sighed. "We've got to. Nick lost his job, I don't earn enough to pay the mortgage, and Mum's disabled."

"I see, if you want, I know of a company who I could talk to. They will need to see one, so you'd have to leave a stone with me. I presume this is all you have?"

"No, we have twenty in total."

He raised an eyebrow. "And you want to sell them all?"

"Yes," Lisa answered quickly.

"Very well, leave it with me, and I'll be in touch."

They thanked him and left the study, Lisa linked arms with her brother.

"Well, I was right, wasn't I? We can easily pay the mortgage now."

"We can, I'm proud of you, Sis, but I think we should keep this to ourselves, mum would think you'd pinched them and be constantly worried the police would take you away."

Chapter 11

While Lisa expected the professor to contact her in days, it was close to a month before he telephoned. "I've sold your stones, subject to the company seeing them, Lisa," he said after the initial pleasantries, "but you'll have to go to London."

Lisa said nothing.

"Are you still there?"

"Yes, but I can't afford to go till I get paid at the end of the month."

"Don't worry about that; it's felt that the stones are too valuable to carry on public transport, so they'll pick you up. But you must have the diamonds with you."

"Can I ring you back after I've talked to Nick?"

"Yes, no problem, I'll speak to you soon."

When Nick arrived home, she told him what the professor had said.

"Then we'll have to go to London," he said decisively, "besides, we don't have an option if we want to sell them."

"No, I suppose not. Will you ring your professor?"

***

Following the call, a car picked them up only a day later. The journey was pleasant in the air-conditioned vehicle. Eventually, they turned into a private underground car park in Central London. As they stopped, a man was already waiting to welcome them, and soon, they were in what looked like a boardroom—very expensive-looking with heavy oak panelled walls. Moments later, three men entered, one in a white coat and the other two in dark city suits.

"My name is Sir John Lions," a tall, well-spoken man with greying hair introduced himself and offered his hand. "My colleagues are Hans Barter and our senior cutter Pier Sandyford. I presume you must be Lisa, and this young man is your brother Nick?"

"Yes," she replied weakly, slightly confused as to why such powerful men in the company wanted to see them.

"Can we offer you coffee or tea before we sit and talk about the diamonds?" he asked.

"No, we're fine. Thank you. I'd like to get on, please. I need to go back tonight, as I'm working in the morning," Lisa replied.

"Of course, I understand. You have all the stones with you?"

Lisa opened a cardboard box from her bag so he could see them.

"There's nineteen here. I'm told you have the other. But before you take the stones away, can I have a receipt, please? After all, the professor said they were very valuable."

Sir John nodded to Hans, who left the room and returned with a typed sheet of company paper. Sir John signed the bottom and handed it to her. In turn, she passed him the box. Pier poured them on the table, picked each one up, and then replaced them in the box before leaving the room. Very little was said for the next fifteen minutes except pleasantries to pass the time. Then Pier returned and spoke softly to Sir John.

"We will purchase your diamonds, Lisa. Our offer is two thousand pounds for each stone, which is in line with the current wholesale value of an uncut class one stone of the size and quality. However, I'd also like you to answer a few questions, not conditional on the sale."

Lisa was stunned at his offer; they were rich, and Jenny had been right after all.

"If I can," she replied after the initial shock of hearing their value.

"You say the stones have been in the family for years?"

"Yes, we inherited them; why do you ask? They're not

stolen, you know."

"I didn't suggest they were. But it is scarce for so many uncut diamonds to be in the hands of, shall we say, the general public. How long have they been in the family?"

Lisa looked at Nick for help.

"We don't know," he replied. "You see, we found them after Dad died."

"Was your father ever in South Africa, maybe there with the forces?"

Lisa sniggered. "Dad in the forces? More like a prison when he was called up. Our dad was a drunk, a sponger who never worked. We hardly got fed because of the drink. If it wasn't for school dinners, we'd have starved."

Sir John raised an eyebrow. "I see; maybe your grandfather or an uncle, then?"

Nick shrugged. "Grandpa was in the army. He may have been in South Africa. I don't know."

"Why are you so interested in our relatives?" Lisa asked.

"A diamond, Lisa, under spectrum analysis, emits a unique fingerprint for that stone. It's so exacting that these days, we can even tell you which mine they originated from, and from the mine records, quite often the day they were mined. We believe, but it will take a little further analysis; these stones are from a batch that disappeared during the Second World War," then he leaned forward, his voice low, "The total value of that shipment is forty-nine million pounds; we want them back, South Africa wants them back. I was hoping whoever brought these stones from South Africa, be it your father, your granddad, or even a relative, might have mentioned a little as to how they came into their possession."

Lisa sighed. "I'm sorry. We'd like to help, but no one told us anything. We didn't even know they would be so valuable until Nick's tutor told us what they might be worth. If Dad had known, he'd have cashed them ages ago."

"Well, think about it. Talk to one or two of your relatives. Someone may be able to shed some light on how they ended up in your family. Would you join us for lunch while I arrange to raise your cheque?"

Both Lisa and Nick were impressed with the dining room—a long polished table in an oak room lit by several chandeliers. Of the three people they had met, only Sir John joined them for lunch, but seven more diners were already standing around the room holding predinner drinks. Sir John introduced them, and they all sat down.

Lisa was particularly taken with a man sitting at her side who'd been introduced as Steven Rankin. He looked around twenty-five, tall, athletic, and good-looking.

"I hear you have just returned from South Africa, Lisa?" he asked.

"Yes, I'd gone to meet my penfriend, but there was a plane accident, and she was killed."

"I read about that. I didn't realise you were the girl who survived. It was a tragedy reported in all the papers. It must have been a shock finding yourself alone in the bush?"

"If you want the truth I was terrified. I'm glad to be back."

"So you didn't like the country?"

She thought for a moment, in some ways not wanting to put Steven off from talking to her. "I suppose I did. What I saw of it, that is. I met some nice natives who looked after me and let me join in the celebrations. I'm not sure what they were celebrating, but it was good besides taking my mind off what had happened."

"That I can understand. Tell me, how did you survive before you found the village?" Steven asked.

Lisa had no intention of making a fool of herself again by claiming Jenny had been with her, as clearly, according to the South African police, she was still on the plane. So, she decided to make her survival story a little more plausible.

"I don't know. I knew it was a waste of time staying around the lake; after all, no wreckage had come to the surface, so after wandering around the edge, I found a path. It was more of a dirt track, and I hoped it led to a town. It went for miles. I was hungry, and if I saw anything on a tree that looked like something from our supermarket, I'd try it. Sometimes it was foul and bitter, and I'd spit it out, but most times it was edible."

"You're very resourceful. But what brings you to see us?"

"We're selling some family heirlooms. We were told your company would give us a fair price."

"You had diamonds as family heirlooms?"

"Yes, not many, but it will pay our mortgage and give us a little extra."

"You should have taken them to South Africa with you. You might have got a better price there."

"I never thought about them. Although thinking about it, they'd be at the bottom of the lake now, so it was a good thing I didn't."

"Fair point. What a coincidence you have diamonds after coming from South Africa, don't you think?"

"I suppose, but you could say that about anything. Like having a stereo made in China after visiting the country. Although, even in South Africa, they'd hardly be scattered around on the ground, and if they had been, I'd have thought they were stones or broken pieces of glass."

Steven laughed. "I'd have to agree with you there. It's similar to London purporting that the streets are lined with gold when all the gold is in the Bank of England."

"Good job, don't you think? Otherwise, the roads would be full of excavators," she answered with a smile.

"Yes, most inconvenient to get around. But, returning to your comment about scattered around, if you found diamonds in South Africa, they would not have been scattered around, more like in a mine or maybe a box."

Lisa looked at him. His statement worried her. Did they know more than they were saying? However, she was pretty streetwise, and often, attack is better than defence. "Am I being a bit stupid here?" she began. "Because it sounds like you're suggesting because I've just been to South Africa, I must have brought them back to this country. If you are, I'm out of here. Besides, if there had been a box hanging around like you're suggesting, surely someone with far greater knowledge of what they were would have noticed rather than rely on a complete novice regarding diamonds. Then, to scoop them up, travel halfway across the world and ask some university boffin what they were. I may as well have picked up a load of pebbles from the beach for what good they'd have done me. I only returned with two boxes of geology stones, for which I paid five quid."

"I apologise, Lisa; I wasn't suggesting anything like that. Just surmising it would be one way you could find diamonds, not that you did."

Lisa suddenly felt embarrassed over her outburst. "I'm sorry, I misinterpreted. My time in South Africa was quite an ordeal and something I'd not like to repeat," she replied meekly.

Nothing more was said about diamonds, and the rest of the lunch was filled with small talk. After lunch, a cheque, made out in Lisa's name, was brought in.

Sir John handed her the cheque and shook her hand. "It's been nice doing business with you, Lisa, and you, Nick. Perhaps we'll meet again?"

Lisa took the cheque, giving a weak smile. "Thank you. Except it's unlikely. After all, you live in different circles than we do, and there's hardly a chance of more diamonds turning up. Unless, like Steven suggests, there's a box full of them, except they are not in our house. We'd have found them by now."

They left the building by a different route, along a corridor to a wide staircase leading down to the reception. Along the walls were portraits with names below. Sir John was telling them who each of the pictures were of. Just as they turned to go down the staircase, Lisa came to a halt. Her body began to go hot and cold; she couldn't move, the fear inside her all too apparent. She was staring at a portrait of the man she'd seen on the plane, by the river, and in the village.

Nick was close behind her and nearly knocked her down the stairs when she suddenly stopped. "What's wrong, Sis?" Nick whispered. "You look as if you've seen a ghost."

Before she could reply, Sir John had closed up to them, not noticing Lisa's reaction to seeing the portrait, just believing she'd stopped to look.

"You may recognise this picture?" he began. "His name's Donald Blackmon, known by everyone as DB, a significant man in the development of the mining industry. He was a famous geologist and an explorer responsible for opening up several important mines, including the ones we own."

"What happened to him?" Lisa asked, trying to act casual.

"He was on a visit to a mine during the war when the mine was attacked by renegade German soldiers. The security and staff fought them off for a time but were overcome. He, as well as the security men, were killed. A large amount of stones were taken but never recovered. His wife was distraught as his body was never found. It left a rumour that he didn't die, but he'd made a deal with the Germans and shared in the diamond haul that was stolen."

"Did that turn out to be true?" Lisa asked, still attempting to show a casual interest.

"We think it's false because no diamonds from the missing batch have ever emerged on the open market. That was until now. Like I said to you earlier, diamonds have a fingerprint of their formation, and the ones you brought in are from that particular area, maybe they are even part of the stolen batch. But to be certain of that will take a great deal of investigation. So you can understand, Lisa, why we were very interested in how they came to be in your possession."

After hearing what Sir John had said, Lisa was about to tell him the truth when she glanced down the stairs. Standing there was the man she'd seen in South Africa, whom she now knew as DB. He looked directly at her and shook his head before the image blurred until he was suddenly no longer there. Lisa stared at the empty stairs, wondering how he could be in London. Had he followed her? If so, this would quickly become a nightmare. She pulled herself together, sensing everyone was watching her. "Well, if we can find anything else out for you, we will let you know," Lisa replied before descending the stairs.

At the entrance, she shook hands with Sir John. "Thank you both for coming. Remember, if you find more information, there's a finder's reward of five percent. That is two and a half million pounds. Worth a little investigation into your family's connection with the stones, don't you think?"

***

Sir John returned to the boardroom. All the other people who had attended the dinner, including Hans, were also there.

"Well Hans, what have you found?" Sir John asked.

"The stones were in South Africa within the last year, Sir John. During dinner, our geologist poured over the stones.

On some, there are clear signs of this year's algae growth. If the stones had been in their family for years, the growth would not exist. Another important aspect is the spores themselves. We are ninety percent certain they come from the area where the plane went down, although you would need to give us more time to confirm that. The consensus is that Lisa has found the diamonds, that is certain."

"So why isn't she biting? After I offered over two million. For them, it's like winning the lottery."

"Fear, Sir John. She's scared of admitting she's brought stones out. But give her a little time, and I think she will come round," Steven suggested.

While the conversation was going on, Hans lit a cigarette and was in deep thought. "The point is, do we need her?" he suddenly asked. "After all, we know where the plane crashed. I have contacts in the police who will give me her route to the village. We also know she was alone and must have stumbled across the stones or maybe even the vehicle carrying the stones. So, we have to assume she brought the ones out to ensure they were what she thought and may be returning for the rest. Now, with her coming to us, it's certain the authorities don't know anything about the find, so it was lucky for us that the professor was researching on behalf of our company. Besides being well aware, we would be interested in anyone turning up with an uncut diamond, let alone twenty. So how about we fly a helicopter over the terrain she took from the lake?"

"Why a helicopter? Sir John asked, now more than interested in Han's suggestion.

Hans smiled. "Put a metal detector system in it, and we'll find the vehicle. If it is there, now we know where to look."

"Do it, use our people, and get a team on the ground. We may have the diamonds under lock and key in days. Besides," Sir John said, laughing, "we get to save two million."

***

When Lisa and her brother left, they said little on the journey home, neither wanting to say anything that might get back, but once they were dropped off and in the house, Nick laid into her.

"You bloody fool, over two million pounds, and you say no. What sort of idiot are you?"

"Excuse me, I've got us forty thousand for doing nothing besides, you don't know what went on in South Africa. I never want to go back to that country ever again."

"Okay, there was a plane crash. You survived. Besides flying back, you weren't nervous on that flight, so what's your beef?"

Lisa grabbed a Coke from the fridge and sat at the kitchen table.

"I didn't tell you everything, Nick, because the police said I was stupid or hallucinating, and it wasn't possible. You see, I claimed that both Jenny and I had escaped from the plane. Believe me, we did, and we found the diamonds together, taking only ten each, leaving the rest."

"So, how did you end up with hers?"

"She'd been bitten by a snake or something like that. I had to leave her to get help but took her diamonds to look after them. I was worried her rescuers would find them, and she'd end up with none."

"But you said she was dead, so her diamonds were yours. What's wrong with that?"

She took a drink of her Coke and then looked at him.

"They found Jenny still inside the crashed plane. She was never with me, so they said. But we walked, swam, and talked, even spending a night huddled close to each other to keep warm. Where did her share of the diamonds come from when I only took ten if she was never there? Then there was this man, or rather not a real man, but a ghost. He said I'd return to South Africa, which was my destiny. Still, everyone else who fulfilled their part of the destiny is now dead. I don't want to die, but if I return and fulfil his so-called destiny, what guarantee have I got of returning alive?"

Nick could now understand her dilemma. Lisa truly believed Jenny had been with her. Whoever or whatever this apparition was had convinced her that if she returned, she'd die, so while she stayed away, she was safe.

"It's okay, Sis. You may not be able to find the vehicle again, knowing your sense of direction. Still, at least we can pay the mortgage off and have a few pounds for a summer holiday. Anyway, what use would we have for millions of pounds?"

Chapter 12

A few days after going to London, Lisa returned home after work to find Nick lounging on the settee, watching television.

"I've been thinking, Sis. Why don't you get a couple of days off, and we take Mum to Blackpool like we used to years ago? We can afford a nice hotel, just this once."

"I like that idea. I've got a few days owing. It will make a change."

"Leave it to me, I'll sort out a booking. We'll collect dinner from the fish and chip shop tonight."

***

The following week, they were turning into the car park of a hotel in Blackpool. After booking in, Mother took a nap while Lisa and Nick went to the spa. Soon, they were lying on tables being pummelled.

"I could get used to this. How about you?" Nick asked.

"I've got to agree with you there. Are we going to the theatre tonight?"

"We certainly are. It's a variety show, and Mum will love it. She always went to one when we came. Then, with Mum's mobility problems, we will have front seats."

"We should book an early dinner mum won't want to eat late."

***

The night went well, and the next day, they all wandered slowly down the seafront towards Blackpool's theme park. The weather was good, and day trippers were beginning to arrive.

"I need to go to a cashpoint, Nick. Do you want to meet on Central Pier?"

"Yes, okay."

Lisa walked through the main shopping area, where the banks were. Using her card, she withdrew fifty pounds.

Returning the way she came, she passed a lady dressed as a gypsy sitting outside a small booth. A poster and photos on the booth claimed she gave horoscopes to the stars.

The lady had been watching Lisa approach. "Beautiful girl, let me read your future," she called.

"Sorry, I don't have the money to waste, maybe some other time."

"It is early and quiet, no charge. Let me show you your future."

Lisa didn't want anything to do with someone else telling her she would travel, yet in some ways, she was interested in discovering her destiny, not that she ever believed people purporting to know the future. Her mother had gone to such people for years and swore by them. Lisa was also curious if this woman could sense if DB was still around or if, as Marcia had suggested, fear of being alone, added to selecting the wrong fruits on shrubs and trees, had enhanced her hallucinations. Then maybe this woman could talk to Jenny, not that she held out much hope that anyone could speak to the dead.

"Go on then, tell me if I'm going to find some dishy boyfriend and live happily ever after."

She smiled. "Everyone's future is written in the stars if you know where to look. Although every girl wants to know if she'll meet the boy of her dreams. I tell them all the same. Their future is already written. Come inside, and we'll see what the cards reveal."

Once inside the tiny booth, the woman shut the curtain and sat opposite Lisa. She picked up her cards and shuffled them carefully before turning over the first two cards.

"I see you have just come back from traveling. You are disturbed and unsure of your future. Am I correct?"

Lisa frowned. How did she know? "Yes, I was in South Africa earlier this year. It's not something I like to think about. What about my future?"

She looked at Lisa, "Sometimes we need to see into the past to know the future. Please bear with me."

She turned to another card, "You have experienced death recently?"

"I was in a plane crash, and everyone died. How would you know that?"

"It's in the cards. I only interpret."

"My friend was killed, yet I was talking to her later. Is that possible?"

The woman shook her head. "No, love. Many claim they can talk to the dead, but that is impossible. The dead cannot hear our words. Although it is said the dead can talk to us, but not with vocal cords; you hear them in your head. Even such claims are suspect when our thoughts can sound real. The cards are different; their energy comes from the stars and the cosmos. Let us look to your future."

After picking up the three cards and placing them to one side, she turned over two more. The small booth became very cold at that moment, and the noises outside fell silent. The woman seemed to go into a trance, staring vacantly at the two cards. When she spoke, her voice had changed to that of a man. Lisa suspected the voice to be that of DB.

"A word of warning, very soon you will return to Africa. Do not trust the people you return with. Dark forces are gathering that will attempt to destroy you. They cannot be allowed to succeed. Already, you are finding that only you can see and hear what others cannot. Be bold and call out for help. Help can only come if you demand that they stand by your side. Remember that. I will be waiting."

"Who am I calling for help? Then why me? Unless you explain, I will never return to Africa. You cannot force me."

"I can sense doubts in your abilities. Already, you have proved you can cross boundaries; others cannot. Such abilities can only increase, allowing you to face what is impossible."

"That's all well and good, but you've still not told me who I call upon."

There was no answer. The sounds from outside had returned, and the woman snapped out of her trance, staring down at the cards.

"I'm sorry, I cannot see anything more."

"Some bloody fortune teller you are when you don't know what you've just said," Lisa came back at her before standing to leave. "If I were you, I'd look for another profession," then she left the booth.

The woman glanced at her watch; they had been in the booth for nearly a quarter of an hour, but that couldn't be; the reading had only just begun. Looking down at the two cards, already turned over, the first showed death, signifying a transition between one phase of life and the next. Alongside the devil, a card of illusion. Tentatively, she turned the third card. This was the hanged man indicating acceptance of loss for the greater good. This combination she'd never turned before. Now, it was time to see the last card. That was judgment. She gasped. Coming alongside death, the devil, and the hanged man, it indicated a destiny where choices must be faced that cannot be changed or avoided. The girl faced a decisive confrontation between light and dark forces in such a combination. How could such a future happen in a young girl's life? She had no answer, but she felt for her. Then what did the girl mean by claiming 'she didn't know what she'd just said'? Had one of the opposing forces intervened, using her as their vessel? The woman was scared, quickly locking her booth and walking away. Today was not a good day to read the cards.

"You've been a long time," Nick told Lisa when she joined them.

"Yes, well, I got dragged into one of those fortune teller

booths. She was rubbish."

Her mother shook her head slowly. "You shouldn't mock such people. I have never found them to be wrong."

"Rubbish or not, has she given you a fantastic future?" Nick asked.

"I wish. The woman had some sort of brainstorm, suddenly telling me she could see nothing. Probably because I wasn't paying after she'd got me in there saying the reading would be free."

"You always have to pass silver across her palm, Lisa. It's expected," her mother commented.

"Then she shouldn't have said it was free. Anyway, forget it; she told me nothing."

Chapter 13

Two weeks after the meeting in London with Lisa, Sir John banged the table in frustration.

"What do you mean they've gone? That girl couldn't have moved three boxes of diamonds alone."

Still in South Africa, Hans was on the other end of the phone, sitting in a Land Rover by the side of the lake where the plane had come down. He sighed. "With coordinates from the helicopter scans, finding the vehicle had been relatively easy, but it was empty; it didn't look like it had been disturbed for years. I tell you, Sir John, this is the vehicle for certain. The number plate tallies with our records, but nothing is in the back or around the vehicle. What I can't understand is that there are three bodies, so that means none escaped the crash; they all died here. I can only surmise the stones must have been taken somewhere else before it crashed, or it could have been found in the past, and someone has them."

"Then where did the girl get hers from?"

"The vehicle had certainly crashed. Maybe a box burst open, and whoever found them hadn't collected all the diamonds that fell. Lisa could have found those."

"Well, keep looking; I'm not prepared to have some stupid pauper of a girl beat us in this. And Hans, I want DNA tests done on the bodies. If DB isn't one of them, we might need to look elsewhere. With that in mind, you follow that track carefully. The records may be wrong; four people may have been in the vehicle, or another vehicle was following with others inside. Maybe that one also came to the same fate further down the track, carrying the diamonds."

"I'm ahead of you, Sir John. I've twenty natives carefully searching the sides of the track. Lisa wouldn't have strayed off the track very far. She'd be too scared."

"That's good, Hans; keep me informed."

After replacing the receiver, Sir John's secretary buzzed.

"I've had someone called Nick Jones on the phone, Sir John. He's called three times. He said he came to see you with his sister Lisa."

"Put him through," he told her, interested in why Nick was calling.

"Am I speaking to Sir John?" Nick asked.

"Yes, Nick. It's nice to hear from you. I believe you've been trying to get hold of me."

"I have. Is your offer still open?"

"Possibly. Does that mean Lisa has admitted that there are more stones?"

"Yes, they didn't come from our family. She brought them out of Africa. She told me there was an open box with diamonds scattered around it. She also said her penfriend Jenny was with her when she found the stones. That doesn't ring true because Jenny's body was said to have been found inside the fuselage of the crashed plane. Do you know if that was the case?"

"I could find out, but did she tell you where the stones were?"

"No... Only that they stumbled on the box while trying to avoid elephants."

Sir John needed clarification. Where would elephants have come from? He'd never heard of any around there, but he didn't pursue that line with Nick; he only made a note to tell Hans in case such information had value. "I see. Can you tell me why you want to know about Jenny?"

"Lisa's confused with this Jenny thing and, like I said, convinced she was with her when she found the diamonds. If I can convince her that it was all in her mind, she'll want to prove that there are at least more diamonds by showing me where they are."

"And what do you want from me?"

"The money, of course, with a bonus for helping you? Lisa's not right in the head, turning her back on a fortune."

Sir John smiled to himself. It was surprising just what the lure of so much money could do to allegiances. This lad couldn't care less about his sister's reasons for not returning. All he could think of was the money.

"Leave it with me, Nick. You test the water with Lisa, and I'll look into the aspects surrounding the crash. Thank you for calling."

After making a few telephone calls, Sir John took a cigar from a box on his desk and smoked it slowly. What Nick had said about Jenny was true. If Lisa was hallucinating, she could also be confused about where the diamonds were. The more he thought about it, the more he was convinced that finding the vehicle was a waste of time because the diamonds were never in it. That means they needed Lisa to tell them where they were. It would be impossible to find them without her.

***

After Nick had finished talking on the telephone, he heard a thud from upstairs. Running up, he found his mother lying on the floor beside her bed.

"Mum…," he shouted, dropping down alongside her, trying to move her, but he felt something wet and sticky on his hand and drew back quickly, finding it covered in blood. Grabbing the telephone from the bedside table, he dialled the emergency services, asking for an ambulance when they answered.

The fifteen minutes before they arrived seemed like hours, but all that time, she never moved. He stood quietly while they checked her over, and then one of them looked up.

"I believe your mum might have had a stroke and banged her head when she fell; we will take her to hospital."

While they readied her, Nick called Lisa, arranging to

pick her up on the way.

***

"How is Mum?" Lisa asked, climbing into his car when he stopped outside the hairdresser's.

"Not to good, Sis, but she's had strokes before, so I expect she'll be okay."

Traveling in silence, they arrived just as the ambulance medics were wheeling her inside. Lisa stayed with her while Nick filled out the forms at reception. He caught up with her sitting outside the curtained cubicle while the doctors conducted tests.

"Have they said anything?" he asked.

She shook her head. "No, not yet, but mum hasn't come round, and it's worrying them."

Without warning, the curtains were drawn back quickly, and the bed was wheeled into another room. Doctors and nurses followed, closing the door behind them.

Nick looked at his sister. "Doesn't look good, Sis."

She nodded slightly. "No."

Inside the room, nurses and doctors were doing everything they could to save their mother. Stood back, away from all the frantic efforts, DB watched and waited. Very soon, everyone stepped away from the bed. "We are getting no response. Is everyone in agreement that we should cease efforts to revive this lady?" the doctor asked.

Each person confirmed his assessment.

"In that case, I will fill in the medical report accordingly," he told them.

DB moved to the bed, unseen, passing through the medical staff to look at the mother. He waited a moment, then satisfied, he slowly faded out.

The doctor left the room where their mother lay and walked over to Nick and Lisa.

"How's Mum?" Lisa blurted out before he could say anything.

"Would you follow me, please?" he asked without replying to her question.

Once inside a small room with the door closed, he shook his head.

"I'm sorry, we did everything we could, but your mum suffered a second stroke. After the earlier one, she couldn't take another and died without regaining consciousness."

Lisa put her hands to her face, her eyes wide, and tears began to run down her cheeks. Nick moved closer to her and slipped his arms around her, pulling her towards him. Now, she was sobbing uncontrollably.

"Can we see her?" Lisa asked between tears.

"Of course, you can stay as long as you want; just inform one of the staff when you leave."

Chapter 14

The funeral of Lisa and Nick's mother finally arrived. Very few came, with none remaining for the interment. Nick and Lisa were standing at the edge of the grave.

He took her hand. "Come on, Sis, it's time we were going."

She looked at him, her eyes red with tears. "I'd like a few minutes alone, Nick. I'll join you shortly."

"Okay, I'll wait in the car."

When he'd gone, she just stood there, not knowing why. In some ways, it was a blessing. The pain, the tablets, and creeping disability were getting them all down, particularly her mother. Not that Lisa complained; she'd do anything for her, but often, she felt helpless.

While she stood there, she sensed someone was watching. Lisa looked up from the grave to see who it was. DB was standing at the cemetery entrance when he began coming towards her. Lisa backed away. Would this man, this apparition, ever leave her alone?

He stopped a few feet away, looked down at the open grave, then back at her, his eyes lifeless, his face featureless. "It is time to return to Africa and fulfil your destiny; your mother is at rest. She no longer needs your help."

Lisa stared at him, realising what he was saying. "You killed my mother," she blurted out, "so I'd have nothing preventing me from going back. Well, get lost, I'm not coming, I hate you."

"You will return, and you will need help once again." Then he turned and walked away, slowly becoming more and more opaque before disappearing completely.

Lisa stared after him, her body shaking, the palms of her hands sweating. Never had she been more annoyed and so wholly devastated to find this man; this apparition would go so far as to kill her mother to get her to return to Africa.

Back at the car, she climbed in and slammed the door, the obvious annoyance still written all over her face.

"What's up with you, Sis? You look as if you've seen a ghost?" Nick said with a hint of humour in his voice.

"That's not funny, Nick," she retorted. "Just drive. I want a drink."

"Okay, calm down. I was only trying to lighten the day; they've got a two-for-one at the Swan, so I thought we'd have dinner like people do after a funeral."

Lisa sighed. "Sorry, Nick, I'm a bit uptight, I'd love to have dinner out for a change."

They said little while eating, but Nick started the conversation after the coffee had been served.

"So, what are your plans going forward?"

She frowned. "In what way?"

"I didn't tell you, did I, with all that's been happening?"

"Tell me what?"

"I have a few companies interested in my sort of work."

"That's good, Nick. Mum always said you'd get a job easily."

"She did. The problem is, they're all in the London area."

"Oh, so nothing local then?"

"No. I'm thinking of going south."

Lisa was shocked. "Well, that's bloody charming. First, mum, now you want to split the family up completely. Why can't we stay together? You could get a job at the supermarket, they're advertising, and then you wouldn't have to go to London."

"That's not fair, Sis, I worked for months, never going out, to get my degree, and you just want me to ignore it all by taking some menial job?"

"No, I don't, Nick. It's just that everything's happening so fast, and I don't want to be alone now. Besides, the diamond money will still pay the bills for ages."

"That may be, but with mother gone, the money from social will stop, and I'm still out of a job. When we run out of money from the diamonds, which we soon will, you know we couldn't afford to live at home on your income."

"So we are selling up. Me to live in a tiny flat, and you going to London? Some family we're turning out to be."

"Don't blame me. You always knew we lived on a knife edge, only keeping our heads above water and relying on my job and mum's social payments. You have never earned enough to keep yourself, let alone contribute."

"Oh, I'm sorry for dropping out of education to look after our mother. If I'd had the chances like you, I'd have a good job now."

"Unlikely, you're not academic; even in year two, they said you'd never get anywhere. Anyway, our current position is your fault," he retorted. "We could be living it up in Spain in our villa, with a swimming pool like you've always wanted."

Her eyes narrowed, beginning to understand. "I see. Now we're getting to the truth, are we, Nick?"

"What are you saying?"

"This is not about me and you. It's those bloody diamonds, isn't it? Do you believe anything to do with diamonds is easy money? Well, my stupid brother, people have died for those diamonds. Not just the driver and passengers of that truck but a plane load of innocent people, including children. I lost my only real friend and now mum. Those are the ones we know about. Do you honestly believe the deaths will stop there? Whoever controls this cannot go any further while I refuse to return. That brother keeps us both alive, so forget any notion of me returning to South Africa. The answer is decidedly no."

While Nick didn't believe Lisa about ghosts and talking to dead friends, his reward and a personal bonus would not happen while she was in this frame of mind. It was time to take another tack, changing her thinking rather than knocking her down.

"You seem to be blaming whatever is in control for our mother's death. If that's true, it didn't stop them getting at her," he replied softly, "That means I, the same as mum, am expendable in this so-called deadly game played out between you and some ghost. The point is, do you go back to Africa, show them where the diamonds are hidden, and perhaps save my life, or stay and I die? Otherwise, whoever or whatever you believe is pushing you to return may just squeeze the screw that much tighter, and it will be me next?"

She sat looking at him, a cold shiver running down her spine. What he was saying carried a grain of truth; DB, if it was him, was determined that she returned, and all she had left was her brother. Would it go that far if she still refused to return - punishing her even further by killing him?

"I need to think, Nick. Mum's only been buried for minutes; let's sort things out first, shall we?"

Nick smiled to himself. He could see his sister was crumbling, and all he needed to do now was keep the pressure up. It was time to negotiate an advanced fee just in case Sir John reneged on any deal that may be struck later. With this in mind, he called Sir John later in the day while Lisa sorted their mother's clothes.

"You say she's prepared to go?" Sir John asked.

"She's a bit cut up about our mother's death, but after that settles, she will go, believe me."

Sir John leaned back in his chair, drawing on a cigar. The telephone was on speakerphone. Opposite was Hans, who'd just returned to the UK after failing to locate the diamonds.

"May I call you back, Nick? I have a meeting I must attend."

"Okay, but can you use the mobile number? Otherwise,

Lisa might pick it up?"

"No problem, give your number to my secretary. I'll get back to you later today."

After passing Nick back to his secretary, Sir John opened a file before him, glancing at a report Hans had made of the search areas before looking up at him. "Seems like the girl lied about her real route from the lake to the police, Hans. Both you and I know the weight of a full box, and Lisa would struggle to lift it, let alone move it some distance. She changed the route so no one would stumble on the box. We've been looking in the wrong area."

"It's a logical explanation. At least after further testing, we are certain the diamonds are from the hoard, Sir John; the identification from records confirms it. This points to the information that originally indicated three in the conspiracy was wrong. There had to be at least one more to have moved the diamonds from the vehicle."

"So you're suggesting that maybe the vehicle has been a red herring, in case anyone was following, and the diamonds were in another vehicle?"

"Maybe or maybe not. If the diamonds were in a vehicle that ran off the track. Possibly, the one following came across the accident and took the diamonds themselves. Except they also met with an accident."

Sir Peter took another long draw of his cigar. "Suggesting two crashed vehicles, Hans, all occupants dead. It's pushing the boundary of coincidence, don't you think? Even so, this is a bizarre situation. I'll remind you that people have searched for years. It was close to a fever pitch when it got out that the diamonds had been lost with a huge reward for their recovery, representing twenty years of income for many who went out looking. Yet, this girl stumbles on them, walking back on a single track from a lake, which others must have searched a thousand times. Surely, someone would have come across the vehicle, being only a meter or so off the track, but no one did. It doesn't add up. Another track, which is not obvious but wide enough for a Land Rover, is pushing it. It would have been found."

"Then all we can do is involve Lisa's brother to make her show us where they are."

"I agree. But he needs to sweat a little, thinking we're not that interested; after all, he has an eye for a chance to make a few pounds out of it. He'll want more if we push him to get her to go."

Hans sniggered. "What's the difference? After we've got the stones? He's expendable, the same as the sister. The last thing we want is them blabbing around where they got so much money."

Sir Peter closed the file before him and placed it in his drawer.

"I'll call later today, set it up for them both to go. Whatever the outcome, the accident must be above board and have no comeback on our company. Preferably well away from the location, do we understand each other?"

"Of course, but it could be costly."

Sir Peter shrugged indifferently. "With a prize of forty million in diamonds, we could buy half the population in that area and still have change."

Chapter 15

The last weeks for Lisa had been an emotional roller coaster. First, she had to sort her mum's possessions, and then there was Nick's constant references to money and diamonds. Additionally, there was the real worry about Nick's safety, which she'd become paranoid about to the point of not letting him near the kitchen knives. As if that hadn't been enough for her, Nick suddenly announced he was taking the train to London, saying he had an interview.

Of course, Nick had no interview. He'd spoken again to Sir John, arranging to meet him the following week in London. However, Sir John had not volunteered to send a car, which Nick would have refused anyway. This meeting had to remain a secret from Lisa, so he couldn't have a car turn up at the house.

***

Entering the boardroom, Sir John walked over to Nick, holding his hand out in greeting. "Nick, good to meet you again. How is your sister?"

"She's well," he began, "but our mother's sudden death has been quite a shock, although we'd been expecting it since her last stroke."

"Yes, I can understand, but is Lisa prepared to return to South Africa."

"She is," he lied, "but it's been a lot of work on my side. God knows why, but she was dead set against going back."

"Well, so long as she's okay about it now. I assume you want money in advance?"

"Course I do, I've not spent thirty quid on the train for my health. A hundred grand is good, half now and the balance when she gets on the aircraft."

Sir John smiled, "I think not, Nick, half when she gets on the plane and the balance when she takes us to the stones."

He shrugged. "That's up to you, but I need money now. You can hardly expect me to push her without an incentive?"

Nick knew he was taking a long shot, expecting Sir John to hand over money, but his need for money was essential. Lisa had given him twenty thousand pounds to pay into the mortgage to reduce the monthly payments. However, he hadn't paid it in. Unknown to his mother or sister, Nick had gambled with it. Not, of course, at a legitimate casino, but in back rooms. He'd been losing consistently but was convinced his luck would change. It did; he'd been dealt a winning hand, or so he thought. Six people were playing, but soon, only three were left. They pushed the pot higher between them until Nick was on loan notes. Even with everyone betting strongly, Nick was still convinced the hand he held couldn't be beaten. But of course, it was, losing not only the twenty thousand but also being forced to borrow the balance owing from a loan shark. He needed Sir John's money desperately; the debt, with such high interest, had already doubled with the loan shark threatening him if he didn't start to make payments.

Nick was brought out of his thoughts when Sir John spoke again.

"I'll give you money in advance, Nick, but you can forget a hundred grand. I'm looking at fifty percent of what you are asking. Ten thousand up front and the balance of fifteen thousand when she gets on the plane, followed by twenty-five thousand when she shows us where the stones are hidden."

"That's not fair to give up half my money for the sake of a week or two?"

"It isn't a case of being fair. It's business. I have the money. You want it immediately, for some reason, rather than wait a short time. So you have a choice, take the money or speculate she'll be on the aircraft quickly, and you get the entire hundred grand, with fifty thousand when she's on the aircraft and the balance when we have the stones."

"I'll take the money now," he said without hesitation.

Sir John picked up his phone and talked briefly before replacing it back on the cradle. He then carried on looking through reports while Nick sat waiting. Shortly, Hans entered the room, passing a large envelope to Sir John.

"Right, Nick, this is your money. Just sign a receipt, and you can take it away."

Nick stood leaning over the desk to sign the note, but Sir John placed his hand over Nick's right hand as he took the pen from the desk.

"Think lad, if you're pulling a fast one on us and the girl's not prepared to go, Hans will come to find you, then break just sufficient to make sure you never come out of a wheelchair for the rest of your life. Do we understand each other?"

If Nick had been scared or intimidated by this man's threat, he wouldn't have shown it externally, except deep down, his stomach was turning. Not expecting a direct threat, he just wanted to get hold of the money and worry about Lisa later.

Nick sniggered. "She'll come, believe me. Besides, she needs the money. What she got didn't even touch our mortgage."

Sir John half-smiled and removed his hand from Nick's. "Then sign and make the deal."

***

Outside, Nick could have jumped for joy, grabbing the first taxi and booking a posh hotel in the city center. Following an early dinner, he pocketed five hundred pounds and placed the balance of the ten thousand pounds in the hotel safe. Drifting in and out of a few nightspots, Nick finally found himself in a drab club on a back street in Soho. Sat at the bar, several obvious hookers approached. He wasn't interested, asking the barman if he knew of any card games. At first, the man was hesitant, telling him he ran a bar and wasn't a tourist information officer. However, he talked softly to a girl sitting at the far end of the bar. She just nodded and, after a few minutes, approached Nick.

"Hi… here on your own, are we?"

He looked at her, then shrugged, "Get lost. I'm not after a lay."

She ignored the comment, taking a seat at his side. "Neither am I. I'm already spoken for, but if you're looking for a game, buy me a drink, and I might be able to help."

Nick called the barman over and asked him to get her another of what she was drinking. Once alone, he turned to her, "Okay, take me."

"You have money?"

"Bit bloody pointless not to," he replied with evident scorn.

Drinking up, she stood, "Come on."

Leaving the club, he followed her further down the street; she turned down a side passage and knocked on a door. Then she left him standing there. A man opened the door, and Nick went inside. Ten minutes later, he was sat with seven others, and his cash turned to twenty-pound chips. They played without a break for the next two hours, and a girl dressed in a scruffy pair of jeans and an old jumper brought drinks when someone asked. Nick's luck was up and down, winning but losing more on bad calls. Eventually, he placed his last chip down, losing the hand and not having cards good enough to bid.

"I'm all out; good game, lads," he said, standing and downing the last drink. "Are you here tomorrow night?"

"Some are, but there's a big-stakes game at another location. Most of us are going there," one replied,

"Sounds like my sort of game. What's the stake?"

"Hundred minimum, but no limit."

"Can I get a seat?"

"Maybe, where are you staying?"

"Palace Hotel on Bridge Street."

"Room?"

"2065."

"Okay, if it's alright with the organiser, Lucy will meet you in the foyer at ten tomorrow night. Give her your stake money, and she'll exchange the money for chips; no one goes in with money, just a friendly game between a few people. She will arrange to pay out any winnings back at your hotel."

Nick had done this many times at home and wasn't concerned. "Cool, I'll see you tomorrow night then?"

On his way back to the hotel, he was full of confidence for the next night. After all, he'd decided to quit when he doubled his money, and that, for a gambler, was the hardest bit to walk away when on a roll, but he was determined to do just that.

Chapter 16

Lisa had expected Nick to return from London the same night. After all, the train journey takes less than three hours, so it would be cheaper to come home rather than stay overnight. When Nick didn't return and she had no contact with him, she was in complete panic, calling the police, the hospitals, and anyone else she could think of. So when, two days later, he walked through the front door as if nothing had happened, Lisa went hysterical after believing he was either dead or injured. Of course, nothing had happened, but he couldn't tell Lisa. She'd convinced herself that this ghost was manipulating her life, and she didn't like it, particularly when it involved Nick.

"Where've you been?" Lisa demanded.

"Don't start, Sis, I'm not in the mood," he retorted.

"Well, while you're in no mood to tell me where you've been, explain a phone call from the bank. They're demanding over a thousand pounds. When I asked how that was possible after you had paid them twenty thousand, they said they knew nothing about any such payment."

"Yeah, I meant to mention that. I was robbed in London; they took everything I had."

She stood back and stared down at him. "You're telling me you were carrying around twenty thousand pounds in cash? Come off it, Nick, even I'm not that stupid."

"Not cash; they got hold of my bank card and drew it all out at different cash points," he lied.

"Show me."

"What?"

"Your statement, anything, but I want to see that money in your account, then taken out by, where did you say, at cash points?"

"I can't; the banks get all the receipts and things; we'll just have to wait for them to investigate."

However, Lisa was not going to be put off. "No, that was my money. If it was stolen, that's their problem. I want it back, so we go down and get it."

"Where?"

"Your bloody bank, where else?"

"They won't just give it to you. I've just said they have to investigate."

Lisa grabbed the yellow pages, looked through, and then began to dial a number.

"What are you doing?" he asked, grasping the phone off her and slamming it on the cradle.

"I'm calling the bank. Let them tell me I can't get my money back."

"They won't talk to you, I'm the account holder."

She snatched it back and began to dial once again. "Well, we'll see, won't we?" then she looked directly at him. "Because Nick, if they don't, I'll call the police. I want that money back, and someone is going to listen."

"But that money came from stolen diamonds. You'll be in trouble," he said quietly, desperate that she abandon her plan.

"No, as far as anyone is concerned, and your professor will confirm, the stones have been in the family for years. Let them prove different. So are you dialling or me?"

He decided that his sister had no intention of abandoning the call to the bank and knowing full well that they would confirm it had been drawn out, but in a lump sum, even before he went to London. Nick knew there was no way out but to tell her the truth. However, he surmised that by going this way, she'd realise that they could lose the house without returning for more diamonds.

"Okay, forget it, it's all a lie. I used the money to pay off debts."

She stood silently looking at him, shocked by his words, "What debts?"

He shrugged, "I have been playing cards since university. I had a bad run and got into a game I was certain I'd won, but I was wrong and had to borrow money. The interest amounted to three times the debt, and with me losing my job, I was being threatened with violence."

Lisa took a seat opposite him. "So you used my money without telling me? How the hell did you think I wouldn't find out?"

"It's worse, Sis. I knew you'd be mad, so I took a risk that you'd go back to South Africa to show them where the diamonds were. I went to see Sir John and said I could get you to go if he gave me money. I stayed in London overnight and went out to play cards. I only lost a few hundred, but they said there was a big game the next night. I knew I could pay everyone back if I played carefully and got out when I'd doubled my money."

She sighed, "So you lost, I suppose?"

"No, I won, but the girl didn't have the money with her when she met me outside."

"What girl, and why should she have the money?"

He told her how these illegal gambling meetings operated, then went on. "She came back with me to the hotel and went to the phone booth in full sight of me to have the money brought. It was then two plainclothes policemen came into the hotel. The receptionist had called them, and the girl was arrested for soliciting. They took her away. I sat there dumbfounded, not knowing what to do. I didn't even know her full name. I went back to the place where we'd played the game, and it was empty; even the room where I went the night before was empty. I'd been set up without proof or names; I couldn't call the police."

"How much are you talking about Nick?"

"Ten thousand."

Her mouth dropped open, "You've got to be joking?" she stammered.

"Do I look as if I'm joking?"

"So you're telling me you lost my original money, then lost another ten thousand on some card game?"

"I'd won twenty-seven, Sis. In gambling, people are honourable; they pay their debts, and winners get their money."

"Does that include idiots in a city they don't know, with people they don't know, and if they win, such people would allow them to walk away with thousands of pounds in cash? God, even I wouldn't have been that gullible."

He glared at her, "That's easy for you to say, but it's never happened before. Anyway, there's not much I can do. You'll just have to go to Africa to get us out of this mess."

Lisa gave a forced laugh. "Oh no, Nick, this is your problem, not mine. What money I've left will bring the mortgage up to date. You also sign a legal document that you owe me twenty thousand pounds, and it comes out your share of the house when it's eventually sold. Whatever you've arranged with Sir John is your responsibility, not mine."

"But I can't," he gasped. "I've just told you I've lost everything. Besides, owing money to loan sharks, when I tell Sir John you're not going, he'll have me sorted out. Those men made threats if I didn't deliver."

"Then go to the police, but read my lips, I'm not returning to South Africa, and that's it."

Lisa left the room, and Nick sat staring at the table. He had been certain she'd go. Now, he didn't know what to do.

Chapter 17

Six weeks had passed since Lisa's and Nick's bust-up. Nick had walked out, telling her she'd killed him. Lisa laughed at his exaggerations; after all, in her view, and as she told him, people don't go around killing others just because they owe money. However, since he'd gone, Lisa had more important problems. The mortgage was too high for her to support alone, even if she paid part with the last of her money, so reluctantly, she put the house up for sale. Several potential buyers came, and she accepted an offer within days. Although the offer was quite a few thousand lower than she asked, it did get her out of the liability, and with the contract signed, she had one week left before she had to be out of the house. As for her accommodation, Lisa settled on a small one-bedroom flat, and the money made on the house was just about paying for it outright. Fortunately, her mother had made her executor before her death, so she didn't have to involve Nick in the sale.

While sorting the house out on Saturday morning, the telephone rang. At first, she ignored it. After all, for the last weeks, she'd been pestered by cold callers wanting to sell her everything from double glazing to replacing a mobile when she didn't even possess one.

However, the ringing was persistent, so she grabbed the handset. "Hello!"

"Where've you been? I nearly gave up?" Nick's voice came down the handset.

"Sorting the bloody house out, you forget you bailed and left me picking the bills up. So don't bother coming home because it's sold, and I'm gone," she retorted.

"Sorry, Sis, you're entitled to be mad at me. But you have to listen to what I have to say. I've only got five minutes, and I won't be able to call again."

"Sounds a bit far-fetched as usual, Nick, so what do you

want."

"I'm in the shit, Sis. I mean serious shit, and without help, you won't see me for twenty years."

"What are you talking about?"

"I'm awaiting trial for trafficking drugs."

"Then you're a bigger fool than I imagined. Not content with gambling, now, it's drug trafficking. Anyway, what police station are you in? I may even come down and watch the trial."

"I'm not in the UK, but the Philippines."

"Excuse me, where did you say?"

"The Philippines. I needed money, so I agreed to help a friend out. Well, not so much a friend, more someone I owed money to. I was just about to leave the country to come back when I was detained by the police. I need help, Sis; otherwise, I'll go down for a long time."

"So, how much have they caught you with?"

"Two kilos of heroin. Here, they throw the key away."

"I agree with you there. Such countries don't like traffickers. Anyway, what do you expect me to do?"

"Money to pay for a lawyer and even feed myself. They give you nothing here. This phone call has cost me my watch."

"We don't have any, Nick, in case you've forgotten. Someone gambled it all away," she answered quietly.

"We do, and you know it. You only need to pick up the phone and call Sir John."

"Oh, I see, you want me to return to South Africa to get you out the shit again?"

He was silent for a moment. "I know I'm not perfect; no man is, and yes, I've been a fool and let you down. But there's only you and I. Say no, and that's it. I'll be an old man when they let me out. I'm asking you to spend a week of your time and help your stupid brother. I won't expect a penny from you beyond what it takes to get me out of here or a very reduced sentence."

"So how's a lawyer going to get you off with two kilos of drugs found in your suitcase or whatever? All I can see is good money going after bad and getting nowhere. In my mind, you've fucked your own life up; you're not fucking up mine."

"I'm told Sir John has influences in this country. Just talk to him. That is all I ask."

"Oh, a diamond merchant can bribe the police over there. Do you know how stupid that sounds?"

"Ask him to explain. Then decide. I'll get a charity to contact you that works in the Philippines helping Europeans who have fallen foul of the law. I have to go now, Sis. My time's up. Please don't leave me to rot here."

The phone went dead. Lisa stood briefly, holding it and listening to the dial tone. She was convinced she was being manipulated, but by whom or what? Except they seemed hell-bent on destroying what little she had left, even taking her brother away.

Walking into the kitchen, she boiled the kettle and poured herself a coffee. Then, as Lisa turned, she very nearly dropped the cup. DB was standing in the doorway to the lounge.

"It's time for you to return and fulfil your destiny," came the voice in her head.

"Why, why me?" she screamed at him.

However, he didn't seem to hear her. "Remember this. Do not trust the people you travel with; they mean you harm."

"And that is a reason to go? Come on, you can do better than that. I don't intend to risk my life for nothing, even for my stupid brother."

Again, he ignored her words.

"I will be waiting for you."

Then he faded before completely disappearing.

Lisa stared at the space. She knew DB's persistence in insisting she return may only stop when she returned to South Africa. But would it stop then, or would it become even worse for her?

Chapter 18

"It is a pleasure to meet you again, Lisa. May I offer you refreshments?" Sir John asked when she entered his office.

This meeting had been hastily arranged following Lisa's call to his secretary asking for an appointment. The secretary asked her why the meeting was taking place, but Lisa wouldn't tell her, asking for Sir John to call her back when he was free. Sir John responded quickly, and Lisa was collected the next day, travelling to London by car.

Lisa smiled softly. "Thank you, coffee white with no sugar, please," she replied, sitting on the opposite side of his desk.

Sir John poured the coffee and sat down. "Well, what can I do for you? Your call did not explain why you wanted to see me."

"Let's not play games, Sir John. You know why I'm here. You want the lost shipment of diamonds, and I know where they are. It's that simple."

"Of course, we knew you'd found them, Lisa. You see diamonds kept in a drawer for supposedly years, don't have particles of soil and fresh plant growth on them. After analysing the particles, we found they originated where the plane crashed. However, what interests me is why you have come now. When, for weeks, you have not even considered returning to South Africa?"

"I'm not here by choice, I can assure you. I'd never have come if it hadn't been for my brother's antics. He needs help, and no matter how stupid he's been, he is my brother and all I've got. I need to sell the diamonds to do something; I can only get at the diamonds with funds. Pointing to my need for a partner."

"I can see your dilemma. I have also read about your brother's case. He is, like you say, a very foolish man. I promise you that if we recover the diamonds, I have the contacts to get him out of the country and back home with you quickly."

Lisa said nothing for a moment, sipping the coffee slowly. Being a streetwise girl and untrusting, she suspected that Nick's dilemma might be a setup, and he was probably sitting in some hotel laughing at her so-called naivety. After all, Lisa had not seen anything in the local paper, and in her view, if a local lad had been caught with drugs, it would have been headlines. Without proof, she couldn't take the chance. Lisa didn't intend to pursue this suspicion; instead, she would keep to the plan she'd decided on.

"I assume, with you not getting back to me, apart from attempting to use Nick to pressure me, you originally tried to find the diamonds yourself and failed?" she asked quietly.

He smiled. "You're very astute, although you could hardly blame us. After it was confirmed by our botanist, the location where the diamonds had been lying was straightforward to find from contacts on the route you took from the lake. You also made it clear that returning to South Africa would not happen."

Lisa gave a hint of a smile. "After my last experience in Africa, you could hardly blame me for not wanting to return." Then she gave an indifferent shrug. "But needs must, and I cannot see an option but to return. As for you not finding the hoard, I knew you wouldn't find them. Jenny said someone might attempt to bypass us. So we moved the diamonds. After all, don't they always do that in movies?"

"So I understand. Besides, it makes a well-trod storyline."

"I'm glad you agree because, like any good movie script, I hold all the cards, and as such, my price to impart information has gone up. I want one million pounds sterling in advance, with a legal document saying that the money is a reward for my assistance in helping the South African government find a lost shipment of diamonds."

His eyes narrowed. He didn't like being caught out like this. "I presume you've thought this out, and there is no negotiation?"

"What is there to negotiate? You can hardly expect to have them for nothing. Of course, there's more to complete the deal."

"And that is?"

"The money must be paid into a holding account, which I can draw on after the diamonds are in your hands, or whoever is with me takes them away. A second million is added to complete the contract between us. Then, to ensure there are no double dealings, like me suddenly having an unfortunate accident and getting killed, all the money must go to a stipulated number of charities of my choosing. It can never be returned to your company."

"But what if you fail to find the diamonds or only a few are left?"

She smiled. "Then we both lose out, but not the charities, although I can assure you there is a box with stones similar in size to the ones I brought back. You'd know if they'd been found in the meantime."

He frowned. "When you say box, you mean there is only one?"

"Yes, why would there be more?"

"We have always understood there were three boxes."

She shrugged. "You may know there were three boxes, but the box I found didn't have a label attached, saying one of three. So why would I search for what I didn't know existed?"

"Then your reward is too high for only one box."

"That's your decision. But my price stays the same, and even with one box, I can't see you losing out. Although if you say there should be three, they may be close by. I don't know. That's a chance you take."

"I will have to speak to my fellow director, Lisa. Would you be willing to stay overnight in London as our guest?"

"I can; after all, one million, followed by one more, is a great deal of money." Lisa glanced at her watch. "I can give you until tomorrow at ten o'clock. I have an appointment with an Israeli diamond company. They seemed interested in acquiring many uncut diamonds and wished to speak to me."

"Very well, Lisa. If you can be ready to leave the hotel by nine o'clock, I'll have my car collect you and bring you here. We will give you our decision then."

After Lisa had left, Hans joined him. Sir John had sat down and looked up when Hans entered the room. "You heard her terms, and she claims there's only one box?"

"I did, but what's a million? For us, it's a donation to charity with a full tax write-off. As for only one box, it's possible. Why should she think there would be more? But if one's there, the others will be very close anyway."

"You could be right. If the other boxes are not around, then beat the truth out of her, just to be sure. I don't want her moving on to the Israelis offering the diamonds to them."

Hans laughed. "Believe me, Sir John, I'll get the truth. We cannot risk such a find getting in the papers. So Lisa will get her wish, and it will all go to charity."

Sir John smiled. "The associates would not be happy if the find became public, so I'll accept her demands. You go to South Africa in advance and get the necessary equipment and transport together. Lisa will join you in three days."

***

Charles Forrester, a geologist working for Sir John, had been handed the twenty diamonds to find where they originated. He had noticed the fresh algae growth on the stones. Charles pointed out to Sir John that they had been picked up recently, passing scrapings to a botanist to pinpoint their location in the world. When the results came back to him, he called a number in South Africa once he had left the office the same evening.

"Charles, it has been a long time. Do you have information on what we have been waiting for all these years?"

"I do. Finally, stones from the lost consignment have turned up. Only twenty, but I suspect whoever passed them to Sir John knows where the rest are."

"Do you have a location? Is it in the general area we know the consignment disappeared?"

"Yes to both. Also, Sir John's man Hans has been out looking for the rest but returned empty-handed. Today, the girl who originally brought the diamonds here is back. I'm told she has been booked on a flight to South Africa."

"So it seems only she knows the location and has been roped in. You have done well, Charles. After all these years, the diamonds will finally come back to their rightful owners."

"They will. I'll contact you when I can confirm the flight number."

Chapter 19

After Sir John agreed to their deal, Lisa remained in London. Her flight wasn't until the end of the week, so she spent the time doing a little shopping, updating her wardrobe to clothing more suitable for the trip, and visiting some of the main attractions of London.

***

Lisa handed her boarding card to the flight attendant, welcoming people aboard. Her ticket, provided by Sir John's company, was for club class, which was far more comfortable than the tourist class. On the previous flight, she had to put up with the person behind kicking her in the back.

As she settled into the window seat, a man took the seat next to her.

"Good afternoon," he began. "As we will be seated together for the next few hours, I thought I might introduce myself. My name is Casper Meer."

"Hi, I'm Lisa. You have a South African accent. Do you live there?"

"I do, and I came to England to meet someone."

"Did you get to meet the person?"

He looked at her for a moment. A flicker of a smile crossed his face. "Of course. And you, do you live in London?"

She shook her head. "No, Manchester. I was in London to meet people before this flight."

Their conversation was interrupted when the flight attendants went through the safety procedures. Lisa ignored them, pulled a book from her bag, and began reading.

"You're not interested in emergency procedures, they are important?" Casper asked.

"They're a waste of time. Sitting in a seat like we are; if it goes down, we're dead. There's nowhere to run, no way of escape."

"That's very cynical, Lisa."

"Yes, well, I've only recently experienced the terror and hopelessness when you have no control of the outcome. All you can do is pray, not that He hears you."

"Again, very cynical, especially after God heard your prayers."

Her eyes narrowed. "How do you know?"

"You're here, aren't you?"

"Yes," she replied meekly, feeling a bit of an idiot with her question. "Except my deliverance, if you can call it that, was not my doing."

"I never suspected it was; after all, the almighty, once he makes a decision, would not need any help."

"I suppose not that I've had a religious upbringing, so I can't understand why he picked me."

He didn't pursue her statement when, at that moment, the aircraft turned onto the runway. It hesitated for only a moment as the engine power was ramped up before the brakes were released, and it began to accelerate down the runway.

Casper sighed. "I love this part, to feel the power before she lifts off."

Lisa didn't comment, looking out of the window. She knew now there was no turning back, besides not even sure if she'd be the next to pay the ultimate price. That's after she fulfilled her so-called destiny.

For the next twenty minutes, Lisa sat reading her book. Casper had closed his eyes, preventing further conversation if she had wanted to talk. But she didn't, content in keeping herself to herself.

Eventually, he opened his eyes. "Tell me, Lisa, I assume by your earlier comment that you had no control over the outcome. Perhaps that was a road accident when you were the passenger?"

She closed her book and looked at him. Why ask now? Had he spent the time contemplating her original statement? By now, she was fed up with reading and happy for a little conversation to pass the time. "No road accident. It was in South Africa, on an internal flight, when the plane crashed. It was in all the papers. All the passengers, the crew, apart from me, died. I felt like a fraud. Everyone on the plane was far cleverer and more intelligent than me. They would certainly have contributed more to the world than I'd ever do if they had lived."

"You are one of God's children and just as important. As it is, if he allowed you to live, you may have everything wrong, and it will be you who will contribute to humanity."

She smirked. "Believe me, I won't. I'm nothing. I can't even keep a boyfriend. I have a fragmented education because of looking after a very sick mother, ending up with a job that couldn't be much lower in the pecking order if I'd tried."

"But you're going to South Africa for the second time. Is that not expensive?"

She didn't answer immediately, allowing her memories of the short time with Jenny to fill her mind. "The last time I was on this aircraft, it took me four years of doing without, saving up to meet my penfriend. All was wasted, including my spending money and personal items, besides my clothes, when on an internal flight, the bloody aircraft crashed. The airline and their insurance company refused to pay, claiming my insurance didn't cover sabotage. What could I do with no money? I couldn't fight them, so I went cap in hand to the British embassy; even then, it was only a loan, and it had to be paid back."

"That sounds very harsh. Insurance companies have a lot to answer for. So is this time different?"

"Yes, I'm coming to sort out something outstanding. Nothing important, but believe me, I couldn't afford the fare. Someone else is paying. Anyway, forget my life, it's boring. So, where do you live in South Africa?" she asked, changing the subject.

"I used to live in Pretoria but moved out into the Kruger working for the government, ensuring the mining companies kept to the rules regarding pollution and other environmental issues. In the past, such things had been ignored in pursuit of money. It's a bit primitive around where I was. I spent time among the villagers and saw the poverty and malnutrition. Yet South Africa is not a poor nation full of valuable natural resources. It shouldn't have ever been like that, Lisa. When the mine was open, there was plenty of work. But as usual, the owners took the profit and gave nothing back to the villagers who still lived in poverty, with many dying in the mines, leaving their families destitute, often starving to death. Then there was the big robbery."

"What sort of robbery?"

"It happened during the Second World War. Most mines in the area produced mediocre stones for industry. Still, at times, one stone would stand out, and every stone found like that was carefully stored to eventually be sold on behalf of the miners and their families. The robbery took all the finest diamonds the mines in the area had produced, including one that is twenty-two carats. According to reports, this was the most flawless and brightest diamond ever mined. The value of that stone is beyond belief. Some say the robbers were German troops; others say it was the owners attempting to get the diamonds out of the country before the Germans took over."

"Did they ever turn up?"

"No, the diamonds were never seen again. All the workers lost out, with no wages, the mines closed, and with closure came poverty. The owners just turned their backs, claiming the mines were exhausted. They never even tidied up when they left, leaving a particularly lethal lake created during the pumping of mines constantly being flooded. Even today, in what was once a fertile area, seepage from the lake has turned the area dead and lifeless. Which is why people like me exist, so it can never happen again."

"I can understand their frustration. We had a local closure, putting a thousand or so out on the street, like my brother. It devastated the local businesses, even the chippy closed. But people get over it, move on, and something always turns up."

"You are correct, of course, but that is in an area where there are many business opportunities, not a remote area of the Kruger, where even the tiniest part of the hoard would have given the villages fresh water, medical assistance, education, and help them to be self-sufficient. Now, they rely on charities to provide the basics city dwellers take for granted. You see, Lisa, the men of the villages were forced to leave their homes, go to the city, and work. The ones left surviving on what was sent home. Because of inflation, less money can be sent home as the years pass."

"So, who would the diamonds belong to if they turned up?"

"That's an interesting question, but it would depend on where they were found, for example, if they turned up in the area where they were lost."

She frowned, "in what way?"

"Mining rights need constantly renewing, so the rights would lapse with no renewal. After all, such rights cost money, so why maintain mining rights if your mines are spent or producing too little to be viable? Under those conditions, the existing miners cannot return and ask for them, mainly because the stones were never registered officially to a particular mine, so they don't exist. Technically, whoever finds them, providing they obtain a license to mine in the area, even if they just picked them up off the ground, could claim they are theirs. Who could object? Diamonds in the past were found scattered around in many areas of Africa."

"And if there were no mining rights and they were found?"

He looked at her for a moment. "Why would such a scenario interest you?"

She gave an indifferent shrug. "More of an interesting conversation about something I know nothing about. Except if the mines are spent, there's hardly likely to be such a scenario; more likely they'd be found locally or in someone's safe deposit in another country."

"Logical assumptions, perhaps. Let's look at the scenarios. Hidden in a safe deposit box is very possible. Even so, they would have no value in such a box and couldn't be used as collateral for a loan. Questions would be asked about where they came from or, more importantly if they were blood diamonds. If they were proven that they were, then the government of whichever country they came from would claim them. If, on the other hand, they were found locally in the mines, which is very unlikely, when over the years, the loss has attracted hundreds of treasure seekers. But let's say they were missed, and with modern search techniques, they were found. While the finders may have had a valid claim to keep them in the past, that is not the case today. The diamonds would belong to the villagers, as the government returned the land to the locals some years ago. Having said that, the stones have a great deal of value, so if the descendants of the miners found their only opposition was a few illiterates from local villages rather than a new mining company, they would crush them, taking the diamonds themselves."

"This would make an interesting story, as a David versus Goliath. With a twist, that the finder runs away with the haul to live a life of luxury."

He laughed. "If only life was so easy, Lisa. But you need to remember that uncut diamonds for the average person would have little value and are not something they could sell to a local jeweller. They would need to go to a cutting company. When not dealing with a registered mine, the company would want to know where the stones came from. Suspicions would be aroused that they might be being offered 'blood diamonds.'"

"You've mentioned blood diamonds twice. What are they?" Lisa asked with interest.

"Blood diamonds are sometimes called conflict diamonds; these are stones mined in war zones, often by forced labour or children. Such stones are traded illegally to finance violent conflicts against legitimate governments. The trade is frowned upon, and companies found to be buying them can lose their licence, and owners sent to prison."

"It's certainly been an interesting conversation, Casper. You know your diamonds."

"Not so much diamonds, more the happenings around such a valuable commodity." He got up from his seat. "Well, nature is calling. It happens when you get older. I enjoyed our conversation, Lisa." Then he walked away down towards the toilets.

Lisa sighed and began reading.

Shortly after, a member of the cabin crew brought her dinner.

Lisa thanked her, but she called her back as she moved to the next row of seats. "A gentleman is also sitting here. Shouldn't you leave his dinner?" she asked.

The woman looked at Lisa. "These seats are vacant. Perhaps the gentleman has moved back to his own?"

"No, he's been here since we took off. You must have seen him. He's just left to go to the toilet."

The woman looked around and then back at Lisa. "I'll be returning shortly. If he has returned, there will be dinner for him."

Lisa nodded and began her dinner. Casper never returned, even when coffee was brought.

Confused, after her dinner, Lisa took a walk down the aircraft, looking for Casper, but she couldn't find him. Going back to her seat, she sat there for a moment. Her entire body was shaking. Was Casper real, or was he yet another dead person like Jenny? Then she thought back to what DB had said while in the fortune teller booth in Blackpool, "Already you are finding only you can see and hear what others cannot. Don't be afraid to call out for help. Help cannot come unless you demand they stand at your side." With such thoughts going through her mind, never had she been as scared as she was now.

***

Lisa looked out of the small window at the landscape below. She'd become fascinated by what looked like a toy town, suddenly becoming houses with real people and cars as the airplane dropped to land.

Leaving the aircraft, Lisa made her way through to the immigration hall. It was there that she saw Casper again. She walked up to him.

"Casper, you never came back to your seat. Are you alright?" she asked, relieved that the man existed but also a little worried. He wasn't, after all, a young man.

"I'm sorry, Lisa. I had not only the wrong seat but also the wrong ticket class to be in there. But it was good of you to inquire about my health. Anyway, I must go. Enjoy your stay in South Africa."

"I will."

She watched him walk away, then joined the queue to show her passport.

Casper made his way out of the airport, climbing into a

waiting car.

"You managed to talk to her, Casper?" the driver asked.

"I did. Lisa is here for the diamonds. I'm certain of that. Do we know if the consortium, headed by Sir John, paid for her ticket?"

"We do; his sidekick, Hans, is already back in the country."

"Then it is time to get the lads together. Our people will not be happy if the large diamond slips through our fingers."

***

Lisa, on her part, was finally standing in front of an Immigration Officer.

"Can you tell me what your visit is for?" he asked while looking through her passport.

"Just as a tourist," she replied.

"You were here not so long ago?"

"Yes, that was also a holiday, but I was in a plane crash, so my holiday was cut short. I'm here to complete it."

He nodded and stamped the passport, handing it to her. "Welcome back to South Africa."

Lisa thanked him, collected her baggage, and went to the arrivals hall. A man stood beside the barrier, holding a handwritten sign high with her name on it. She walked over and introduced herself.

"I'll take your bags, Miss. I have a car waiting outside," the man said, taking over the trolley.

The car was comfortable and air-conditioned. After about an hour's drive, they turned through double gates and stopped at an imposing entrance to a huge house. A lady ran down the steps and pulled open the car door.

Lisa climbed out, and then, after an exchange of pleasantries, she followed the lady through an impressive entrance hall into the lounge. Two men were waiting, standing as she entered. Lisa recognised Hans from when she originally went to London.

"It's good to see you again, Lisa. I trust you had a pleasant flight, " Hans said.

"Yes, thank you."

"I'd like to introduce you to Sam Strange. He will be our guide on the expedition."

Sam was well over six feet and well-built. To Lisa, he looked ex-army with his close-cut hair and tattooed arms.

"Hi!" she said.

He shook her hand, his grip tight, nearly shaking her arm out of its socket. "So you're the little lady who will show us where the diamonds are?"

"Yes, that's if I can find the place again. I'm hopeless at maps and things."

"You'll be alright. It'll all come back when you're there."

"Shall we have dinner?" Hans asked, cutting the conversation short.

***

Later that night, Lisa lay in bed, wide awake, staring at the ceiling. Unable to sleep, she climbed out of bed, slipped on her dressing gown, and went onto a veranda. The usual sounds of the night had gone, the silence overwhelming. Lisa pulled her dressing gown tighter. She was leaning on the rail, looking across the neatly trimmed gardens. The sizeable ornamental pool was glistening in the moonlight. By the side of the pool, she saw DB standing watching her. However, she was no longer frightened or even annoyed at him. She was back in Africa and felt calm and safe with him being there as if she had a friend watching over her.

Eventually, she returned to her room and lay down in bed. Lisa sat up. She knew DB was in her room. In seconds, he was at the end of her bed.

"You have, as foretold, returned; it is time to right the wrongs of the past. Never feel you are alone; call out for me, and I will come. Be warned, call only when your life is in extreme danger, too often, and each time I become weaker. Follow your instincts, and you will succeed."

"How do I call for your help?"

However, she had not received an answer, and DB was gone.

"Well, that advice was a waste of bloody time," she said out loud. "It's always half a story with him. Jenny's ghost was better. At least we could talk to each other."

She lay back down, deep in thought.

Chapter 20

The next day, Hans joined Lisa out on the veranda. She'd had breakfast and was reading a magazine.

"Good morning," she said when he approached.

"Morning," he came back at her curtly. "There's been a delay. We'll not be leaving for two days."

"Does that mean I can go into town and look around?"

"Why not? I'll have one of our drivers drop you off at Menlyn Park. It's the largest shopping centre with over four hundred stores. You'll not get bored there. Call us when you are ready to return, and we'll collect you."

"Sounds good to me, I'll go and get ready."

***

Lisa walked into the centre, casually looking in windows and entering stores. All the time, she watched to see if anyone was doing the same thing, checking if she was being followed. But she saw no one, or they were very good at using more than one person. Finding a small coffee shop, Lisa sat down with a coffee and biscuit and looked through a flyer that offered discounts at certain shops.

She had been there for fifteen minutes when a voice she recognised came from behind her.

"We meet again."

Lisa turned to see Casper standing there. She smiled. "Casper! We do. Would you like to join me for coffee?"

"Thank you, I believe I will, but let me buy. It isn't right for a lady to buy."

"That's the past. We have equal rights, but I'll not argue the point."

"Then I will go and collect them," he told her, walking to the counter.

Soon, he was back, taking the seat opposite. "So, are you enjoying the shopping centre?"

"I am, except everything I see in the shops I like, is way

beyond my meagre funds."

"Isn't that always the case? Tell me, are you remaining in Pretoria? If you are, we should meet again."

"Sorry, I'll only be here a day or so before going into the Kruger. I should be back in a couple of weeks. If you leave me your number, I'll call. Then, if you're free, we can have lunch, and I'll tell you what I've been up to."

"I'll look forward to it. You must like our national park with you returning."

"Yes, and one village in particular I want to visit again. I owe my life to them, and I'd like to find out if I can do anything to improve their lives."

"Take care, Lisa; these are proud people; they don't take charity."

"I'd not be offering charity. I just want a clearer understanding of their lives. Maybe I can set up a fundraising page, like Umbra, to get them a well."

He frowned, "Umbra has a well now?"

"Yes, brought about when the rescue services and engineers came to the area to raise the crashed aircraft."

"That is good, but your idea is very ambitious."

"Anything's possible, Casper, if you want to do it. But one step at a time."

They chatted generally before going their separate ways. As Lisa walked away, a man approached Casper.

"I believe she is going to take them to the diamonds. Are our people in place?" Casper asked the man.

"Yes. We have also been watching Hans. He's brought in three vehicles. They are currently being prepared."

"Then you join our team immediately. Keep in close communication, and I'll send in a helicopter after you confirm you have the diamonds."

"What are your instructions for Hans and his crew?"

"Mining can be dangerous; accidents happen constantly, and Hans is not immune."

"I understand, consider them gone."

Chapter 21

Following a very early breakfast, three days after arriving in South Africa, Lisa joined Hans and Sam, along with four others, standing around three Land Rovers. All the men were white. They carried sidearms and some rifles.

"You're in the first vehicle with Sam. I'll be in the second," Hans said as Lisa handed him her bag.

She nodded and climbed into the passenger seat. Within minutes, the small convoy was turning onto the main road.

***

Lisa had not returned to the shopping centre. Before they left, she spent the rest of the time around the villa relaxing beside an outdoor swimming pool. She also attended several meetings where the expedition was discussed, as Hans liked to call it.

Among those discussions was basic safety, recognition of insects, snakes, and other possibly harmful residents she might encounter when they were in the bush. Particularly if Lisa left the perimeter of the camp. Naively, she'd ask why she'd do that. The answer was filled with laughter after she was reminded that there was no toilet block and a wash would be a dip in a river.

Hans told her they would not be flying, mainly because there was nowhere to land except the lake. They had already been to the lake and found several partially submerged hazards, making any sort of landing extremely risky. Although they could use a helicopter to land by the lake, they would still need a route march to the diamond's location. Because of this, they faced a three-day journey, fifty percent of which would be on what they referred to as tar roads, before turning off onto narrow single-track unmade roads.

***

The first night had been in a hotel. Now, they had turned off the tar road and made their way slowly, first along a wide track, before far narrower tracks that had been little used. They were constantly being held up by fallen trees and rain-damaged tracks, leaving large potholes that had to be made good to a reasonable extent just to get through. Lisa would try to help, but most of the time, she'd be standing around watching.

They parked up, and tents were erected. No campfire was used, rather a double burner portable gas stove.

Lisa settled down, leaning against a large stone, working through her hot stew, which she had brought along with her can of Coke.

Hans joined her. "Not far now, Lisa. Are you enjoying the trip?"

She gave a light shrug. "We got here quicker by aircraft. But I am seeing the Kruger this time, without the pressures that were on me after the crash."

"Yes, I can believe that. But you have never told us how you came across the diamonds."

She placed her stew down for a moment. While she was going to tell the truth, it would be a more acceptable version of events, rather than mentioning Jenny. "It was raining. I was on a track leading from the lake when I heard rumbling. You know, like loads of horses galloping. Then I saw them, large black things, coming towards me on the track. I think they were elephants, but I'm not sure. Anyway, there was no chance of me stopping them, so I panicked, trying to get out of their way, and tripped, falling face down. After whatever it was had gone past, I pushed myself up. It was then I touched the tipped box. Wondering what it was and why it was there, I pulled the grass away. The lid was open and contained what I believed were rocks."

"So you didn't know they were diamonds?"

"No, I'd never seen a raw diamond. All I've seen is

what's in the jewellers windows."

"So what made you take some?"

"I thought whatever they were must have value to be collected and boxed. So, I intended to ask Jenny's dad. He's a geologist."

"He is, but you never showed them to him."

"No, they were so distraught at losing their only daughter; they weren't very sociable to me. I believed they'd rather have Jenny survive than me."

"I can understand that. So you left the box then?"

"I did, but I decided to move it to a place I could find again if Jenny's father wanted to see the rocks. So I found a landmark and dragged it there. It wasn't far, but easier to find than in the scrub."

"You know there were three boxes?"

"So Sir John told me, but I only found one. I don't know if there were others around, nor did I bother to look. It was difficult enough moving the one I'd found so it didn't enter my head there may be more. Then, I didn't know what I was looking at. So it would have been stupid to look for more when they may only have been something used in the local tribal rituals and be valueless."

"Can you show us where you originally found the box you moved?"

"I don't know. It could be challenging with all the rain and how the forest grows."

"But you'd know how far you dragged the box? Besides the direction."

"I'll try, but it was quite a time back, and everything was confusing and mixed up."

"Well, let's see, shall we? It may all come back to you when you're there."

Hans moved away and joined Sam. Telling him what Lisa had said.

"It sounds feasible," Sam said, lighting a cigarette at

the same time. "She certainly didn't know what she was looking at. Then she'd have no idea there were three boxes. But where there's one, the others must have been there. Whatever happened, with her finding the box and not the Land Rover, makes what went on all those years ago even more puzzling."

"It does, although a more acceptable explanation would be that there were more than three people in the vehicle, and the box Lisa found had been thrown out before the fatal crash? If that did happen, any people surviving the accident took two boxes, ignoring the third."

"Lisa could be far more astute than she's acting and has decided to admit to only one box, knowing that the money she would be paid for the box contents would allow her to return for the other two."

Hans grinned. "It will be interesting to find that out when she's strung up, and we begin to beat the shit out of her."

Sam nodded. "It will, but let's keep it all sweet until we have the first box."

Chapter 22

By lunchtime the following day, the small convoy was running alongside a river, approaching the track leading off to the lake, where the aircraft had come down.

Lisa had been looking at the river as they travelled along. Since the last time she had been here, it had dropped considerably; in fact, it was now far less wide than when she had first crossed it with Jenny. "Are we in a dry season now?" Lisa asked.

"Why do you ask?" Sam wanted to know.

"Just with the river being so low, that's all."

"In this area, heavy rain and flash flooding are quite regular. You need to watch the weather. It comes in very fast."

"Tell me about it. I'd only just dried after crawling out of the lake when I was soaked by a heavy downpour again."

He laughed. "It's good you understand. The flooding in this area has caught a lot of people in the past, and many have died. Anyway, have you begun to recognise the landscape?"

"No, it all looks the same to me."

Before he could comment, the satellite navigation began to bleep. Sam pulled in and climbed out of the vehicle. Hans came to a halt behind and joined him.

"This is the track Lisa took from the lake. I suggest we walk from here. If we use the vehicles, Lisa may not recognise landmarks sitting high up in a vehicle. Then, last time, if she found the box close to the wrecked Land Rover, we'd struggle to get a vehicle down that far. Over time, the track has closed up to just being a walking track."

"So, how did the rescue services get to the lake?" another man who had followed Hans asked.

"They bulldozed a new road some half a mile closer to

Umbra. To have widened this track would have taken them close to old mine workings, making the land unstable. That is probably why they never found the crashed Land Rover. If they had, they'd not have left the bodies inside."

"How far is it to the wrecked Land Rover?" the man persisted.

"We'll have a good day's walk, maybe into the next if we have to cut our way through. When we searched last time, we landed a helicopter on the bank of the lake. Coming from the lake direction would have been easier. Still, I suspected it could have confused Lisa about which track she had taken. From the dirt road, she'd know where she emerged from the forest."

Sam glanced at his watch. "We can go no further today. I'll get the lads to set up camp."

Lisa had left the camp area. She needed the toilet, and as Hans had told her, with a great deal of laughter from the others, there was always behind a bush. Now, running her hands in the river and drying them with a small towel she'd brought with her, Lisa looked up to see DB standing a short distance from her.

He seemed to be just watching. Then, Lisa was distracted by a voice from behind.

"There you are, Lisa; you must keep close to the camp," Sam told her as he approached.

"I'm coming, but you must find a bush when there is no handy toilet block when nature calls."

He smiled. "You do."

DB watched them go. Sam never saw him, but Lisa did, as he'd not moved.

***

The following morning, after breakfast, they all set off, on foot, along the track that eventually led to the lake where the aircraft had come down. Lisa, with Hans, was a short distance ahead of the group.

"Take your time, and you'll begin to recognise landmarks you didn't realise you'd notice coming the first time," Hans told her after she had commented on how much everything had changed.

That was the truth on Lisa's side; she had recognised nothing. She also realised that there would have been no chance of finding the boxes if Jenny had not suggested landmarks that wouldn't move or disappear, no matter how the forest grew.

Time went on, and then Lisa suddenly came to a halt. To the side of them was the stone jutting above the scrub. While she knew this was the marker for the location of the two boxes, she intended only to show them the location of the single box. "I remember that jutting out rock. I was going to put it at the bottom, but the vegetation was too dense, and I couldn't get close."

"So, where did you end up hiding it?" Hans asked.

Lisa stood momentarily, then turned to face the way they had come. "I counted seventy steps beyond the jutting-out rock before finding a place to put the box." Then, without another comment, she set off, carefully counting her steps.

Everyone moved out of her way. Coming to a halt, Lisa pointed into the vegetation at the side of the track. "It's a bit overgrown now, but five steps in is where I left the box," she told Hans.

He nodded to two men, who immediately began cutting the vegetation clear.

Twenty minutes later, after careful searching, they had found nothing. Lisa watched without commenting.

"It's obvious you have the location wrong, Lisa. You'd better start thinking. We're not here for our health," Sam told her with a hint of aggression.

"It's alright for you, I was on my own, and the box was heavy."

"Tell me, did you drag or carry the box when you

counted your steps?" Hans asked.

"I couldn't carry it. I dragged the box and counted as I progressed, looking for a suitable location. Why?"

He looked at one of the men. "Give her a bag with a couple of rocks in it. Lisa, drag it along the path back to the pointed rock, and let's count the steps."

She did as told and dragged the bag towards the pointed rock, counting the seventy steps again. Lisa stopped; she was still a distance from the pointed rock. "That's strange. I'm sure I counted right," she commented.

"You did, but dragging the box made your steps shorter. Do seventy from the pointed rock, but you drag the bag this time," Hans told her.

"Okay, but let me get my breath back first." Lisa took a few gulps of her water, returned to the pointed rock, and began again. When she arrived at seventy, the two men began clearing the scrub. Also, on Hans' instruction, the search to either side of the new location was widened. Fifteen minutes later, the box was found.

As soon as one of the men shouted, he'd found it. Sam pushed him away, dragging the loose lid off the box. He froze, his eyes wide with terror. Seconds later, the snake struck, sinking its fangs into his arm. By now, he'd pulled away and was screaming that he'd been bitten. Meanwhile, the snake slipped away into the undergrowth.

"Look after him," Hans told one of the men, completely ignoring Sam's dilemma and directing his interest to the now open box. He was already feeling a little putout. He'd expected the box to be full. It wasn't, being less than half full. Poking around the stones with the tip of his rifle, not prepared to take the chance; something else was inside the box, he was looking for a particular stone, but it wasn't there.

"You told us it was full, Lisa," he said, obviously annoyed.

"I never said it was to the top; I just said it was full of stones, then a few of them may have fallen out while I dragged it. But you've got the stones. What more do you want?"

"We want the other two boxes; one will have a stone inside, purporting to be the largest stone ever mined. I believe you are hiding the real story of what happened. Perhaps believing you can come back and collect the rest yourself."

"You're mad. If you remember, I was never going to come back. It was you lot that had me come. Then how the hell could I drag three boxes?"

"You didn't; you left the other two where you found them all, taking one box as insurance so as not to share all the finds with Jenny's father."

Lisa shrugged. "Believe what you want. As far as I'm aware, this is it; there's nothing else apart from what's in your mind."

"Then you take me to where you found this box."

"How can I do that? There's no landmark; that's why I moved it."

"You would know how many steps you took before you reached the pointed rock."

"Why would I count before the pointed rock? I was looking for a landmark." Then she hesitated. "There was something I saw."

"What?"

"Deeper into the undergrowth, there was a vehicle of some sort. I never investigated; by the look of it, the vehicle had been there a long time."

Hans suspected she was talking about the Land Rover, not that he was certain, but he'd not found any others. "And the box was close to the vehicle?"

"Yes, mind you, I'd not have found the box if the bloody elephants hadn't forced me to get off the track pretty sharpish. I think they had been spooked by the thunder coming close to the lightning."

Hans stood. "Right, back to the Land Rover. Then Lisa can show us exactly where she found the box."

"What do we do with Sam? He's deteriorated even though I tried to suck the poison out," one of the men asked.

Hans was annoyed at what had happened. He looked at Sam, sitting on the ground, his head slumped forward. Hans was confused about what sort of snake bite reacted this fast, particularly in this area, where highly venomous snakes were unknown. "Make a makeshift stretcher and two of you will take him back to the vehicles. Then drive to the village and see if they can help."

With this agreed, Hans, Lisa, and the last two men returned to the pointed rock.

***

Soon, they were at the crashed Land Rover. Hans stood for a moment. "Was that the vehicle you saw?" he asked, pointing to the Land Rover.

"I think so, mind you; all I saw was the shape of one, where this vehicle someone has cleared all the vegetation covering it," Lisa told him, attempting to sound confused.

"We did last time we were here. So where was the box exactly?"

Not wanting to include the vehicle, Lisa walked back a few paces and pointed to the ground. "It was just off the track tipped on its side."

"Sounds like the box she found fell out before the crash," one of the men suggested.

"Maybe, but they weren't in the vehicle; then, if the other two boxes did fall out, they are not here now; we've already searched the area," Hans commented.

Happy, Hans seemed to accept her story, and Lisa was ready to go.

"I've kept my end of the agreement; now I want to go home," Lisa told him.

"You're going nowhere until I'm satisfied you've told us the truth. So shut up," Hans retorted.

"I see. What do you intend to do with me? Use thumbscrews? Because whatever you do, I can't materialise three boxes from one. I'm not a bloody magician."

Hans grinned. "We don't use such basic methods. I've got a far better option that's bound to loosen your tongue," he looked at one of the men. "It's time for a bit of fun. Bring her; I have the ideal location."

Before Lisa could run for it, one of the men grabbed her while another pulled a rope from his bag. The next moment, her wrists had been bound together, and she was led further down the track into a small clearing that looked like a location where people here before had set up camp.

"You see, Lisa, we were here not so long ago and had already set up a nice campsite but had to abandon it. Too many biting insects for my liking, but it will be ideal for loosening your tongue."

"I've told you everything I know. You're wasting your time. Just accept that the other boxes you claim to be here are not," she retorted.

"Perhaps you are correct, but I was a mercenary for years after my army service, and many then would claim they knew nothing. Most didn't, but some certainly did. I soon had them begging for their lives and telling me everything. You will do the same. Release the rope and strip her."

Lisa was in a panic. They intended to rape her. But no matter how much she struggled, they soon had her naked. The rope again was tied around her wrists, and the other end was thrown over the branch of a tree. Following this, the rope was pulled, first dragging her arms up above her head and then literally lifting her entire body, leaving her feet just able to touch the ground.

Hans walked up to her, his face inches from hers. "You're stupid and naive, having the belief you'd leave here alive. But believe me, before you die, you will have told me the truth and begged me to end your life."

She just looked back at him. "Well, at least I've done something good in my life, and children will benefit."

"Whatever," he answered, taking a jar of honey from his backpack. He opened the top and poured the contents on Lisa's forehead. He watched with satisfaction as the liquid trickled down her face, body, and legs until it dripped below her feet. Satisfied, he came around to face her.

"You have time to think, Lisa. Within the hour, ants will have found the sweet honey at your feet. They will bring others, climb up your body to get at the rest of the honey, cover your face, and go up your nose, into your mouth, up your backside in their search. By then, you'll be in hysterics, trying to spit them out, but you cannot stop them; they will come in their thousands, crawling all over you. Attracting even worse insects that will bite and, of course, snakes. Attracted by your screams and sweat, some even feast on the ants. I don't envy you, and believe me, when I return, you'll be telling me everything, even begging me to kill you. I won't; your death will be slow, painful, finally leaving only your bones unless I'm happy with the words that come out of your mouth."

"Then you'd better kill me. I can't tell you anything more," she told him bravely.

"We shall see. Let's go, lads, so she can contemplate her position during dinner. Enjoy the experience, Lisa. I'll be back later to see if you decided it would be prudent to tell me about the other boxes." He and the other men began to walk away.

"I hope you have a good explanation for the police when you return?" Lisa called after him.

He ignored her words and carried on walking.

"Besides the British Embassy?" she added.

Hans stopped and turned. "What are you on about?"

"I'd a feeling I might not be going home? So, I sent the safe deposit box key to the British Embassy and a letter to the police telling them where the key was. With the key were instructions on which bank the safe deposit box was, and if I went missing, they were to open it. Inside the box is a letter and a recording of my last meeting with Sir John. The letter is a complete statement of everything that has happened to me, besides naming everyone I've met and where, as well as Sir John. I told them everything, even how you'd put money into an account for me and why you were taking me back to the scene of the accident. So go ahead, kill me, but believe this, I will have the last laugh when the police knock at Sir John's door to arrest him for complicity in murder. Would he take the fall without implicating you and your other men? I think not somehow."

"You're lying. You never went anywhere without us watching."

"That is true, but if you check with the people watching me in London, they will confirm I went to a bank with safe deposit boxes. As for the two letters, I posted them in the hotel post box. So, go on believing I didn't do as I've said. After all, I won't be there when they come for you, and they will come. My death will be the catalyst."

One of the men nudged Hans. "I'm not going down for her murder," he said quietly.

"Shut up, she's all talk, she never went anywhere. We'd have known," Hans came back at him.

"So why take the risk? It's obvious she's not got any more diamonds," the other man commented.

Hans turned to them both. "If it makes you happy, I'll call Sir John and get him to ask the men who were watching her if they saw her going to the bank."

"See, you fucking do. Otherwise, we let her go," one threatened.

"We'll check out your fantasy. In the meantime, enjoy your experience with the ants," Hans shouted back at her and walked away.

Chapter 23

Lisa had been left alone for some time. She could see ants around the honey that had dripped off her body to the ground. Lisa had tried to slip her hands out of the rope and even lifted herself to use her teeth to pull on the knot, but all it did was tighten, hurting her even more. Then, not a gymnast in any respect, she attempted to swing, believing she could reach the tree trunk with her feet and walk up the side of the tree to finally get her legs around the branch the rope was over. However, she couldn't reach the tree trunk without swinging, which was painful when she touched the trunk with her feet, and she just swung away again. Failing to escape, Lisa was now concentrating on keeping her feet off the ground. Still, the strain on her arms was too much, and she was forced to take the weight off her arms by touching the ground. She could feel insects crawling up her legs, forcing her to shake her legs, trying to get them off, but while a few fell, most clung on, determined to get at the sweet honey.

Now, she was panicking, her thoughts returning to what DB had told her to do if she was in serious trouble. In her view, this couldn't be more serious. But what could a ghost do in reality? Realising shouting out for DB wouldn't work; he'd never once responded to her questions, Lisa concentrated hard on his vision and began silently calling him in her mind, asking him for help. But nothing happened.

"Please, DB, whoever you are, I don't want to die; I want to help the villagers. I can't do this alone," she whispered in a last-ditch attempt to reach him.

Lisa didn't see DB standing a short distance away. He watched for a short time before looking up. The sky was darkening as heavy storm clouds began to form, immediately followed by rain. It came down in torrents. Lisa was freezing and drenched, but what honey she had on her body was washed off. The ants, unable to hold on, followed.

Besides the rain, there was thunder in the air. The flashing of lightning, followed by the thunder immediately after, meant it was getting closer all the time. Lisa was terrified; the noise and the rain lashing down stung her face and body, forcing her to keep her eyes closed tight. Then, lightning struck a tree behind her. The bolt of lightning split it in two, and as it fell, one part hit the end of the branch, and the rope securing Lisa had been thrown over. The branch snapped, and Lisa went crashing to the ground.

She lay there stunned, except the rain was not letting off, effectively bringing her out of the shock of falling to the ground. Lisa, with her survival instinct kicking in, sat up. Then, using her teeth, she pulled at the knot around her wrists, slackening it sufficiently for her to wriggle her hands out. Standing gingerly, she found her discarded clothing and quickly dressed. Not waiting around, she headed towards the lake, away from the direction Hans and the men had gone.

Lisa had no idea what she hoped to achieve, but at least for the moment, she was free and alive by some quirk of fate, and she intended to remain that way if possible.

***

Hans and the two men had deliberately moved out of sight of Lisa to add to her fear and nervousness at being alone. While the ants would only be irritating, she would soon be covered in them, making her dilemma much worse before Hans replaced this with beatings and cutting her skin to allow the blood to flow, attracting more deadly insects besides snakes.

"Are you calling Sir John?" one of the men asked Hans, between mouthfuls of bread and cheese.

"I am, but there's no rush; I'm eating first; she's going nowhere."

They all fell silent. Once they had finished their dinner, Hans raised his satellite telephone and dialled. Soon, a woman answered.

"It's Hans, I want to talk to Sir John. Tell him it's urgent," Hans said, cutting short the woman's standard welcome.

"Hans, is all going well?" Sir John asked.

"One box and that's only half full. The girl claims she's only ever seen one box and knows nothing of the vehicle. We've left her to contemplate her position."

"She'll break. The girl's weak. Just keep the pressure up."

"I intend to, but she made a statement, and I need clarification," Hans said before repeating what Lisa told him to Sir John.

After listening to Hans, Sir John said he would call back in half an hour. Hans cut the connection. "We wait, he's checking it out," was all Hans said to the men with him.

Shortly, one of the men looked up at the sky. "I can't say I like the look of those clouds; rain may be on the way," he commented.

They all looked up. "Maybe. That's one thing I don't like about this area. Rain comes without warning," Hans added, pulling out waterproofs from his backpack just in case. The others followed suit.

Hans' comment about the rain coming without warning was valid. They all grabbed what they could and moved deeper into the forest, trying to use the tree canopy to protect them from the worst of the downpour. However, the sky cleared as fast as it came, leaving water dripping off the trees.

"What about the girl? Shouldn't we check on her?" one man asked, pulling off his waterproofs.

"I wanted a comeback from Sir John first, but you're right, we should check," Hans agreed.

Making their way back to where Lisa had been left, all of them stopped dead, surprised she'd gone.

"She'll not have got far. Find the bitch," Hans demanded.

Everyone spread out, with Hans running down the track towards the lake.

As he ran, he looked for footprints in the muddy ground, but there were none. Eventually convinced Lisa couldn't have come this way, he returned to find the others.

"Well, what about tracks?" he asked the other men.

Both men shrugged. "I could find nothing. It's as if she has never left," one man commented.

Hans stood looking up into the trees. "You might just have it. With not even one footprint, there's no way she walked out, so she's up a bloody tree and close by. Look for anything, signs of climbing, broken branches, disturbed climbers on the tree trunks."

They spent time carefully retracing their tracks, looking for signs that would have been obvious if someone had tried to climb a tree. Again, they drew a blank.

As Hans returned to join them, his satellite telephone began to ring. Pressing the answer, he was put through to Sir John.

"Well, what have you found out?" Hans asked.

"She did go into a bank. Spent fifteen minutes there. We can't be sure about any letters being posted, as the box is in the hotel reception where she stayed. So bring her back once you're sure she can tell you nothing."

"Yes, okay, I'll see to it," Hans answered, cutting the call. He had no intention of telling him Lisa had escaped. Not that he considered her recapture would be a problem.

Chapter 24

The track Lisa took towards the lake was running with water, leaves, and other debris forced along by the water, all contributing to wiping out her footprints. However, if Hans had gone further towards the lake, he'd have found signs Lisa had made after the rain stopped, although weak and partly washed out,

After a two-hour walk, Lisa came out of the forest by the side of the lake. She stood for a moment looking across the still lake; the memories of the crash came flooding back, making her go cold inside. After a short time, and not dwelling on those thoughts, she headed in the opposite direction she'd initially come from following the original accident. Why did she do that? Lisa wasn't sure; it seemed right to go that way. Besides, she'd surmised, there was nothing in the way of tracks leading from the lake the other way, or rather, she and Jenny hadn't found any. However, if she had gone that way, she would have come across the new bulldozed road made by the rescue teams and ended up closer to the village and safety.

Following the lake round, Lisa came to an abrupt halt. Fifty yards in front of her stood DB. He looked directly at her, then turned and walked into the forest. Lisa didn't wait for long, setting off towards where he'd been standing before she could see where he'd gone. The track wasn't obvious. It was narrow enough to allow a single file rather than the much wider track on which she'd come to the lake. Lisa didn't hesitate, pushing her way through the partly overgrown entrance, and set off again. She was hungry and aware that no matter what, she'd need to spend a night on this track. Lisa felt confident that Hans would struggle to find where she had gone.

***

Unlike the track Lisa had come on, this one was climbing.

It was not steep initially but was becoming more difficult. With no knowledge of where she would end up, Lisa could only place her absolute faith in DB. He hadn't let her down so far, even if, in her view, he was a figment of her imagination. When considering this, she couldn't understand why her imagination allowed her to know another track leading from the lake. It was as if she'd been there before, which, of course, she hadn't. Unless that is, she had lived another life? Lisa smiled to herself at the thought. What would she have been? A man, a girl, maybe an animal? She had no idea, but it sounded as feasible as seeing and relying on her imagination for a guide.

The skies soon began darkening, and she needed shelter to see the night through. While she was hungry, Lisa wasn't prepared to eat anything growing for fear of poisoning herself or at least making her ill. She trudged on.

Lisa finally came to a halt. It was so dark that she couldn't see anything in front of her, so she was risking injury. Sitting at the side of the track, leaning on a tree, she closed her eyes. Lisa had had enough. As a city girl with no hiking experience back home, this was another world, and she was entirely out of her depth.

While she slept, DB stood at her side. His presence left the small area where she slept completely void of any life, whether an insect or a large predator. All avoided the tiny little circle surrounding Lisa.

***

"Hey, come on, wake up, sleepyhead," a girl's voice shouted, gently shaking Lisa.

She opened her eyes and gasped. "Jenny, you're here. That can't be. I've got to be dreaming?"

"Hardly, Lisa. Anyway, what dream collects a few berries and the like for breakfast?"

Lisa looked at the small pile on a large leaf before accepting that this wasn't a dream and standing, giving

Jenny a long hug. "God, you're cold. Don't you have anything warmer to wear?"

"No, what about you? You're freezing and hardly dressed for the cold nights," Jenny said.

"I never thought about that. I've missed you, but the police told me you'd died in the aircraft and claimed they had your body. No one would believe me when I told them it wasn't possible, that we'd left together. So where have you been? Why didn't you wait by the track while I brought help?"

Jenny pulled away and shrugged, picking up what looked like a small apple from the leaf pile, and handed it to Lisa, who took it gratefully.

Both sat down while Lisa carried on eating.

"You've not told me what happened to you yet," Lisa commented.

"I don't think I was bitten by anything particularly dangerous, but waking up and finding you not there, I think I must have set off down the track to find you," Jenny said after some thought. "I couldn't believe you'd gone so far, so when I found a small settlement, I remained there, not feeling very well."

"Well, you're going to confuse your parents, wondering who they buried. But that was months back. You couldn't have remained in the settlement for this long. Why didn't you go home?"

"You're wrong, Lisa, I've only been there a few days."

"Hardly, I've been home and come back, and why are you on this track?"

"I was told you were lost and needed help, so I've come for you."

"Was the person that told you an elderly man by any chance?"

"Yes, do you know him?"

"Sort of, not to talk to, he turns up, telling me strange

things, never replying to my questions before going away again. It's very disconcerting."

"I can imagine. You didn't tell anyone about our diamonds, did you?"

"I'm sorry, but it's a long story, and I was desperate. In the crash, I lost everything and went into debt to get home."

"Didn't my family help?"

"You have to be joking. Apart from interrogation and obvious innuendos as to how I survived and you didn't, I was ignored. The police made me feel like I'd sabotaged the aircraft. When I said you were still alive, they put me with a shrink, finally deciding I must have been eating something similar to magic mushrooms, and my head was scrambled. If when you'd woken, you'd gone the same way as I did, it would have saved a lot of hassle. Back home, things just got worse. Mum died, and my brother is now in prison, facing twenty-five years. So I had to sell some diamonds. Only the half box, as well as the twenty, we took out. No one knows of the two full boxes. I got two million pounds, well I would have if the people who brought me here hadn't decided I'm expendable. So I can't see myself getting paid."

"I'm sorry you've had to put up with so much. Anything to do with diamonds brings out greed in people. So what's your plan now?"

Lisa grinned. "Apart from surviving, I have no idea. Mind you, that's not quite true. I was talking to a man during the flight from the UK. He told me the rights to mine must be paid for, and you lose your rights if you don't keep paying. He also said you need permission from whoever owns the land."

"That is correct. My dad often applies for mining rights when he's studying an area. The rights allow him to dig around and take samples. The application is made on the internet these days."

"So you don't need to be experienced or have certificates, then?"

"No, why do you ask?"

"If I got mining rights, I could legally claim any diamonds found. After all, I'd be a miner."

Jenny thought for a moment. "You know, you're correct. But we are talking millions in value. Do you need that sort of money?"

"I'm not looking at keeping the money; the villages in this area desperately need help. Not that they would admit it or even accept charity. I was told they are now the landowners; if I made an agreement with them in exchange for their permission for me to mine, they could receive a percentage share of anything I find. That's not charity. It's just business. The money gained in selling the diamonds could bring fresh water to all the villages, genuine health care, and education. We could clean the poison lake up. Buy tractors to farm more efficiently, and the list goes on. Most would say they are managing and don't need help, but we live in a different world; it has to be embraced, even in small bits. Otherwise, poverty takes over."

"You would do that?" Jenny asked.

"Of course, the diamonds belong to the villagers and the miner's family, not me. This is a legal way they can all benefit without the diamonds being claimed by the government and the local areas getting nothing."

"It's a good plan, Lisa, but to do this, you don't want me turning up suddenly and opening more police and press involvement."

"What are you suggesting?"

"I, for the moment, must remain in the background. No one will be affected because everyone believes I'm dead. Even so, we will work together, and I'll find contacts and places to go so you can set up your mining rights."

"It's probably the right thing to do. The papers would have a field day, making the police investigation look pathetic. Although I still have an immediate problem with people who want to kill me, so I have to assume they are still searching."

"Well, let's concentrate on your problems. First things first, did you meet any villagers you could trust, or did they keep away from you?"

"No, I got to know loads, and there is one, Joshua. He speaks good English and was educated in a university. He could act as a middleman for us."

"Then he's your first port of call. Anyway, it's time we moved on. What was the name of the village Joshua lives in?"

"Umbra. Have you heard of it?"

Jenny fell silent for a moment. Lisa believed she'd not heard and was about to repeat herself when Jenny nodded her head up and down slightly. "Yes, I know where that village is. We will go the wrong way if we continue on this track. Sorry, it means retracing your steps, but not down to the lake. We will skirt around the upper, outer edge."

"How long will it take? We need to eat."

Jenny smiled. "We'll be fine, let's go."

Chapter 25

Hans and one of the men had finally come down the track as far as the lake. That was after the other man, Chas, decided Lisa hiding in a tree to be rubbish. She had to have followed the track heading towards the lake. Taking it upon himself to ignore a tree search, he headed directly towards the lake. In doing this, he picked up her tracks well beyond where Hans had turned back. Radioing the others, he sat by the side of the track, waiting for them to catch him up.

"Call yourself a fucking tracker, Hans, when it was obvious her first footprints would have been washed away. In doing that, she's got quite a lead on us. I also know which way she turned, and it wasn't towards the new road laid down by the rescuers."

Hans shrugged. "So she got a head start; she's a bloody city girl with no idea how to move around in this terrain. We'll have her before dark, that's certain. So let's move."

Lisa may have been from the city, but she was bright enough not to walk on the bank by the lake but to stay in the grass. This effort did not deter Chas from tracking her, apart from slowing him while looking for fractured vegetation rather than clear prints she'd have left by remaining on the bank.

"Not that easy, then?" Hans mocked after Chas had come to a halt, carefully looking at the vegetation.

"Fuck off, such terrain is never easy, move further down and see if you can pick her tracks up again."

Both looked and searched but found nothing.

"This can't be," Chas said annoyingly. "We should backtrack and check if she turned away from the lake earlier."

Finding earlier tracks, they both looked into the dense vegetation.

"What do you think, Chas? Did the idiot decide to leave and head back into the forest?" Hans asked.

"Without a machete, she'd be mad, but we are talking about a girl with no concept of how difficult it can be off track. Either way, we don't have an option but to wade in ourselves and pick her trail up. She'll not get far and will have snapped leaves and twigs to get through."

"Then we have her, but now it will need to wait until the morning. It will soon be dark, and I'm not stumbling on such a narrow track, unable to see hazards. Not that it will matter; Lisa won't be able to move either. We set off first thing."

With this agreed, they set up camp at the entrance to the track Lisa had taken.

***

They woke up at first light and, after breakfast, set off into the undergrowth, looking for signs that Lisa had taken this route.

The third man, known as Gareth, finished packing the equipment and stood on the bank watching. He was not a tracker, leaving the search to Hans and Chas. Glancing back the way they came, he saw several figures approaching.

"Looks like we've company, Hans," he called.

Both Hans and Chas returned to the edge of the lake. Hans took binoculars from his backpack and studied the people heading towards them.

"They're not locals, they look Caucasian, all carrying weapons. I don't like it. They could be after the diamonds. We'll go into the forest, find Lisa, and lose the followers."

***

Samuel Ritter, with four other men sent by Casper to follow Hans and retrieve the diamonds, needed clarification about what was happening. He sent up a drone, complete with an infrared camera, allowing him to follow Hans' progress, even in the dense vegetation of the forest, using Hans' team's heat signature. The drone had been obtained from a company supplying the military. Virtually silent and able to remain in the air for several hours, Samuel would use it for an hour, check progress, and then bring it back for recharging so it was fully charged when needed.

Hours later, observations made it clear they were going no further. Samuel saw the group split up, with three returning, including one injured on a stretcher. Deciding they were no longer important, he returned to the ones left. Samuel watched Hans string Lisa up, move a short distance away, and settle down. Samuel wasn't sure why he had done that unless it was some punishment to force her to reveal where the diamonds were hidden. Then why would that be the case? After all, she'd gone with them to retrieve the diamonds.

When the rains came, Samuel had no option but to bring the drone back or lose it. When he could put it back in the air, he could only count three figures; the last one was missing. By the way, they were acting. it seemed they were searching for someone. It could only be Lisa. Finally, the three headed toward the lake.

As time passed, Samuel realised they were tracking Lisa, but with apparent difficulty. Now, dark was coming, and like Hans, Samuel decided to set up camp.

"We camp here, and in the morning, we intercept them," Samuel told the others. Then he looked at one of the men. "You, Kirk, first thing return to the Land Rover, take the new road to the lake, and meet us there. I'll call you if we turn off before meeting the road."

Chapter 26

Jenny stood for a moment, looking back the way they had come. "We're being followed. They are close." She hesitated as if watching for signs of movement. "It seems not just one group, but two."

Lisa looked in the same direction as Jenny but could see nothing indicating one group, let alone two. "How do you know? If we are, then it will be Hans. I've no idea who the other lot are, unless Hans had requested more help."

"I don't think they are together. I sense aggression between them. As for how I know, I've been in Africa all my life, Lisa, I can read the signs." She looked up at the sky. "It seems the weather is coming to our assistance. They will be delayed, allowing us to move on."

As happened yesterday, storm clouds began to form, quickly gathering together.

Lisa felt the first spots of rain. "Not again. I got soaked last time. We need shelter."

"We're fine; we are just on the edge of the downpour; come on, let's move on and gain distance."

Lisa followed Jenny, feeling no more spots of rain. However, Lisa was concerned. How did Jenny know people were following? Then it seemed so convenient, the rain coming once more. Was it a coincidence, or was DB around but not showing himself? Did Jenny and he communicate? If so, why was he leaving her out of the conversation? Lisa began to suspect that everything was not right with Jenny. Was she here, or was DB so powerful that he could bring Jenny back like he'd done when she escaped the aircraft? If that was the case, was all this all in her mind? The reality was that she was alone. The more she thought about it, the more she decided that could not be. She didn't have the skills to feed herself safely, let alone find her way across a confusing terrain without becoming hopelessly lost. Jenny had to be real. There was no other explanation.

"Is it a long way to Umbra?" Lisa asked as they walked.

"Half a day, not much more. You will be there early afternoon."

"So if you're not coming into the village? Where will you go? I can hardly ring you when I need assistance sorting the diamonds out. Then, sometime in the future, you have to go home. True, it will raise a few questions as to how they decided you'd died in the aircraft, but those questions will need to be addressed one day, now you're better, that is."

"I'd not thought that through yet. To tell you the truth, I thought it had only been days. Now you're saying it's months, which makes it a little more difficult to just turn up. My parents would have heart attacks."

Lisa sniggered. "Only your family? I nearly died being woken up by you. Talk about being famous. You'll be in every paper worldwide, let alone the social media going berserk. People already buried don't often turn up months later unless they're in a zombie story."

"I suppose you're right. I must begin a new life away from my family to prevent a media circus. I'm broke if I don't return home, so you'll have to put a few diamonds to one side."

"Can't see that being a problem, but you've still not told me how I get in touch with you."

"I'll wait at the cave we slept in. Don't delay too long. It's not exactly an ideal place to sleep."

"I'll do my best, but it's one thing convincing Joshua. He has to convince the elders, who may be far more difficult."

"I can't see why. There's no risk to the villages permitting mining in their area. You're not asking them to help."

"True, but moving two boxes of diamonds worth

millions of pounds will need protection. I can hardly do that myself."

"You'll find a way, Lisa. But first things first, get your mining rights."

Lisa sighed inwardly. Why does everyone believe she can go up against multinationals, gunmen, and all and sundry? She can't unless witnessing a fight between forces beyond the understanding of mortals. 'Oh, come on, Lisa, such things don't exist; they only exist in storybooks and nothing more.' Yet, while she told herself this, she couldn't explain why a person like DB would follow her across the world and persist in telling her she would return to Africa. Then there was Jenny. Her parents must have identified her, and probably DNA also confirmed whoever they found on the aircraft was Jenny. Yet, she was here, and unlike DB, she could speak and hold her. Jenny was no ghost; if so, she was a bloody good one.

As time passed, Lisa began to recognise the terrain; they were less than a mile from Umbra.

"I'd never have got here. Mind you, to be fair, I'd not have taken the turns you have. I bet you'd make good money as a tracker, Jenny."

"I prefer sitting by the side of a pool, with a glass of wine in my hand, rather than traipsing around in old jeans and a T-shirt. It's hardly sexy compared to a bikini."

Lisa laughed. "At least you could wear one. I'd look like a beanstalk. Then, at this moment, I'd be happy with a hot bath, but not that I'll get one in the village. They wander down to the river."

Shortly, Jenny came to a halt. "This is as far as I go. Talk with Joshua, and meet me back at the cave. I'll be waiting."

They hugged before Lisa set off to the village.

Jenny watched her briefly, then turned away, fading as she walked until she was no longer there.

Chapter 27

Hans, using his binoculars, looked back towards the lake. "It's bloody uncanny. Whoever is following has also turned and is still heading towards us. Do we wait and see what they want, or set up a defensive position and wipe them out?"

"I vote for the latter. We can't risk it when carrying a few million in diamonds. That must be why they're following. They want the diamonds," Chas answered. "Besides, we all get a cut. I'm not sharing my cut with others."

"What about you, Gareth? Are you in agreement with Chas?"

"With Sir John not believing the girl's claim she'd only found one box and your insistence she had to know where the other boxes were, we've ended up with very few to what I was told we were getting. So there's no way I'm letting others take what we've already got. I say we either attempt to outrun them or take them on and risk a gunfight with possible injuries on both sides."

Hans shook his head slightly. "To outrun them isn't an option. Gunning them down, as you say, carries risks. Then, we don't know if they are after the diamonds. Letting them catch up is the only way to discover what they want. I suggest we hide the diamonds. If it's just a coincidence they're going the same way as us, that's fine. We hang back until they are gone. If they were here for the diamonds, we would tell them Lisa couldn't find where she had left them. We didn't believe her and decided to beat the truth from her. She escaped, and we're tracking her. We gun them down if we can't work out something between us."

The other two thought for a short time.

"It could work. Then, she'd have both groups tracking her. When we find her, she'll tell them she'd already found the diamonds, and we have them," Chas commented.

"True, but before that happens, we split up from them, widening the search area. Once out of sight, we backtrack, legging it to the vehicles and getting out fast," Hans suggested.

"It could save a risky gunfight, Hans," Gareth added. "But we all have to know where the diamonds are hidden."

"That goes without saying. So let's find a landmark to allow us to set a returnable location."

Moving on faster, all of them searching for a good location. It was Gareth who found a good position. He called them back, pointing to an established tree. "Line the tree up exactly between those distant converging hills, and we count several steps beyond the tree in a direct line."

All agreed, and the diamonds were soon buried at sixty-eight paces.

Once this was done, they moved on before settling down to eat.

***

Samuel and his team caught them up in three-quarters of an hour.

"All right," Hans said casually to Samuel as they approached. "Are you following us for some reason?"

"Don't treat me like an idiot. The diamonds. Where are they?"

"Why do you have this idea that they belong to you?"

"We work for the original owner's relatives of the mines operating in this area. They own and want the diamonds stolen from their grandfather's mines. You can have a five percent finders fee, but we take the diamonds."

"Is this fee in advance, whether we find them or not?" Hans mocked.

"Don't get smart with me. We pay in exchange. So hand the stones over."

"Yes, well, it's like this, the girl's a fucking idiot. She claimed she hid them but couldn't find the location again.

We scrambled around in the thicket, where one of the lads got bitten by a snake and had to send him back, but we found nothing. Then she claimed there was only one box, not three. So you can imagine we were pretty pissed off when she couldn't even find the one box; deciding she needed her tongue loosened, we strung her up naked with honey all over her. An hour or so with ants crawling over her body would help to remind her how serious we were, but the fucker escaped in the downpour earlier. Gareth here reckons she's about half an hour in front of us. We'll collect her after a bite to eat. She's going nowhere fast."

"Any objections to us checking your backpacks?"

"None; look for yourself while we prepare to move on."

While Samuel did a quick check, Gareth looked up at the skies.

"I don't fucking believe it, the rains are coming again."

Samuel's team began to open their backpacks, taking waterproofs out, except the rain hit in seconds. The downpour was so great that the sloping terrain suddenly became a river from the water crashing down. No one could stand up, all stumbling about being washed down the slope, grasping anything they could and holding on. While the time of the downpour was short, the damage was extensive. Each man retrieved their backpack; most had burst open, spilling the contents.

Again, the rain lasted less than ten minutes, but twenty minutes before they were ready to leave.

"Everyone okay?" Hans asked.

They all mumbled a yes but complained their rations were ruined.

"I've been here several times and never seen anything like that," Kirk, from Samuels group, commented.

"I have to agree with you there. Two in a matter of hours is unusual. The problem I can see is it will have wiped out the girl's tracks—that's if she survived. Wearing jeans and a jumper would have been hell for her," Chas said.

"Either way, we move on together," Samuel added.

With this agreed, they all set off.

Shortly, they stopped.

"It's hopeless. The rains have wiped out any signs of anyone coming this way. Normally, I'd find broken twigs and odd places of crushed grass in soft ground, but the rain and river have made it one big disaster area."

"What are you saying?" Samuel asked.

"We should spread out; the girl could be injured or cowering following the storm. She could be fifty meters from us if we don't, and we'd miss her."

"No need. Get the drone out, Allan. Our drone will seek out the heat she's giving off. Even someone dead will show a temperature difference to the surrounding area for quite some time after death."

Gareth looked at Hans, only shrugging. They hadn't seen that coming.

"So that's how you found us?" Hans asked.

"Of course, we even saw you scrambling around in the undergrowth and when you separated yourself from the girl. We'd have had doubts if your story hadn't tallied with what we had watched. Not that it was clear you'd not found the diamonds. Which is why we caught you up."

By now, the drone had been launched. Allan and Samuel were studying the display, trying to see Lisa. Time went on, with nothing displayed on the screen that could have been human, be it someone on the move or stationary.

"She's not in front of us, that's for certain," Samuel eventually said as the drone returned.

"That's impossible. We tracked her walking alongside the lake. When the tracks finished, we turned to enter the scrubland and forest, finding indications that was the direction she went," Hans told him.

Samuel gave an indifferent shrug. "That may be, so

she's progressing faster than you anticipated. Looking at the terrain, I can't see it, or she doubled back, finding the area she was travelling through far too difficult."

"Then send the drone towards the lake and search the banking," Hans suggested.

"Do it, Allan," Samuel told him.

Again, Samuel watched the screen, but there was nothing.

"Well, Lisa's either dead and covered with debris, or she's travelled further and faster than you thought," Samuel commented.

"In that case, I'm calling it a day if your drone can't pick her up. You can keep looking if you want," Hans decided.

Samuel said nothing, walking away, using his satellite telephone to call Casper.

"Sir John's group doesn't have any diamonds with them. They could have stashed them earlier, but we can't even find Lisa to confirm if they were found. Then, according to Hans, she told him there was only one box. What do you want me to do?"

"You're still with him?"

"Yes."

"I can't see him returning to pick up diamonds if he has hidden them while you're around. What's the chance of watching what they do covertly?"

"Hans is no fool and a good tracker. Now they know we have a drone, they will be watching. I'd struggle to get close enough to see if they have stashed the diamonds."

"Then we can't do anything. Do you think Lisa managed to get out of the area?" Casper asked.

"I think she was moving far faster than Hans believed. I've had the drone up. Something would have shown up even if she was dead."

"You call it a day and return to base. All is not lost. Even if Hans has managed to collect a few diamonds, it's certainly not the full haul, so Lisa has pulled a fast one over Sir John just to placate him. I have an idea that will help Lisa a great deal and, more importantly, gain her trust."

Chapter 28

Lisa walked into the village of Umbra. This time, unlike when she was last there, all the vehicles had gone, along with 'tent city. A few children playing saw Lisa coming and ran to meet her. Many recognised her, hugging her tightly, preventing her from moving forward. Villagers began to come out of their homes to find out what the commotion was about, among them Joshua. As soon as he saw who it was, he quickly went over to her, sending the children away to play.

"I must say, you are the last person I'd expect to visit us, Lisa. Don't tell me you've had another accident and fallen out of the sky?"

"Not quite, but I have a slight problem, transport-wise. Although my problems aren't yours, I am here for a different reason and need your assistance."

"You're always very welcome, as I told you when you left. As for needing my assistance, if I can, I will. First, may I offer you refreshments? Then you can tell me what I can do for you."

"That would be good, lead on."

Going inside Joshua's home to eat, out of the sun, Lisa sat down after being welcomed by his family.

"We had visitors yesterday, Lisa. Were they anything to do with you?"

"Had one been bitten by a snake?"

"Yes."

"What happened to them?"

"We could do nothing. In fact, I don't know of a snake around here that could bring a man down so quickly. I suggested they call the Red Cross and find out if there was a doctor in the area. One was in a village some distance from here, and they left to catch him up."

"It is good they have moved on. Before we go any

further, I'm not here and have never been here. That is important, Joshua."

He frowned. "You are suggesting we could have more visitors?"

"It's possible, but steps have been taken to deter that. Even so, you should send someone down the road to warn me if they have followed me here. Then I'll move out quickly, so there is no risk to the villagers."

"I understand. Although I can assure you, we can look after ourselves."

Lisa shook her head. "You can't believe me. These are not nice people, and they carry guns. Which is why, once we've spoken, I have people who will look after me."

"Please tell me what is on your mind."

"I understand the government has given the villagers this land?"

"It was always our land, Lisa. That was until diamonds were found, and our rights were conveniently pushed to one side. When the mining finished, the government had no intention of being liable to clean up the mess the miners left, including the poisoned lake, so it was handed back to us using a legal statute. Now, miners can only register to mine on our lands with our permission. I can assure you that will never be given."

"I fully understand after seeing the damage mining has left for you to sort out. I'm with you all the way. Except I would like to make a mining application, and I ask the elders to agree."

He stared at her in astonishment. "You want to mine?"

"Why not? I'm used to hard work."

"But the mines are spent, Lisa. I say spent. There may be a few inferior quality diamonds around, but nothing that could cover the cost of opening up a mine."

"So I understand, except you are not quite correct. There are still diamonds in the area. At least enough to pull the villages out of poverty, give them all freshwater, tools to make their fields more productive, educate your children, better healthcare for everyone and all that goes with it."

He shook his head. "There are no mines still containing diamonds. So tell me what this is all about? Is this something to do with the lost diamonds, and you like hundreds before you believe you know where they are? If so, forget it. For years, treasure hunters have searched for those diamonds without success. It is believed they were taken from the area years back and stored in the vaults of diamond centres worldwide."

Lisa knew how much easier it would be to tell him about the diamonds, but if the news got out, people like Hans would be the least of their problems. Everything must move softly.

"I'm not another treasure hunter, Joshua, but I can assure you a mine does exist with a few diamonds that could change your lives."

"If I believe what you're saying, how do you know this?"

"Since the crash, but with all that was going on and being told Jenny was dead, diamonds were the last thing on my mind. But one night, I found a small cave, probably the beginning of a new mine, I don't know. But I was sitting inside watching the moonlight reflecting off a few stones on the ground. Thinking they were glass beads or something like that, I took some home. Not so long ago, I remembered they were still in my bag, so I took one to a local jeweller to find out what it was. Believe me, Joshua, they weren't glass. I'd brought back diamonds. After reading about mining in South Africa, I learned that to be able to claim them, you need a mining license. Even landowners can't claim them; I'm told they'd go to the government."

"I know a little about the mining industry, and you are

correct in your assumption. If you have the mining rights, what you find would be yours. And you want to use them to make our lives better? Why would you do that?"

She sipped her drink, saying nothing for a moment. Joshua didn't push her for an answer. He suspected there was more to how she found the diamonds than what she'd told him.

"They are not mine. They belong to the people of South Africa. Not a girl living in the UK who has never spent years working in appalling conditions to get them out of the earth." She hesitated for a moment. "There is another reason why I need to do this."

"And what is that?"

"Let me explain. I was invited to a celebration after I was cured of poisoning after swimming in the lake. I also attended a celebration in your village before I left. In both celebrations, several men would dress up to banish evil spirits from the village and call on the villagers' ancestors for their continued help."

"You have the gist of such a celebration, Lisa, but it is far more complicated to explain to an outsider who doesn't know the old ways."

"That goes without saying, except to conduct such a celebration, there must be a belief your ancestors could be called upon or spoken to."

"You are correct again. Where are we going with this?"

"Soon, you will understand. Tell me, do you believe a city girl could survive around here without help?"

"Anything's possible, Lisa, and they may last a day or so before ending up eating something wrong and being poisoned, or like you, ignoring obvious signs to us around a lake that something wasn't right."

"Precisely, that is me to a tee. This brings me to Jenny, a girl found to be still in the aircraft, turning my claim that she escaped the same as me to be words from a raving loony."

"I'm not sure they said that Lisa, more that you were traumatised, and picked the wrong shrubs to take berries from."

"Perhaps, but it was easier to agree with the police that eating berries could have affected my reasoning, particularly when everyone was insisting the body found aboard the aircraft was identified as Jenny. So how would you explain away that for the last two days, I've been with Jenny once more? She told me she hadn't been bitten too seriously, coming around reasonably quickly. After waking, she went in the opposite direction to the one I took to your village and ended up in what she called a settlement. It was a strange name when everything around it was called a village. But if we forget that small point, she claimed she'd only been there days, not months. If that's not enough to convince you, the man I kept seeing and speaking to, I found his portrait in a diamond merchant's office in London. They told me his name was Donald Blackmon, or DB for short. How could a dead man tell me, time after time, it was my destiny that one day I would return to South Africa? He was correct; I have returned, but only after he began interfering in my life. You may still tell me it is all in my mind, but since returning, DB caused a storm, allowing me to escape some bad people. Jenny sensed I was being followed, and in seconds, she, too, created a storm to delay my followers. I'm not going mad, Joshua, things are not right. As for my destiny, I believe it is to bring out the last of the diamonds to help like I said, the villages."

Joshua listened carefully to what Lisa said. This was not a time to mock; the girl truly believed what she was saying. "I'm not going to tell you such visions are a dream, Lisa, because superstition, fear of the dead in this country, go back hundreds of years. In the remote villages, before

Christianity came with the explorers, all had their own beliefs. The natives would rely on their medicine men to talk to their ancestors on the village's behalf. Donald Blackmon is a well-known name from the past, a man who caused unspeakable hardship for so many around here in his pursuit of diamonds. The villagers believe he, like many who destroyed so many lives, walks this land, unable to move on until the wrongs of the past have been corrected, which could never happen. It is their punishment for eternity. Donald Blackmon may have sensed your weakness, which allowed him to believe you could free him from his perpetual torment. If so, the village elders will know we cannot stand in his way. Now he has you, touching us from beyond the grave until we, through you, do his bidding."

Lisa was relieved that Joshua hadn't mocked her, but she felt used by DB. "You're right, Joshua. I cannot fight him when he can even bring my friend back from the grave. I tried by refusing to return to a country that was a nightmare, but he mocked me and showed me how insignificant I was to what was playing out around me. So, no matter what, I'll see it through and make sure none of you lose out this time. DB has already warned me dark forces are building. I don't know if what I've decided on is what he wants from me or if he is part of the dark forces, where the diamonds play an important role beyond my understanding. I may even be discarded, like Jenny, after playing my part?"

Joshua shook his head slowly. "I cannot tell you that, Lisa. We are taught from childhood that the forces of good and evil are in constant conflict and will always be. Some of us will take one road, others another. By what you are saying, maybe DB is standing outside, attempting through you, to prevent evil from taking him."

"Maybe, Joshua. He deserves to be taken, but while

he hasn't, I will use him the same way he's trying to use me. Your job is to convince the village elders they must permit me to mine. That is their only involvement. I will do the rest. No one must know, not even the elders, that this permission has anything to do with finding a few diamonds."

"Why not the elders, Lisa?"

"You've been shafted in the past. If it gets out diamonds have been found, you can be sure diamond fever would be rife. The villagers' rights would be completely ignored again, and hundreds would demand that the government allow the issue of mining permits once more. I'm hoping that by making the first accepted application, with the landowners' permission, the government could not issue more permits without similar conditions. Meaning you could refuse anymore."

"I can understand your thinking, but it will be a hard sell to the elders."

"Then you must work on superstition and fear of the dead. Tell them DB is back and is controlled by me. I read on the internet that his body has never been found. Maybe you could tell them you believe the mine he led me to also contains his remains, and by giving him a proper burial, he'd be allowed to move on."

"It might work, Lisa. You make the application, and I'll lay the path down to get it accepted by the elders. If I can't, we will look at another approach."

"I'll do that. Now I must leave. I feel it's far too dangerous for the village for me to be here."

"You are sure you are going to be alright? After all, you are alone, and if you rely on the dead, you can't guarantee Jenny will still be waiting for you."

Lisa shrugged. "I've no idea, but I can only do what I can do."

As they left Joshua's house, he had an idea. He told her

to wait a few minutes. Running deeper into the village, he was soon back with a bicycle.

"This is one of three left by the rescuers. All were wrecked, thrown to one side, but we have made two out of three, so take this. It will be quicker for you."

"Thank you, it will certainly save a long walk. I'll let you know where I've left it."

Joshua watched her peddle away. Now, he had to put together a convincing reason why the elders should accept the mining request. To do that, Joshua needed to think. He was just about to go back inside when he froze. Standing a short distance from him was a man dressed in clothes not seen for seventy years. Immediately, he knew he was looking at Donald Blackmon. Blackmon began to walk towards him; Joshua was rooted to the ground, unable to move. Their eyes met, Blackmon's black and lifeless, yet Joshua couldn't tear his eyes away from those lifeless sockets. Blackmon never moved his lips, but Joshua could hear every word inside his head.

"You have been given a task. All elders must agree without question what is asked. I will be there, watching. Those who refuse should be reminded that the living must never question those who walked before. When the time comes for such disbelievers to pass through my world, such actions will be called to account."

Blackmon turned and walked away, fading until he was no more.

Never had Joshua been so scared. Everything Lisa had told him was true. She walked with the dead, protected by them, to fulfill her destiny. Quickly, he joined several elders in another hut, telling them to send runners to other villages for an essential meeting of all the village elders in four days. He added that all must attend to avoid retaliation from those who watch. Every elder would know what he meant in saying, 'those who watch.'

Chapter 29

Lisa soon arrived at the other side of the river from the cave. The shallow water allowed her to push the bicycle to the cave entrance.

"Jenny, are you in there? It's Lisa?" she shouted into the cave entrance.

"No, I'm behind you."

Lisa spun around. "Where were you hiding?"

"I was a little further down the track, foraging, and saw you cross," she answered, handing Lisa a large rolled-up leaf. Inside were different berries and tiny apple-looking fruits. "This will see you through the night before we move on."

Lisa sat down on a rock and began to eat the food. Jenny remained standing, looking around.

"I spoke to Joshua, and he will put my request to the elders. Hopefully, it will be agreed. Otherwise, I may have to tell them more."

"Joshua has been visited already. He will get the elders to agree. Your job is to return to Pretoria and make the necessary application."

"You know this because?"

Jenny turned and looked at Lisa. "Let us be truthful with each other, Lisa. I am here because you feel comfortable around me, even though you believe I'm probably just a figment of your imagination."

"You can hardly blame me when you were identified by your parents. DNA from a body still in the aircraft confirmed it to be you. Yet we walked and talked together, and I was finally made out to be some sort of loony when I'd got search parties looking for you. Now it's happening to me again. So yes, let's be truthful with each other."

Jenny sat down on another rock and sighed. "It was your fault for having people come out and look for me. Can you remember my words before you left for the village?"

Lisa thought back. "It was something about your work being finished, but you didn't explain what work. You also said it was up to me now, but I didn't understand. Then DB turned up, appeared like he does, and told me where the village was. He also said he'd look after you."

"And has he?" Jenny asked.

"Hardly difficult if you weren't even there, but some sort of ghost. Going back to us, Jenny, we've been writing to each other for years, even though my life and education were worlds away from yours. I'll never know why you kept writing unless…" she hesitated, a slow realisation coming into her mind. "DB talks to you, doesn't he? So when the school put us together as penfriends, the same as others in the class, DB guided the teacher to match us."

"Yes. The same as you, I had no option. It was written."

"So DB has been coming to you since we were fourteen?"

"He has. Always at night in my bedroom. I'd suddenly wake to find him standing at the end of the bed. I was terrified at first but unable to shout for help, not even move. He'd speak to me in my head. I didn't want you as a penfriend."

"Why not?"

"We live in different worlds. Your letters were just a jumble of incoherent words, the spelling so bad I'd spend time correcting them before even attempting to read and understand what you were on about. But DB told me I could not refuse. I had to keep you as a penfriend. Admittedly, you improved your writing over the years, and while I said we were worlds apart in many ways, I looked forward to your letters. You were a welcome change to the girls I hung out with at school and home."

"I also looked forward to your letters, painting a life I could only dream about, yet I believed you liked me. When

I met some of your friends at the funeral. I could sense the hostility when one asked me if I was the poor, illiterate girl from the UK, followed by them all bursting into laughter. It hurt, Jenny, knowing you thought of me that way. Even your parents shunned me, adding to me wishing I'd never come. It took years to save up to come and see you. Then, I lost everything in the crash. Because the insurance refused to pay any compensation, I had to pay my hotel bill and borrow money to stay here until they let me go home. I'll be paying off my debts for years."

"I'm sorry for the way you have been treated, Lisa. While I was making drinks downstairs at one of our sleepovers, Agatha went rummaging in my drawers to find your bundle of letters and all my corrections. I had to make a story up about why I kept writing to you, and yes, I didn't paint a pretty picture, I made out it was more that I felt sorry for you. These were my so-called friends. Without them, life would have been hell for a fourteen-year-old, you must understand."

"I do. I was having the same trouble at school. We had little money, struggling to even feed ourselves. I wanted to go around with the coolest girls in the class like any girl would, but they'd meet in the burger bar at weekends to plan nights out and in the week for a coffee. I couldn't afford the coffee, so I never got to go to the meetings. They would only talk to me when they wanted a laugh at my expense, then they'd notice me. Most of my lack of funds was I was saving to come here. Once, the school arranged a trip to London to visit the museums. I wanted to go, paying a small amount from my weekly paper round. A day before the trip, I suddenly went down with a nasty bug, putting me in bed. I was lucky; the coach crashed on the return from London. Two girls who oddly enough were the most vocal in pulling me down all the time ended up with life-changing injuries, and another girl died."

"How did you feel about that?" Jenny asked.

"Outwardly, like everyone, I showed the usual concerns; inwardly, it was another story. I felt they deserved it for all the horrible things they had done to me. I know it wasn't very Christian thinking, but when you hate people so much, I didn't care," Lisa hesitated. "You don't think it may have been DB's doing, do you?"

"I honestly don't know, except similar happened to me. Agatha, cycling home from school, hit a pothole and fell in front of a truck. She was pretty badly injured and now uses crutches."

Lisa shrugged. "Whether DB has anything to do with these accidents or not, it seems he's winning and keeping everyone in line. It leads me to ask you again: Do you exist, or are you a figment of my imagination?"

Jenny shook her head. "I wish I knew. In my mind, I'm Jenny. But you tell me I'm dead. I don't feel dead, except there seem to be so many blanks, like when you left for the village, then you were back, and I seemed to have been looking for food but couldn't remember doing it. It's as if when you are around, everything's normal, but when you're not with me, everything begins to blur. It also begs the question, are you alive? They didn't find your body in the aircraft as well, did they?"

"Unfortunately, I'm very much alive and being used as a punchbag by everyone. I may be thick, Jenny, but I will win, if only for the villagers' sake."

"Yes, I believe you will."

Lisa stretched. "I don't know about you, but I'm completely knackered," she said, then hesitated. "Can you be knackered?"

Jenny frowned. "Good point, I need to think about that. Even so, you should get some rest; we'll move on first thing."

"Should I call DB for protection like he did for me in

the forest?"

Jenny shook her head. "No. I'll be around and call him if there are any problems."

Lisa lay down and was soon asleep. However, Jenny's statement that she would be around would not be true. As Lisa fell asleep, DB appeared, and Jenny faded. He set up an area similar to the one he had done in the forest last night around Lisa. Then, he stood gazing out at the entrance to the cave.

***

Lisa was awake early. Jenny was sitting on a rock at the cave entrance.

"Good morning," Lisa said, "I'm going to the river for a wash. Are you coming?"

At first, Jenny didn't seem to react to her comments, and Lisa believed she hadn't heard her. Then suddenly Jenny reacted, turning her head. "Morning. Did you sleep well?"

"I did, thank you. It's so much better knowing someone is watching. I hope you weren't too bored?"

"No, I was fine, I've been watching the sunrise. You get a wash while I sort out your breakfast."

True to her word, Jenny had found more fruit, and they both sat at the entrance, looking out, while Lisa ate. Soon, Lisa had finished her breakfast.

"Now you have finished, we should move on," Jenny told her.

"What should I do with the bike?"

"We will leave it in the cave. The villagers will be told where to find it."

Lisa didn't comment. They would probably be told by DB where their bike was.

Crossing the river and keeping to the dirt road, they set off in the opposite direction from Umbra village.

"Don't tell me we're walking to Pretoria. It took three days by car?" Lisa asked.

"No, where you left the transport to go down the track, there are two vehicles. The man bitten by a snake has already left the area with two others; these last vehicles are for Hans and the men with him."

"That sounds great, except I'm not exactly an experienced driver; I've only just passed my test."

"This is where I've been told you should go, so arrangements must have been made."

Lisa rounded a sharp bend and came to a halt. As Jenny had told her, both vehicles were there, but standing alongside them were Hans, Chas, and Gareth.

"Looks like we've problems, Jenny," Lisa said quietly. Jenny was no longer at her side. "I should have known. Like DB, you bail when the going gets tough."

By now, Hans had seen Lisa approaching. "Enjoy your walk, Lisa?"

"Why not? The weather is good. So, have you finally decided there are no more diamonds?"

"You're lucky; Sir John wants to see you. Otherwise, I'd have beaten the shit out of you."

Lisa grinned. "Why's that? Was he expecting more than a handful of diamonds, and your commission is down? Not that I can see why anyone's complaining. I always said there was only one box."

"Shut up and get in."

She climbed in the back. They travelled for some time before Hans broke the silence.

"How did you escape, and where did you go?"

"I untied the ropes, which were not exactly difficult; they were loose, and I've only got small wrists. Then I went down to the lake, finding a track heading away from the lake."

"We tracked you, then you disappeared; even a drone couldn't find you."

Lisa knew what drones were. Her old boyfriend had

one, and they went into a field once, and he gave her a go. "You know, I wondered what that funny sound was. So it was a drone looking for me then. It'd not work. I was sitting inside a cave on the river's other side, waiting for the rains to go."

Hans didn't answer; he should have realised her disappearance would have a simple explanation.

"So how much is Sir John paying you? After all, he's already down a million and still owes me another. Let's hope the stones are worth more and you get something."

"You expect to get two million? In your dreams. You'll be lucky to hang onto the million," Hans said.

"Then you have a bit of a conundrum. If the money does not come to me, then the charities of my choice get the money. So it makes no odds if I live or die or even if you find the other diamonds. As for the second million, maybe a step too far, but we'll see."

Chapter 30

Four days after Lisa left Umbra, elders from other villages began to arrive. Many huddled in groups, wanting to know why they had been called together. None could tell the curious why.

Later that day, in the only building large enough to house everyone, the elders gathered in the hospital; the doors closed, and Joshua went to the front as everyone sat down.

Joshua looked around the room. "Since the aeroplane crashed into the great lake, our lives have changed. Fresh water came to Umbra, and more tourists are arriving, tramping through our lands, leaving their rubbish, and camping in our cultivated areas. While we own the lands, we cannot prevent or control this intrusion."

"We all know this, Joshua. Why are you calling us together to tell us?" one elder asked.

"I am coming to that. Many of you have met the girl Lisa. A girl who survived the aeroplane crash. Swam in the poisoned lake. Everyone knows few survive the lake, yet she did." He fell silent, and his features changed. "We all know of Donald Blackmon. A man from the past who first brought in the mining companies. Their destruction of the area has lasted for three generations, making mining companies millions, yet we still struggle to survive. The government gave us the land, telling us to tidy it up ourselves if we wanted to use it, as they were uninterested. We know we cannot do that. The cost is beyond us. Our only advantage is that no mining company can set up again without our permission. Why am I speaking of Blackmon or spelling out the future he left? Blackmon is back; he came to me only days ago."

"That cannot be. Our mungome banished Blackmon from our lands," an elder shouted.

"So I understood, and for years, he has kept away. We even believed he'd gone forever, but he hasn't. I will read out what he said to me." Joshua took a sheet of paper and slowly read DB's words to the elders. After finishing, he pocketed the paper and looked around. The fear in the room was palpable.

"Who is the one who walks by his side?" an elder asked.

"The girl, Lisa."

Everyone began talking to each other, and another elder shouted to Joshua, "Why are you saying this? The girl is not South African, and what are we supposed to do for her?"

"We are to give her mining rights?"

"No, no, no," lots shouted at him.

Joshua expected this reaction. "We must, or we incur the wrath of Blackmon."

"Mining rights mean she or Blackmon believe there are diamonds when we all know there are not. Why is Blackmon wanting this to happen?" the elder persisted.

"I agree, but I don't think this is about diamonds. I believe Blackmon will guide the girl to his remains. He wants them taken from this land, back to Pretoria, and buried in consecrated ground. Only then will he be able to move on, leaving this land forever? I don't know about you; that is one man I'd like to banish."

An elder who hadn't spoken stood. "I believe Blackmon, even from the grave, has cast a shadow over our land. If Joshua is correct in his thoughts that Blackmon is using this girl to find his remains, we should allow her the mining rights."

Others began to express verbal agreement. However, not all were convinced; some shouted down the ones in agreement.

Joshua held his arms up. "Please, let us not argue with each other. We are better than that. Everyone can voice their arguments for and against. However, keep in mind the chilling warning given to me by Blackmon. Those who oppose will risk retaliation against that person and maybe their family from Blackmon. While Blackmon may be weak in entering our world, one day, all of us must pass through his to join our ancestors. Our mungome will admit they do not have the power to control the dark forces in Blackmon's world. You never want to see him standing there in front of you, his eyes boring into you, unable to tear your eyes away. You cannot block his words by covering your ears; they are inside your head. You cannot converse with him. You can only listen. Blackmon is not just mine but everyone's nightmare. Lisa was selected by Blackmon. She had no choice but to walk by his side. Blackmon followed her across the world. The girl, Jenny, Lisa insisted escaped the airplane crash, yet searchers found her still in her seat, has returned. I believe Blackmon sent Jenny to keep Lisa company because she told me she had just returned from being with Jenny. Many of you know that in times of stress, within your family or village, an ancestor will come at night and offer advice and comfort. But none has materialised and walked at your side. This is the power of Blackmon, a ghost controlling the dark forces. We must do as he demands."

Even with this strong argument, many doubters pointed out that once they permit one mine, mining companies will hear and believe diamonds have been found again.

At that moment, the room began to get very cold. Everyone had fallen silent, fear quickly spreading. Blackmon began to materialise by Joshua's side. Soon, everyone could see him. As Joshua told them, he'd heard Blackmon's voice in his head; everyone this time heard his voice.

"You will accept the girl's request without question. My warning to those who refuse. Their family will be dammed now and in the future."

Then Blackmon was gone. Everyone in the room was terrified at what had just happened.

"You can now understand what we are up against. Does anyone still doubt we must do what Blackmon demands from us?"

The room remained silent.

"Very well, I accept your silence as a no. Raise your hand if you agree, and permit Lisa to mine on our lands."

Everyone raised their hands.

Chapter 31

After three days, Lisa arrived in Pretoria with Hans. They had returned to the house she had been taken to when she arrived from the UK. Going directly into the main lounge, Sir John was already in the room, standing by the large fireplace.

"It's good to see you are safe, Lisa, particularly after running away from my people. It is a dangerous country for those who don't know how to survive."

"You question why I ran away? Sounds pretty hypocritical after Hans left me naked, hung from the branch of a tree, before pouring honey over my body to attract the ants?"

"Such abuse never happened, Lisa, and you know that. I've spoken to Hans and the lads with him, and nothing has been mentioned of any abuse on their part."

She shrugged. "If you say so. Anyway, you've got your diamonds. I want my money? Then we part."

"What diamonds? You couldn't find them."

"I see; you are not only liars but thieves by claiming we never found any. Whatever, I'll survive, the same as I've always done, then you've donated a million to charity, which is always good."

"It's tax deductible. Also, it gives the company good PR. So you did us a favour."

"I don't suppose you're going to help my brother?"

"No, he can rot in the prison. Not that we could have done anything without a few backhanders. So, no diamonds, no brother. As it is, you've got your return ticket to the UK. If I were you, I'd leave as soon as you can. Girls alone in this city are often targeted by undesirables. I'd feel responsible if you were hurt in any way."

"I'd not concern yourself or lose any sleep over it; I can look after myself. I'd like to be taken to a hotel or given a taxi; I've no intention of sleeping in this house."

"I'll have my car take you to a suitable hotel. Before you leave, a word of warning. If you've been holding out on us and know where the rest of the diamonds are, Hans will come and find you. You wouldn't want that, Lisa."

"You don't give up, do you. Why's that? Is the lure of diamonds so great that people lose the sense of reality for a bit of shiny stone?"

"To you, maybe, but you're a pauper. You have never known a life where diamonds are displayed in rings, watches, necklaces, the list goes on, and more importantly, they show you have arrived."

"Then you can keep them, I'd rather be normal."

"Clear off and let it be a lesson to you not to meddle in areas you don't understand."

Lisa stood and began to walk to the door, then turned. "You know Donald Blackmon won't allow you to take the stones. They are cursed and belong to him. Without his consent to take them away, they are worthless." Why did she say those words? Lisa had no idea; she just did.

"Yes, little girl, but you see, such stories may be good for the natives, but in the real world, it means nothing."

"You have been warned," then she left the room.

Sir John shrugged indifferently. He stood to make millions once the stones had been cut.

***

After Lisa left, Hans joined Sir John.

"Do you believe she ever knew where the rest of the diamonds were?" he asked.

Sir John shook his head. "She's not bright enough to have hidden them separately. Even so, we will keep an eye on her. Anyway, let me see the diamonds."

Hans opened the bag he'd brought and poured them onto the large table. Sir John looked at a few carefully.

"Well, are they as you expected?" Hans asked.

"Many times more, I wish we could have found the rest, particularly the twenty-two-carat single stone, supposedly flawless. That Hans was the one I wanted to see. Pack them up. I'll take a selection to London with me. I'll also sort out the commission for you and the lads."

"When do you intend to return to London?"

"Weekend, I have a few meetings before then."

Chapter 32

The hotel Lisa was staying in couldn't have been more downmarket. Yet Lisa was fine. She had little money and wanted to avoid repeating the situation where the British embassy had placed her and handed her a bill to be paid when she returned home.

Coming out of the shower, sitting on the edge of the bed, and drying her hair, Lisa noticed an envelope had been pushed under her door. Going over and picking it up, she saw her name and the hotel written on it. Someone had also written her room number down on the envelope by hand. Lisa surmised that the hotel had written the room number before slipping it under her door. Opening it, she pulled out a single piece of paper. The name of a solicitor, their address, and an appointment time for tomorrow were written on the paper.

Later, sitting in her room watching television, a knock came to her door. Lisa wasn't sure if she should answer but decided to anyway.

Pulling the door open, Lisa gasped. Standing there was Jenny.

"Hi, are you letting me in?" Jenny asked.

"Yes, of course. But how did you find me?" Lisa wanted to know, shutting the door after Jenny came inside.

"No idea. I just found myself in the hotel corridor outside your room," Jenny commented.

"Well, I'm glad you did. I was already feeling lonely and hoping you were not confined to the village of Umbra."

"So, did you get anything out of Sir John?"

"You have to be joking; apart from being threatened, he'd send Hans to sort me out if I held out on him. I'm finding where diamonds are concerned, they bring out the animal in people. Besides being stitched up, with Sir John claiming we never found any diamonds, what money I relied on to cover costs has gone."

"Don't be concerned about Sir John cheating you out of the diamonds. Unless DB allows it, those stones cannot leave this continent. Anyone attempting that will not succeed."

"But I took some," Lisa reminded her.

"With DB's consent, not that you had to ask him. It just happened."

Lisa sighed. "It's all getting beyond me, Jenny. Things are happening that logically can't. I know the term 'there are more things in heaven and earth'; it's one thing to create people and conditions in your mind to overcome the sense you are alone. Still, everything is becoming far too real for me. I'm seriously scared and out of my depth."

"I can't disagree with you, but then look at me. I'm supposed to be dead; well, everyone believes I am. Yet I don't feel dead. Neither do I believe DB means you any harm. Try looking at him as living in another dimension. Diamonds have no value to him, but they mean much to the villagers and can pull them out of poverty. However, doing that has a cost, if only to keep the stones out of greedy hands. People, including me, have made the ultimate sacrifice to get you where you are now. DB will not let you down. You're his only link to this world."

"So what does he get out of this?"

"I believe he wants peace, to move on. You can do this for him. In turn, with the diamonds, you can help the villagers."

"How can I do that? I'm struggling to sort my own life out."

"I don't know, Lisa. As time goes on, it will all become clear."

"I suppose. Are you hungry, or can't you eat?"

Jenny thought for a moment. "That's a good question. Either way, I'll go with you to find a restaurant if you want me to?"

"I don't want to go on my own, even if you can't eat, I've had nothing since breakfast, and that was pretty crap."

"Come on, let's try and find a fast-food restaurant."

***

"I don't believe it, you've got a McDonald's," Lisa commented, seeing the sign a short distance down the road they were walking along.

"Why shouldn't we?" Jenny asked.

"No reason, I am just surprised. It's like being at home when you see the sign. Shall we go in? At least you know what you're getting?"

After they agreed to this, they went inside. Jenny found a seat while Lisa went to the counter and ordered. Soon, she was back.

"What did you order for me?" Jenny asked.

"A small burger and a drink, at least if you can't eat. I can take the drink back to the hotel and get two burgers."

"I think you might have to do that, Lisa; look at the mirror over there; I have no reflection."

She looked over. "Oh, shit, you're right. I'm sorry, Jenny, it does look like you're dead."

"It's okay; at least it answers some strange happenings like me suddenly finding myself outside your hotel room. As well as where I've been for the last months."

"I suppose it does. It also begs the question: You may not have a reflection, but can anyone else see you?" She hoped they could; otherwise, Jenny was a figment of her imagination.

A girl came over with the order and left them alone, but she never commented that there were two meals and that she was alone.

Lisa finished her food in silence. Jenny seemed to have gone into a trance, as if visually there but not. Lisa wondered if her thoughts controlled what Jenny said or did or even her actions. After all, as soon as she spoke to Jenny, it was as if she'd switched her on, and then Jenny seemed to wait until she was ready to talk to her again. All in all, it was very confusing.

"Well, I enjoyed the burgers; sorry you couldn't," Lisa commented at the same time, putting the unused drink into her bag. "Shall we go back to the hotel?"

Walking back, Jenny suddenly stopped and waited. Lisa also stopped and turned to look at her.

"Problem?" she asked.

"You are being followed; I sense danger; I will call for assistance. Please do not move."

Seconds later, DB was walking towards them, at first a weak shadow but soon turning to a solid vision. Jenny moved towards him. They looked directly at each other. They didn't seem to be having a conversation, or rather, Lisa wasn't given the impression that they had talked, yet DB set off the way they had come.

"Come on, Lisa, let's return to the hotel. You will be safe now."

As they returned, Lisa wanted to know what had happened, asking Jenny.

"A girl walking alone sometimes attracts interest from the unsavoury. It is essential you are kept safe, Lisa. I don't have the power to do that, but I can sense danger. DB can call on forces beyond your imagination; he will always come if he is called. That is all you need to know."

"It is good to know, although DB told me I could call for assistance in the past but never told me how. Shouldn't I know, just in case you are not around?"

"It's straightforward. Call DB in your thoughts, demand he comes, and stand at your side. It would be pointless shouting for help vocally. He is not of this earth and would not hear you."

"Could he refuse to come?"

"No, you were selected many years back to link reality to the light and dark forces. DB was made your protector. Until the day he moves on, he will obey your call. If you are stressed and don't call, he will sense that and stand by your side. DB protected you when you escaped Hans and spent the night in the forest. Nothing could come near, from a tiny insect to a beast. I was called to be with you when you awoke."

"I wish he'd told me he was around. I was shattered but terrified of going to sleep. So when I sleep tonight, will he be there?"

"I will be there and, like now, will call him."

"I'd like that, Jenny, I've felt alone for so long. With mum gone, my brother taken from me, leaving me struggling to understand and scared of people like Sir John and Hans."

Later that night, Lisa lay in bed. While she couldn't see Jenny, she knew she was there watching. In lots of ways, she felt sorry for her. It would seem impossible for Jenny to pass on to where the dead go. Forced to remain in limbo like DB to fulfil what Lisa still could not understand. Then would DB allow her to take the diamonds to use for the good of the villages around? Lisa had doubts; after all, DB had not given her the impression he had any affinity with the villagers.

Chapter 33

The following morning, Lisa took a taxi to a large multistory building in the business center of Pretoria. At the main reception, her name was checked against appointments, and she was directed to the twentieth floor after receiving a visitor's badge.

Arriving at the floor and facing yet another reception, she approached it.

"Hi, I'm Lisa Jones, I have an appointment with Mr. Chapman."

"We were expecting you, Miss Jones. If you take a seat, Mr. Chapman's secretary will be out in a few minutes," the girl answered with a smile.

Lisa sat down; no one ever called her Miss Jones; she felt rather important being addressed that way, not that Jones was a very sophisticated name. Picking up a magazine, she began glancing through the pictures, wanting to avoid getting into reading an article. It was the right thing to do; in minutes, a girl came through to the reception, walking directly over to her. Lisa was jealous. This girl was attractive, wearing a perfectly fitted skirt, top, and high heels. Lisa felt uncomfortable in jeans, jumper, and trainers but had nothing else.

"Miss Jones, I'm Mr. Chapman's secretary. If you come with me, Mr. Chapman is waiting."

They went through a far door down a wide passage into a large room at the end. A long meeting table ran down the middle, with large picture windows filling the room with light.

A man around six feet tall, dressed in a pinstriped suit, stood as she entered and approached her, offering his hand. "Miss Jones, it is very nice to meet you. Please take a seat. May I offer refreshments, perhaps coffee and biscuits?"

"Thank you, that would be nice. Can you call me Lisa?

Everyone else does, and Miss Jones sounds like something official is happening."

"Of course, and you must call me Cyril."

In minutes, after hearing Lisa wanted coffee, the secretary returned with a tray, placed it on the table, and left, shutting the door after her.

Cyril poured them both coffee and sat down himself.

"My position in the company is looking after the corporate side of the business. I must confess, Lisa, when I was told of your visit yesterday, I was somewhat surprised by what I was to prepare. Even my appointments were moved or taken by others to accommodate you this morning."

"I'm sorry to have disrupted your day."

"I assure you that is not a problem, especially when a request comes from the practice's senior partner. Anyway, to business. I've been instructed to form a company and register a mining license in the company name. The mines are in the Kruger, on land passed over to the villagers there. I'm also opening a bank account for the mining company, to be capitalised with a directors loan of one thousand rand, to be added to our fee. You will be the director and the single signatory of the bank account. Both are simple to do, and I understand permission for you to mine will be given by the villagers. Is this your understanding?"

"That is correct."

"I'm happy to hear you know of the arrangements. Another point is that the area designated covers several spent mines. I took the opportunity this morning to look into previous mining operations in that area, mainly to ensure there are no active mining rights. All the reports declare they are spent mines or mines unable to produce diamonds of any quality and quantity to cover the overheads with no active mining rights. Given what I've read, forming a company to commence mining again seems a costly mistake, and I feel duty-bound to ask if you are being forced into this arrangement against your will?"

Lisa thought for a moment. Forced... probably. Cajoled into something she didn't understand... definitely. Did she have any option... no. However, outwardly, she gave him a nice smile. "Thank you for informing me of the past mining reports, Cyril. I have my reasons for obtaining the mining rights, which I prefer not to elaborate on."

"Very well, Lisa, with such assurances, we can proceed." He opened a folder, took out papers, and passed them to her. He also included a blank sheet of paper and a pen. "I will leave, allowing you to read through all the documents at your own pace. Just lift the telephone receiver and let my secretary know when you are finished. Don't feel pushed, Lisa. Take as long as you want. When I return, if you have any questions or need clarification of a section, make notes of page numbers and paragraphs on the paper. I will be happy to discuss such concerns with you. Once you understand and are happy to proceed, I will call in a partner who will witness your signatures. Do you have any questions before I leave you?"

"Will I have to pay the fee you mentioned today?"

"No, I understand one of our senior partners will sort that out."

"Okay, that's all I need to know. I'll go through the papers now."

After Cyril left, Lisa began to read the documents. Nothing sounded logical or in a language she understood.

"You look confused," Jenny said from behind her.

Lisa felt relieved to hear her voice. "God, I'm glad you've turned up. I've no idea what I'm looking at."

"Don't worry about anything written there. It is all in order. We'll wait around fifteen minutes, then call him back in again."

"Has Joshua managed to get the villagers to agree?"

"I will need to check on that, but they will agree. It is also prudent to ask to meet the partner who arranged everything. He will explain where you go from here."

"He is a real person then?"

"Why shouldn't he be?"

"It's just that one moment I'm talking or rather listening to the dead, the next I'm with people who I think are alive. So I assume this partner is being told what to do by DB?"

"I don't know, Lisa, ask him. It's a reasonable question."

They both looked at the documents before Lisa called Cyril back. Neither understood what they were reading.

"Have you any questions, Lisa?" Cyril asked.

"No, everything is in order. However, with no reflection on you, I must talk to the partner who set this up before I sign."

He looked confused. "Are you suggesting you knew nothing about this? After all, you didn't give me that impression earlier."

"I've not discussed this plan directly with anyone, so I want to know if the partner was under instruction or was doing this for your company or himself." Lisa was quite proud of how she had answered his question. She couldn't have done that six months ago.

"I understand your concern and will ask the senior partner to talk to you."

***

Lisa had been taken for dinner after Cyril found the partner was not in the building until early afternoon. He had agreed to see her immediately when he arrived.

Now, she was in his office. His name was Thomas Grobler, a white South African.

"You have requested to speak to me, Miss Jones, before you sign the documents. Do you have a problem with what has been set up for you?"

Lisa decided not to ask this man to use her Christian

name. It didn't seem appropriate. "I don't, Mr Grobler. I need to know who instructed you to form the company and arrange mining rights because it certainly wasn't me?"

"I received instructions from a client who has been with our practice for many years. Client confidentiality for our practice is essential, making me unable to give you their name."

"Then you had better get in touch with your client and have him speak with me, or I will not sign the documents."

He looked confused. "I understood from Mr Chapman that you seemed aware of the documents and their contents."

"Correct, but I had the intention to do this myself. As I told Mr. Chapman, I was surprised someone knew my intentions and arranged to prepare documents, look after the fees, and fund the account. That is not right in my book, so I want answers."

"Of course, you are entitled to know the full facts. I will call the client immediately and talk to him. It will be a confidential conversation until I receive further instructions."

"That is expected. Do you want me to leave the office?"

"I wouldn't think of it, Miss Jones. I will use another office if you will excuse me."

He left the room. Lisa saw Jenny standing in a far corner.

"You're becoming quite the businesswoman, Lisa. It will be interesting to know who this person is."

Lisa grinned. "I don't know how it just comes out. Let's hope it isn't DB who set this up, or we'll both be in trouble. He will then be annoyed at my messing about."

"I think I'll go walkabout if he turns up," Jenny answered.

"Chicken."

***

Thomas Grobler returned to his office, sitting down at his

desk. "I'm sorry for the delay. I have spoken to the client and have been permitted to give you his name. His name is Casper Meer. Do you know this man?"

"I do."

Grobler looked relieved. "Mr Meer has asked if you would go ahead and sign the documents. There is no catch, and you control the mining operation and the bank account. I can confirm that as the documents are set up, he cannot interfere. I will give you his contact number. He has asked if you would call him and arrange a meeting, then he will give you his position."

Lisa looked beyond Grobler towards Jenny, who was standing listening. She nodded to do as Grobler asked.

"Now that I know who it is and that it is a person I have met, I will sign the documents."

After signing, Lisa left the building and returned to her hotel.

Jenny was sitting on the bed. "That was fun, don't you think?"

"Maybe for you, but I'm living it, Jenny. This guy Casper was a man I spoke to on the flight here. Which means him sitting on the seat next to me was intentional, not that I can see what part he plays in the overall scheme."

"Well, the only way to find out is to call him."

"I'm certainly going to do that. He's got a lot of explaining to do."

Chapter 34

Lisa took a taxi to a small restaurant in central Pretoria the following day. When she went inside, she saw Casper standing at the bar. She walked over.

"I must say, for your name to be mentioned at the solicitor's offices was quite a surprise, Casper. What is it all about?" Lisa asked, not giving him time to even welcome her.

"You're certainly direct and to the point, Lisa. Shall we eat, and I'll explain everything?"

"Very well."

Soon, they were sitting in a booth, the starter in front of them.

"I'll not go into fine detail, Lisa, save to say we first knew about the diamonds you found from a contact in Sir John's company in London. After examining the flora found on the diamonds, Hans returned to South Africa armed with that report to search for the rest. Of course, he didn't find them and needed you to show him where they were. You will know about this, but I'm only repeating it to show you how much we know. Fortunately, I was in London when you came to London to see Sir John.

After finding out about the flight you booked, I secured a ticket. Our meeting and conversation on the aircraft were to give you a potted version of how mines operate under mining licenses, and obtaining such a license is something anyone could do. On top of that, I wanted you to know where the diamonds came from in case Sir John told you something different. Are you following me so far?"

"I am."

"What you don't know is we were following and watching you when you were with Hans. We also saw you tied up and your eventual escape during a freak storm. When Hans was tracking you, we caught them up, but they had hidden the diamonds you had taken them to. A drone was sent up to find you, but there was no sign. You were either dead or out of sight of the cameras. There was nothing we could do but come back and wait for your return to Pretoria. I assume they did find the few diamonds you told them there were?"

"They did. Sir John claimed when we got back, they'd found nothing, and I was getting no money. What could I do? A charity will benefit as they get all the money under the agreement, so it was alright. I don't understand how you knew I was forming a mining company?"

"From an elder who was at a meeting organised by Joshua. We couldn't understand why, but then I realised you were following what I told you on the flight. As a miner, if diamonds were found or mined in the registration area, they would belong to the mining company. That was smart thinking, Lisa, I applaud you. So, armed with this information and the elder's confirmation, we knew exactly what you wanted and ensured it was certified legally. Without help, you could have used a small local company. Such companies having someone wanting to register a mine suspect there may be a find. They'd tell you to come back the next day, and by then, they'd have your documents ready. Except most are in contact with large mining companies. They'd immediately be on the phone, giving them the locations you want to register. By the next day, after checking, they'd claim you were too late. A mining company would already have the rights."

They fell silent as the starters were removed and replaced with the main course. Apart from compliments on the food, the conversation didn't begin until they were finished and had coffee in front of them.

"I appreciate your help, Casper, but why?"

"I represent a large number of people who are distant relatives of the owners of the mines, as well as important white employees whose ancestors lost everything when the diamonds were stolen. You have to remember in those days, black South Africans had no say, used only as slave labour. For them to own land legally would have been unheard of. But I digress. For years, relatives have watched and waited as treasure seekers scoured the area for the missing diamonds. They also had watchers in the large cutting houses watching and waiting to see if any of the diamonds turned up. The relatives believed they could make a legitimate claim, receiving a large percentage of their value if they had. It isn't certain. Only the courts could ultimately decide that, but legal advice gave hope. So, while the villagers refused mining rights on their land, the diamonds, if ever found, the relatives would follow that route. We suspected you had lied to Sir John and knew the location of the rest of the diamonds. This was confirmed when you had Joshua convince the villagers to allow you mining rights so they would legally be yours when you brought them out, and no one could claim differently."

"I'm not bringing them out for myself. They are for the villagers, to bring them out of poverty, repair areas like the poisoned lake, and buy agricultural equipment."

"I know your intentions, Lisa, but you have no concept of the haul's value. What you intend for the villagers is a few million. That probably won't even amount to the interest from the sale of the diamonds if you left the money in the bank. I don't think it is out of the way to help others who lost their life savings, most ending up in poverty, just like the villagers. All I'm asking is that you consider all these points. Then, a final word of advice, don't sell everything as rough diamonds; select the very best and have them cut. Such stones can multiply their value by ten times."

"I understand what you're saying. The stones look nothing like what you see in the jewellers. I need to think about what to do from here."

"Whatever you do, the diamonds must be secured in bank vaults before anyone knows they have been found. To do that, they need to be extracted by helicopter, not road vehicles."

"Where will I get a helicopter from, and how much do they cost?"

"A lot of money, Lisa. If you are prepared to work with me and the others who lost out beyond the villagers, I can raise the funds to do this for you."

"I need to think, Casper, I will be in touch." Then she changed her tone. "While I do, a word of warning. I found the diamonds in their boxes lying a meter off the track in the back of a crashed truck. By the number who have searched that track, none could have missed the wreck still with the bodies inside, as well as the diamonds in the back. They weren't found because they are protected by forces you and I cannot imagine. Why was I allowed to find them? I cannot answer, except if you are thinking of cheating me and taking all the diamonds yourself, the same as Sir John, it will not happen. The forces protecting them will not let them be taken. Even I don't know, at this stage, if I can."

He looked at her while he sipped his coffee, thinking back to the conversation with the elder, who had told him of Blackmon's appearance and the terror he instilled in every man in the room.

"This force you suggest that protects the diamonds. Would that involve Donald Blackmon?"

"He takes a major role, why do you ask?"

"According to the elder I spoke to, Blackmon appeared during the elders meeting with Joshua. Everyone in that room heard his threat if they didn't do as you asked. He is a persuasive guy to have on your side; he terrifies everyone."

She smiled. "DB gets around, I'll give him that. Since I first came to this country, he's been at my side, pulled me out of the lake after the crash, brought villagers to help me when I swam in the poisoned lake and has remained at my side, keeping me safe. Blackmon even brought the rain to enable my escape from Hans. I believe I know why he needs me, although the diamonds are a side issue and will only serve to better the lives of the villagers. So, for your safety, Casper, don't laugh it off because while I can call him to protect me, I cannot control his actions."

"I've lived in Africa all my life, Lisa. While Christianity was forced on the population in modern times, beliefs surrounding the power of the dead go back thousands of years. To this day, rituals are still practiced in the villages. A man is a fool to ignore such rituals that have sustained beliefs for so long, in talking or calling on the dead. I suspect Blackmon is stuck between light and dark; whether he is capable of thought as we understand it, I don't know, but like those called back from the dark side by medicine men and tribal dances, their powers have been demonstrated so many times. You have the means to let him move on. I can assure you, I will not do anything to attract the attention of whatever he's become when, even in life, he was responsible for so much pain and suffering."

"In that case, we have an understanding and can move on together. Thank you for a lovely meal, I'll be in touch, but now I have things to do."

Casper watched her leave, climbing into a taxi. Samuel Ritter, also inside the restaurant having dinner, joined him.

"She has the diamonds, Samuel. She also believes she's being protected by Blackmon. She gave me a direct warning not to double-cross her."

Samuel grinned. "Not the Blackmon who died during the war?"

"The very one. Come to this country and allow yourself to get involved in the beliefs of the villagers, and it just goes to show how stupid you can be."

"So, how are you going to play it?"

"We go along with what she wants until the diamonds are safely in our hands, then unlike Sir John did with her, claiming they never found the diamonds, so she gets nothing. I'll tell her the diamonds disappeared from the boxes as the helicopter moved away from the area. Suggesting it must be Blackmon and his dark forces preventing them from ever leaving the forest."

"And she'll believe it?"

"The girls so up Blackmon's arse, she'll believe anything."

"Then we will be rich?"

"Stinkingly rich."

Chapter 35

Sitting in an empty office of his company in Cape Town, Sir John was on the telephone with the supervisor, Mark Talbot, from the cutting room in the UK.

"What do you mean there is something wrong with the stones, Mark?"

"I've had our best people on them, Sir John. Already, two have completely disintegrated during cleaving and another during sawing. That was after hours of studying the correct way to cut them. We're scared of trying another."

"I can understand that, but we've had stones shatter before. Have your people looked at the shattering and come to any conclusions?"

"I agree, it does happen, but normally it's the result of a serious fissure break, and expected. These stones shatter like you get with a car windscreen. The bits are very tiny, full of fissures themselves, and useless. We have looked at each shattered stone under powerful microscopes; the fissures were not there when I originally studied the stones, and now they are covered in them."

"Have you another stone ready for sawing?"

"Yes."

"Then try again."

"You are sure about that, Sir John? When we don't know what is happening."

"Just do it and call me back."

After finishing the call, Sir John walked over to the wall safe and took a diamond from the batch Hans had brought back. Pocketing it, he went to a room in the basement of the building. Inside, two technicians were working.

"Mbuyiseni, I want you to look at this diamond," Sir John said, pulling the stone from his pocket and handing it over.

"What am I looking for, Sir John?"

"Talbot in the UK claims the stones are shattering when they attempt to cleave and even saw them. It could mean some have an abnormality from a particular mine, but we know they came from several mines, so they can't all have this problem."

Mbuyiseni placed the diamond under a microscope. "This one looks perfect, not even a fissure. This is a very rare stone, Sir John."

"Rare or not, select an edge and cleave. I want to see if we get a repeat of what London is finding."

Mbuyiseni frowned. "May I first attempt a simple brut? Suppose the diamond is under an unusually high tensile strain in its formation. In that case, it will show up immediately without too much damage."

"Very well, set it up, and I'll return."

After leaving, Mbuyiseni mixed a small amount of cement, filled his cupped stick, and pushed the diamond into the cement, exposing one corner. Then, he placed it on one side to allow the cement to harden.

Later in the day, Sir John was back with Mbuyiseni to watch the bruting of the stone.

Mbuyiseni had also set up a similar arrangement on another stick, using a diamond from the cutting room. With great skill, he began to rub them together to create a simple facet on the stone brought by Sir Peter. As he rubbed them together, looking at them under a large illuminated magnifying glass, everything began to follow what was expected.

"The stone is responding as normal, Sir John. Should I continue or stop until we have studied the stone for the perfect preparation?"

"Go a little longer. I need to be certain what Talbot reported wasn't just a coincidence."

Mbuyiseni carried on, now a little more confident all was well. Suddenly, Sir John's stone exploded. Mbuyiseni pulled back in shock; he had never seen this happen before. "It's gone, Sir John. All that's left is dust," he gasped. "A three-carat diamond has destroyed itself."

Sir John stood there in silence, his thoughts returning to Lisa's warning about the stones, that they were cursed. This couldn't be. There had to be a logical explanation. "You suggested earlier that the stones could be under unusual internal strain. Explain this concept."

"The best way to describe it is glass. We harden glass to turn it into safety glass, so when it breaks, it shatters rather than leaving very sharp pieces. I have heard you can overharden glass, forming massive stress, and even the lightest bang can shatter it; sometimes, it will spontaneously shatter. I have never seen natural hardening in diamonds go to this extreme. If they are all like it, they are worthless."

At that moment, Sir John's mobile began to ring. It was Mark Talbot. He answered the call. "I hope you have better news, Mark?" he asked before Mark could speak.

"I'm sorry, Sir John. This last diamond has done the same. Until technical experts can tell us what is going wrong, I recommend no more be touched."

"Very well, stop all work on them and get the pieces to a lab for analysis."

Mbuyiseni looked towards Sir John. "Was that another from the original twenty?"

"Yes, they have all come from the same box. Could it be possible the box when stolen that the thieves didn't know it was a box of rejected stones?"

"Looking at them under the microscope, there would be no reason to reject them. A better option would be if they came from a particular mine where none of the stones from that mine had been cut."

Sir John shrugged. "It would be logical. Not that I've seen any documentation from the archive records of mining that referred to stones that shattered on testing."

"Would anyone want to admit a problem like that? It could make all the diamonds from the mine or even the area suspect and unsellable."

"True, even today, the big mines are very secretive about the yield and initial test results for fear of upsetting the prices. If it suddenly became common knowledge uncut diamonds coming from South Africa were shattering during cutting, the losses would be astronomical; no cutting company would want to take a risk."

"If they got on to the market and were failing, the industry would be in serious trouble," Mbuyiseni added.

"That doesn't bear thinking about. All we can do now is wait for our technical team in the UK to report what the problem is."

***

Later in the day, Sir John was back in his office when his telephone rang. He looked at the caller: Marvin Draper from the Diamond Consortium.

"Marvin, what can I do for you?" Sir John asked, answering the call.

"I've been ringing around, John, to others in the consortium attempting to get information about a Miss Lisa Jones, who has registered mining rights in a large area in the Kruger. It went through after the local villagers who now own the land gave permission. We can't have renegades entering the industry without our consent. Do you know anything about her?"

"Why would someone register that area? We all know the diamonds are spent, and even the roughnecks couldn't make a living and pulled out."

"Precisely, so what does this miner know we don't?"

"Unless it's another treasure hunter after the stolen haul of diamonds. After all, if they have mining rights, claims of ownership by relatives of the original miners wouldn't hold water unless they could prove ownership by initial registration, and we know none were registered."

"I'd forgotten that possibility, John. This is dangerous. Could this Jones woman know where the diamonds are, which is why she registered? If that's the case, such a haul flooding the market could destabilise the industry. I will urgently call a senior members meeting and invite Miss Jones. Can you attend?"

"Unfortunately, on this occasion, I can't. I'm committed to finalising a contract and will be leaving for London in a matter of hours. I will ask my South African representative to be there and forward me a meeting report."

"Very well, I'll talk to you later in the week."

Following the call, Sir John called Hans into his office.

"Lisa's registered mining rights across the entire old mining area. That could only mean she knows where the rest of the diamonds are."

"I suspected that. How do you want to play it?"

"The consortium is calling her in. They want to know what she is up to, so we stand away and watch. Soon, she will make her move and return to the Kruger. You must be in a position to keep close to her. There is something strange going on. The stones she gave us originally and the ones you brought back cannot be cut. They shatter. I'm having our people find out why. I've also looked through old reports of stone quality coming out of the area when the mines were in full production, and there is nothing about failures; the quality was never questioned. It was a pity the mines gave out as they did. Even so, it's completely illogical."

"That's not good. What if she dumps the lot into the market? Would it have any effect?"

"I don't think she'll be allowed; the consortium would buy the lot off her. Otherwise, the market would collapse."

"Would they not realise the diamonds are rubbish when

they make a test cut on one before paying her?"

"I can't see them test cutting, and why should they? No one would suspect they can't be cut; after all, they, like me, would have their specialist report of good-sized diamonds in front of them, all with the highest clarity rating. Based on that, they would want the lot in their hands before auctioning between themselves for future cutting. If the buyers cut in advance, Lisa may catch on to the diamond's potential value and have the diamonds cut on her behalf, making the big money the buyers would want to make. Believe me; most are so greedy; they'd not give her a chance, virtually paying her as the boxes arrived."

Hans gave a hint of a smile. "It could cost them millions. Share values could collapse. Then, with you buying none, you could take over dealers."

"Precisely. Besides, after my people finish their tests, we should know how to get around the shattering. Anyway, one step at a time, first we watch and wait."

Chapter 36

"Why the concern, Lisa?" Jenny asked.

"I received a phone call from the secretary of the chairmen of something called the 'Diamond Consortium' She asked me if I could attend their main offices tomorrow at ten. I told her I'd never heard of them and wasn't looking to join any association. The girl said it wasn't usual to talk to owners of potential mining operations, mainly to make them aware of how diamonds are distributed and sold in this country and give them an understanding of what the consortium could do for them."

"I know of the consortium; Dad often worked for them studying the geology of certain areas."

"So what do they do?"

"By what I remember, they are made up mainly of buyers of uncut stones for turning into jewellery, along with representatives of all the main mining corporations. They will want you to sell them any stones you find because it enables control of release and keeps the price high."

"Is that a direction I should be taking?"

"Who knows, but uncut diamonds are no good to you. You need the money to do as you want. So if they will pay for the lot at a good price, why mess about attempting to sell them yourself?"

"You have a point. I wouldn't know how to sell the stones without returning to Sir John or Casper. Then, I'm not overconfident that Casper won't try to pull a stunt like Sir John. But if I go to a consortium, they could hardly cheat me. Some would have principles."

"Hopefully, so are you going?"

"I'll think about it," she grinned, "after all, the big boss has summoned me. Not that it phases me."

"You're getting very bolshy, Lisa."

"Never, it's the northern English way; no one tells us

what to do."

***

Lisa entered the building, went to a security desk, and told them who she was and that she had an appointment. A uniformed man with 'security' displayed on epaulettes escorted Lisa via a lift to the fourth floor, where she was met by a middle-aged lady who took her directly into a large room. Down the center ran a table. To either side of the table, fifteen men were sitting, all looking at her as she entered.

Sitting at the head of the table, a man stood and walked down towards her. "Thank you, Miss Solgen." Then he looked at Lisa. "My name is Marvin Draper, Miss Jones. Thank you for coming to see us if you will follow me."

He pulled out an empty chair at the top of the table for her. "May we offer you coffee?"

"I'm fine, thank you," she answered softly, completely overawed by the number of people in the room. None looked friendly; if looks could kill, she'd not have reached her seat.

Marvin gave her a potted version of what the consortium did. When he finished, he asked if she had any questions.

"I'm not really into how business works, Mr. Draper, but by what you seem to be implying, you are against entrepreneurs."

"Excuse me, in what way?"

"Well, you seem to want all diamonds found in Africa or anything beyond chippings for industrial use to go through your consortium. Why is this? Do you like to keep the price up artificially, for, I suspect, control of the price, thus larger profits?"

Draper wasn't happy with her analysis, but he smiled weakly. "To the layperson, it may seem that way, but you see, Miss Jones, the mining and finding of a stone is a tiny fraction of the work that must go on in turning a diamond into something of beauty. Many people in this room will tell you that because we are dealing with a natural gemstone, some stones of equal size and quality can take weeks of studying to make the first cut, and others only days. Both stones, when finished, will look their very best. Except one may cost five times as much to achieve the final result. If you only went by the work involved, one would represent a considerable loss, and the other would meet the required profit. Our position is to set a price that reflects such discrepancy between stones of similar brilliance and size so all of the cutting houses and, of course, the mining companies can operate on an equal playing field. What are the advantages of selling to us? The cutting houses will look at the report describing each stone's size, clarity, weight, etc. Many within the consortium are bidding against each other, with the bids reflecting the final price offered to you. It also guarantees everything you produce equals or exceeds the two carats we will purchase. Some members specialise in the smaller stones. They will talk to you individually about purchasing your stones under the required size. Surely a guaranteed purchase must be good business and less stressful?"

"Yes, it does sound like a sensible approach."

"I'm glad you agree. I also have a few questions raised by the members that I want to ask you. If we are to do business, it's prudent to know who you are, where you come from, what makes you want to mine, and what experience you bring. I'm assuming you would have no objections?"

"Not at all,"

"We know you came from the UK. What background do you have in diamonds? Perhaps a geology degree or your family's already in the mining industry?"

"Sorry, no degree, no family member already mining. My parents are dead, and my stupid brother is facing twenty years in the Philippines for drug smuggling. I'm here on my own."

Her answer took him aback. "Are you telling us you have never mined? Perhaps you are working or have worked in the industry?"

"Again, no to both; mind you, I've been watching videos online to find out what to do. Not that I visualise myself in dungarees with a pick over my shoulder, singing 'yo, ho, ho, it's off to work I go.'" Lisa added the last sentence in the hope that someone might have smiled rather than scowled at her. None did, making her feel even more intimidated.

"We are not understanding, Miss Jones. Do you realise you've registered mining rights across an extensive area already mined and declared effectively empty for any commercially feasible operation? Do you intend to mine, or do you intend to sit about, perhaps in a golf club, claiming you own diamond mines?"

"Mr Draper, please don't treat me like a fool because I am not. In Lancashire, where I come from, our working men's club is the poshest club. No one there would be interested in me owning a diamond mine. I assume you asked me here to agree to sell any stones I find to your consortium? How I intend to extract such stones from mines in an area already declared by miners as exhausted is surely my business. You can hardly expect me to explain my intentions with these mines in detail?"

"Miss Jones," one of the members cut in. "It is you who are treating us as fools. Mining is a serious and often dangerous enterprise, with documented operation methods that keep you and your workers safe. So if you don't intend to mine using any recognised method, are you a treasure hunter looking for the lost diamonds and have registered mining rights to keep what you find legally?"

She looked across at him. "Again, Sir, my intentions are my own business. However, I believe that setting up any treasure hunt, or even a mining operation, costs a great deal of money, money I don't have. However, suppose I stumble across diamonds lying around during my time in the Kruger. In that case, I assume I can come to your consortium, and you would make an offer?"

"Stones laying around are very unlikely, Miss Jones. Such a scenario is confined to adventure books. Extracting stones is a formidable task and requires great expertise to avoid damaging a potentially large and valuable stone," the member added.

Marvin decided that continuing this meeting was a waste of time. "If you find such stones laid around as you suggest, you can bring them to us, Miss Jones," he said mockingly. Then he carried on more seriously: "Thank you for coming and explaining your position; we won't keep you any longer." Effectively, he was asking her to leave.

When Lisa left, a member stood, ready to go. "What was that all about, Marvin? The girl's a bloody idiot when she believes videos off the internet will teach her how to mine when she openly admits with no money. I've better things to do than sit and listen to that dribble and naivety."

Marvin splayed his hands out in a gesture. "When someone registers for mining rights in an area owned by the local natives, who gives her permission to mine, it is important to understand her intentions. After talking to her, I agree with you; she's a fool and will fall flat on her face as she attempts to mine her claim. Nothing she said offers any risk to the consortium."

"I wouldn't discount that girl so easily," another member commented.

"Why would you say that, George? You heard her, the same as us, she's no idea what mining entails."

"I agree, by what little she understands about mining, it's clear she's not here to reopen the mines. We only assumed she was because of her actions. However, the more I consider her answers, the more I believe we have unearthed the seeds of a large scam."

"On what basis do you believe it a scam?" another in the room asked.

"It has to be to get back the money already spent. The girl flew halfway across the world and walked into one of the top legal groups in South Africa, formed a company, and registered for mining rights after obtaining permission from the landowners. We all know the thoughts of those villagers in the area and what they think about mining. They've made it abundantly clear that never again would they allow mining on their land. Yet this girl gets it without a single objection. So I ask myself, what is going on? What have we missed? Maybe she's offered a cut of the profits to the villagers, which is why they are permitting it, and she's not going to mine anyway. Considering what I've said, Miss Jones is working with scammers. The mining rights registration gives credence to reeling in fools believing they will become rich."

Another member nodded his agreement. "I think you've hit the nail on the head, George. If any are naive enough to fall for it without the usual due diligence, let them."

"If it is a scam, by the area of registration covering a large number of mine workings, it is going to be big, in fact, large enough to affect our reputation," Marvin added.

Yet another member cut in. "I also agree with George and Marvin that we have uncovered a scam. Most, if not all of us, come from a long line of miners and cutters. The last thing we want is for our industry to be involved in a scam. I'm proud of what I do. No cocky kid is going to make a fool of me."

Everyone remained silent for a short time, mulling over the possible ramifications of what had been suggested of Lisa's intentions.

Marvin looked around the room. "Like many here, I assumed this was the beginning of a new mining operation. It isn't. George reminded us our thinking was too narrow, and mining had never been her intention. I don't believe she knew we'd want to talk to her. Then, she panicked with our questioning and held back by refusing to elaborate on why she wanted the mines. After listening to Miss Jones and other possible alternatives from members in this room regarding why she is here, I believe this is the seed of a scam. Due to the possibility of damage to an important part of this country's economy, we must pass our suspicions to the appropriate authorities. If everyone agrees, this is the route we should take. Please raise your hand."

Everyone raised their hand, and the decision was made.

Chapter 37

Lisa, still planning her return trip to the Kruger, had come down for breakfast and found a table in the corner of the dining room.

Bapota entered the hotel, spoke to reception, showed his police warrant, and walked through to the dining room. He saw Lisa and went over to her.

"Lisa Jones, seeing you back in South Africa is a surprise. Would you mind if I joined you?"

"Do I have an option?" she asked.

"Of course, although the alternative after your breakfast is to accompany me to the police station."

"On what charge?"

"To assist us in our inquiries following a telephone call from a concerned member of the public."

"I see, but if I'm only to assist, you may take a seat. Would you like me to order you coffee?"

"Thank you, that would be much appreciated."

Coffee was brought, and he added sugar, stirring it slowly.

"I must admit, I was surprised to hear you had returned to South Africa. Last time we spoke, you didn't give the impression this country would be at the top of your list of go-to places."

She shrugged. "Circumstances change, then apart from the experience of crashing into the lake and all that followed, I got on well with the people I met in the villages. So I decided, with them saving my life, I owe them a great deal and came back to see what I can do for them."

"Then you came into a lot of money, perhaps high insurance payouts?"

"Yeah, like that was ever going to happen. You made out it was a terrorist bomb that brought the aircraft down, and what do you think happened? The insurance people pointed out their get-out clause; they don't pay for terrorist acts."

"I must admit initially that was suspected, and it was picked up by the media, who like to run with those scenarios. It sells papers."

"Then you're saying it wasn't terrorists?"

"No, the final report concluded there was fatigue in the aircraft frame. Although the airline did have an up-to-date safety certificate, the fatigue was in a location that was only subject to inspection once a year. I understand all the passenger's relatives are in the process of settlement, but it seems, you being in the UK, no one deemed it important to let you know."

"Story of my life, but knowing my luck, they'd remind me I'm still alive, paying me only for my lost suitcase and then deduct the emergency two hundred they reluctantly gave me to buy some clothes."

Bapota wanted to laugh but instead pulled out his notebook and a small card with his name and telephone number on it. Going through his book, he wrote down a number and name on the back of the card, handing it to her. "Call that number and speak to Mr Shoemaker. He is the assessor who looks after all the claims for the insurance companies. You'll certainly be in line for at least a hundred thousand Rand, maybe more, with how you've been treated."

"Thank you. I'll give him a call. Although I don't think you came here to check if I've received any compensation."

"I didn't. Lisa, you set alarm bells ringing at the Diamond Consortium. The South African government hasn't any issues with anyone applying for mining rights. However, someone coming to our country on a visitor visa to want to mine would require a new application to work here and show they have the initial funds for any undertaking they want to carry out. I assume you have that in hand?"

"I'm aware of the visa situation. My solicitors are currently sorting it out. But why is the consortium concerned?"

"Lisa, please don't take everyone for fools. An eighteen-year-old female who barely survived when she was last here and broke on her admission, having no idea how to mine old workings, who has applied for mining rights in the Kruger is unheard of. You have to admit that alarm bells would begin to ring."

"Are these alarm bells created by the consortium because I may not sell any diamonds I find to them like they want me to?"

"Not at all. They don't believe you are going to mine. Apart from the fact there are no diamonds of any value left in the mines you have registered, everyone knows that. The consensus is you are sowing the seeds for an elaborate scam, selling shares to unsuspecting investors worldwide with the promise of untold profits. With any investor looking into your proposal, they would find the mines exist, and you have the mining rights. If that is your intention, Lisa, I will tell you now the slightest hint of you attempting to offer shares in these spent mines, your rights will be withdrawn, and if you return to this country, you will be arrested and imprisoned. Our laws differ slightly from how the UK operates, which you will find to your cost. I'm telling you this because I don't think you are the person behind such a scam, more someone who has got herself mixed up with the wrong people, and they see a way to exploit you. Maybe by claiming while you were in the forest, you stumbled across diamonds scattered about an entrance to a mine."

"It certainly sounds like one idea to fund my mines, Bapota; you should take a punt and buy a few shares from me, just in case I've found a mine brimming with diamonds," she mocked.

"You have been warned, Lisa. I think you should go home, take any compensation offered, and never return. South Africa is not the sort of country that likes to be exploited."

Lisa smiled. "That's bloody big of you to claim I'd be exploiting your country. For a start, it isn't your country; your ancestors have been stripping this country for hundreds of years of its natural wealth and its people, the same as the Europeans did to the Indigenous Americans and the Australian Aborigines. When I walked into the consortium's plush building, the only black person I met was the security man at the entrance, probably the lowest-paid person there. Everyone attending the meeting was white. It is all pontificating that they control the diamond industry in this country. I'll tell you this, I'm not here to scam anyone, although it would be nice to shake the big fat arses of the people in that room by hurting them where it hurts the most, their pockets. So why am I here? If you must know, I'm here to contribute, to give back to the people of the villages who saved my life and have been exploited for years, besides being robbed of their dignity. How I'm going to do that is my business. You, like everyone, will have to wait and see."

He shook his head slowly. "Naivety, Lisa. You cannot change the world as much as you believe you can. To run any country, it is not the politicians running it. They come and go. Nor the dictators lining their pockets to eventually get their comeuppance; the very clever people in the background know how to create wealth and, as such, make a country rich. And yes, you may disagree with the consortium, but they have generated more wealth for the country by controlling the diamond trade than those who exploited the country's wealth. This is the same as every other natural resource in South Africa; people are working to maximise the returns. Okay, they will get rich, but the country does as well; it is not being ripped off."

At that moment, Lisa sensed she was not alone. Looking towards the doors leading out onto a terrace where more tables were laid, DB was standing there. Then he began walking towards them, passing through tables, chairs, and even diners to halt at her side. She knew he could see DB by the look on Bapota's face.

"Do not question this girl's destiny. When she calls for help, you will respond. Dark forces that seek to disrupt are already building. Ignore my words at your peril."

DB faded to nothing.

"Did you see him?" Bapota stuttered, obviously very shaken.

Lisa gave an indifferent shrug. "I assume you're talking about DB? He's always around. He spoke to you then?"

"You didn't hear his words?"

Lisa had but decided not to admit it. "No, you only hear him if he wants to talk to you. Not that you can ask him questions; he just ignores them. What did he say?"

"He said I shouldn't question you about what you are doing, and when you want help, I must give it."

"Sounds typical of his normal threats. I'd not discount anything DB says; he can get quite nasty."

He frowned. "Are you suggesting he talks to you as well?"

"Of course. Sometimes, DB sends Jenny. Not that any of you believed me. So you can understand why I was a bit angry when everyone kept saying I was some loony. These days, I'm quite used to him coming and going. He's the one who's driving me forward, but I'm still determining what the outcome is at this moment. But hey-ho, I can only humour him and go along with what he wants."

"Are you going to enlighten me about what has happened, Lisa? I'm already feeling out of my depth?"

"Join the club. I've been in that situation since the

aircraft crashed and someone pulled me out, but no one survived, so who was that? As it is, I can't tell you anything unless DB tells me I can. Well, I say I can't. You shouldn't know until the time comes when I may need your help." She lowered her voice. "It would seem that what has always been taught that only heaven and hell exist isn't quite correct. From what I now understand, there is also a dark side, a parallel world between us and a perceived heaven and hell. DB walks in that world, and I believe Jenny cannot move on until DB has completed whatever his intentions are. The villagers, particularly the elders and the medicine men, the locals call mungome, have always known about this world, and it terrifies them, even though the bible pushers for years had attempted to discount it."

He nodded. "I've always been sceptical of what the villagers claimed. Mainly because I come from a very religious family, and yes, I was only ever taught of two places to go when you leave this world."

"You should be aware, Bapota, that DB is not just a vision that plays on fear. He is capable of killing to get his way. I've witnessed many times just what he's capable of. He's also not opposed to targeting your family to force you to do what he wants. He killed my mum, or rather accelerated her demise."

"Would this be why the villagers gave you mining rights when they were always adamant that they would never again allow mining on their land?"

"You mean, did DB visit them? Believe me, if he wanted me to have those rights, he would, the same as he's shown himself to you."

"I need time to think, Lisa. Take care. This entity posing as DB looks to be very dangerous for you. I will mark off the complaint as investigated with no basis for escalation. You have my card if you need to get in touch directly."

"Thank you, but I've lived with DB for some time, so

I know what he's about. There is one thing I'd like you to look into for me: a white South African named Casper Meer. He's given me some help, except I'm not a trusting person anymore, so I must know his background to see if it aligns with what he's telling me."

Bapota stood, looking down at her. "You will have the information you ask for as soon as I can. I'll leave it at your hotel reception," he said, then walked away.

Lisa watched him go inwardly, smiling. DB came by at just the right time. Bapota should be scared, particularly for his family, because they could be in great danger if he didn't cooperate. She also wondered if DB had involved Bapota so she could have Casper looked into. In her view, everything was falling into place, but not because of her.

***

Back at police headquarters, Bapota sat quietly at his desk. The appearance of DB had shaken him far more than he had displayed to Lisa. As he sat there, thinking back to when he was in Umbra, even then, nothing seemed right. The plane crash, Lisa wandering around in the forest and claiming she'd been with Jenny; it all made sense. Yet how could he put this down on paper? He, like Lisa, would be laughed at. Picking up the telephone handset, he dialled Marvin Draper.

"Bapota, thank you for coming back to me so quickly. What are your thoughts after speaking to the idiot?"

"I can find no basis to believe she is involved with any scam, Mr. Draper. The girl has every intention of visiting her mines. You should put it down to another person with diamond fever, believing they can find diamonds when we know she's only wasting her time."

"What about her visa? It must only cover her as a visitor. Can't you throw her out of the country for violating the rules?"

"I could if she does, except her legal representatives have

already applied to change the visa. She'll get it, providing she does nothing to violate her existing visa conditions before the new one is granted. But tell me, why are you so interested? After all, if she finds a few diamonds that have been missed, it makes no difference to your members?"

"That is not the point, Bapota. Our mining corporation members don't like being made to look foolish. We see ourselves as a professional organisation that has matured from the days when lone prospectors would pile in, and stake claims all over the place when someone found a diamond or a nugget of gold. Then, if she does find diamonds, the government handing over the land to illiterates has effectively blocked us from sending in the big mining groups to blitz the area without us buying her claim out. If she'd even sell."

"I've been to the area, Mr. Draper, after an aircraft went down. Looking at the condition you left the area following your last intrusion, it is good that you will be blocked."

"Keep such opinions to yourself, Bapota. One phone call, and you'll be back on the beat. I'd advise you to pull out all the stops, get the girl deported, and strip her of the mining rights." Draper cut the call.

Bapota replaced the handset. That wasn't going to happen, not on his watch. He also hoped that Draper would get a visit from DB; he'd like to see how cocky he was then.

Chapter 38

Two days after Bapota came to see her, Lisa received a sealed letter from him that had been left at reception. Returning to her room, she lay on her bed reading the report.

'Casper Meer has been in the mining industry all his working life. Important to you, most of his recent work was in the Kruger. He held a government role to ensure miners holding mining rights made good and, importantly, safe, the working areas covered by the issued certificates after finishing their mining operations. Several complaints were received then that Meer was taking backhanders to ignore shoddy tidy-up operations. He was replaced following a devastating report on a lake he'd cleared as safe, but it turned out to be poisoned with heavy metals and arsenic. His name has recently been linked to dealing with blood diamonds and is under investigation. If he is making any approach to you offering assistance in any way, I recommend being cautious. He's an opportunist and should not be relied upon.'

Lisa placed the letter down and leaned back. Why does everyone lie to her? Casper, on the face of it, seemed plausible. Had DB stepped in and made Bapota aware that he existed so she could be warned about Casper? Lisa no longer knew what was going on. However, no matter what, she had enough money to buy a vehicle and was leaving for the Kruger tomorrow. Hopefully, DB would further guide her on what he wanted of her this time. Lisa had also telephoned Mr Shoemaker, as Bapota suggested she should. His secretary told her he would ring back later that morning. Lisa wanted to see if Bapota was correct and if she may be in line for at least something. Her savings were quickly depleting, and if the diamonds didn't come good in any way, however small, she would be in trouble financially. Not that Lisa held out much hope the insurers would cough up; they had been pretty aggressive to her the last time she contacted them. However, if he could get her costs back, like the hotel the embassy had put her in, it would save on the payments she was still making to the government. Lisa also wondered where Jenny was. She was usually around quite often. Lisa couldn't believe she was actually missing Jenny, even though she had convinced herself Jenny was a figment of her imagination.

***

Returning from a walk to clear her mind, the telephone was ringing when Lisa entered her room.

"Lisa here," she said, grabbing the handset.

"Am I talking to Miss Lisa Jones?" a man asked.

"Yes, who's calling?"

"Mr Shoemaker, Miss Jones. My secretary informed me that you had called my office earlier today; how can I help you?"

"Inspector Bapota told me you were handling the compensation claims for the aircraft that went down on a flight between Pretoria and the Kruger National Park. Am I correct?"

"That is true, judging by your accent. Were you the English girl on the stricken aircraft by any chance?"

"Yes, I was wondering if you could help me?"

"In what way, Miss Jones?"

"My insurance company didn't want to know when I claimed for a lost suitcase and clothing. It wasn't lost; they pulled it out of the hold after recovering the aircraft, but everything was ruined. I would like you to get the airline to cover my hotel costs while waiting to return home and my damaged property. I even got charged seventy-five pounds for a new passport because the original went missing in the crash. Without it, I couldn't leave South Africa."

"That is ridiculous. Of course, I can help you. Looking

at my computer records, we wrote to you, but the letter was returned as gone away. We asked the British embassy if they could find where you had moved and are still waiting for a response."

"I had to move, my mum died, and my brother lost his job. I didn't put a forwarding address down or keep the telephone number. I was getting numerous calls from people trying to sell things."

"I understand, and I'm deeply sorry to hear of your mother's death. I also noticed the number you gave is here in Pretoria, South Africa. Are you in the country?"

"I am. Is that a problem?"

"Not at all, in fact, advantageous. Is it possible for us to meet while you are here?"

"I'm moving into the Kruger tomorrow and still determining when I'll return. I could call when I'm back."

"Can you be free later this afternoon? My diary is empty after three."

"Yes, where do you want us to meet?"

"What hotel are you staying in?"

"Hotel Neptune, is it close to your offices?"

"No, but it is on my way home. I will come to your hotel if you are agreeable."

"No problem, I'll be in the main lounge from three."

"I look forward to our meeting. Can you make sure you have your passport with you when we meet? Before we can talk, I will need to check your identity with the details I already have on you."

"I understand and will have it with me."

***

Mr Shoemaker was on time, and after checking Lisa's passport, they sat down with coffee in front of them.

"I'm representing all the accident victims, although I'm not representing you, Miss Jones. Based on what you told me on the phone, you've not talked to a solicitor, even in the UK?"

"I couldn't see the point. The insurance told me they didn't pay out on terror incidents and virtually put the phone down on me. I didn't know the police had changed their mind; it was now an accident. Then the papers in the UK never mentioned it."

"Even so, Miss Jones, you should have talked to a solicitor. You still had rights, which have been ignored by people who should know better."

She shrugged. "I suppose, but I was left destitute in a country I didn't understand; even the embassy told me nothing apart from land me in debt."

"Well, that is all in the past. Would you be agreeable for me to represent you with the underwriters?"

"Will it cost a lot?"

"As I've already mentioned, I'm representing all the other victim's families; I'm happy to add you to the list at no cost to yourself. Why am I doing that? As a surviving passenger on the aircraft with no obvious signs of life-changing injuries, your claim is clear-cut. So you will be compensated at a recognised standard rate across the industry, including all your costs. My work is to negotiate the extenuating circumstances immediately following the accident on your behalf and come to an acceptable figure. My fee will be added to your settlement, so you won't be out of pocket."

"On that basis, I'm happy to leave it to you."

Shoemaker opened an attaché case he'd brought in with him, taking out papers and placing them in front of Lisa. "If you can fill in your new address in the UK, your bank and account number, and then sign, I will inform the underwriters of my representation on your behalf."

Lisa filled in the documents and signed the bottom.

Shoemaker put everything back in his attaché case. "Thank you, Miss Jones. I will be in touch once I have an offer. The way negotiations are going, I would expect two, maybe three months for settlement."

"That's fine."

"May I ask why you are back in South Africa?"

"I'm finishing my holiday and looking up some of the villagers that helped me survive and saved my life."

"I read the report; they were very good to you. I believe they will appreciate your visit." He glanced at his watch. "I won't keep you any longer. Please enjoy your holiday. I will contact you as soon as I have any news." Then he finished his coffee before standing, nodded, and walked away.

Lisa leaned back. It had been a good meeting, not that she held out any hope of him getting much compensation. After all, he looked after families that had lost breadwinners and children without parents, and she had walked away unscathed.

Chapter 39

Lisa left Pretoria for the Kruger after purchasing an old Land Rover from a backstreet car dealer. The vehicle had certainly seen better days, but it was all she could afford, and it did start the first time, as well as being fitted with recently replaced part-worn tyres. After Lisa told him she intended to go into the Kruger, the dealer was concerned about her taking such an old vehicle. Going into the back, he brought out two jerry cans and a spare wheel at no extra cost to her. They were now firmly strapped in the back.

On her way out of the city, Lisa stopped at a large superstore that had a sale. There, she found a small tent, cool box, and camping set containing a plastic plate, dish, mug and metal cutlery, a single burner gas stove, and a water bottle. Lisa also stocked up with basic food, such as tins of stew and soup. With never going camping when young, Lisa relied on advice from a store assistant who seemed to know what she should have with her. Although he was surprised when she told him where she was heading, he added a basic first aid box, 'just in case' he had told her.

Lisa had only passed her driving test a month before initially going to South Africa. She thought of eventually starting a mobile hairdresser, but the promised training beyond washing hair had yet to transpire. Even so, at least she had a license, enabling her to drive a vehicle, but next to nothing in driving experience. Added to this inexperience, once off the tar road, she was finding it hard going with the old Land Rover's suspension, not in the best of condition and being firm, making the ride particularly uncomfortable and very noisy. After four hours on this road, Lisa pulled off and took a break. Sorting out a peanut chewy bar and opening a can of Coke, she sat on the drop-down tailgate of the Land Rover, enjoying the break. There was no rush; no one was waiting for her, so it was pointless not making regular stops. Lisa had also remembered the last time she'd been on this journey, Hans had pulled into a gas station and filled up before turning off the tar road. She had done the same, so there was plenty of fuel in the tank, although she was surprised just how much fuel had been used to get this far and glad the car dealer had made sure she had extra fuel with the jerry cans.

Jenny was suddenly by her side. "Where are we going?" she asked.

Lisa was no longer surprised by how Jenny turned up, taking her appearance in her stride.

"I'm returning to the village of Umbra. I hope to be able to hire a few villagers to take me into the area of the mines."

"Why would you go there? Is it just to collect the diamonds and bail, I would."

"I had thought about that, but it's wrong, Jenny. DB needs me for something else; the diamonds have little value to him. Unless I find out what he wants of me, it won't finish."

"So you think you'll find the answer by entering the mining area?"

"Not so much the answer, but more guidance on the direction he wants me to head or what he wants me to do for him. To tell you the truth, it's a flyer. I could be completely on the wrong track, and he wants nothing beyond me helping the villages by using the diamonds. It's difficult when I can't have a conversation with him. Doesn't he tell you anything?"

"Since meeting you again, I've seen no one."

By Jenny's admission, Lisa was becoming increasingly convinced that her own mind was creating the image of Jenny. Such an image gave her confidence that she wasn't alone and allowed her to converse with herself, working through situations in her mind as they came up. If it hadn't been for Jenny's company, Lisa knew she would have given up and returned home long ago.

"I was thinking, Jenny. There's every chance I'll be closely followed by Sir John's lot, particularly if Sir John found out I've registered mining rights. Then Casper could be hanging around because the more I think about his story, the more I believe he's another conman like Sir John. What do you think?"

"Trust no one where diamonds are concerned. Lean closer to the villagers; they will look after you; they know all the back ways and are very good hunter-trackers. Something they have done for hundreds of years."

"I'll remember that. If I'm in trouble, maybe with Hans or Casper around, and you are not with me, can I call DB?"

"I told you, you can always call him. He will come."

Lisa finished her Coke. "Time to move on. Are you coming?"

"Course I am."

They travelled on in silence, and Lisa finally broke it after the road improved and became less noisy.

"When this is over, will I ever see you again?"

"I wish I knew. We get on well, and to tell you the truth, you are all I have left. I'm frightened, Lisa. I don't know where I'll end up."

"I'm the same. You're my only friend these days. Back home, no one talks to me. My brother's a complete plonker, and I probably won't see him again for years."

"You'll be rich."

"Great, a bit pointless if you've no one to share it with."

Jenny laughed. "We're a hopeless pair. But seriously, you'll meet someone while sitting around on a beach with a gin and tonic in your hand."

"I suppose, but DB never thought this through. I'd have been better dead and you alive. At least you had a family to return to and help sort this mess out."

"Never think that, Lisa. I've always believed life has a destiny, which cannot be swapped about at will. When your time comes, that is it."

"So if you'd known in advance when your life in this world expired and you moved on, would you have done anything differently in your life?"

Jenny remained silent for a short time, then sighed. "I don't think so. My life has been good. Yes, like everyone, I've had down days, but they didn't last. How about you? Would you have changed your life?"

"God, yes, mine's been a nightmare ever since I could walk and talk. All the dreams I had for my future were shattered, and often treated like shit at school. A skivvy at home, looking after a mum who, over time, I began to suspect put on her disability to keep her high dependency allowances, as well as having me do all the housework while she lounged about complaining all the time about anything and everything."

"Why would you say that? I thought you loved her?"

"Don't get me wrong, I did love my mother, but at the same time, I was growing up and beginning to notice that what she would say sometimes was not always true. Then, she had no trouble feeding herself and entertaining her friends while I was at school, yet her problems were back when I was home. Even my brother robbed me. Now, I've nothing to go home to, apart from a crappy one-bed flat I had to move into when the mortgage company wanted to repossess the family home. I'm not like you educated and confident. Even Sir John laughed when I asked for my money, virtually kicked me out of his office, and threatened me. All my life, everyone has taken advantage of my naivety and crap education. I suppose that's why DB selected me: I'm easily manipulated and won't complain when I've completed my so-called destiny, which will probably leave me destitute. Even now, I've had to take so much crap not only from the police but every man and his dog."

"You don't sound thrilled, Lisa?"

"You can say that again. I would have if I could have gotten DB out of my life easily. He could keep his diamonds. I may be broke, but I would survive like I've always done."

"You should be looking for somewhere to park up, Lisa. It'll be dark soon," Jenny advised, changing the subject.

Lisa slowed down, saw a track, and turned off, following it a short distance before coming to a halt. "What do you think? Is this place okay?"

"Yes, you'll be fine. It's also about time you tested DB."

"In what way?"

"Once you settle down for the night, call DB and demand he protects you."

Lisa grinned. "You know, I think I will. Otherwise, I'll be terrified all night, wondering if anything or anyone is watching me."

"It's right to call him, at the very least, for a good night's sleep."

***

Later, Lisa, after sitting and talking to Jenny for some time, decided to call it a day. After Jenny left, Lisa lay in the tent, listening to the night-time noises of the insects and other noises she couldn't place. Lisa was very scared, and no matter what, she would not sleep tonight without help. Sleep was needed after the long hard drive. It was time to test Jenny's theory that DB would come.

Lisa began to call him in her mind, demanding he look after her. As she did, the noises outside the tent fell silent; Lisa knew he was there even though she couldn't see him, and soon she fell asleep.

Chapter 40

When Lisa left her hotel in Pretoria with the old Land Rover, Hans, Chas, and Gareth followed. They even pulled up not far from her when she entered the store.

"Right, Gareth. She's inside. Go and attach the tracker to the vehicle," Hans ordered.

Gareth climbed out and quickly ran to the Land Rover, attaching the magnetic tracker under a front wheel arch. He was back in minutes.

"You should see it, Hans; it looks even worse in the close-up. The dealer certainly saw her coming," he said, climbing into the back of the car and switching on his computer pad. "Trackers working, she'll not lose us now, that's for certain."

"What's she up to?" Chas commented when Lisa eventually came out with her purchases on a trolley and loaded them in the back of her vehicle.

"It looks like she's intending to go mining. Shouldn't we remind her she needs a pick and shovel?" Hans mocked as they watched what she had purchased.

"Maybe lend her ours when we catch up with her so she can dig her own grave," Gareth added.

Hans laughed. "I like that."

They fell silent, watching Lisa. Then, when she set off again, they followed at a distance, pulling short when Lisa eventually turned into the petrol station.

"At least she has some sense and is filling up before leaving the tar road," Garth said as he pulled up.

"I'm surprised that the vehicle's still running. It'll not get far on the dirt road," Hans commented, looking up from a book he was reading.

"What happens if she breaks down?" Gareth asked.

"I've got that sorted—Frankie is on her way to join us. If Lisa breaks down, she'll go ahead to help her. Frankie turning up will be hardly likely to raise Lisa's suspicions when attached to her vehicle are red crosses on both doors. Frankie will claim to be delivering extra medical supplies to the doctors visiting the villages. She's even got a few boxes in the back with appropriate medical labels attached," Hans told him.

Gareth smiled. "Sneaky, but why couldn't we just pick Lisa up? Except this time, she wouldn't escape."

"Sir John didn't want to take the chance. The last thing he wants is for her to be so badly injured that she is incapable of taking us to the other boxes. This time, he wants the boxes in her hands when we move in. Then it's not a beating. We cut her throat and bury her. A fitting end to a girl who has given us the run around with her stupidity."

Chas, watching the computer, looked up. "Pull over, she's stopped about a mile ahead."

They pulled over, and Hans called Frankie on the radio to join them and not go past. As time went on, Lisa was on the move once more.

Little was said, but the light was failing before the tracker indicated Lisa had pulled off the road and come to a halt. They also pulled off, quickly setting up tents.

"Would you believe that heap of junk is still running?" Hans told Frankie as she settled down to eat.

"She's not exactly rushing, which is probably why. Then it's a long drive for one person, even I'm tired."

"I can understand that. Now you've caught us up, we'll share driving. We'll know if she stops, and you can take over your vehicle and go ahead."

"I've been thinking, Hans, somehow I can't see Lisa collecting the diamonds and returning to Pretoria. Besides, it would be risky to carry so many diamonds, worth tens of millions, in a vehicle that could break down at any time and leave her stranded. Even she can't be that stupid to take such a risk," Frankie commented.

"I've thought the same, and I'd agree she'd have been far better off hiring guards or arranging a helicopter for her return. But it must be remembered that she's very short of money looking at what she has purchased, even less when Sir John refused to pay her for the diamonds she took me to. She has no option but to take the chance."

"Well, better her than me; I'd not take the chance alone in this area. There are roaming gangs from Mozambique and various animals who would see her as their dinner."

"She's got guts, I'll give you that. Then, as far as we're concerned, it'll be like taking candy from a baby," Hans added, laughing simultaneously.

***

The following morning, they were up early with the vehicles packed, waiting for the tracker to indicate she was again on the move. It was after nine when Lisa finally set off.

With Gareth driving Frankie's vehicle, she was sitting in the other vehicle alongside Hans, who had just turned on the ignition. When he pressed the start, nothing happened. He pushed again, but still, there was no response.

"Bloody strange, Chas, have a look under the bonnet."

Frankie grinned. "Seems it's one to Lisa, then? At least her heap of junk must have started," she mocked.

Hans didn't comment, getting out of the vehicle and going to the front to see what Chas had found.

"Well, what's the problem?"

"There's nothing obvious. It could be in the engine management system; if so, we're fucked. We should call for assistance; you can't repair those on the roadside."

"That's all we need. It'll be hours before anyone can get here."

By now, Frankie had also climbed out and was standing listening. "Should I take the tracker receiver and go on alone? If she breaks down, I couldn't afford to have someone in the vehicle she'd recognise."

"There's no option. We'll join you as fast as we can," Hans told her.

With this agreed, Frankie set off alone to follow Lisa.

Standing away from the group, DB watched, then slowly faded.

Chapter 41

Casper had sent a satellite telephone to Lisa's hotel to take with her into the Kruger, so when she collected the stones, she could call him, and he would send a helicopter, but he couldn't trust Lisa would do that.

Because of such doubts, he, like Sir John, had Samuel following her. However, unlike Hans, Samuel had gone ahead and set up camp close to the entrance of the track Lisa had originally been taken to by Hans. His camp was on the opposite side of the river, and in such a position, the camp would only be seen if Lisa and whoever had joined her crossed the river, which was unlikely. Samuel was convinced the diamonds were hidden somewhere along that track, mainly because that was the track Lisa had initially taken from the lake, and being alone, she couldn't have moved them far.

Kirk, who was with him, scooped a little bacon from the pan onto a plate and passed it to Samuel.

"Has Casper called with Lisa's position yet?" Kirk asked.

Casper could do this because the telephone he had given Lisa would periodically send a signal, giving its position, enabling Casper to watch her progress.

"He sent a message last night to say she had parked up. He was estimating another two days before she would arrive. Why?"

"I was thinking of doing a spot of hunting today, and we'd have fresh meat tonight. What do you think?"

"Why not? Hans is behind Lisa, so we'll not miss him. Besides, it's better than sitting around and the rivers too low for decent fishing."

"Those were my thoughts. Are you coming?"

"I think I will."

***

The two of them had been out for over three hours; they had seen zebras and buffalo; such animals were far too big, with the buffalo being extremely dangerous and to be avoided. They were after a bushpig or even a scrub hare. Both made good stews.

Kirk was on his tummy, scanning the area ahead with powerful binoculars. A short distance back, Samuel was sat down, leaning on a large rock.

"There's a native hunting group coming this way, and it looks like they have been successful. We should stop them and look at what they've got," Kirk suggested.

"We should. Time's going on, and we should be returning to camp."

Both men set off to intercept the natives, quickly catching them up. They could see a zebra being carried by four natives using a long branch passed between the front and hind legs, which had been bound together. Three natives had hessian sacks over their shoulders.

"What's in the bags?" Kirk demanded.

"You want to buy?"

"Yeah, like we're going to pay, open the fucking bags?" Kirk persisted, drawing his handgun.

The natives looked at each other, and a man carrying one of the bags placed it on the ground, pulling out a hare.

"That will do. Leave it and fuck off," Kirk told him, at the same time shooting the handgun in the air.

The natives ran and were soon out of sight.

Samuel stuffed the hare back in the bag. "Well, that's one way of hunting, and we get fresh meat tonight."

***

Back at camp, Kirk skinned the animal, cutting it up and throwing the carcass in a pan of boiling water over an open fire. He wrapped the legs in foil and placed them on the fire.

Samuel, while Kirk sorted the food, called Casper.

"Where is she now?" Samuel asked Casper.

"Lisa's parked up, and it looks like she's stopped for the night. She's probably been held up with obstacles on the road, judging by her little progress."

"Do you reckon she'll be in the area by tomorrow?"

"With a clear run, yes, but it'll be close to darkness. I believe this time, Hans will wait, like us, until she has collected the diamonds before moving in."

"Then, we should eliminate Hans and his team before she collects the diamonds. There's a great deal of value in those two boxes. If we leave it too long with only two of us, we'll end up in a pitched battle. It's best to catch them unaware to avoid any injuries."

"I agree; Lisa will probably go on to the village to hire workers. Hans, like you, will hang around the track entrance. Take them out when they arrive before Lisa returns with her workers."

"I'll do that. Keep me informed if there's any change."

Samuel joined Kirk, who had pulled out the bones cooking in the foil and put Samuel's on a tin plate.

"Casper said it's okay to take Hans and his men out as soon as they arrive," Samuel commented while unwrapping the foil around the meat.

"Very sensible. I didn't relish a gunfight along that track. I'll get out the sniper rifles in the morning, check them over, and set up the sights while you find us two good vantage points."

Samuel nodded as he began eating. "This tastes good. You can't beat freshly killed meat."

Later, the two men settled down for the night.

***

While the men slept, others from Mozambique met up with the hunting party Samuel and Kirk had robbed. If they had known the natives were, in fact, from Mozambique, both would have thought twice about stealing from them. Such groups often illegally crossed the border, taking spoils back to their own country. The gang leaders who employed the hunting team were unhappy to hear somebody had robbed them. It may have only been one hare, but it represented lost income. To this end, a gang leader decided that one man from the hunting party would join his gunmen to track Samuel and Kirk back to their camp.

When Samuel woke, he gasped in fear and kicked Kirk to wake him up. Standing around them were five men, four holding rifles.

"You two, on your knees, hands behind your heads," one of the gunmen demanded. He was a large man with an ammunition strap over one shoulder, sitting diagonally across his chest. He was wearing a dirty T-shirt and old jeans with a handgun stuffed in a belt holding up the jeans. He watched until they had both done as he'd demanded. "You use your weapons to rob unarmed locals trying to feed their families. Why are you here? You don't have any hunting equipment?"

"Why are you?" Samuel came back at him. "You're not from the Kruger."

"We're from Mozambique, supporting the hunters of this area."

"Yeah, like ripping them off, giving them a pittance."

"At least we give them something. We don't steal. You're coming with us; maybe you and your equipment have value to someone."

Samuel panicked. "Then you should know, the person we work for will come for you… be warned, you wouldn't want that."

"Who is this man?"

"Casper Meer."

The man narrowed his eyes. "If Meer is involved, you're here for diamonds. What's going on?"

"Leave us alone, and you will be well rewarded. Casper

will see to that," Samuel replied.

"Meer would only volunteer payments if he was up against the wall. I want to know more, particularly why he would want to reward us."

"The stolen diamonds have been found. There's money for everyone, provided we're not hampered," Kirk suddenly blurted out.

Samuel glared at him but never said anything.

"That's not possible. People have been searching for years. Where have they been found?" the man demanded.

"Local, that is why we're here. But we don't know the diamond's exact location and are waiting for the person to arrive who does."

"Then pay the hunter for his hare. He will be happy and leave. We will remain here with you. I want a cut of the diamonds."

"Pay the man, Kirk," Samuel told him.

After the hunter left with his money, the atmosphere became more relaxed. The man from Mozambique introduced himself as Munis.

"There is a problem, Munis," Samuel said while Kirk cooked breakfast.

"What?"

"Another group, which has nothing to do with us, is also determined to get the diamonds. We were setting up today to take them out. This still has to happen. Otherwise, we could end up in a gun battle on a narrow track. You are used to fighting in this terrain and should understand."

"Then carry on and set up. I'm not sharing with others."

Chapter 42

Lisa was on her way again, and her next stop was Umbra. She'd been held up several times with a badly potholed part of the road, very nearly losing the front suspension as one wheel crashed into a particularly deep pothole. Such was the shock to the vehicle, and unknown to Lisa, the tracker attached to the underside of the wheel arch was thrown off, sinking into the muddy waters of the pothole.

Lisa climbed out and looked at the vehicle. Everything looked okay to her; the wheel was still on and the tyre hadn't deflated.

"Having trouble," Jenny asked from behind her.

"Oh, you're back. I'm still getting used to this driving thing. I nearly lost a front wheel; the pothole didn't look that big."

"It happens, particularly in this area. It all goes to show that they knew how to build vehicles in the past; a modern one would have lost the suspension."

"I suppose, but they could have made it more comfortable while doing these clever bits to keep it all together. I'll end up with a bruised bum, with every other bone getting a workout with all the shaking before I arrive."

Jenny laughed. "They charge for that sort of workout in the health spa. Here, you get it free."

"I wouldn't know. I've never been to one. The closest I got was the exercise room at the swimming pool I used to go to. Then most of the equipment was always out of order." Then she hesitated. "Although thinking about it, when I was in Blackpool with mum, Nick and I went to one of those health spas in the basement of the hotel and included with the room."

"Come on, at least tonight, you'll have somewhere more comfortable to sleep," Jenny urged.

***

Frankie, now alone and following Lisa at a distance, pulled up and checked the computer displaying the tracker signal. It had stopped around a quarter of a mile ahead. She sat there, taking a can of Coke from her bag and drinking it slowly.

However, as time went on, the tracker didn't move. Frankie refreshed the screen to check that everything was working, then stared at it. The tracker signal had disappeared.

"Shit, that's all I need. I'll have to catch her up; otherwise, I'll lose her completely," she commented aloud, not that anyone was there to hear.

Setting off again, she speeded up, not knowing how far Lisa could be ahead.

Rounding a bend, the pothole that caught Lisa unaware caught Frankie. However, Frankie was not so lucky. Her speed was twice Lisa's, and when the wheel dropped suddenly, it wrenched the van around, virtually ripping the wheel off, before careering down an embankment. Frankie was screaming in terror, with no seat belt on; she was thrown around inside like a rag doll, hitting her head and passing out. The van finally ended up halfway down the embankment and a total write-off, trapping Frankie inside. Following the noise of the crash, now there was silence. Standing at the side of the road, DB looked down at the wreck; he showed no expression of satisfaction or concern at Frankie's fate. Slowly, he faded out.

***

Hans had tried to raise Frankie to find out her progress, becoming more concerned when he couldn't get in touch. They had also lost a day before the repairs to his vehicle could be completed.

As soon as they had, they were on their way.

Gareth was the first to see Frankie's van down the embankment, immediately telling Hans to stop. It was a good job he did. Hans stopped only feet from the pothole that had caught out both Lisa and Frankie.

They were all out of the vehicle in seconds, running down to the wreck. It took two of them to wrench open a door before Hans could get inside to Frankie.

"Is she alive, Hans?" Gareth asked.

"Just about, but it looks bad; she's got a head injury, and blood is still seeping out."

"What do we do besides calling a helicopter to take her to the hospital?" Chas asked. He was stood a small distance away, watching.

"If we do, we're fucked with time; Lisa could be at the track by now or soon will be," Gareth added.

Hans came out of the vehicle and stood looking at it momentarily. "Frankie's had it. We can do nothing. Roll the fucker further down the embankment, and we'll set fire to it."

Chas looked shocked. "How can you write her off? The kids are not even twenty, and we're not prepared to help her?"

Hans sighed. "The point is, Chas, what do you want us to do? Sir John would be the first to have us put a bullet in her head. It was her fault for coming off the road. She knows, the same as us, just how dangerous these back roads can be. So it's her or the diamonds; there is no other option."

Chas shook his head. "I'll not kill her or leave the kid for dead. Call in help, I'll stay. You two go on. I'll join you as fast as I can."

Hans shrugged. "If that's what you want, I'll call for help. You stay to look after her."

With this agreed, Hans called for assistance and left Chas.

"It was the right thing to do, Hans," Gareth commented as they left.

"Maybe, but we're one man down, and we know Casper has sent people."

"Then you suspect we may end up in a gun battle this time?"

"Without a doubt. Samuel won't mess around. Casper will make sure of that."

"If that's the case, it would be prudent to pull over short of the track and check it out."

"I agree; after all, we know Lisa must end up at the track, where the diamonds are hidden."

Chapter 43

When Samuel saw Lisa's Land Rover pass, he ignored it, knowing she would head for Umbra to hire villagers. She could hardly do anything different, as the weight of the boxes would be too much alone. He wanted the diamonds, not her. He also knew Hans would be close behind, and to ensure a straightforward collection of the diamonds from Lisa, Hans and his people must be eliminated. Following them, Munis and his gunmen needed to be taken out. Casper wasn't in the business of dealing with criminal groups from Mozambique.

"You ignored that Land Rover. Why is that?" Munis asked.

"The vehicle contains the person who knows where the diamonds are. They will be back with help to move them. That is the time we move to collect the diamonds. The group following, who are also after the diamonds, are the ones we want to take down first."

"If we had stopped that vehicle, we have ways that would soon break the occupants, and they'd take us to the hiding place," Munis came back at him.

Samuel shrugged indifferently. "Bloody pointless. When will they bring the boxes out for us, and then we take them? Anyway, our biggest threat is the people following. First, we concentrate on getting rid of them."

"So long as we don't lose the diamonds, messing about with these followers."

"How the fuck are we going to lose the diamonds when they are hidden down the track opposite, so no matter what, they have no option but to go down the track to collect them? It's time to take our positions; soon, the followers will arrive."

Munis never commented. This white man's time will come once the diamonds are in their hands.

***

As Gareth suggested to Hans, they had pulled off the road half a mile short of the track. Armed with sniper rifles and handguns, they began moving forward after crossing the river and climbing up the steep incline. They wanted a position that would look down on the track entrance.

The going was hard, and the ground was covered with random clumps of shrub, which provided some protection if needed. Even so, after two hours, they had a high position that looked down at the track entrance. Also below them, Samuel, along with five others, was in a position to watch anyone approaching on the road.

"This will be easier than I thought, Gareth. We take the outer ones first, trapping the inner ones with nowhere to hide," Hans commented.

"Sounds good, but with so many, taking out two, the others could scatter."

"True, but we don't let them. From this vantage, there is nowhere to hide out of range of our rifles. Then, you notice that two men in the cluster of four aren't even holding their rifles, being more interested in lighting up. We take them last. We should have them before they can even load up. Check your weapon. We can't afford a jam. We go in one minute."

In precisely one minute, all hell was let loose. Hans and Gareth quickly took out the two outer gunmen, including those not holding rifles. Still, Samuel and Munis were onto their positions in seconds, returning fire, forcing Hans and Gareth to reposition.

It had become a stand-off between the two groups, each watching for a chance to gain the upper hand.

"They have us pinned down, Hans. It will be dark before we can move," Gareth commented.

"Yes, it's a pity we didn't hit those two first. The others were inept. Even so, we're on high ground. Can you reach my backpack?"

"Give me a minute.... got it, what do you want?"

"In the front pouch, there's two grenades."

"Where did those come from?" Gareth asked, surprised Hans would have such items with him.

"I brought them in case we had to blast a partially blocked entrance to a mine. After all, we'd no idea where Lisa had found the stones."

"Wow, it's a bit over the top; even so, they could be handy to scare the shit out of the gunmen below us."

"Scare, I think not. We blow the fucker's to bits?"

"It's tight, Hans. They are around fifty meters away. You'd need to stand to throw that distance."

"True, but we're looking at seconds. With one of us constantly firing over their heads, they will keep down and not dare to raise their heads to see what's happening and risk being hit by a bullet."

"So, which of us is taking the chance and throwing the grenade?" Gareth asked.

"I'll throw it. You're a far better shot than me."

"Very well. Tell me when to begin shooting, and I'll keep heads down for you," Gareth answered while rolling one grenade toward him.

Hans readied himself and pulled the safety pin from the grenade. "Right, I'm ready. Begin firing."

Gareth fired time after time, achieving what was hoped would keep the men's heads down. Except Munis, coming from a military background, recognised this tactic as a cover for something far more dangerous to come.

"They're attempting a distraction. Don't raise your head, only your gun, and keep firing in their direction," Munis shouted.

Samuel did as Munis wanted, so bullets were flying both ways by the time Hans had stood and threw the grenade. One caught Hans in the stomach as the grenade landed, exploding in seconds, catching both Munis and Samuel. Munis rolled over in agony, his eardrums shattered, fragments of the grenade embedded into him. Yet he held onto his gun, seeing Gareth standing quickly to direct his rifle at whoever came out of hiding following the blast. Minis saw his chance and fired repeatedly until he ran out of bullets. Several bullets caught Gareth directly. He fell back, fatally wounded.

The sounds of the area fell silent as DB materialised, walking slowly towards Samuel and Minis. Munis was already dead; Samuel lay back, his wounds severe, and gasped as he saw DB walk towards him and look down.

"Who are you, or rather, what are you?" Samuel asked.

DB looked at Samuel, speaking to him in his mind: "No one is coming to help. You will soon pass through my world and discover who I am. While death waits to take you away, you will have time to contemplate your life and the foolhardiness of you and your friends taking on one who walks with the dead."

DB turned away, heading towards Gareth and Hans. Both men were unconscious, seeping blood, and desperately needed medical care, the same as Samuel. Of course, there was no such care, and soon, the predators of the forest would sense easy pickings. DB showed no emotion, seemingly satisfied with the outcome, and slowly disappeared. In seconds, the sounds of the area returned.

Chapter 44

Lisa had arrived at Umbra, and as usual, Jenny was no longer around. She stopped outside the hospital building and climbed out of the Land Rover. Joshua was hurrying to meet her.

"Welcome, Lisa. You are getting to be quite a regular," he hugged her. "And what is this?" looking at the vehicle. "Don't say you've driven it from Pretoria?"

"Why not? It's not let me down. Mind you, it could be a little better in the comfort zone. Anyway, thank your elders for agreeing to my mining application. From tomorrow, I'm no longer just a visitor to your country; I have a new visa that allows me to work here."

"And that is important?" Joshua asked.

"Of course. I can hardly work in the mines on a holiday visa or employ people. They'd kick me out of the country. With a working visa, I've got five places on my work team to fill. The work is very light and well paid."

"What are you doing then?"

"I want to go to the old mine workings. In particular, the mines Donald Blackmon was involved in."

He frowned. "For what reason?"

"I've no idea. It's just a feeling I have as to where Donald Blackmon wants me to go. Refrain from mentioning that to potential villagers wanting to come. Just tell them it's a survey of the mine area. I can only pay two hundred and fifty rand a day for a maximum of two weeks."

"Are you sure, Lisa? That is a great deal of money for us."

"I'm sure it's hardly a minimum wage in the UK; I'm not prepared to pay any less."

"Then you will have more than enough volunteers to take the jobs. I will be with them to interpret, but I don't want any payment. I'll be there to make sure you remain safe."

"I'll not argue. Now I need something to eat and then rest. I've been on the road for what seems like a lifetime." Lisa wasn't worried about Joshua not getting paid. She knew very shortly that once the diamonds had been securely stored in a bank, there would be more than enough money to change their lives and futures forever.

Joshua arranged for Lisa to stay in the hospital building, with villagers setting out one of the stacked-up beds used by the hospital. Following food provided by Joshua, Lisa was alone in the hospital sorting out her bed. It was then Jenny joined her.

"You notice I got here, Jenny, with no breakdowns. That Land Rover may look rough, but it keeps going," Lisa told her proudly.

"I have to agree. You have surprised me. So what's the plan from here?"

"Hopefully, DB can give me some sign about what he wants unless I'm only here for the diamonds, which I'm still not convinced is the only reason he followed me across the world."

"I understand, but I really can't help you, one way or the other. You will have to wait for DB to make the next move."

"Yes, that worries me; he's not exactly specific; trying to interpret what he's on about is virtually impossible. If I still have people following, should I call on DB to protect me, even in the village?"

"Why not?"

"It's just that one time he was on his visits, DB told me if I kept calling for his help, he would become weaker to the point he could do nothing. There again, there was no mention of just how many times I'd have to do that before he's no use anymore for protection."

"I can see your point. Again, I can't help because I don't

know."

Lisa didn't expect Jenny could; after all, she was now more than convinced Jenny was part of her mind in as much with no one to talk over her issues, she had created Jenny. In fact, Jenny acted like her own sounding board. However, there were odd times when Jenny would do or say something she could not make up.

"I think I'll leave calling DB tonight. I may need him in the mining area, so I can't have him burning out too fast," Lisa said after some thought. Then she had an idea. "If you're doing nothing, you could be an early warning system, giving me time to call DB for help."

"I could. But how could I wake you?"

Lisa shrugged. "I've no idea, then who says you can't? You may have powers you don't know you have. In the worst case, you'd have to call DB yourself, telling him I was in danger."

"In that case, I'll try. It's going to be a bit boring sitting around watching."

"Why? You don't just sit in here; you'll need to wander around the village or whatever. After all, you're on guard to watch for intruders. It'd be a bit pointless sitting at my side all night. That would hardly be an early warning when they also stand by my side."

"I never thought of that. Mind you, it can get freezing outside at night."

"Jenny, if you've not forgotten, you're dead. You're hardly likely to catch a cold or even feel the cold for that matter; you're already cold."

Jenny looked a little putout. "You don't need to rub it in. I don't feel dead. Thinking about it, I don't know how I should feel."

"Well, I'm sure I don't." Lisa glanced at her watch. "Right, I'm calling it a day; I'm completely knackered. We'll talk tomorrow; don't disappear on me."

"I won't. Have a good sleep."

Jenny stood quietly as Lisa fell asleep. She knew that she could not protect Lisa on her own. Closing her eyes momentarily, Jenny opened them to find DB at her side. They looked at each other, and Jenny slowly faded. Lisa would be safe now.

DB looked down at Lisa. Dark forces were building, and she could delay no more before the darkness overpowered the light; if that happened, there would be no return.

Chapter 45

After hearing from Hans that he had arrived and was close enough to watch Lisa following Frankie's accident, Sir John could return to London. The diamonds worried him, although he knows people in the UK universities who, using very specialised equipment, could tell him what was going wrong, particularly why the diamonds shattered.

However, before leaving, he decided to stop at the hospital to see Frankie. After arriving, he was shown to a private room where Frankie lay. The doctor met him in the room. Frankie was asleep and was attached to all sorts of monitoring equipment.

"What's the chances, doctor, of her recovering?" he asked.

"Frankie is very poorly, Sir John. We believe she will pull through. Although we don't believe she will ever walk again, such was the damage to the spine."

"Thank you for the information. Can you keep my office informed of Frankie's progress?"

"I will, Sir John."

Sir John's satellite telephone began to ring when he was inside the car heading towards the airport. The caller was Chas.

"Have you joined up with Hans, Chas?" Sir John asked.

"I have found them, but there has been a gunfight. There are eight dead. Both our lads, another I recognise as Samuel Ritter who was with that lot who caught us when we'd collected the diamonds, the others I'm not sure who they are, except I think one of them was with the Ritter lot."

"I don't believe this, what the fuck's been going on? What about Lisa's Land Rover? Is that around?"

"No, the point is, Sir John, should I be calling the authorities?"

"Are they all over the road?"

"No, I found Hans' vehicle and walked from there. The fight was on the slope opposite the track's entrance on the river's far side, where Lisa was expected to go down."

"So you would need to search to find any victims?"

"Yes."

"Forget it, then. We're not a funeral company. Take anything off the bodies and inside the vehicles that link Hans to us and move on to the village. Find out if Lisa is in the village, has been there, or is out on her own."

"Should I leave the vehicle?"

"Yes, once the authorities are involved, they need to see how the groups arrived; no vehicle should indicate others are involved."

"I understand. I'll be in touch as soon as I've located Lisa. Tell me, how is Frankie?"

"She's still unconscious. If she pulls through, she'll never walk again."

"When she can talk, find out if Lisa did this to her. I'll kill the bitch if it was."

"All in good time, first the diamonds, then you can do what you want with her. She's expendable. Keep in touch," Sir John cut the call.

Sir John arrived at the airport for first-class check-in before walking through security. He placed his bag on the scanner and watched it go through.

A security officer approached Sir John. "Please come to the desk, Sir. Bring your hand luggage."

He did as the officer requested.

"Can you open the bag and stand away, please?"

Sir John, not overly concerned, opened the bag. The security officer emptied the bag, Taking out an inner package.

"The scanner couldn't determine the contents. What is inside this package, Sir?" he asked Sir John.

"Rough diamonds. I have the paperwork."

"May I see the paperwork?"

Sir John pulled an envelope from his inside pocket, took out a document, and handed it to him. He took it away to a back office.

Soon, he returned. "Please, can you follow me, Sir?"

They went into an office. A man was sitting at a desk, and he asked Sir John to take a seat.

"What is the delay? The flight leaves in just over an hour?" Sir John asked.

"This should only take a few minutes. You see, there is a problem with the declaration, Sir John. Can you tell me which mine these diamonds came from?"

"Why?"

"Your export documentation does not state the particular mine or mines the stones originated from. There are also no registration numbers for the stones stated. You should know that to take uncut diamonds out of the country, the source or sources must be declared along with registration numbers."

"I apologise; my office must have failed to do that. I believe they originated from the mines in the Kruger."

The man keyed into his computer, pulling up the registered mines. "It seems there are several mines registered, in fact, to the same person—a Miss Jones. Are you saying she supplied the diamonds? If so, she has not registered any findings to date. Although her registration is only a matter of days old, the recording of the stones may still be going through."

"They came out of the area, I understand, before this woman registered her claim."

"I see... If that were the case, whoever brought them out, if they didn't have mining rights, would mean the diamonds were effectively stolen. Technically, they would still belong to the mine they were removed from, and because

Miss Jones now holds the mining rights across the entire area, she could claim them. Because of this possibility, they cannot leave the country pending a decision from the authorities as to who owns them legally."

"In that case, you must secure them while I sort out ownership. Bear in mind there are potentially over five million dollars in diamonds in that package. Lose them, and you will be liable."

"We are well used to holding contraband, so a few diamonds will not be a problem. We will count the diamonds in front of you, take photos, and give you a document to say that the government is holding them, pending clarity on the true ownership of the diamonds and how you came to have them in your possession."

Sir John knew he couldn't argue the point. Whoever had informed the security knew what they were doing and was intent on ensuring the diamonds did not leave the country. Even so, he couldn't believe Lisa was bright enough to do this alone, so who had she joined up with?

"I hope this error in paperwork by my office will not prevent me from leaving the country?" Sir John asked.

"I don't have the power to detain you, although if you still want the diamonds, I'd advise you to sort out ownership."

"And how would I do that?"

"In my view, how you managed to get hold of them is not my business; it is for others to determine. As there is only one registered mining operation in the Kruger, you should contact Miss Jones, who can get you out of this mess. Have her register the find and list them. Then, obtain the necessary sales documentation from her. That is a route I advise you to pursue; otherwise, given their value, you could be charged with theft and attempting to leave the country with the goods if you ever return to South Africa. Such a charge would certainly attract a prison sentence followed by deportation."

"I know this woman. I will contact her."

"Very wise, Sir. I will have seizure documents made out, listing the seizure of the items because of incomplete documentation and awaiting completion. Have Miss Jones register the find; your office should put the reference numbers on the export document. It must also include the bill of sale from Miss Jones to not delay any release from our customs."

Later, sitting in his seat aboard the aircraft, Sir John was livid. He'd already lost a million pounds and all the costs surrounding Hans' operation. The man at the airport was right. If this wasn't sorted out, without Lisa, he faced prison if he ever returned to South Africa, and his business relied on him returning regularly. To do that, he'd have to go cap in hand to her and negotiate the purchase, and she wouldn't be that cooperative after what she'd been through; he knew that. Even so, he couldn't help but remember her words from when they last met. "You know Donald Blackmon won't allow you to take the stones. They are cursed and belong to him. Without his consent to take them away, they are worthless." How could she have known this would happen? He'd been taking stones out for years and had never been questioned before. Then, he was sure his office would have entered a mine reference number, which was always required. So why had they failed to do so? Such an error must be sorted out when he returned.

Chapter 46

Joshua found four villagers who were more than eager to take Lisa to the old mine workings. So the following morning, armed with picks and shovels, the four men, including Joshua, left with Lisa in her Land Rover. They would visit the mines close to the poisoned lake to give Lisa an overview of the area where she had mining rights.

The vehicle was helpful because it saved hours of walking and carrying tools when the track was wide and good enough. Of course, what is a good track still needed, at times, to be cleared of fallen branches to allow the vehicle through. Later the same day, they arrived at the poisoned lake. For Lisa, the memories came flooding back, and she kept well away from its edge, setting up camp beyond the dead vegetation area.

"This is as far as we go by vehicle, Lisa," Joshua told her. "From now on, we will walk."

"How far are the mines?"

"They are all around this area. Unlike the big mines in the west of the country, which move huge amounts of materials before sifting them, these are small mines, hand dug, and using pans by the streams leading down to the lake. Later, they brought in larger sifters. Fortunately, the mines were deemed spent before the big earth-moving equipment arrived in the mining industry; otherwise, this entire area would be like an open quarry, and the area would have been destroyed. Tomorrow, I'll take you to the largest of the mines."

"Are they tunnels or opencast?"

"These are tunnels, but there are a few opencast mines. They are not as large as in other areas of South Africa. They are on the far side of the lake where the aircraft came down. These days, you can see very little of the workings; the vegetation has finally hidden all the scars. I understand it used to be good land to grow food, but scraping the topsoil left only clay and rocks, allowing only the hardiest plants to take hold. Donald Blackmon has a lot to answer for. Have you any idea what you are looking for?"

She sighed. "Hopefully, I'll know when I find it."

"We will set up camp and prepare food. You take it easy; it's been a difficult drive for you."

"That's fine, but I think I'll go for a short walk. I'm stiff."

"Then keep well away from the lake."

She smiled. "That, Joshua, is my first intention. I've not forgotten my last encounter with that lake."

Lisa wandered away. Once out of sight of the men making camp, she sat on a stone and looked across the water.

"Looks beautiful, doesn't it?" Jenny commented.

Lisa looked at Jenny, who now stood by her side. "Beautiful, yes, but deadly. Soon, the clean-up will begin. I intend to return this area to what it was before the miners turned up."

"I believe you will succeed, Lisa. There is something you should know; I've got a feeling that I'll be moving on very soon."

"How do you know that?"

"It's just a feeling as if I'm drifting away. Maybe you are coming to the end of this destiny DB keeps talking about. I don't know, I'm terrified, Lisa."

"I'll not let you go; we get on well together. I'll make it a condition that you stay with me, even if DB wants to move on himself."

Jenny shook her head. "We don't have any control, Lisa, you know that. I wish we hadn't crashed before going to the cabin; we'd have had a great time, and I'd planned so much for us to do."

"No, you're wrong. I've enjoyed our time together;

even though you keep appearing and disappearing, we've still had some great adventures."

"We have, haven't we?"

"Yes. Anyway, don't worry. You'll see. I'll find a way for you to stay with me."

A short distance away from Lisa, Joshua, concerned about her leaving the camp alone, watched her sitting on the stone. He was scared and confused; it was as if she was talking to someone, not aloud, yet her mannerisms and movements indicated that someone was by her side. At that moment, he saw DB approach Lisa. However, before approaching her, he turned and looked directly at Joshua. Joshua was terrified. He began to back away, turned, and ran back to the camp as fast as possible. Others looked at him as he stopped close to the campfire, his eyes wide with terror, shaking uncontrollably, squatting down by the fire, trying to warm himself up.

"What is wrong, Joshua?" one asked.

Joshua had no intention of scaring the others by telling them that DB was around, so he devised a viable alternative. "I nearly walked into a buffalo; it turned, and I was afraid it would attack me. I ran. It was scary to see such a huge animal in the dark."

They all knew a buffalo could be very dangerous and is always best avoided, particularly when one is alone.

"You should remain close to the camp; this is a dangerous area; animals drinking at the lake are often followed with intense pain in their body and their heads; they become violent, rushing around uncontrollably. Even a bullet, at times, will not stop them."

"I went to ensure Lisa remained safe when she left the camp."

The man shook his head slowly. "When you gained your education, Joshua, it required you to leave our village for a long time. Education often dulls the belief in the old ways, particularly when they claim no one can communicate with their ancestors. You, of all people, should know we will always need knowledge from those of the past. Our mungome talks to them for us, asks for advice, and obtains guidance. In the case of Lisa, the mungome are powerless; it is as if a dark wall has been built, and no one can see beyond. Lisa walks with the dead. She cannot be hurt; the dead will protect her. No person can explain why a woman has come across the world to our village, but while she is here, we will respect and help her in whatever the dead demand. To not do that risks the dead being displeased. If she leaves the camp, it may be to converse with the dead. You should keep well away."

"I understand and will not do that again." Joshua was not going to admit he had seen DB. It would only strengthen their argument.

***

Jenny, still with Lisa, suddenly looked up. "I must go, DB is here," she said, then faded.

Lisa watched him approach.

"You must enter the largest mine. Take care. It is unsafe. There, you will find part of why you are here."

"I'll be going to all the mines. But tell me, is Jenny moving on?"

For once, DB seemed to understand her question. "Soon, Jenny's time with you will come to an end. When that time comes, you must let her go. Otherwise, I will be gone, and she will remain for eternity wandering the earth. Without my protection, the dark forces would constantly attack her, making her time on earth a living hell." Then he faded out.

Lisa walked back slowly to the camp. With such a possibility, Jenny had to move on no matter what, although she would miss her.

Chapter 47

Following breakfast, Lisa and the villagers headed towards the old mining area.

"I want to visit the largest of the mines first, Joshua," Lisa told him as they walked.

"Is there a reason for this?"

She shrugged. "It seems logical, particularly with you telling me back in the village, there are a considerable amount of mine workings; many just dug looking for a particular seam that would indicate the possibility of diamonds being there."

"If that is what you want, Lisa, it's the largest mine workings first," Joshua replied. However, he suspected her request was more an instruction from DB, not that he would get her to admit it.

Following a good three hours of challenging walking along virtually impassable tracks, made only passable by the villagers with Lisa, clearing the path, they came to an open area, now a mixture of rusted equipment that could only be described as large bins on railway wheels, winding gear, small stacks of thick wooden posts used to hold the tunnels up, partially hidden by the creeping vegetation. Beyond was a large entrance to a cave. Blocking entry were slatted wooden gates with a faded notice 'Keep Out - danger of sudden collapse'.

As Lisa gazed at the entrance, she saw DB waiting for her.

"The entrance is larger than I thought, Joshua; how many workers would be working this mine?" she asked.

"Up to a hundred."

"It would support that many?" She was surprised by his answer.

He sniggered. "You mean, did it support slaves that cost nothing?"

"Enough said," she answered. "As it is, this is the mine I'm to go inside; none must follow. You have to make that very clear."

He looked at her in astonishment. "You're going in alone?"

"Of course, that's why I'm here, although I can assure you it isn't my choice. I just wanted to go home and never come back. As for going in alone, I'll not be; DB is waiting. First, we eat, then ask the men to open the entrance for me, please?"

As they began eating, Joshua told the others what Lisa wanted.

The man, who had spoken at length last night, nodded up and down knowingly. "We all know, with the supports weakened over the years by termites, how dangerous it is to go into any of these old mines. Lisa is correct; no one must follow her inside. Lisa walks with the dead; she will be safe."

"We only believe she does, but can we allow a young girl who knows nothing about mines to go inside?" Joshua replied with obvious concern.

"Have you asked Lisa the reason she wants to go in?"

"Yes, she claims DB wants her to go inside."

"Then we should do as she asks. Our teachings warn us never to ignore the instructions from the dead."

"Is everyone in agreement that we let Lisa go in alone?"

All the men nodded their agreement.

Joshua turned to Lisa. "I'm sorry for talking in a language you don't understand, but it was essential for all the lads to be aware of what is wanted. I still have concerns for your safety inside this mine," Joshua said.

"I really do understand. Why must I enter the mine? I'm not entirely sure, only that I must. In fact, while we were eating, DB stood watching, waiting to take me inside. If you've all finished, could you open the mine while I collect my torch, and then I can get it over with?"

After clearing the entrance, the men watched Lisa go inside. Then, they retired to the camp they had set up earlier to await her return.

Chapter 48

Entering the mine, Lisa was surprised at how high it was. However, the large area ended abruptly in minutes, with at least six lower tunnels going in different directions. Still trying to figure out where to go, she had come to a halt, waiting to be shown.

"It's the third tunnel to the left, Lisa," Jenny advised, suddenly appearing at her side.

"I'm glad someone knows after all, DB's done a runner," she said, more than happy to have Jenny at her side. "What's down there? Should I be going deeper? Everyone's telling me it's hazardous."

"It's not fallen in for fifty years, so it's hardly going to decide to do it now. After all, you're not going in with a pickaxe, chipping the walls looking for diamonds."

"I suppose that sounds logical; even so, I'll keep clear of the wooden pillars holding the roof up."

Using her torch and the tunnel height, which allowed her to stand, apart from at times having to duck under beams that had shifted, they came out into a large chamber, again with tunnels going off. These were very low, needing to be down on hands and knees, crawling.

"This is as far as I'm going, Jenny," Lisa told her, but Jenny, who had been following her, was no longer there. "God, I wish that girl wouldn't keep coming and going. Now, what do I do?" Lisa muttered to herself.

At that moment, everything began to change. Lisa was no longer in the cave; she seemed to have moved into another world. One side was dark, billowing black clouds along the edge. The other side was bright, with the same clouds but in white, again billowing at the edges. She was standing between these two clouds.

DB began to materialise a short distance in front of her. "Welcome to the world I'm forced to live, Lisa."

"You can talk?" she asked, surprised he wasn't as usual in her head.

"Here I can, outside this world, all I can do is project my mind into yours. Neither can I hear what you say; I can only sense your thinking."

"Can you talk to Jenny?"

He smiled, "Jenny is you, or part of you. It's difficult to explain, but the human mind is very powerful. We only use a tiny part of it. Save to say you can protect yourself, the same as I have done to bring you here."

"Yes, I suspected she was a figment of my imagination. So if Jenny's a figment, are you the same?"

"Again, it is complicated, but in essence, no. For thousands of years, people have believed you move on to another life when you die. The Egyptians went one step further, believing their Pharaohs were actual gods and needed slaves to take them to the afterlife, the same as their goods and a means to travel. You don't, or rather, you cannot take anything with you."

"You are in this world, if you can call it that, mind you, with so many people dying over the years, I'm surprised it's not crowded. So where is everyone?"

"You assume a person should look like they do when alive on earth. They are not; they are life forms, so minuscule, millions can exist on the top of a pinhead if they lived, but a life form neither lives nor thinks on its own; it is either part of the dark or the light, so I'd not be too concerned about it becoming overcrowded."

"So the white side are the good people, and the black are the bad?" Lisa asked, believing she was seeing good and evil.

"Sorry to disappoint; there are no good and bad places. All that exists is a balance between two huge entities of billions of life forms. We are in no-man's-land, where each entity attempts to take over. Each side is usually balanced, taking life forms as they pass through."

"Does one side ever win?" she asked.

"If it did, then that would be the end of the world as you know it. Even so, this balance is always in conflict."

"So what can I do? I can hardly prevent one side from winning against the other."

"Of course, you can't, but you can contribute to keep the balance."

She scrunched her nose. "I wouldn't think so, but if you suggest I can, how?"

"The balance does not depend on how many go through; the imbalance is caused by people like me who cannot go through. While I'm here, I'm attracting the dark side, causing it to slowly move forward. I must move on to prevent the dark side from overcoming the space between, but I can't. I believe, because of my actions while alive, I prevented hundreds of victims who helped dig this mine and those trapped there from passing through, creating this imbalance."

"Are these people still alive?"

"No, but there are entities still wandering around the mine, trying to find a way out."

"Like you?"

"No, they haven't even come into this place we are in; if they do and, like me, cannot pass through, then black will take over this world, and white will pull away."

"So if that happens, the world is stuffed."

"If you mean by those words your world would no longer exist, then yes."

"Well, that was a bit remiss of you placing humans in such a precarious position, and they don't even know. So how can we put this right, if we can?"

"I believe the only way to release these people is to blow open the mine entrance."

She stared at him in shock. "Excuse me, you want me to

blow open a mine. How am I going to do that?"

"You own the mining rights. It is reasonable for you to purchase explosives and employ an expert to do the job."

"I suppose, but that's assuming I've got the money to do that. The diamonds I've already got are causing a few problems, attracting people determined to take them off me for nothing. They even kill people who get in their way. I could afford a few fireworks at this point, which would make quite a bang, but I do not believe that would open up a mine."

He smiled. "The diamonds you originally took with Jenny and the ones taken from the box were worthless. All came from a mine that the owner believed would make him rich. He soon found they could not be cut. No one ever found out why. The general opinion was that they were subject to excess pressures over thousands of years, causing them to be brittle. I've seen it with many semi-precious stones. Still, it is scarce with diamonds, particularly seemingly perfect stones."

"So the other two boxes, are they good or bad?"

"The boxes you saw don't exist; they were in your mind."

"That's charming. The boxes were bloody heavy for something that doesn't exist."

He shrugged. "It was your belief that the boxes would be heavy, but that is how human minds work: picking up visual information in advance, creating an expectation that may not be correct."

"So if the diamonds are crap, are there any good ones I can sell to buy this gunpowder you want?"

"Of course, they are in the mine where the victims are and always have been."

"Oh, come on. If the diamonds are inside the mine, I'm supposed to blow. How do I buy gunpowder to do that?"

"When you return to your world, I will show you where

two good diamonds remain in this mine. That should give you enough money to buy everything you need."

"That's fine, so why have the diamonds never been found?"

"If the treasure seekers had searched properly and found the mine, they would have released the victims to move on, and I'd not have been in this situation. All I can assume is an abandoned mine that looked collapsed was ignored."

"So that vehicle had nothing to do with moving the diamonds?"

"The mine owners believed the Germans intended to take everything, so the owners decided to hide the best diamonds. Unfortunately, they took the wrong route, coming off the track and crashing. However, there weren't one but two vehicles. Realising the error, the two men in the one following took the diamonds to an abandoned mine, placed the diamonds inside, and blew up the entrance."

"Then those two men didn't survive the war?"

"One died after joining the army. The other survived the war to live with his children and grandchildren."

"And you know this because?"

"I was the man who survived."

"But you never came back for the diamonds. Then, the reports claimed you had died during the war."

"Reports are only good if whoever writes them has the real facts. I didn't die; I had to make it look as if I had, so I disappeared to avoid people looking for me. As for not coming back for the diamonds, I had every intention of doing so, but that was becoming more and more difficult due to the political situation. I was without funds and afraid of involving people with contacts and facilities to assist me. Time caught up with me; I fell ill and was no longer interested or capable of returning for the stones."

"Then it seems logical for you to know where the diamonds are. So, where do I come into this? Did you use a pin on a map to end up at our house?"

"Speak to any of the villagers, and they will tell you that the Mungome can only contact the dead relatives of a particular villager who wants assistance. That is the same for me."

Lisa stared at him in astonishment. "You are suggesting I'm related to you somehow?"

"Not suggesting, Lisa, you are, which is why you're here. You are not the daughter of your mother?"

"Oh, come on, I'm not falling for that. Apart from the fact I knew my father and both of my parent's relatives. Although, if you are suggesting I'm effectively an orphan, how did it happen, and why didn't Mum tell me when I reached the age of eighteen?"

"Your mother and father didn't know. Let me explain: your birth mother, my great-granddaughter, died on the operating table while giving birth to you. The doctor wasn't registered as a doctor, although he had a clinic and made lots of money. In his ignorance, he allowed her to die; you, of course, survived. Did your mother ever mention she went into labour on a bus?"

"Yes, she was on a trip to London and very proud to tell me I was born in a posh clinic. I wasn't due for three weeks, but Mum had gone out in the morning without Dad to do some shopping. He, as usual, was in bed getting over one of his regular drinking sprees from the night before. The bus stopped outside a clinic, and everyone panicked when Mum went into labour until one pointed out where the bus had stopped. The driver ran into the clinic, asking for help. That's how I was born in a posh clinic."

"You are correct, except the doctor pulling your mother's baby out broke the baby's neck. He panicked, knowing your mother's baby's death would be investigated, maybe even involve the police, and he'd end up in prison for operating with no medical licence. Your mother never knew her baby was dead. The doctor handed her you as her baby."

"And my real mother and mum's baby, what happened?"

"She was dumped in a shallow grave along with the child. The doctor left the UK soon after. I caught up with the so-called doctor after our granddaughter suddenly stopped writing. Her final letter told us she was pregnant, had found a good clinic to look after her, and intended to have her child before leaving the UK. She wanted the baby to have a UK passport. With a little persuasion, the doctor came clean, telling me what he'd done. He didn't survive the interrogation, neither was he able to tell me who the other mother was or where she'd come from."

Lisa didn't know what to say. To be told her birth mother died and she didn't even have a brother. "How did you find me?"

"The advantage of living in limbo like I am, no matter where you were, I was drawn to you. I've been watching you most of your life, guiding your friendship with Jenny, and placing in your mind the desire to visit Jenny here in South Africa. You see, Lisa, time is different for me in terms of how you experience time. I don't sense time, but I do sense if you are in trouble and will come if you call me."

"I will need to think about all you've told me. How long until this black smoke covers the no-man's-land?"

"I cannot tell you; time here, as I said, is not measured in hours, days, or years; it just happens. Now you know what must be done; get on with it."

"You are sure the balance will return if these entities are released?"

"No, Lisa, I'm not; all I know is if their release allows me to move on, maybe then the creeping black will draw back."

Lisa thought for a moment. "One thing is bugging me. You say these entities are trapped in a mine, yet you put the diamonds in the same mine before blocking the entrance. Why didn't the miners escape before you closed the mine?"

"When we blew the mine, Lisa, we had no idea that around sixty people were still working inside. They died of suffocation and possibly starvation because of us. I believe that is why I cannot move on until these miners are allowed to move on themselves."

She nodded her understanding. "I suspected as much, yet it sounds illogical they couldn't just pass through blocked walls, not that it matters, as these people died eighty or ninety years ago. Didn't the local relatives attempt to find them?"

"The miners weren't locals; most came from Mozambique and beyond. It was quite normal; the wages in South Africa were so much higher, allowing workers to send money home. These workers would drift between jobs, taking the highest pay and moving on when the work ceased or finished. Relatives would never know where they last worked when they didn't return home. Those days, the authorities wouldn't look into where they were. It was a white government, and the blacks, particularly migrant workers, had no rights."

"Well, it all sounds a bit iffy to me; even so, it's time I returned to reality and my world and at least obtain the explosives. Please show me where the diamonds are so I can get the funds together. I also need to know where the mine I should blow open is."

"We will speak again. Jenny will show you where the diamonds are. The mine I will take you to when you return to this area. Call me if you are in trouble. I will assist."

The next moment, Lisa was back in the mine.

"Hi, you're back then?" Jenny asked.

"Yes. Apparently, you know where there are two good diamonds?"

"I do, and I sense it is time you had them. Come on, I'll

show you."

"No pickaxe, Jenny, I'm not digging in this death trap."

She laughed, "No digging, I promise." They came back to the main entrance and went down another tunnel. Then Jenny stopped, pointing to a rock at the side of the tunnel.

"They are under the rock."

Lisa rolled the rock back and felt among the dust underneath, pulling out two diamonds. They were larger than what she had previously held.

"So where did these come from, and who put them here?" Lisa asked.

"Found and hidden by miners probably, to collect later. It looks like the thieves didn't survive to collect their booty."

"Well, they now belong to me; I own the mine."

"You do, so how are you going to sell them?"

Lisa grinned. "I'm looking forward to walking into the Diamond Consortium and seeing their faces when I place them on their posh table."

By the time Lisa left the mine, Jenny was gone.

Joshua ran up to Lisa. "I'm happy to see you safe, Lisa."

"I told you I'd be looked after. Now I need to return to Pretoria."

"Are you coming back?"

"Of course. But I want to take the Land Rover only some of the way. Once I reach the tar road, I can catch a bus, and someone can bring the vehicle back to the village. What do you think would it be useful?"

"When we return to the village, Let me talk to the elders, but first, we will seal up the entrance."

Chapter 49

After watching Frankie airlifted to Pretoria, Chas caught a lift from an attending emergency vehicle to the tar road. He booked into a local hotel to wait for a hire vehicle to be delivered.

The following morning, with the hired car, Chas didn't delay but returned to join Hans. After finding the results of the gun battle and calling Sir John, he carried on to Umbra. Chas could speak the local language and approached an elder sitting outside his home.

"Has a white girl come to the village?" he asked.

The man nodded. "Come and gone."

"What are you talking about, gone?"

"Hired several villagers and left."

"Where did they go?"

He shrugged his shoulders.

Chas walked away and called Sir John. Once he answered, Chas told him what he'd found out.

"Lisa has become very important to me. She must not be harmed in any way. Offer help if she needs it."

"I wish you'd make your bloody mind up. So what help should I be offering?"

"She's not used to the country, so you can be certain any help offered by one of her kind will be appreciated. Local villagers cannot do anything for her beyond act as guides."

"Then do you want me to wait until she returns or try to find where they have gone?"

"Why chase after her? She's bound to return; after all, she has villagers with her; they will want to come home."

"Very well, I'll be in touch. If anything changes, let me know."

Chas pocketed the phone and went back to the elder. He threw a small amount of rand down on the ground. "Sort me out food while I'm here. You'll get more when I leave. I'll bunk in the hospital."

The man nodded his agreement.

***

Three days after Lisa left the village, she arrived back, surprised to see a modern four-wheel drive parked close to the hospital. Chas was sitting outside in a dilapidated, easy chair.

"This doesn't look good, Joshua. Don't get involved. Such men carry guns and have no compunction in using them," Lisa warned him.

"Will you be alright?" he asked.

"I will. I have my own protection."

Lisa climbed out of her vehicle and walked over to Chas.

"You call that a vehicle; it looks like a heap of rust on wheels," Chas said.

"Maybe, but it's not your problem, so don't let it concern you. Why are you in the area, or has Sir John still not accepted there are no more diamonds, or rather I don't know where they are?"

"I should be asking you the same question: why are you here?"

"I own the mining rights, so I'm looking around my empire," she mocked.

"Come off it, you are here for the diamonds."

"Sorry to disappoint. You're welcome to search my vehicle if you don't believe me. Ask the villagers who took me to the poison lake; they will tell you the same. We're not diamond hunting or collecting these so-called boxes of diamonds, Sir John claims exist. Although I understand if any diamonds are found in the area my mining rights cover, they would belong to me. Aren't I the lucky one?"

"Why the lake?" he said, ignoring her comments.

"I'm raising money back in the UK to clean it up."

Chas suspected Lisa had no idea where the diamonds were or what she was doing. Even so, he walked over to her vehicle, looking in the driver's cab and the open back. There were no signs of any diamonds or even their boxes.

He returned to his seat and sat down again. Lisa had collected a folding chair from the hospital and was already seated. She was eating from a small bowl brought by Joshua's mother.

"Find any, did you?" she asked.

"What are you playing at?"

She looked at him. "I'm playing no games; the villagers near the lake saved my life. It's my turn to help them as much as I can. Maybe I'll find the lake a step too far to put right, but I'll certainly raise enough to drill a borehole and bring water to the village. Anyway, the villagers have shown me the problem; I'm finished here for now, and I'm returning home to begin my campaign. I'm leaving for the tar road in the morning and catching a bus into Pretoria. You can follow if you want; I'll not be stopping to collect the mythical extra boxes of diamonds I'm supposed to have."

"Why are you going by bus?"

"I don't want the Land Rover with me; there's nowhere to leave it while I return to the UK. Then it is a bit old and could break down. I'll ask Joshua to return it to the village and look after it."

Lisa needed a vehicle that could travel backward and forward to Pretoria. She was considering something larger and more comfortable, but that would depend on the funds raised from the sale of the diamonds.

"It's pointless for me to remain here. I was supposed to meet Hans and Gareth, but they have returned to Pretoria. I'm going back to, so I'll give you a ride. If you trust me, that is?"

Confident that DB would look after her, Lisa agreed

and went to find Joshua to tell him.

"Will you look after my Land Rover?" she asked while counting out payment for the villagers who had gone to the lake with her. "I did say two weeks, but after going inside the cave, I understand more. Even so, circumstances have changed, and I will need the men for a few days when I return, so each man will receive his two weeks in advance. There is also payment for your time as well, Joshua. Please don't refuse. I couldn't have gone without you because of the language barrier."

"I'll happily look after your vehicle, but there's no need to pay us upfront. We are used to being paid when we complete the work. I'm also concerned about you going back with Chas. Would you not be safer to keep well away from him?"

"I'll be fine. DB will look after me. As for payment, it's pointless taking all the money back to Pretoria."

"If you are certain, then thank you. Every rand is essential, particularly for purchasing even the basics to survive."

"Then you are more than welcome."

Chapter 50

The journey to Pretoria was uneventful; Chas was quite chatty. However, Lisa, being a streetwise girl, knew how to avoid probing questions, so over the long journey, Chas was no wiser as to her real intentions. That is apart from how she intended to help the villages with clean water, better tools, and maybe machines to make cultivating their fields more manageable. To him, this sounded like the pipe dream of someone who needed to gain knowledge of the cost of such projects. Notably, she claimed the money would come from fundraising. He could also get no concrete reason why she wasted money securing the mining rights if the only diamonds found were the few Sir John had taken off her.

Once back in the hotel where she had previously stayed, Lisa contacted Marvin Draper from the Diamond Consortium.

"What can I do for you, Miss Jones?" he asked after his secretary put her through.

"The last time we met was a little strained, with your membership virtually calling me an idiot. That may be true. So I'd appreciate advice on how I'd recognise a diamond. Is there a chance I can visit your offices, and you can give me perhaps half an hour of your time?"

"Of course, we are always open to talking to potential miners. However, we normally expect miners to come to us with at least a basic knowledge of mining and geology. I will make an exception and talk to you this time, as you clearly need guidance. I have time tomorrow afternoon around three. Can you be here then?"

With this time agreed, Lisa replaced the handset and leaned back on her bed, a hint of a smile crossing her face. He still had the same attitude in his voice, that she was an idiot and he was just placating her. The next call was to the solicitors she had signed for the mining rights, asking to talk to Thomas Grobler. She was lucky he was in and between clients and could take the call.

"Miss Jones, I trust you are well?" he asked.

"I am, Mr Grobler. Would your partnership consider taking me on as a client when you also have a client in Casper Meer?"

"On what basis, purely personal or representing your mining operations?"

"I'd like both if possible. However, I do have an urgent need for representation. During a recent visit to one of my mines, I found two stones I believe the Diamond Consortium would be more than interested in purchasing. I will see them tomorrow, but I need someone to act as a witness that I'm not being cheated."

Grobler wanted clarification. "Excuse me, you say you went to one of the mines and found a couple of diamonds? I'm not a miner, Miss Jones, but are you sure they are diamonds? I can't imagine stones you could pick up not being missed by previous miners?"

"Sometimes people miss the obvious, or maybe they dropped them and didn't notice. I need funds, so they have to be sold."

"Very well, then we are happy to take you on as a client. What time are you due to see the consortium?"

"Three tomorrow afternoon."

He went quiet for a moment. "I will adjust my diary and meet you at the consortium's offices, Miss Jones. Is that acceptable?"

"Thank you, Mr. Grobler. I can assure you that your practice won't regret taking me as a client. You'll find I'm straight to the point and keep my word."

"Yes, I believe you are; we shall meet tomorrow."

Lisa's next call was to Bapota's office. He was available at the end of the week, being on a course in Cape Town. As it wasn't urgent, a message was left for him to contact her the following Monday.

***

Lisa found herself in Draper's office with Mr. Grobler the following day at three o'clock. She was impressed. The office was large, panelled in oak, with a huge desk and a meeting table. It was at this table that she sat down. Coffee was served, and Draper sat down opposite her.

"What can I do to help you, Miss Jones?" he asked while sipping his coffee.

"I've just returned from a short survey of my mines and found some of what I believe are diamonds. I wanted to show them to you so you can confirm I'm on the right track."

He grinned. "Miss Jones, let me assure you, diamonds don't just lay around on the ground, particularly inside a spent mine."

"Yes, you made that point last time I was here. Even so, I followed the online videos and sure they are diamonds. You can laugh; I'll not take offense if I've got it wrong."

She pulled a cloth bag from a plastic carrier bag she'd brought in, took out the two diamonds, and laid them on the table.

He reached over, picked one up, and stared at it in absolute disbelief. He placed it to one side and looked at the second stone.

"You say you picked these up from the ground?" he asked weakly, pulling a magnifying glass from his pocket.

"Yes, and like I said, I followed a video and looked for the ones that they showed in the video. So, was I correct, and they're diamonds? They look larger than the video showed."

"Just one moment, Miss Jones. I need a second opinion," Draper told her. Reaching over to his telephone, he asked his secretary to have a man named Stefan come to his office.

Stefan, a small man with a balding head and heavy-rimmed glasses, came into the room a minute later.

"Ah, Stefan, can you please look at these two stones and give me your opinion?"

Stefan sat down and pulled an eyeglass from his pocket, studying each diamond. Then he put the glass down and looked at Draper.

"Well, Stefan, what is your verdict before I give you my observations?"

"We are looking at two diamonds that would cut to at least four carats; from what I can see, the clarity is close to the finest. Diamonds of this quality are scarce, Mr Draper. Which mine did they come from?"

"They came from what we understood to be a spent mine. Is that not correct, Miss Jones?"

"Yes, but mining is not easy. I spent at least two hours looking around, where the video gave the impression that they would be everywhere." Lisa enjoyed pulling mining down, explaining she had to look for two hours before finding the stones.

Draper and Stefan looked at each other. Was this girl for real?

"Miss Jones," Draper began. "Miners spend years looking for their first diamond; I can assure you two hours is nothing. Thank you, Stefan. You may leave us."

"Of course, Mr Draper," then he left the room.

"These stones must be registered as a find, Miss Jones. If agreeable, I can do that for you and offer them for bids from consortium members."

"What sort of value am I looking at?" Lisa asked.

"If Stefan is correct, and I'd certainly trust his initial observations, I'd expect bids of around half a million dollars for both. It would seem, Miss Jones, you have got off to a flying start in your mining operations. I would also like to develop a contractual arrangement with you to cover future finds. We offer a holding fee, which is non-refundable even if you find no more diamonds. We would require a first call on all your finds, and it would last for a minimum of a year."

"I have no objection, but my solicitor will guide me. What do you think, Mr. Grobler?"

"We will look at the contract, Miss Jones, before going forward with any agreement. Please send the documents to my office, Mr. Draper. Given the estimated value of the stones, until registered, the stones must be kept secure. Can you facilitate that for Miss Jones, Mr. Draper?"

"We certainly can. I will photograph the stones in your presence, complete an initial specification, and issue a receipt, storing them in our vault pending your decision. We would still like to purchase the two stones even if we have no ongoing agreement. If you agree, I will contact consortium members, asking them to make their bids."

Lisa thought for a moment. "What sort of timescale?"

"By the end of next week, the consortium will have completed the in-depth inspection of the stones required to offer them for sale. The seven days following will be when sealed bids may be submitted. At the end of the seven days, envelopes are opened in front of all the bidders, yourself, or your nominated person. If you accept the top bid, payment is transferred to a bank of your choice within twenty-four hours. I must point out that the consortium will charge five percent if no bid is submitted or the top bid is rejected. Our charge covers the storage and the in-depth inspection before the auction, you will also receive a copy of the report to sell the stones privately. There is no charge to you if a bid is accepted; the winning bidder pays the cost of the report. Your nominated representative must have written authority to accept or reject a bid if you are unavailable. On a personal note, I have been valuing stones for forty years. On the initial inspection, I believe the stones are of such high quality that ninety percent of the members will make a bid."

"What do you think, Mr. Grobler? Could you act as my representative, as I will unlikely be in this area?" Lisa asked.

"The method of sale is in line with previous sales where we have represented a client, and if you want to sell the diamonds, this is certainly one way to obtain their true value to the trade. We can also represent you for the opening of the sealed bids."

"Very well, Mr. Draper, can you arrange for the auction among your members?" Lisa asked him.

"I'll be delighted, and let us hope you will come to us many times even if you don't accept our sole rights contract. Is there anything else I can help you with?"

"There is one thing. Again, I've been looking at the internet. I need an explosives expert or a company that deals with such things. Apparently, several acts govern how explosives are used and transported."

"There certainly are. I will have my secretary forward you recommended companies with all the necessary certificates. Individuals are not the correct route for you, as they may only hold a blaster license. However, transport, storage of explosives, etc., are controlled under different licenses, so others still need to be brought in. I'd be interested to know why, at this stage, you would need such expertise?"

"One or two mines have had falls at the entrance, so I want to open them up. I understand blowing them is the fastest and safest way."

"Perhaps, but I'm no expert. The companies we pass on to you will know what can and cannot be achieved. If you have no more questions, we'll move to the workshop and photograph and describe the stones for registration."

Chapter 51

Chas called Lisa, arranging to pick her up and take her to a meeting with Sir John. Of course, he wasn't in the country; it was to be a video call held from his Pretoria office.

Lisa wasn't worried about going there; she trusted that DB would look after her. Soon, she was in an office, sitting in front of a monitor. Sir John's live picture came on.

"Thank you for coming to the office, Lisa."

She shrugged. "I had nothing else on, so what do you want? Have you had a change of heart and have decided to pay me for the diamonds?"

"You knew those diamonds had a problem?"

"Excuse me, I was a bloody hairwasher, so how would I know? Anyway, what sort of problem do they have? They are rocks out of the ground, not manufactured in a factory?"

"You said the diamonds couldn't leave South Africa; how did you know that?" he continued, ignoring her question.

"Believe me or not, and even the villagers in the Kruger will tell you, Donald Blackmon protects the diamonds. Until he decides they can leave, no matter what you do, they will never leave. Although you will be happy to hear I'll soon be sorting that out."

"If that's the case, now you hold the mining rights. I want you to register them and give me a bill of sale."

"You want a bill of sale without any payment for them? That's not going to happen," she came back at him.

"You'll be paid a fair sum."

"Yes, I'm getting to understand what you call a fair sum, and it sounds pretty biased your way. When Hans looked at the stones from the same box in your office in London, he reckoned them to be at least VS1, with a clarity of I or H, some even better than that. According to the internet, such stones fetch at least 100,000 dollars. There are certainly over a hundred stones. So how much are you offering?"

"You can have the million already in the bank, and I'll give you another million."

"The chance of getting any of my diamonds at those prices is long gone. You should have paid up when you had the chance, now I've had time to find out what they are worth. As a special offer, I want fifty percent of the value. That's five million."

"Are you mad? Two is more than sufficient; they cost you nothing."

"Then I'll take them back. I'm currently on the edge of signing with the consortium for all finds to go through them. Unless you make a better offer, they can go that way, and you can bid for them alongside other dealers."

Sir John knew that mustn't happen. If he returned to South Africa, he would be charged with handling stolen, unregistered stones and risk imprisonment.

"Three and not a penny more."

"How about we go fifty-fifty between what I want and your bid and settle at four million, paid in advance to my account. That's fair."

"Very well, when the money is in your account, you sign both documents. The registration and the bill of sale."

"I'm happy with that. I'll contact my solicitor. He will sort out the registration and then issue a bill of sale once he gets confirmation of the payment. I'm leaving the area very soon and won't be contactable."

After leaving the offices, Lisa took a taxi back to the hotel. Once in her room, Jenny joined her.

"A busy couple of days then?"

"Yes, I've done a deal with Sir John and the two stones from the mine are going to sealed bids at the consortium. It's all looking good, Jenny. At least I'll no longer be living hand-to-mouth."

"That's fantastic, so what are you doing now?"

"I've got a director of a company licensed to use explosives coming to see me tonight. He's even paying for dinner. I'm getting to like this business world, Jenny. I've never eaten so well, and often it's free, which is always good. Hopefully, Bapota will call me on Monday."

"I'm surprised you've been able to do all you have, particularly on your own."

"I wouldn't have if I wasn't confident DB was watching over me. I'd have fallen apart before returning home a gibbering wreck. Even now, what I'm saying are my thoughts or if DB is driving me."

"I can understand that; everything sounds very complicated. What are you going to do about Nick?"

"Nothing at the moment. Then, I don't consider any of the money made from diamond sales to be mine. Later, I may get a small percentage and use the money for expenses. Still, I don't intend to use it to attempt to buy out a criminal, particularly now I know he's not my brother."

"That's hard, Lisa."

"I was never a hard person and would help anyone, but that man stole what little money we had, left me destitute, and I had to sell the family home. Even then, after getting himself in serious trouble, he only called to have me take Sir John to the diamonds so he could get out without considering the risks on my side. If it hadn't been for DB, I would have been in serious trouble or dead. It's the same as Sir John, treating me like shit until the time came when for some reason, he needed documents for the diamonds he stole from me. Like Sir John, Nick found that when he wanted my help, I needed a bloody good reason why I should; otherwise, he'd be out my life forever," she sighed. "Anyway, I'm running a bath for a good soak before getting ready to see this guy later."

***

The man Lisa was to meet introduced himself as Dennis Du Toit, but he insisted she call him Dennis. After collecting drinks at the bar, they ordered dinner in the hotel restaurant.

"My secretary, making the appointment, never told me I'd be sitting down to dinner with a beautiful young lady, Lisa. Not that I am complaining, it is a welcome change, when normally my work is with builders or their representatives, looking for demolition. So what is your requirement? We offer the complete service that includes land clearance ready for building."

"I have mining rights in the Kruger, and an existing mine entrance needs to be blasted open. I know it's not a large job, but using explosives requires licenses and experience."

He smiled. "Understandable. We do many jobs for the mining industry, and in my book, everyone has unique problems and is just as important. With you talking about the old mining areas in the Kruger, we will send our team by helicopter. The cost is high but in line with sending a team on a three to four-day round trip by road. On a personal note, do you realise we are talking close to fifty thousand rand? Are you certain entry into what is a spent mine is worth such an investment?"

Lisa took out her calculator, found it represented around twenty thousand pounds, and then looked up at him. It didn't sound expensive, not that she would say that. "I have my reasons for opening the mine, Dennis. Considering your cost based on the UK pound, I'm prepared to pay you 47,000 rand. That cost must not rise, so don't return to me wanting more because you'll not get it."

"I like your style, Lisa, and yes, we'll do the job for a fixed price. The only condition is that if the explosion causes rockfalls inside the mine workings beyond the entrance, we will not take any responsibility. Our people are experienced and will be very careful how they place the explosives for maximum impact at the blast point and very little beyond. You must understand that we cannot see the condition inside."

"That's fine. Just open the entrance, and I will sort it from there."

"Very well, I will send a fixed quotation. Are you going back there by vehicle?"

"I am, why?"

"I would like to send one of our experts ahead of the team so he can assess what is needed and how close we can get with the helicopter."

"I'm okay with that. Will you want payment in advance?"

"You are a registered mining operation, I assume?"

"I am, with substantial assets," Lisa said, tongue-in-cheek. After all, at present, she had no money in the bank and couldn't pay a deposit.

"Then a deposit is unnecessary."

By now, dinner had been served. With the job already discussed, they reverted to casual conversation for the rest of the night.

Chapter 52

The following Monday, Bapota contacted Lisa, and they arranged to meet in a local cafe. Bapota was sitting at a table when Lisa came in. She walked over and took the seat opposite. Coffee and cakes arrived, and it was time to discuss why she had contacted him.

"I don't believe I need to explain how I know, Bapota, but there's a mine whose entrance was blown up and sealed. Around sixty workers were trapped and allowed to die inside. What would the government's position be if such people were found, particularly those from other African states?"

He sighed. "It doesn't surprise me, Lisa. Life was cheap, and greed high. Since the 1994 elections that brought a black majority into government for the first time, no person of colour has been treated differently. So yes, the police would investigate what happened and ensure all are removed, identified, and buried with dignity."

"Being aware there may be criminality, even though it took place many years before, would you want to be there when the entrance is opened?"

"More than that, Lisa. To preserve evidence, the mine must be opened by the police. It may have happened eighty years ago, but the crime must still be investigated to enable the file to be closed."

"I've arranged for a demolition company to quote for blowing the entrance. Although, with what you are telling me, would the authorities want to do that?"

"They would. However, we would use such expertise if the team you have approached carries all the necessary licenses. They must also be on the government register of approved contractors. But we will look into that. Tell me, Lisa, why are you doing this?"

"DB told me I had to. Although he still needs to take me

to the mine in question. But he will."

"This sounds as if he had something to do with the blocking of the mine?"

"He and another blocked the mine, or so he told me. I believe he wants it opened, telling me the victims of his actions are entitled to be buried with dignity. I don't believe he's had an epiphany; more that he believes that admitting this crime is the only way he can move on. If DB can move on by disclosing this, he will no longer haunt the area, terrifying the local natives."

Bapota nodded his understanding. "If he'd not appeared to me, I'd have thought you insane. Now, I genuinely believe what you're saying has come from him. How that can happen is beyond me."

"Tell me about it; his coming and going is unnerving. I'll be glad when he's finally moved on."

"How did you intend to fund a demolition team, among other costs?"

"Again, no one would believe me, but I was shown the location of two diamonds inside one of the open mines. They are currently registered as a find, and the Diamond Consortium will auction them between its members. So I would have the funds to do what was necessary."

Bapota shook his head slowly. "If the world knew that people from the past can actually return to earth and literally control what happens, there would be panic."

"It's worse than you think, Bapota; I left this earth and joined DB in a world where we could converse. There is no heaven as we all envisaged; in fact, there is nothing apart from dark and light in the form of mist facing each other. Which side you go to depends on what side needs more to maintain balance. DB is upsetting the balance by not passing through, as well as the entities of these murdered miners, so one side is gaining on the other. Too much imbalance will lead to the world's end as we know it."

"Wow, has it really gone that far? Why did he choose you to help sort it out?"

Lisa explained what DB had told her about what happened at the clinic and then shrugged. "I wouldn't have believed it, but for one thing. Joshua from Umbra told me that you can only communicate with your own deceased relatives. It's okay to hear his voice in our heads, but he can't hear us or have a conversation. So, he was telling me what to do in a way that I couldn't ask questions or let him know if I understood what was required. Once in his world, we talked like you and I are doing now. For that to happen, it would seem I had to be a relative, but such beliefs are only held by locals and may not be the reality. It all sounds far-fetched, I know, and even if Joshua is correct, it won't help me in finding who my mother really was since they are both deceased."

Both fell silent for a moment, taking the opportunity to sip their coffee. Bapota broke the silence.

"I think the way to approach this is, you have reported to me, while surveying the area, of talk among the natives that many miners who had gone missing during mining operations were, in fact, trapped in a mine that you have bought mining rights to. You have requested that police be present when the mine is opened to confirm whether such an appalling situation is true. I've decided that if the natives are correct, we could look at a crime scene that must not be contaminated. We will open the mine. The ramifications of leaving this mine sealed are too high."

"I'd appreciate people with me who, like you, actually understand what's going on, with everyone else believing I'm some idiot. You should have seen Draper's face at the consortium when I turned up with two stones, particularly after they had literary thrown me out as another treasure seeker."

"Yes, I can imagine. So when do you leave?"

"I'm off to the bank to get an advance on the sale of the stones. Then, my solicitor will ring to confirm additional funds are in. So let's say two weeks before we return to the Kruger."

"Very well, I'll be ready."

***

Lisa walked into the bank, holding the account set up by Cyril Chapman from her solicitors. She was shown into a small office. Inside the office, behind a desk, was a man of around forty with heavy-rimmed glasses. He looked up at her.

"Please take a seat, Miss Jones. My name is Bolton, and I am the bank's small loans manager. What can we do for you?"

Lisa sat down. "I've substantial funds due, but I need working capital beforehand."

He looked at her account. "I see you've only just opened the account. When you say substantial funds, how much?"

"Five million dollars."

The figure took Bolton aback but pulled himself together, showing no emotion. "These funds, where are they coming from?"

"From the sale of diamonds."

"But you've only just begun mining, and you tell me you have already found stones worth five million dollars. It's hard to accept, Miss Jones."

"Are you suggesting I'm a liar?" she asked directly.

"No, Miss Jones, this is only an observation because of the considerable value. How much are you asking for in advance?"

"Five hundred thousand rand, which I believe is around 20,000 in UK pounds. Hardly a fortune."

"Because you have no track record, and your address in South Africa is a hotel, the bank making such a sum available would require supporting collateral from you,

Miss Jones."

She stood. "You know, in the UK, that sort of loan can be done over the internet without collateral or anything. In fact, as a property holder in the UK, I could probably do it from my hotel bedroom and then transfer the money from my personal account. Tell you what, forget it, but I can guarantee your bosses will ask questions when they find out how large this account will be in the next few months when I move it to another bank," then she walked towards the door.

"Please, Miss Jones, let me talk to the manager. Looking at your original telephone inquiry notes, you requested to speak to someone who could sanction a loan, so you were directed to me. I'm a personal loans adviser who arranges long-term loans. After what you say, it sounds very much like you are looking for a business overdraft, not a loan, to cover short-term expenses pending the completion of sales. Is that your understanding?"

She shrugged. "I suppose," Lisa answered, although, in reality, she had no idea.

"Then it's out of my remit. I will bring in a business manager who deals with such funding."

She sat back down. "Very well, talk to your business manager, but if he's messing around wanting personnel guarantees, forget it; I'll go elsewhere."

He quickly left the room. Jenny, who Lisa hadn't realised was in the room, grinned. "You terrified the poor man, Lisa. I have to admit you're getting very bolshy these days."

"Well, in the UK, for twenty thousand pounds, no one would ask for collateral these days, so long as you have a decent credit score. I don't have one, or it would be abysmal if I did. Anyway, where have you been? I was sat alone in my room last night; I could have done with some company."

"It's your fault. If you want me, call the way you do with DB. Otherwise, I could be doing something else."

"Like what?" she mocked.

"I can't tell you now; the guy is returning with another man," she faded.

"Chicken," Lisa called after her.

Mr. Bolton and another man dressed in a smart suit entered the room. Bolton took his file and left.

"I'm Mr. Todd, Miss Jones. I'm sorry for the mix-up. When you booked your appointment, they didn't understand what you wanted. Of course, you can run into an overdraft. We will set it at a hundred thousand dollars. If you require more, please don't hesitate to contact me. Mr. Bolton mentioned that you already have stones going through the sales process. Are these stones registered and being sold through the Diamond Consortium?"

"Two with an estimated value of half a million dollars are with them. The other sale is through a single company. My solicitor is sorting out the documentation and payment for both sales."

"That is perfectly in order. Would you require us to transfer funds above the overdraft limit into an interest-bearing account?"

"Yes, so long as it's accessible when needed."

"Of course, a no-notice account will give you instant access. Can we do anything else for you?"

"I need a credit card tied to the business account. I'm using my own at the moment."

"I will have it delivered to your hotel by the end of the week. I'm assuming you have a personal account in the UK?"

"I do. Why do you ask?"

"Well, to save exchange costs, etc., it would be prudent to open a personal account here in South Africa. That will allow you to separate your spending between business and personal. We will set an overdraft of a thousand rand and include a debit card for the account when we deliver your business card."

"Thank you, Mr. Todd. I hope I didn't upset your colleague?"

He smiled. "I don't think so, he quickly realised your requirement was for a business overdraft and beyond his remit."

***

Lisa left the bank; she was happy; everything was falling into place, and hopefully, there was an end in sight.

A car pulled up alongside Lisa, its front window sliding down. A man looked at her. "Into the back, Casper wants to talk to you."

"You don't need to be rude about it," she returned at him, grasping the door handle, opening it, and climbing inside, finding Casper sitting there.

The car they were inside was a limousine. The passenger area was sectioned off from the driver's, with seats facing her.

Lisa, at the side of Casper, smiled inwardly. Directly opposite, sitting on one of those seats, was DB. Of course, Casper couldn't see him, but he was clear as day to Lisa. He was also, in Lisa's mind, protecting her. She couldn't help contemplating what the world would think if they knew she could not only see but talk to the dead. For how much longer, she had no idea, but time was ticking to save the world, or at least get rid of DB and give the villagers peace. However, even though DB had taken her to what she presumed was the much misinterpreted heaven, for her to actually be saving the world sounded corny as if she was part of a child's story. Yet she knew what she was about to do was very real.

"You seem to be doing a lot of running around, Lisa. Have you not collected the diamonds yet?" Casper asked.

"A bit of a problem there. The boxes have gone or been taken. I found two on the ground, which must have fallen out, pointing to the boxes being found, opened, and taken away. Was it your people or Sir John's?"

"It certainly wasn't my men; I've not heard from them. I assume Sir John has taken the original lot you found?"

"He has, but there's a problem. Those came from a source that produced inferior-quality stones. They cannot be cut; something about them being too hard, they shatter when being worked on."

"I've heard that a tiny percentage of the larger stones can break apart. Such stones are used in the low end of the market as fillers. So, are you going home?"

"Not yet; one of my mines, I'm told, could contain miners that were trapped years ago. The police want me there because I own the mining rights when they open it."

"Could the diamonds be inside?"

"No idea, but unlikely; it was a working mine then. I can't see such a large haul left in a mine with miners walking about. Then, if they are, the police are there, and any diamonds would be taken away, with the courts deciding if I, or the state, own them."

"You have a point. You'll have to keep your fingers crossed they find nothing."

"Why should I worry? If there are any ownership problems, you can be certain I'll not spend years attempting to claim ownership. I'd rather go home and pick up my life once again. Putting it down to experience."

Casper had fallen silent. He had decided that Lisa had been a waste of time. She had no real idea where anything was anymore, although he was concerned for the men sent to watch her.

"How long have you been back from the Kruger?" he asked.

"I got back at the beginning of last week. Why?"

"And you return again when?" not answering her question.

"Later next week with the police."

"You should sort that out and go home, Lisa. Your actions to date have shown how out-of-depth you are. At least you will be going home with something."

"And you, where do you go from here?"

"We watch and wait, as we have done for years. Mind you, if the diamonds are found while you hold the mining rights, we could call on you to register them and arrange their sale."

"That's fair enough. Then, even when I go home, I'll not allow the licenses to lapse. The villagers trust me, and I will protect them."

"May I drop you off at your hotel?"

"I'd appreciate that."

"Have you enjoyed South Africa, Lisa?" he asked, changing the subject.

"It's big, I'll give you that. Although it would have been nice to go on a real safari and see the wildlife. Even so, the strain has been too much for a city girl, and I am facing business people who constantly look down on me. I'll be glad to go home. In a city, you can lose yourself in the crowds; I hate standing out and purporting to be something I'm not."

"Yes, business is a hard taskmaster. Most who succeed are born into an environment with a well-rounded education and bags of ambition to succeed. Mind you, it is good everyone is not the same, or we'd have no foot soldiers."

"True, then I'm happy to be one of the foot soldiers," she commented.

The car drew up outside the hotel; DB had faded.

"Thank you for the lift. I'll be in touch if anything changes."

"Look after yourself, Lisa,"

Lisa left the car, and Casper sat there contemplating as they set off. Why didn't he believe her? She wasn't a bright girl, unable to hide what she was really thinking. You would walk away if you took what she said literally, but he wouldn't do that for now. Already, she had bucked the trend, and she could continue to surprise him with her stumbling about in the dark.

Chapter 53

The time had come for Lisa to return to the Kruger. Then, following a phone call from Bapota, she would be travelling in a helicopter with several other personnel rather than by car. Bapota had already gone back to Umbra after natives, on a hunting trip, had found bodies, reporting them to the local police. A murder investigation was in full swing by the time Lisa arrived.

Bapota met her from the helicopter, and they went to the hospital building, which was again used as a police operations room.

"What happened?" she asked once they were alone.

"It looked like a shoot-out, but I'd no idea what it was about. At least two are from Mozambique; they are on our police computer as being wanted for murder; the rest we haven't identified."

Lisa had an idea. "Between you and I, Sir John and Casper Meer are still convinced I knew the location of the diamonds stolen or lost during the Second World War. Sir John's people were almost certainly following me last time I came to the Kruger, maybe Casper's people too."

"Did you ever meet these people?"

"I met Sir John's."

"Would you look at the photos of the victims and tell me if any are Sir John's?"

She looked at him nervously. "I suppose, do they look pretty bad?"

He smiled, "better than having to look at the actual corpses, but still disturbing. Lisa. But if you don't want to, that is okay."

"No, I'll look; at least I'll know if this has something to do with them following me."

Bapota opened a filing cabinet and took out a folder. Returning, he spread the photos from the folder onto the table.

Lisa looked at them for a while, then took three photos, placing them to one side. "Those three I can identify. This man was with Sir John. I knew him as Hans. This one was also with Sir John. His name was Gareth. This last photo is a man I've seen with Casper Meer, but I don't know his name."

"That's good; at least we have leads to follow up. Do you know the location of the mine that needs opening yet?"

"No, but give me the rest of the day, and I'll attempt to contact DB. Hopefully, I don't need to return to the mine where I transferred to his world. It's a couple of days walk."

"Forget walking; we'll use the helicopter and take you directly to the mine. The demolition team is on the way. The company you approached to look at the demolition job has been canceled; now the police are involved; like I mentioned, we can only use companies listed as government-preferred contractors." Bapota glanced at his watch. "Time to eat. Are you hungry?"

She smiled. "I am, and I love the food they produce here. Very basic, but good."

"You'll not be eating the local food; they don't have enough for themselves. We have our own catering. Come on, let's see what's on the menu."

***

Later, Lisa left the village alone and headed away from the police activity. Jenny soon joined her.

"Where's DB, Jenny?"

"Why?"

"I've got everyone here, demolition, police, forensics, and workers. He'd better not be making a fool of me with all his talk."

Jenny was going to say something but stopped and slowly disappeared; DB was walking towards Lisa.

Joshua, told by Bapota to keep an eye on Lisa, particularly if she left the village, was hiding watching her. It was not because Bapota didn't trust her; it was more about ensuring she was kept safe. Like it or not, this was a dangerous country for the unwary, and while she told him DB would protect her, he had to be sure.

Lisa saw DB, but he didn't come to a halt in front of her; he passed directly through her. The next moment, she was back in DB's world, the billowing white and black smoke on either side of her.

Joshua, watching from a distance, stared in disbelief. Lisa had disappeared in front of his eyes. Even though Joshua had been educated, to witness what he'd just seen instilled absolute fear in him. Lisa was truly walking with the dead, or she was also an apparition. Joshua stood, turned, and ran for his life. You never interfere with the dead.

Bapota was leaving the medical center when Joshua nearly ran into him. He grabbed Joshua. "Where the hell do you think you're going, and where's Lisa?" he demanded.

"She's gone, taken by the dead," he gasped.

"Get a grip, man, explain," Bapota demanded.

"I followed her as you told me to. She seemed to be talking to someone, but no one was there, then she faded to nothing."

Bapota gave a hint of a smile. "That is good; she's joined DB. There was no need to return to the mine."

Joshua stared at him. "You expected her to disappear?"

"I expected her to talk to DB; she can only talk to him in his world. You've just confirmed they are together. Now go back and wait for her to return."

Joshua raised his hands, backing away. "Oh no, I'm not going anywhere near the dead. They can be unpredictable, and many have been taken and never returned."

"Nonsense, man. DB doesn't want you. Now, do your

job and protect her in this world. The world as we know it depends on this meeting. We should do our part."

Realising he wouldn't let him return to his home, Joshua reluctantly began to walk back to where Lisa had disappeared.

Chapter 54

"You've returned to the Kruger, Lisa. Does that mean you have sold the diamonds and obtained the explosives needed to open the mine?" DB asked.

"I didn't need the diamonds; I used the policeman you once appeared to. With there being potentially dead miners, they are going to declare it a crime scene. As well as open the mine for me."

"Since when have the police been interested in blacks, particularly ones coming from other countries in Africa?"

"The worlds changed. No one says blacks; everyone is South African, no matter what their colour. These days, every crime, whoever it is directed towards, will be investigated."

"It had to happen; in my day, the blacks were valueless. So with this new government run by the black majority, has this worked?"

She shrugged. "I'm not political; there's still crime, still corruption, and the rand is pretty well on the floor, value-wise, but that's the same in any country."

"And you, how has your life been?"

"The mother I ended up with pretended to be more disabled than she was to get extra state payouts. She wasn't, just lazy, with no intention of working, so life was pretty crap, apart from being constantly broke. That's all behind me now, and I intend to live a little."

"Do you hold anything against me?"

"Why should I, apart from you being a pain in the arse coming and going with cryptic sentences. But knowing and talking to you, I'll miss discovering more about your life."

They fell silent; Lisa looked at the dark swirling smoke. "Has this moved closer since I was last here?"

"Correct, it's accelerating, maybe because you are here,

disturbing the balance even more."

"That's all we need. We'd better try your idea out smartly. You still have to give me the location of the mine I'm supposed to blow open. Then once open, will I ever see you again?"

"Nothing personal, Lisa, but I hope not. Jenny will take you to the mine. I can't do that. I can't remain visible to you long enough while we go there."

"But with Jenny being part of me? How could she lead me to the mine?"

"It is more complicated than how you describe Jenny, Lisa. Yes, she exists in your mind, but she is also a drifting sole that allows me to communicate with her. In fact, I can give her instructions away from our world. This is why she will know where to take you."

"Fair enough, I assume the diamonds are in the same mine?"

"They are. Stand just inside the entrance, looking into the mine. Look up on the far wall before the smaller tunnels go off, you will see a narrow ledge inches from the top of the cave. You will need a ladder to get up. The diamonds are in canvas bags laid flat across the ledge, so looking up, you cannot see them. What will you do with the diamonds?"

"Help the villages out of poverty, attempt to clean up the poisoned lake, give back valuable agricultural land poisoned by the mine workings. I don't know how much it will cost, but I must do something for them."

"I'm proud of you, Lisa. I was a criminal, profiting from people who couldn't fight back. You will be able to give back on behalf of our family what has been taken. I'll also miss talking to you. If we had the time, I'd like to hear how the world has changed."

"I could have done more for you if I'd been able to go to university and get a decent job. But that wasn't going to happen because of that corrupt doctor."

"Don't be hard on yourself. You have done well and learned quickly. Now it's time for you to go. If we don't meet again, take care of yourself. There are many sharks out there disguised as people offering help. You have grown up streetwise and can see through such people."

"You can say that again; the area I lived in at least teaches you how to look after yourself. Can we hug?"

"We can't. You may be here, and we look like ourselves to each other, but in a solid form, I am not. It is time for you to leave, and Jenny will be given the directions. Goodbye, Lisa. Take care."

Lisa was back on the path leading away from the village. Jenny was leaning against a tree a little further on. "You've got someone watching you, Lisa. Get rid of him, and we will go to the mine."

She turned and walked towards Joshua, who was attempting to hide. "It's no use, Joshua. You can't hide from me; I know you are there."

He stood. "I saw you disappear, Lisa; what are you really?"

Lisa decided to play on his fears. "It's not what I am, but who I'm with. It's perilous for you to be close to me. They will take offense, believe you are a threat, and could turn on you. I don't want anyone harmed, but I have things to do and need to be alone."

"I'm sorry. Bapota was concerned for your safety and wanted me to watch you."

"I'll speak to him, but you should return to the village. Unless I ask you, please never attempt to follow me again, no matter what anyone else says. You know DB is involved. He is not a man, alive or dead, to cross."

"I understand, it won't happen again." Then he turned and ran back down the path towards the village.

"Come on, let's go," Jenny said.

"Is it far? Should I get warm clothing, maybe some food?"

"You will not get back before dark, that's true. But you're with me. We will find somewhere to sleep and food. We've done it before."

"Yes, it's alright for you; you're dead, and don't feel the cold; I do. Then a few nuts are great for an emergency after a plane crash, but I need a bit more than that."

"I suppose you're right in a way. The problem is, Lisa, I'm not certain how long I will retain the directions as to where it is. We can't take a risk and delay."

"In that case, it looks like nuts for dinner tonight. Let's go."

They walked together for nearly three hours, eventually turning onto a very narrow track that was virtually invisible at times but climbing.

"It couldn't have been easy in those days; I'd be surprised the path was wide enough to take a vehicle," Lisa commented as they walked.

"I think you're right. I'd hate to have lived in that time."

"I'm with you there. What confuses me is how you would find places to dig. I can understand them coming to an area and completely bulldozing it like the big mining companies. Here, there seem to be small mines scattered everywhere."

"Don't ask me; you should have asked DB that question."

"He's not that easy to converse with, but he mentioned I could be disrupting the balance even more while I was there with him. With that possibility, we cut short any further conversation."

Jenny suddenly stopped, seeming to go into a trance. Lisa had seen this before and knew she was talking to DB.

Lisa had found the climb far steeper and the terrain more challenging, so she was glad for the stop. She also had a satellite telephone and often checked it to determine her position. Each time, Lisa stored the result. With this help, she could find her way back to the mine with the police and demolition company. During this break, she took the opportunity to add another waypoint.

Suddenly Jenny was back.

"You've been speaking to DB?" Lisa asked.

"Yes, DB called me. The rains are coming."

Lisa sighed. "You know it's a great country if it didn't threaten to drown me occasionally. And here's me wearing jeans, a T-shirt, and a jumper; I'm hardly waterproof. Why didn't you see it coming?"

"You should know, Lisa, these rains are not normal. DB created them to wipe out your tracks, so anyone following will not find you."

"You mean someone is still attempting to follow me, but you didn't detect it?"

"I can only see if someone is close. DB knows if they are far away or if I missed the signs. This journey is important, and he has decided to intervene. I will be waiting for you," Jenny said, then faded.

"Hey, don't go and leave me in the rain. You should get wet as well," Lisa called as she disappeared.

However, there was a reason why Jenny went; DB appeared and offered his hand. Lisa naturally went to grasp it, but as she did, she suddenly felt very strange. Everything around her seemed to blur and then fade away until all that was left was darkness. The next moment, she was back. Jenny stood there.

"Excuse me, what just happened?" Lisa asked quietly.

"DB took you out of this world after your whinging about getting wet."

"Oh, come on, even DB wouldn't be bothered if I got rained on, probably laugh; after all, he caused it."

Jenny grinned. "You seem to have the measure of him,

Lisa. In fact, you've lost nearly an hour of your life. No big deal, you'd only have been trying to hide out from a torrential downpour or asleep in bed."

"How could he actually do that? Mind you, it could be advantageous if someone was chasing you."

"It would if it wasn't such high risk. DB brought you to the edge of his world, and you remained in neither this nor his."

"Why is it high risk?"

"Listen, Lisa, I don't know everything. I know that disruption worsens every time you leave this world."

"Well, at least I seem to be in one piece, with no bits of me left hanging about in DB's world."

Jenny laughed. "You read too much science fiction. This is reality, Lisa. You're currently living between your world and that of the dead. This should never happen; no one should see what happens when you leave your mortal body. Such knowledge of your destiny may overtake your mind in the coming years, even sending you insane. You'll need a strong will to ignore it. We'll head for the mine. There's an open mine on the way, and we'll stay there overnight. As for the followers, they searched for you after the rains, found no sign, and are heading back in the direction they came."

Chapter 55

Sir John couldn't find a way to avoid paying Lisa, especially when her solicitors, who were handling the transaction for the sale of the diamonds, informed him that the diamonds were now registered and that payment was required, or they would need to be returned. Returning the diamonds would mean admitting quite a number of them were in customs, which would incur a criminal charge for attempting to take out unregistered diamonds, risking a jail sentence. Therefore, returning them was not an option, so he paid. This proved costly, and he was more determined than ever to obtain the two boxes of diamonds.

Sir John, already aware that Hans and Gareth had been killed, reading on the news feed of their bodies being found. Calling people he knew in the police force for further information, he'd also found out the police were mounting an operation to open an old mine where it was suspected miners had been trapped inside during or after the Second World War. If that wasn't enough, it was Lisa who had made the report. Deciding this could lead him to the boxes of diamonds, which Lisa claimed she knew nothing about, he instructed Chas, along with a tracker, to return to the Kruger and watch Lisa closely.

***

To this end, Chas and a tracker known as Justin returned to the Kruger and were watching Lisa when she left Umbra with Joshua following.

"Where do you think she's going?" Justin asked.

"Don't ask me. The girl is not equipped; it's like she's on an afternoon walk. No one goes into the forest dressed the way she is."

"So do we keep following, or is she, like you suggest, going for a walk and will return to the village?" Justin asked.

"We were told to go where she goes, and that's what we'll do."

Their tracking skills and ability to stay out of Joshua's sight were far better. So when Joshua turned and ran back towards the village, they moved forward, only to find Lisa had somehow evaded them.

"Where the fuck has she gone?" Justin commented after going to Lisa's last position. "The grass has been made flat by her prints, then it stops. Tracking tells me she's effectively stood here but isn't."

"Then you'd better learn how to track, she's hardly a fucking bird," Chas commented dryly.

Justin didn't come back at him, preferring to carefully increase his circle around where Lisa had last stood, looking for any sign of her continuing, but there was nothing. "I can only assume she's gone back the way she came; how we missed her passing us, I don't know. I can't believe it, but it's the only option."

"Then we retrace our steps just in case she'd turned off."

As they retraced their steps close to the village, they saw Joshua returning. Both men darted to one side, allowing him to pass them unseen. Then they turned, followed, and watched.

Arriving back where they had lost Lisa, Chas gasped. "This can't be happening; she's back."

"She's seen the African and is going over to him," Justin commented.

They watched her talk to Joshua, and he turned, heading towards the village.

"Interesting; I wonder what she said to him?" Chas commented.

"Whatever she said, she's on the move, and it's not towards the village," Justin added.

"Well, that's one good thing."

They followed in silence.

"You know, I cannot believe this girl can just go for a walk; we are at a distance when to return to the village would be virtually impossible before dark. Is she heading for a shelter, do you think?" Justin asked.

Chas looked up at the sky. "Then she'd better get a move on; those clouds are storm clouds, and they will be with us in minutes."

Justin looked up and then back towards Lisa, but she was gone. "I don't believe it; the girls disappeared before us again."

"Circle the area fast; if the rains come, we'll never know which way she ran."

Both men searched until the first sign of rain came, then gave up, pulling out waterproofs. They had no choice but to sit out the storm.

The rain was torrential; however, everything was back to normal in ten minutes.

As they wrapped up their waterproofs, it was Chas who spoke.

"During the storm, I thought about what had been happening, and something was not normal around here. Twice, Lisa has managed to lose us, disappearing, leaving no tracks and no indication of how she did it. You're a tracker. Is it possible?"

"If we were following someone very experienced in hiding their tracks, maybe, but a city girl wet behind the ears, absolutely no chance. I've lived in this country for thirty years doing this job for the big game hunters. I'll tell you animals have instincts, senses when being followed, and an arsenal of things to put off a predator, but they leave something. This girl makes them look pathetic. She can literally disappear in front of us, that is, if we take our eyes off her for a few seconds. If I were a native, I'd say she walks with her ancestors; as a white man, I like to believe I'm intelligent and discount such beliefs. She has no ancestors in South Africa; she comes from the UK. So what's going on? Is there something Sir John hasn't told us?"

They finished packing, and Chas looked at him. "I have the same thoughts; we can't chase a bloody ghost. What is your suggestion?"

"There is a determination, by her or persons unknown, not to allow us to follow. We should return to our vehicle. You and I know you don't get rains in this season. Yet, we've just been in a downpour, which conveniently came, the girl disappeared, and the rains wiped out any possible tracks. Now the rain's gone as if it never happened. We should also find that native and speak to him; he must know more about what is happening; he spoke to her."

"I agree. We will collect our vehicle and go to the village. I know that man; he'll talk, believe me."

Chapter 56

With the followers turning back, Lisa and Jenny moved on. The terrain was rugged and climbing all the time. Eventually, they came to a flat area. To the far end of the flat, in front of them, were vertical rock faces rising around thirty meters. Plants hung down the face in a dense mass.

Lisa looked up at the vertical face. "I hope you are not expecting me to climb that? Because I'll tell you now, in jeans and trainers, there's no way I can. I'm also completely knackered," Lisa commented, checking the geolocation before adding the result to memory.

"We go no further; we're actually here. The entrance is covered by the undergrowth. The demolition company will sort out a way to get inside."

Lisa sat on the grass, Jenny by her side. "Well, that's good news. Then what about tonight? Unlike you, I can hardly sit here. I'll freeze to death or, at the very least, end up with pneumonia."

"Come on, I've no intention of sitting here all night listening to your whinging? About five minutes away is the entrance to another mine. That one was abandoned after finding no stones before they dug this. DB showed me where it was. It's surprisingly clean, dry, and safe. You'll be fine there. I'll find you food, and I promise I will keep you company all night."

"I knew you'd have a plan of some sort. I asked DB if you'll be able to return once this mine is open. DB wouldn't answer me directly," Lisa said.

"I've no idea either." Then Jenny's tone changed to a more serious one. "You are all I've got, Lisa. When we are not together, I drift into a weird world. It's so quiet and lifeless; the land is completely flat, the sky a dull white, with no clouds or even sun. I don't want to remain there; it depresses me, and I feel so lonely and scared."

"Neither would I want you to, but what can we do? We can't dictate our lives. It's as if everything's been preordained." Lisa grabbed Jenny's hand. It was cold but still comforting to hold. "I hope if DB moves on, our relationship doesn't change. We've had some good times, weird, yes, but I'd not change a thing."

"Me as well. Anyway, let's go to the old mine, then I'll find food for you. Vegetarian, of course."

"So, no burger then?" Lisa commented.

Jenny smiled, "That's not good for you. I only bring healthy food," then she hesitated. "Mind you, what I'd give for a burger and fries."

"Thanks; now I'm even more hungry," Lisa said, standing. "Lead the way."

They set off again, but Jenny's five minutes was close to fifteen and through thick ground cover. Even so, Lisa was soon standing inside a prominent entrance to a mine, quite a large area with five lower tunnels leading off.

"I have to agree; you were right at the state of the mine entrance; I'll be fine here. Pity you got the timing wrong for getting here and the difficulty. I could do with a shower or even a swim to clean myself up," Lisa commented, walking around the area.

"You're too fussy; the next thing you'll want is blankets. Anyway, I'll be back shortly." Jenny faded out, preventing Lisa from commenting.

Lisa smiled inwardly; whatever Jenny was, she couldn't help but like her and hoped that the opening of the mine workings and DB moving on wouldn't take her away. Wondering around the cave, she found somewhere to sit, leaning back on the wall, which allowed her to see outside.

The silence was overwhelming to what she'd been used to back home. If it wasn't for noisy motorbike screaming past, often doing a wheelie down the street, sirens would go off from emergency service vehicles day and night. Using her satellite telephone, she checked her emails. There were three from Nick, the first asking if she'd met Sir John, the second asking if her meeting had resulted in an agreement, which she thought strange; after all, she'd not replied to the first, so who had told him they had met? The last email claimed that his legal adviser had told him the authorities had been talking about twenty years. He begged her to sort it out with Sir John, who promised he'd arrange his release. Reading between the lines, certain anomalies in his words made her believe the emails were untrue. With the authorities talking about years of imprisonment, in her view, the case had gone too far for Sir John to buy off a few local policemen. However, if Nick was lying and there was no such charge, would he come home, pretending that Sir John had got him out after she had handed over the diamonds. Either way, she wasn't going to fall for it. Lisa began to type a reply.

'Nick, there is nothing I can do. Your friend Sir John got what he wanted, so you'd better call him to help you. Please don't mail me again. In my mind, what you have done to me and the continuing veiled threats clearly show we are no longer brother and sister. You're on your own, the same as I am now. Enjoy your life.'

After writing the text, Lisa looked at it over several times. Can she write off her brother like this? After all, if they are not brother and sister, they had spent their lives together, that must mean something? "No," she said aloud softly. "It may have meant something if he'd been honest with her, and she would have stood by him, but he, like everyone else, had used her to their own ends, disregarding her feelings. Even now, she had no idea if she would survive, to be pushed to one side as she had completed her task."

Sending the text, Lisa went to look at other emails. Most were offers, scams, and adverts. However, one mail from the solicitor confirmed Sir John had paid. The solicitor also confirmed he had attended the sealed bid opening at the Diamond Consortium and accepted an offer of two hundred and sixty thousand dollars bid for each diamond on her behalf. He had also received the promised contract that they were offering a retainer of twenty-five thousand dollars a month from the consortium, having the first option on any diamonds produced from her mines for the next twelve months. He said it was a good deal and recommended she accept. In the long run, it would save a great deal of administration in registering and offering more diamonds on the market.

Again, she replied to the mail, telling her solicitor she agreed the diamond offer was good but asked him to hold on to the contract until she returned. She wanted to sit down with him and understand the contract. In many ways, Lisa couldn't believe she could know to any degree how business worked and even make decisions she'd never thought she could make. With millions of dollars in the bank, she finally had the power to make a difference in people's lives.

Jenny suddenly appeared at the entrance to the mine. "I'm back with your dinner. Well, lots of really nutritious vegetarian goodies."

Lisa stood, walking over to the entrance. Outside were three large leaves with various berries and larger fruits like apples. This was different from her idea of food, but she knew Jenny was doing her best. "They certainly look good. Which do you recommend I begin with?" she asked with enthusiasm.

"The leaves with the berries and for your desert, the larger fruits."

They sat together, and Lisa munched through the various items.

"I'm sorry, it's not very good," Jenny commented.

"It's not a typical Uber delivery, I'll give you that. Then, apart from a few bitter berries, the fruits are really nice. There again over the years, back home, I've had days when we were down to dripping and stale bread, then running down to the cash machine around midnight to get the next week's disability payment out before mum's creditors got their hands on it."

"So, what are your plans now you have the location of the mine?" Jenny asked.

"I'll go back to the other mine entrance, call Bapota, give him the coordinates, and bring in a helicopter with the appropriate people aboard to look at what needs to be done to open the entrance. At that point, it becomes a crime scene until they say otherwise."

"But it's still your property, or the mining rights, that is?"

"Of course. I also need to be here when the police break into the mine and sign a waiver if they cause serious damage in their attempts to get inside. Sounds a bit over the top; after all, what more damage could they do than what has been done in the past?"

"Yes, I see your point. Then I don't suppose the police will want to tidy up; they will just take out the victims and leave you the mess."

"Probably. But it will give the locals some paid work to sort it out for me."

"You'll be stinking rich at the end, Lisa. I wish I'd also survived the crash; we could have had a ball in the playgrounds of the rich."

"We could, and you never know; hopefully, you will still be with me. Then, while the money belongs to the local villagers, spending a little for a good holiday wouldn't do much harm. I've earned at least one perk."

Jenny smiled. "I don't believe you comprehend just how much money will be under your control. Rebuild all the villages, give them water and maybe solar power, tractors for the fields, and a few lorries to move their goods around. You won't even dent the bank account. In fact, all that I've suggested could be covered with the interest alone."

Lisa shrugged. "Maybe you're correct, but I can only do what I can do. Then I've only got DB's word about where the rest of the diamonds are. The miners inside could have found them, hidden them somewhere else, hoping they would get out, and could return and collect them. Or... DB is lying, and the story he's told me is a complete fabrication, and I'm unleashing something far more dangerous when the mine entrance is blasted."

"Why do you say DB could be lying? What advantage would it be for him?"

"None that I can see, except if I accept the miners were trapped, and strangely, no one seemed to bother why the men hadn't returned to their camp, so they died; it raises an obvious question. Well, not obvious at first for me, but after some thought, it does."

"I agree it would be strange if no one was looking for them, but what's the obvious question?"

"People die every day, under many different circumstances all over the world. Is DB suggesting the ones who die and can't see the light of day are stuck, not allowing them to pass on until someone opens a door or drags them out? I can't see that being the case if you take earthquakes as an instance. Lots of victims are never recovered, when buildings collapse. Particularly in the past when heavy moving equipment didn't exist. Millions could be in the same situation as the miners over the years. What will a few more do to balance the two opposing entities?"

Jenny said nothing for a moment, considering what Lisa had said. "Putting it that way, nothing, except these miners were trapped by DB, and now he is paying the cost of doing it by remaining in limbo."

"Then let's hope it's been a quirk by whoever controls the afterlife, leaving DB in limbo."

It was getting dark by now, and Lisa settled for the night. While she slept, Jenny faded out to be replaced by DB. Although Jenny said she would look after Lisa, she couldn't and had to call DB.

***

When Lisa woke, DB had gone, and Jenny was sitting at the entrance to the cave with Lisa's breakfast.

"Sleep well then?" Jenny asked after they'd wished each other good morning.

"I did, thank you," taking one of the fruits from the leaf. "Today, we return to the cave, and I'll call Bapota. Have him bring in a helicopter, with specialists onboard, to look at the mine entrance and take me back to the village so we can all discuss the next move."

Jenny shuddered a little. "It's getting scary now."

"It is. All I can hope is that I'm doing the right thing."

Chapter 57

After returning to their vehicle, Chas and Justin went to Umbra. Chas had attempted to talk to Sir John, but he'd been unavailable, so they assumed he'd agree to them going to the village.

Since the police and all their support staff, including reporters, had come to the village once more, enterprising villagers had set up stalls selling goods they'd made and local fruits in an attempt to make a little extra money. Chas found Joshua with his mother selling carvings carved by the family at one of these stalls.

"You and I should talk; follow me," Chas demanded.

Joshua followed him, and they left the village, joining Justin standing by their vehicle.

"What do you want?" Joshua asked.

"We watched you following Lisa; why were you following her?"

He shrugged. "Inspector Bapota didn't like her leaving the village alone. Lisa's a city girl and wouldn't see danger, so he told me to watch her."

"Yet you ran back to the village, leaving her out there, then you returned only to be confronted by Lisa, who I assume sent you back to the village?"

"You wouldn't understand if I told you."

"Try me," Chas demanded.

"Do you believe in the old ways and, importantly, that the mungome can call your ancestor from the next world to converse with you?"

Chas shrugged. "I've been in this country all my life and seen many happenings science and logic could never explain, with many documented instances that point to such conversations happening. Why do you ask?"

"Lisa has gone one step beyond; she walks and talks with the dead and can pass through to their world. I saw her pass through, and it terrified me. I ran as if wild animals were chasing me. Bapota was annoyed I'd panicked, and he sent me back. She knew I was watching, warned, I believe, by the dead who she was with."

"When you say, saw her pass through, what do you mean by that?"

"Lisa disappeared in front of my eyes. She passed through to the other side. People with such power you step away from. They are more than capable of destroying you."

"How could she do that? The girl carries no weapons or even knows how to use a gun," Justin asked.

Joshua shook his head slowly. "What use are human weapons for someone with the power to enter your mind, mess about inside, turn you mad, or even force you to harm yourself? You should walk away if you value your life? Even the men the police are investigating end up fighting each other to the death. You know that isn't right, so who was controlling the outcome, certainly not the victims."

"Did Lisa issue any threats when she spoke to you?" Chas asked.

"Lisa didn't need to threaten. All she said was Donald Blackmon was in the area. You may not know that man, but every village, every person in the village, knows of this man. If Lisa walks with Blackmon, you can be certain that the powers from the dead he wields are available to her. The mining areas have always been subject to several happenings that can not be explained. Since Lisa came, the activities have become far more regular and dangerous. Go home, don't become victims like your friends. Lisa will always win, no matter what you believe." Joshua walked away, heading towards the village.

"Well, Chas, do you believe him?"

"Fucked if I know. What we do know and have witnessed is that Lisa can disappear. That's not right in any respect. My mates are dead, and I don't intend to add to the statistic. Even if she has the diamonds, with all the police around, what could we do? They would secure the finds and fly them back in a helicopter to be placed in a secure vault. I'm returning to Pretoria, stay if you want?"

"No way; if you're off, so am I. Apart from being too public, what's happening around here can't be explained, and I'll tell you this: that girl couldn't have lost me if it had only been down to wiping out her tracks. That fact alone will remain with me for many years because we both know what we witnessed was impossible."

Chapter 58

The day arrived when everything was in place for the demolition team to blow the entrance to the mine. The demolition people, Bapota, police officers, and forensics had set up camp close to the mine entrance. Several meetings had been held following the removal of dense undergrowth around the entrance.

The final agreements were put to Lisa as the holder of the mining rights to be signed. What else could she do apart from trust what they were proposing? However, she did ask who would make it safe after any investigation. After being assured it would not be left in a dangerous condition, Lisa signed.

Lisa walked away from the camp, sitting down on a banking. Jenny joined her.

"How long have we got before they blow the mine, Lisa?" Jenny asked.

"Around an hour. I'm scared, Jenny. Something is niggling me, I'm not sure what, but I don't believe we should be going into that mine."

"Can you stop it?"

"I don't think so. The police are determined to look inside. Then I signed permission to open the entrance, so I could hardly change my mind without an excellent reason. Have you asked DB about your position?"

"He's not communicating with me. Although, since I took you to the mine, he's been looking after you at night. I was sent to my sterile world to wait for daybreak."

"It must be awful for you, Jenny, I wish I could do something to help."

She gave an indifferent shrug. "I suppose this is what death's like? If only people knew what was awaiting them."

"Bloody good job, they don't."

"Must go. DB is here," Jenny suddenly said, then faded.

Lisa stood, and DB approached her, grasping her hand. The next moment, she was in his world.

"I thought we were not going to meet again? I also notice the dark side has moved even closer."

"We have a short time to talk. As for the dark side, you are correct that it has moved, but it will soon be corrected. I've been sensing through Jenny that you are having doubts, perhaps about being used for something far more dangerous."

"Can you blame me? I've lived all my life in a council house, and finally, mum bought it at a heavy discount, except my brother and I had to pay the mortgage. Often, people living in such estates are treated as the lowest of the low. We're put on, lied to, and considered spongers and criminals. Ninety percent are nothing like that; they are hard-working and vulnerable, yes, mainly because of their education, but streetwise. That means we don't completely believe what someone tells us. I'm taking your word that what I'm doing is right, but it doesn't stop me from doubting the logic. And believe me, the logic is crap."

"If you believe I understand what is going on, I don't, only that I'm stuck in this world between yours and where all who die end up. I've had many years to consider my position, watching the black mist moving inextricably in closing the gap. I'm convinced, what has been put in my mind, that opening up the mine is the right thing to do."

She looked at him. "Put in your mind? By who?" she asked, obviously deeply concerned.

"You can never understand, Lisa. There is no who, no names, nothing. We are part of the universe, insignificant, not even a blip on the age of the solar system. We have no right to dictate, to decide our future, our destiny. You ask what the light and dark mists are, but you should ask what the mists are concealing to understand. Can I answer that question? Of course, I can't. I know what you are doing was decreed, along with images you are comfortable creating, like Jenny and myself. Will you ever see either of us again? Unlikely, as we don't exist in your understanding that people you see and hear should be flesh and blood like yourself. If what you do destroys your world, your destiny was mapped out before you existed."

"Well, that's bloody charming. It seems you are like everyone. You treat me as a fool, lie to me, and persuade me to do something I don't want to do by convincing me to believe I'm doing the right thing for your needs, not mine."

"Where's the convincing? If all goes well, you will be a wealthy young lady, making up for the years you've been living hand-to-mouth. That's apart from deep inside, your greed will get the better of you, outwardly telling yourself you are doing it for the village people whose ancestors paid a dear price, yet all the time knowing the value of such a haul will change your life forever. Living what everyone calls the dream."

"That may be your thinking, but don't accuse me of living like you lived on earth. You'll find you picked the wrong person in me, and I will complete my plan to give back to the descendants for all past wrongs. Not overnight or over a lifetime, but I will try. I will never walk away."

DB began to fade along with the black-and-white mist at that moment, leaving Lisa standing or floating on nothing. There was no horizon, no ground below, and the sky was completely black, yet she could see as clear as day—if there had been anything to see.

Lisa's words were calm, and she assumed that whoever was there would hear her without shouting. "I suspect what has been going on has been all in my mind and, as you say, constructed to make me feel comfortable. If this is your real world, it's time to show yourself and what you really are; that's if you have the guts to appear in front of a human being who is not frightened of you or what you represent."

The answer came as words, not in her mind but all around her, as if the world was talking. "I am showing myself; it is just that you cannot see or comprehend what your eyes tell you, human. Yet only you, out of all the humans who have played my games over the years, have surprised me with your ability to adapt to change. You have been a true adversary. Your reward is waiting for you."

"A game was it. Do you know people died in this game?"

"Not in the game; they died because of their greed. Observing you over the coming years will be interesting to see if you succumb to the same."

"You will certainly be waiting a long time if you expect me to lose sight of my goals. So what do I call you, and where do you come from?"

"Time in my world is not based on ticking clocks; time for me is infinite; you humans are just a blip. As for my name, why would I want such a label? There is only myself to converse with. Where do I come from? Such a question comes from someone living on a lump of rock, where I know no bounds or limits. I am all around you, the universe, the controller of worlds."

"Oh, come on, if you are so powerful, what's this, playing silly games with something you consider a blip in your universe? You can do better than that. Because I'll tell you this, if I were the controller of the universe, I'd not be messing around with a few simple minds on a planet billions of miles from other possible civilisations. Unless there is only us, I'd understand you getting bored on your own all the time. How about I throw the gauntlet down? If you are so powerful, prove it; show me your universe, the civilisations you control."

The voice didn't react for a short time, and she was

going to ask where it had gone when the voice replied. "I like you, human; you have something about you that others on your planet lack. I'm sorry to disappoint; you are not alone in the vastness of space and time. Over billions of years, civilisations have come and gone, the same as your own planet will, in time, be extinguished when your life-giving sun no longer shines. As for showing you my world, you are already there. What did you expect, a house or a palace like the ones you humans built? As to show you other civilisations, even existing outside your body as you are, you would not survive travelling across the universe."

"It all sounds very convenient. Could it be your claim of powers doesn't amount to much?" Lisa mocked, actually enjoying the conversation, which seemed one-sided and in his favour. "So now I'm in your world; I have a question, what happens to us when we die, and why is DB still around in a no-man's-land?"

"What happens to you? That is a fixation of people who are dissatisfied with existing for a short time; they want more. So, to answer your question, nothing is ever destroyed; it just changes into something else. Like the water you drink, destroy it, and it becomes gas; light the gas, and it turns back to water. So, too, are the complexities of life. You ask about the person you call DB and maybe the girl Jenny. Humans go through their lives seeing only certain dimensions: sight, smell, and taste. Many humans touch, at times, other dimensions. You see a dimension where the remnants of people in what you call ghosts, even they, over time, fade out."

"DB is taking his time, then."

"Refusal to accept the inevitable, like the water, can slow your change. Now it is time you returned to your world. You have been an interesting person to talk to."

"You too, will we ever talk again?"

"Only if I want to. There are no plans, so get on with

your life. Maybe I'll let you forget this short time out of your world. I will consider that."

"What about Jenny? Can you at least let me say goodbye?" Lisa asked, more interested in Jenny's fate.

"The human mind is a mighty weapon once the person finds how to use its powers. Jenny is part of your inner world. Call her if you want to talk."

At that moment, Lisa was back, sitting on a rock. She couldn't believe the conversation she'd just had. Was she actually going insane, seeing and talking not only to the dead but also to something that lived in and claimed ownership of the universe? Lisa glanced at her watch. She'd been gone for only minutes, although it seemed much longer. Lisa decided to call Jenny in her mind.

"Hi, you're back then?"

"I am. This time, I've been speaking to something else. I say something as it hasn't an actual form or a name. It's all very bizarre, Jenny."

"It sounds to me like you're going loopy. I'd find yourself a therapist. Everyone who's anyone in America has one," she mocked.

"Yes, that's the Americans; we're not that stupid in the UK. We prefer to avoid filling the pockets of so-called experts on life. But something good has come from my meeting. You're going nowhere. I can call you at any time."

"So we can go on holiday to really cool places?"

"Why not? You'll be cheap on travel, accommodation, and food," Lisa grinned.

"Yes, I suppose I would. I must go; someone is coming," Jenny said, then faded away.

"This is where you are, Lisa," Bapota said as he approached.

"Yes, I had to get away for a short time. Is the demolition team ready to blow yet?"

"It's all set up, and everyone has moved away. You're

coming, I assume?"

"I am."

"Shall we go back then?"

They joined several other people well away from the mine entrance. The man in charge of the demolition team turned to Lisa.

"Would you like to press the button? After all it is your mine?" he asked.

"Yes, please. I've never made anything explode before."

"Very well, I will sound the warning and lift the safety cap over the button. Then it's ready for you to press."

The warning siren went off, and half a minute later, Lisa pressed the button.

There was a large but muffled explosion, with hardly any dust apart from a bit of smoke billowing out, followed by silence.

Lisa felt a little letdown, expecting something more spectacular. However, as everyone watched, the ground began to shudder.

"What's happening?" Lisa asked the man leading the demolition team.

"I don't know, the explosive is spent; this has nothing to do with us."

They didn't have long to wait for the outcome. The entrance to the mine blew out with such force that what few stones were left disintegrated, followed by a roar of wind coming out from inside the mine.

Lisa stood watching; everyone around her seemed to freeze in time, staring blankly towards the mine. She could see shapes like people leaving the mine, carried on the wind, their faces and bodies distorted as they flew out. They passed directly through the police, demolition people, and others, even inches from Lisa before moving past.

Lisa wasn't shocked or frightened. She was half

expecting to see the entities of the dead finally escape; after all, she was probably one of the very few on this earth who had left this world and seen beyond.

As the last of the entities left the mine, Lisa gave a hint of a smile. Coming from the mine but walking and far more solid than the forms of those who had already left was DB. Lisa broke away from the people she was with and went towards him.

"It seems you were trapped in the mine as well. That was a little remiss of you not to mention that small point, don't you think? Unless, as I always suspected, you had an ulterior motive in keeping such a fact to yourself?" Lisa commented as she got closer.

"You are correct; there were particular reasons why you shouldn't have known, which I won't bore you with. In fact, the charge went off prematurely while I was inside. The miners were whipped to within an inch of their lives, but they couldn't work hard enough to clear the entrance before the oxygen in the air ran out. Each died one by one, their entity's constantly provoking me. If I'd not been trapped, I'd have returned and blasted the entrance for the diamonds. You, Lisa, have freed me to walk again on this earth as a human rather than an entity. I'm fast becoming as human as you. I'm also rich, but not you. The diamonds are mine, and you can be sure I'll not be playing the good Samaritan as you intended, using my wealth to enter politics to eventually rule the country, this continent, and put the natives back into their place. I was getting fed up with you and your messing around. I offered you a fortune even that didn't push you forward, always wanting to go home. Your mother was dead, your brother's supposed to be facing years in prison, and still, you dithered when all the time the chances of me escaping in human form were diminishing."

She shrugged. "Maybe, but where I come from, someone coming into your life bearing gifts, you naturally think it's a scam; no one in their right mind believes you get something for nothing; there is always a catch. So tell me, how long have you planned this escape of yours? And now you are free, it sounds like you want to rule the world? If so, a word of warning: those who attempt such a feat are always consumed by their greed, wanting more and more, and all end up dead."

"Perhaps. It takes time to find a mind that is susceptible to suggestion. I sensed I'd found that person in you, and it was confirmed finally when you were close to the mine; my power increased a thousand times, enabling me to enter your body, pulling you out of the water. Everyone else's fate was sealed, and I could only take one. My time to walk this earth as a human was in my grasp. As for ruling the world, my immortality will see out all the competitors, and I will accumulate the knowledge and wisdom to control over time. So yes, I will eventually take over the world. Still, in my own time, I have multiple lifetimes to realise the dream."

"When is all this going to happen? You're still not quite as human as you believe. Look around. Everyone is frozen in time except me. I'm the only one who has left their body, which is probably why I can see you."

DB looked around, only now realising what Lisa was saying correct. This wasn't right. He'd been promised immortality as a human, not some ghost, yet he put on a brave face.

"It's very complicated to form my new human image immediately, but it's only a matter of time before I'm complete."

She shrugged. "I can't see how it's possible that while being confined to your small mine, you were able to protect yourself and plan a complex operation involving humans to escape. I suspect someone else orchestrated all of this with the promise of immortality. I also suspect that I know who is behind it."

DB frowned. "What are you talking about? Who do you believe is behind this?"

She smiled. "Believe me, DB, I know much more than you think. Was this assistance offered by something that has no name and exists in a world of perpetual dark? A world with no beginning or end. If so, I've been there and conversed with it, and it told me one important fact. Would you like to know what that is?"

"You cannot have been there; you are human, and no human could enter such a world. As for an important fact, what are you talking about?"

"Human or not, I have been there. I suspect you, like me, are in a game; this entity, for a better word, is playing. Promises made are as empty as the entity, which has no true existence aside from being a part of the universe. You should go back and converse with it to ensure you understand what is being offered. I don't believe it can promise or offer anything. If that's the case, immortality was not something on the table. It's just words and part of the game this entity plays with the living and the so-called dead."

"You talk rubbish. Soon, I'll be complete and in your world once more."

"We shall see. As for your wealth, you must remember I own the mining rights. Find anything, and it belongs to me. Believe you can just take the diamonds, and you will find the laws differ from those of your time. Today, we have money laundering laws, so unless the stones are registered, they would be treated as Confederate or blood diamonds with little or no value on the open market. It would all be via back doors, the value on the floor."

He smiled. "Believe you are clever, do you?"

"No, but you very quickly learn what you can or cannot do, no matter what the business is, when money is the driving force. Returning to your particular situation, when will these people be released, or is that beyond your control now that you are virtually human once more?"

"Why should I worry? You have been useful in getting me to where I am. Now, it's time for you to go back to your pathetic life. We'll never meet again, but only you and I know where the diamonds are hidden; keep away from them; they are mine."

She gave a hint of a smile. "If you say so, but tell me, the birth, was that all crap like everything else coming out your mouth?"

He shrugged. "Believe what you want, then you must have realised that whatever the mungome believe, the dead has the ability to make themselves known to others besides their relatives. As for us, now that I'm in your world, you can be certain I'll never admit to having a nobody like you as a relative, no matter how distant."

"It's good to know what you really think of me. So I'll place you on notice, succeed in entering this world; believe me, it won't be as before. You'll also have one hell of a fight to hold onto the diamonds because every way you turn, I will be there, making out you're a thief. Unlike you, I already hold the mining rights and have sufficient money in the bank to protect my assets."

"I'll look forward to taking you on if only to teach you a lesson," he said, turning and walking away.

Lisa watched him go; however, as he walked, he became less transparent and more solid, like a real human being. At that moment, Lisa was back in the world of darkness.

"I had a feeling I'd be back. Miss me, did you?" Lisa mocked.

"I don't know the meaning. I sense the spirits trapped in the mine are free. You completed your task."

"My part, yes, but by allowing them to move on, you have been playing both sides of the fence and keeping quiet that you've made a deal with DB to allow him to return as a human on earth. According to him, he has the impression he's immortal. I think you have mistakenly allowed someone who should have moved on more time back on earth."

"I do not understand the word mistake. Nothing, not even DB, can go back in time; time can only move forward. Yes, your passage to the next time in your life can slow, as DB believes has happened to him, but ultimately everyone must pass through."

"Even so, you've let a murderer free to live out his life as a piece of shit he always was. Like it or not, it is you who will have blood on your hands. Because if I'd have known there was even the slightest chance of him returning to continue his criminal life, I'd have walked away and wrecked your little game."

"I do not control how a human lives out their life. Only time itself can do that. Although there are drawbacks to delaying the inevitable. The longer you delay moving on, the memories of the past fade and organs dormant for so long are placed under strain in an attempt to work effectively once again. I could go on, but you should understand. DB may have gained a few more years on earth, but will these years be worth it? Not when you must learn to think, speak, and move once more in what will be a forgotten time of your life cycle."

"By what you are suggesting, you seem to have some belief DB will not remember anything from his past because I've got news for you; he's just left me, and his memory has not been affected."

"Maybe he is still between worlds. Everything I have told you will happen as he leaves his current existence to live again in your world."

"That is good. DB is a very dangerous individual. And me, will I forget?"

"If I choose for you to forget we ever talked or that you came to my world, I've still not decided. Your time on earth that came before and how you arrived at this point of your life, no, that will always be remembered. Now, the energy that is holding back your world must be released. Go and live your life."

Lisa was back, and everyone was no longer frozen in time. People in white suits were making their way to the mine entrance.

Bapota joined Lisa. "We'll soon know if what you told me is true," he commented.

"It's true, unlike you, I witnessed their entities leaving the mine."

Bapota never commented on how she had done that, suspecting DB was still in control. "Now they have gone. Do you believe DB will remain in the area?"

"He's gone and no longer a threat. We've done our job, Bapota, not that anyone will thank us."

He laughed. "Join the club; no one thanks the police for finding and jailing a criminal or murderer. We just do it, often getting abuse from criminals' relatives claiming he was a family man or a nice little boy and would never do as we claim."

While forensics checked the mine, Lisa sat with the disposal team and police, eating. A lady in a white forensic suit approached the group, carrying a large evidence bag.

"How are you doing, Margaret?" Bapota asked.

"We are progressing well. The intelligence was correct. We have found the victims; they are being photographed before removal. What I have in this bag needs to be secured, so I've brought them to you. Inside are sixty-four diamonds scattered around the mine entrance. Considering the value, I have carefully ensured everyone has been picked up and accounted for."

"Thank you, Margaret. We will take responsibility for

them."

She left the bag and walked away.

Bapota looked at Lisa. "It looks like one of your mines still has diamonds. As this is a crime scene, we must look after them. I will have them collected by our armed unit and flown back to Pretoria. Your solicitors will make the ownership claim for you."

"It would seem my little foray into mining has already shown results, and I've not lifted a spade yet. Was this a good investment, then?"

"I think so, and for the villagers, I suspect?"

"That goes without saying," Lisa answered, glancing across the forest's edge to where Jenny stood watching. They exchanged a soft smile. It would seem she still had a friend, dead perhaps, but that's just a minor problem.

After finishing her meal, Lisa went to a table with soft drinks and fresh coffee. Filling a paper cup with coffee, she wandered from the camp, finding a rock to sit on. Jenny joined her, grasping her hand. Lisa was happy with the outcome, no matter what; even if the remaining lost diamonds were not where DB told her they were, she had sufficient value in what had been found so far to start giving back to the villages, much of what had been taken from them over the years.

Ghost Diamonds

Have you enjoyed Ghost Diamonds? If so I hope you will look into other titles I have published. While Ghost Diamonds is the second of my paranormal titles, I have a titles covering international crime. fantasy and romance. The most important books are the international crime series of twenty-one titles that follow Karen Harris from the age of seventeen to taking command of Unit T?

While the first two titles are a must-read in understanding Karen, all the other titles are stand-alone, yet follow Karen on the journey to where she is now. Listed below are the key titles in the series, where her friends and sometimes her enemies become part of her life.

The start of Karen's journey.. The People Traders

Why Unit T was formed ..The People Trafficker

Karen's struggles to keep her charity... Kreisen Cartel

Karen finances LBNF ...Unit T - Special Forces

Karen meets Sherry Malloy .. Goin Goin Sold

Karen becomes Lady Harris ... The Royal Grandchild

The loss of Karen's parents ... Nigerian Connection

Karen looks for her sister Sophie .. Russian Connection

Karen and the contract killer Jasmin... Circulo

Karen meets Midnight ... Covert Operator

Karen's worth £500,000,000 ... Jasmin - Contract Killer

Karen meets Sir Richard Knight .. Contracted to Kill

Karen leaves Unit T ... Hoxa Cartel

By the Same Author

International Crime featuring Karen Harris
    The People Trader
    The People Trafficker
    Kriesen Cartel - The early years
    Lost But Never Forgotten - The early years
    Unit T Special Forces
    Goin Goin Sold
    The Royal Grandchild
    Nigerian Connection
    Russian Connection
    Italian Connection
    Romanian Connection
    English Connection
    Irish Connection
    Spanish Connection
    German Connection
    Circulo
    Jasmin Contract Killer
    Covert Operator
    Contracted to Kill
    Chinwe
    Hoxa Cartel

Crime
    Girl in a Web
    Corrupt Money

Romance
    Catwalk Supermodel
    Gemma's WhiteCliff

Fantasy
    Plagarma (Teenage novel)
    Timeless Chamber (Teenage novel)

Paranormal
    Ghost Diamonds
    Tall Ship Magic

Fairies
    Sparkle and the Insect Collector
    Sparkle and the Hole in the Ground
    Sparkle and the Whirlwind

Audio

Nigerian Connection	15 Hours
Russian Connection	9 Hours
Italian Connection	11.5 Hours
Corrupt Money	7.58 Hours

Read the first few chapters of all the above books free at

http:// www.keithhoare.com